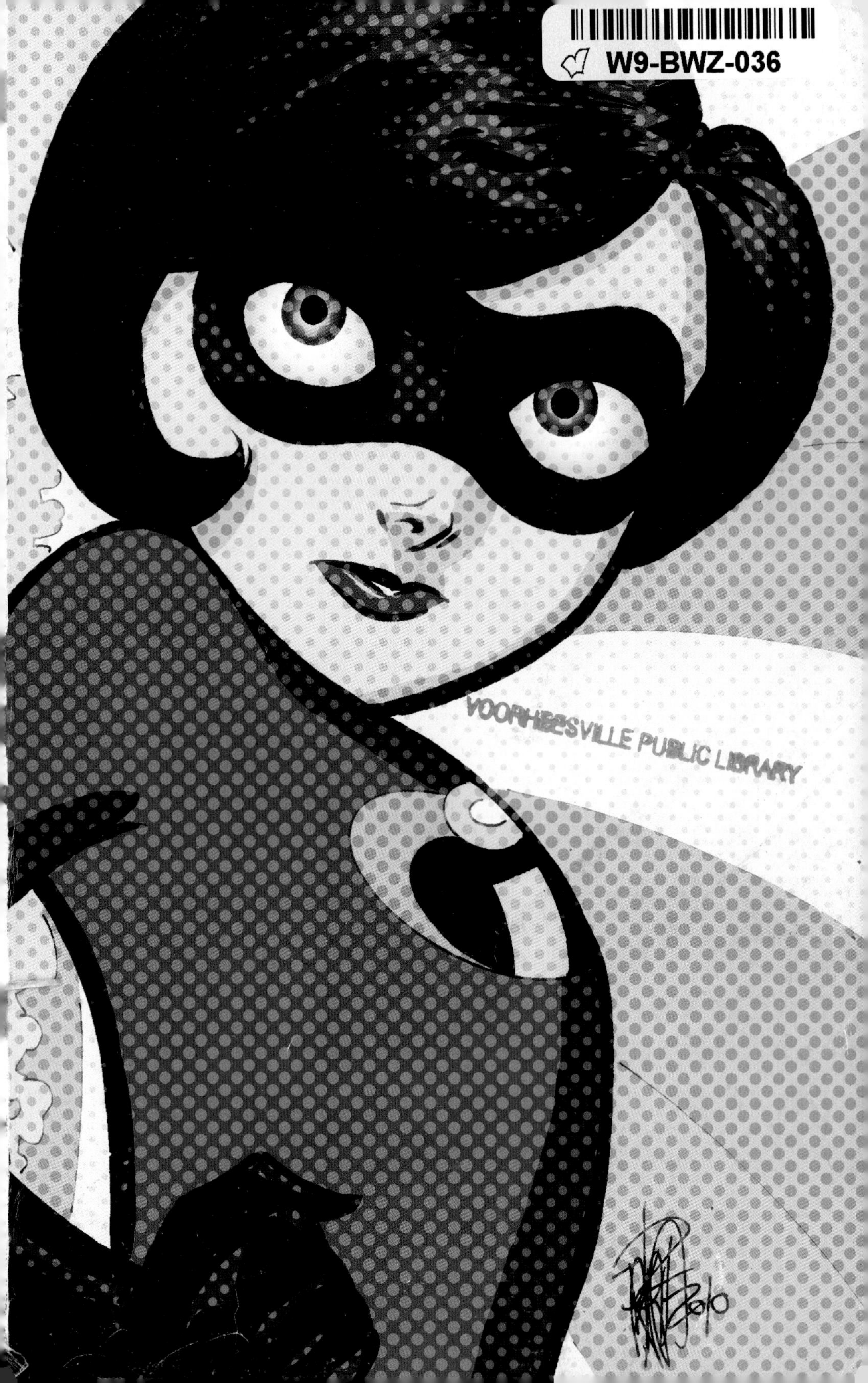

Disney · PIXAR

THE INCREDIBLES
SECRETS & LIES

BOOM KIDS!

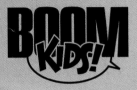

ROSS RICHIE
chief executive officer

MARK WAID
chief creative officer

MATT GAGNON
editor-in-chief

ADAM FORTIER
vice president,
new business

WES HARRIS
vice president,
publishing

LANCE KREITER
vice president,
licensing & merchandising

CHIP MOSHER
marketing director

FIRST EDITION: JULY 2010

10 9 8 7 6 5 4 3 2 1

FOR INFORMATION REGARDING THE CPSIA ON THIS PRINTED MATERIAL
CALL: 203-595-3636 AND PROVIDE REFERENCE # EAST –67432

Office of publication: 6310 San Vicente Blvd Ste 404, Los Angeles, CA 90048.

A catalog record for this book is available from OCLC and on our website www.boom-studios.com on the Librarians page.

WRITER:
   LANDRY WALKER

ARTIST:
   MARCIO TAKARA

COLORS: ANDREW DALHOUSE & RACHELLE ROSENBERG
            CHAPTERS 1 - 3   CHAPTER 4

LETTERS: TROY PETERI

COVER ARTIST: MARCIO TAKARA
      COLORS: ANDREW DALHOUSE

ASSISTANT EDITOR: JASON LONG
EDITORS: AARON SPARROW & CHRISTOPHER MEYER
DESIGNER: ERIKA TERRIQUEZ

SPECIAL THANKS: JESSE POST,
LAUREN KRESSEL, ELENA GARBO, LISA KELLEY,
STEVE BEHLING AND KELLY BONBRIGHT

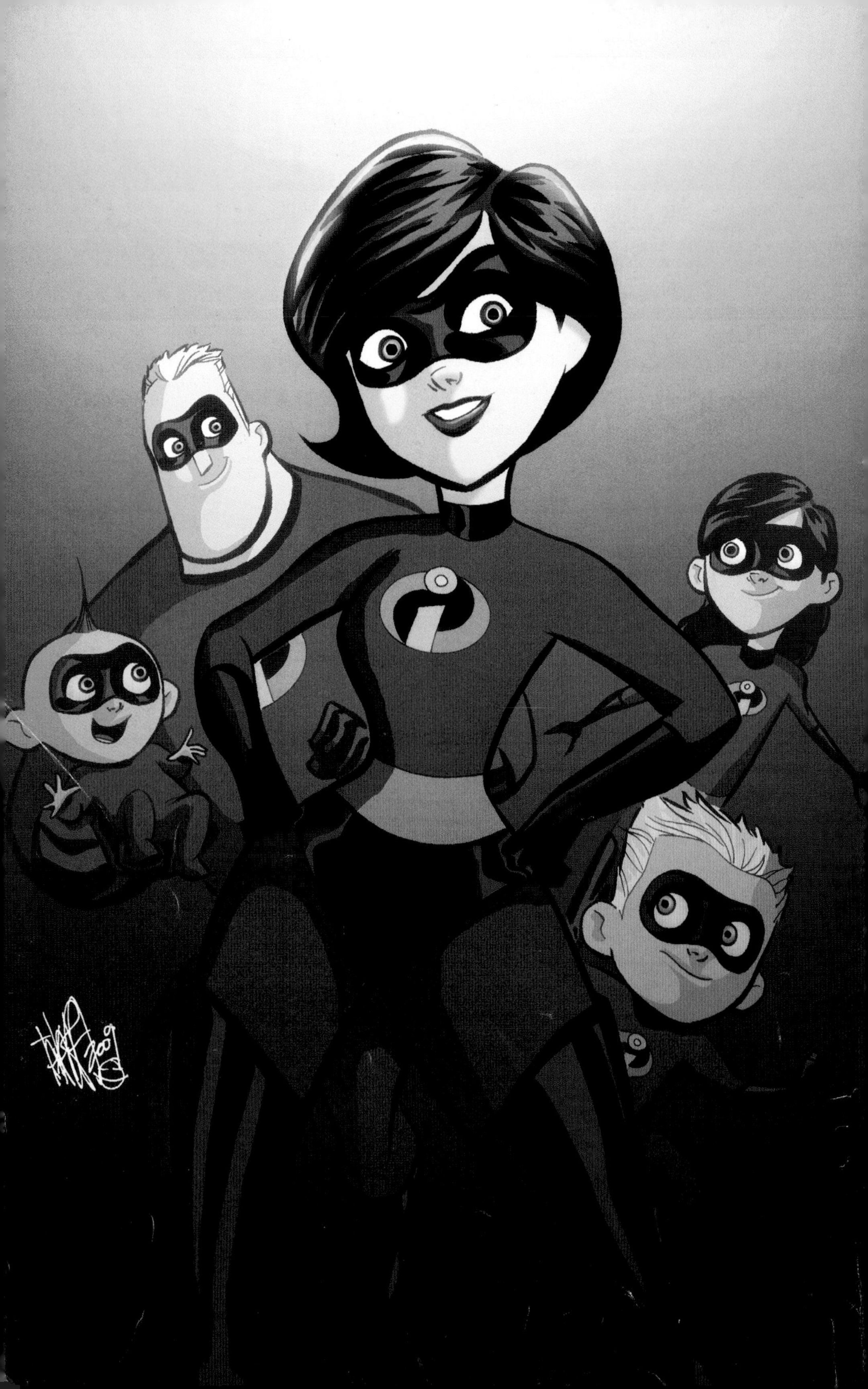

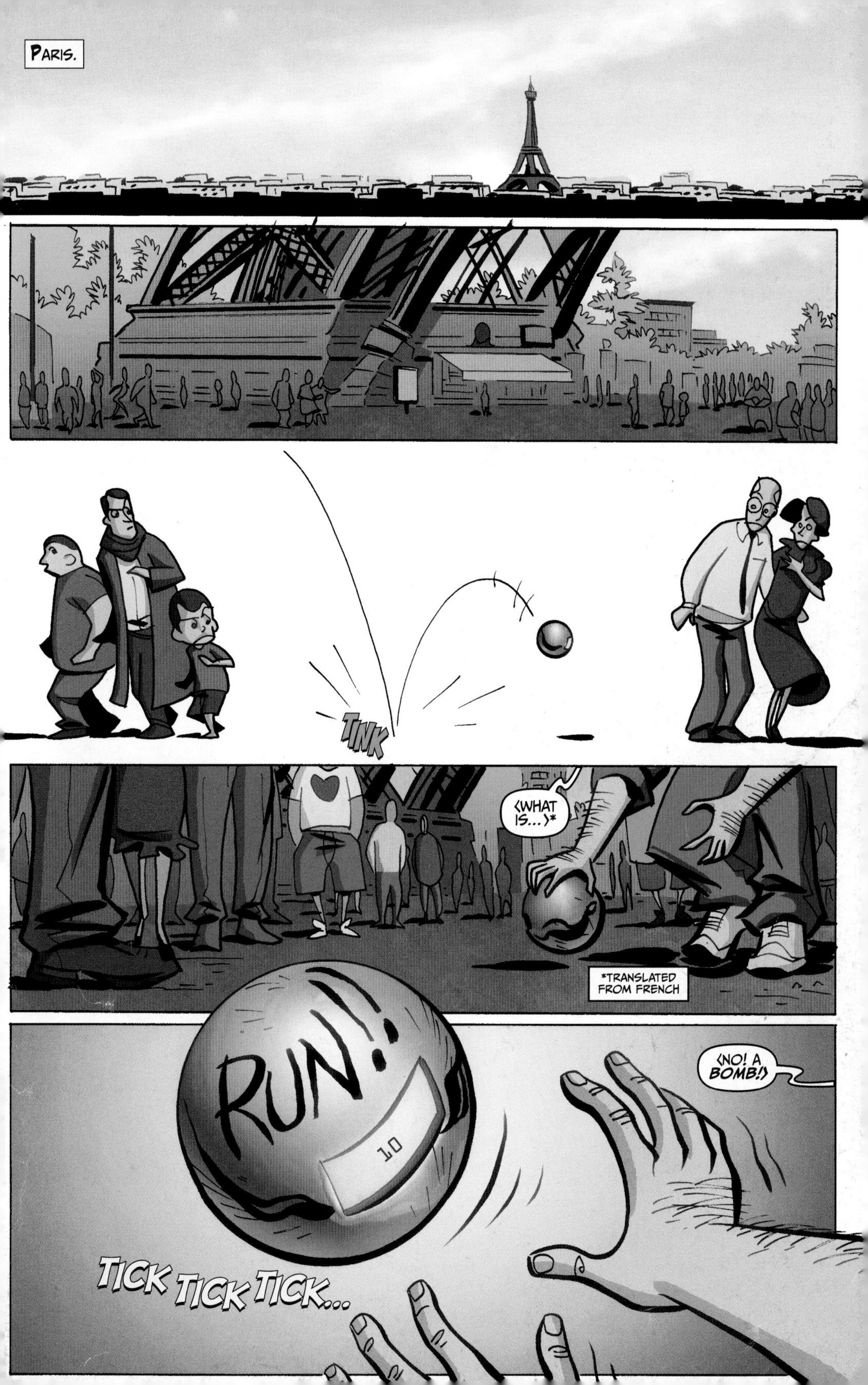
PARIS.
TINK
‹WHAT IS...›*
*TRANSLATED FROM FRENCH
RUN!!
10
‹NO! A BOMB!›
TICK TICK TICK...

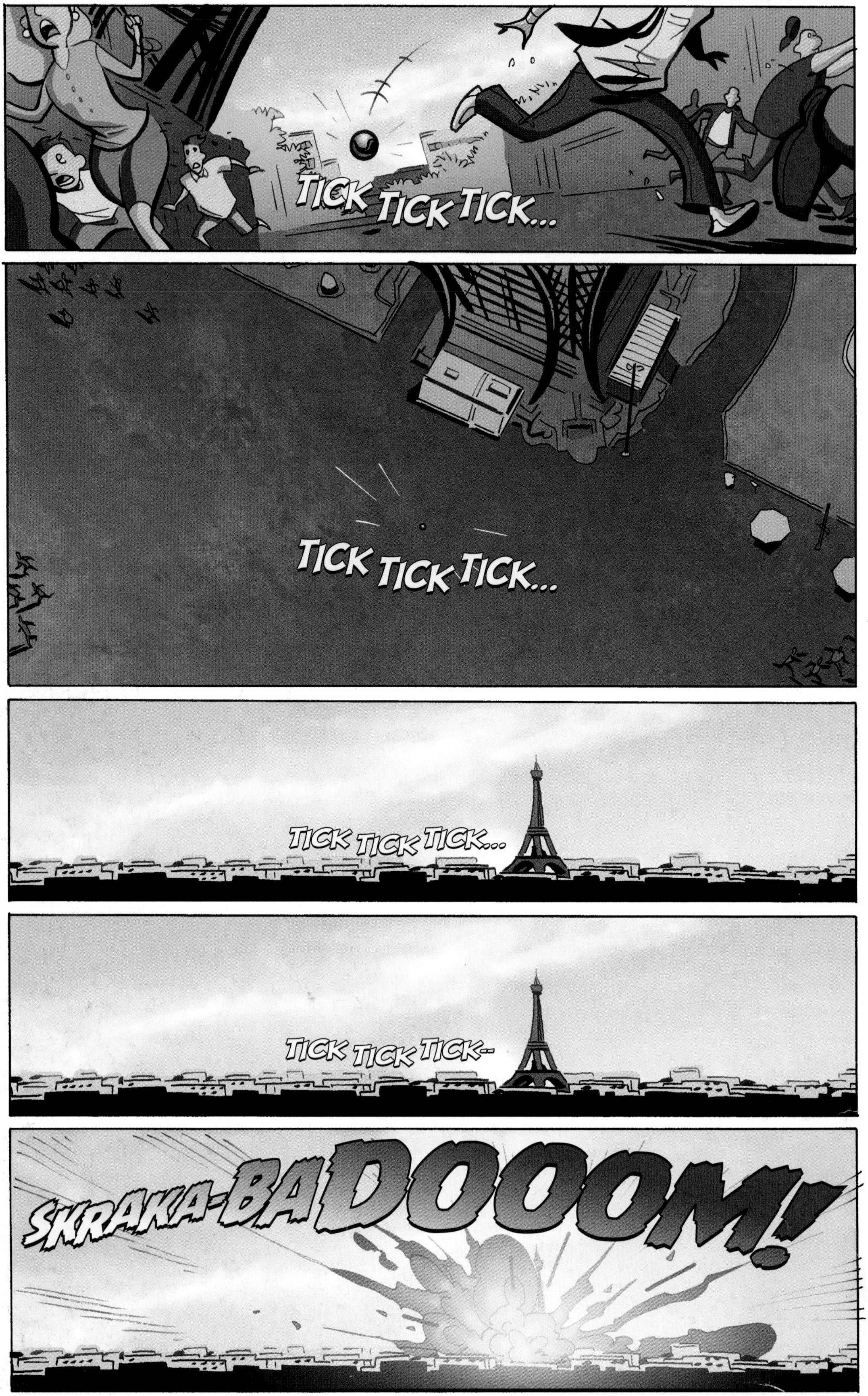
TICK TICK TICK...
TICK TICK TICK...
TICK TICK TICK...
TICK TICK TICK--
SKRAKA-BADOOOM!

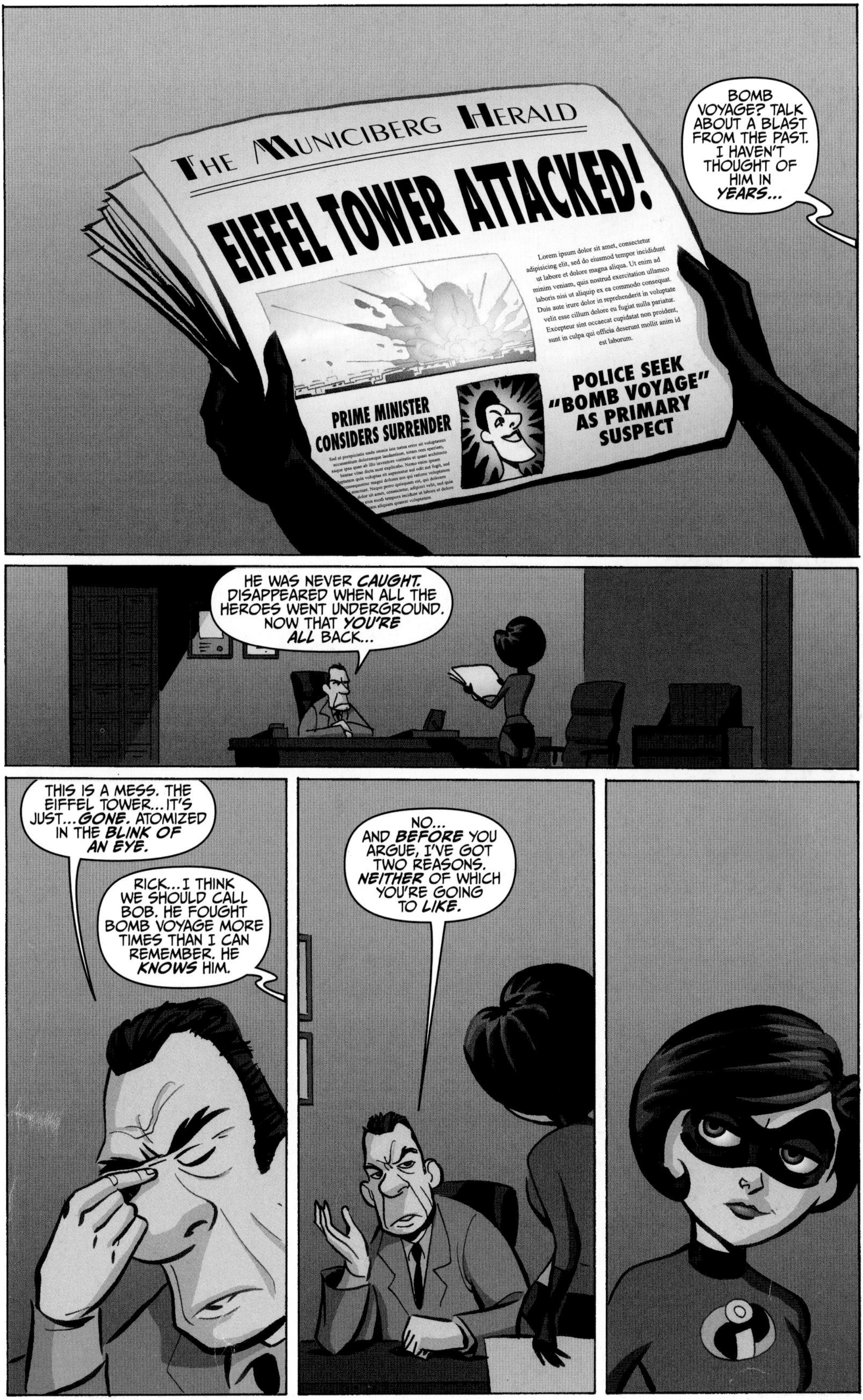
THE MUNICIBERG HERALD
EIFFEL TOWER ATTACKED!
Lorem ipsum dolor sit amet, consectetur adipisicing elit, sed do eiusmod tempor incididunt ut labore et dolore magna aliqua. Ut enim ad minim veniam, quis nostrud exercitation ullamco laboris nisi ut aliquip ex ea commodo consequat. Duis aute irure dolor in reprehenderit in voluptate velit esse cillum dolore eu fugiat nulla pariatur. Excepteur sint occaecat cupidatat non proident, sunt in culpa qui officia deserunt mollit anim id est laborum.
PRIME MINISTER CONSIDERS SURRENDER
POLICE SEEK "BOMB VOYAGE" AS PRIMARY SUSPECT
BOMB VOYAGE? TALK ABOUT A BLAST FROM THE PAST. I HAVEN'T THOUGHT OF HIM IN YEARS...
HE WAS NEVER CAUGHT. DISAPPEARED WHEN ALL THE HEROES WENT UNDERGROUND. NOW THAT YOU'RE ALL BACK...
THIS IS A MESS. THE EIFFEL TOWER...IT'S JUST...GONE. ATOMIZED IN THE BLINK OF AN EYE.
RICK...I THINK WE SHOULD CALL BOB. HE FOUGHT BOMB VOYAGE MORE TIMES THAN I CAN REMEMBER. HE KNOWS HIM.
NO... AND BEFORE YOU ARGUE, I'VE GOT TWO REASONS. NEITHER OF WHICH YOU'RE GOING TO LIKE.

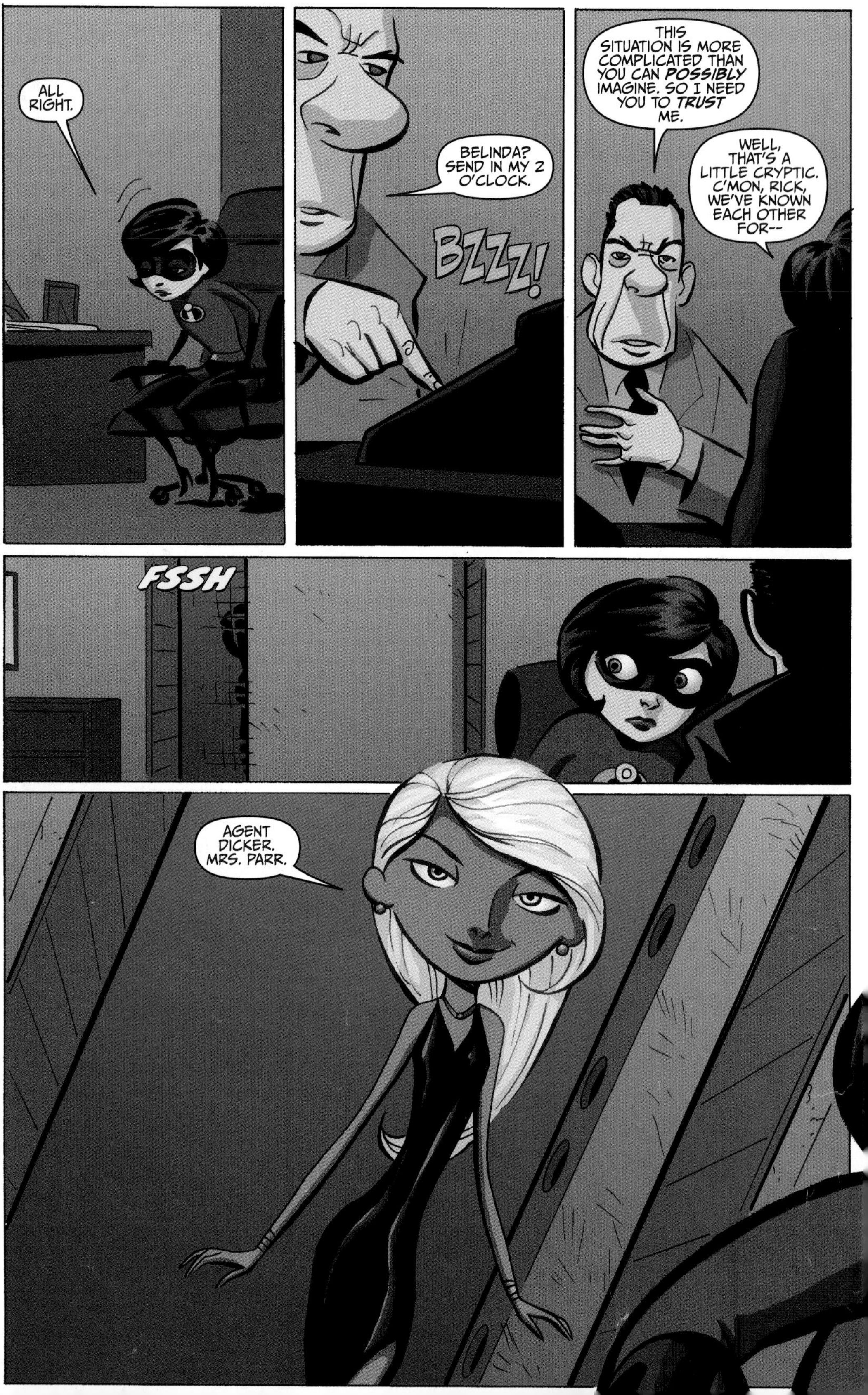
ALL RIGHT.
BELINDA? SEND IN MY 2 O'CLOCK.
BZZZ!
THIS SITUATION IS MORE COMPLICATED THAN YOU CAN POSSIBLY IMAGINE. SO I NEED YOU TO TRUST ME.
WELL, THAT'S A LITTLE CRYPTIC. C'MON, RICK, WE'VE KNOWN EACH OTHER FOR--
FSSH
AGENT DICKER. MRS. PARR.

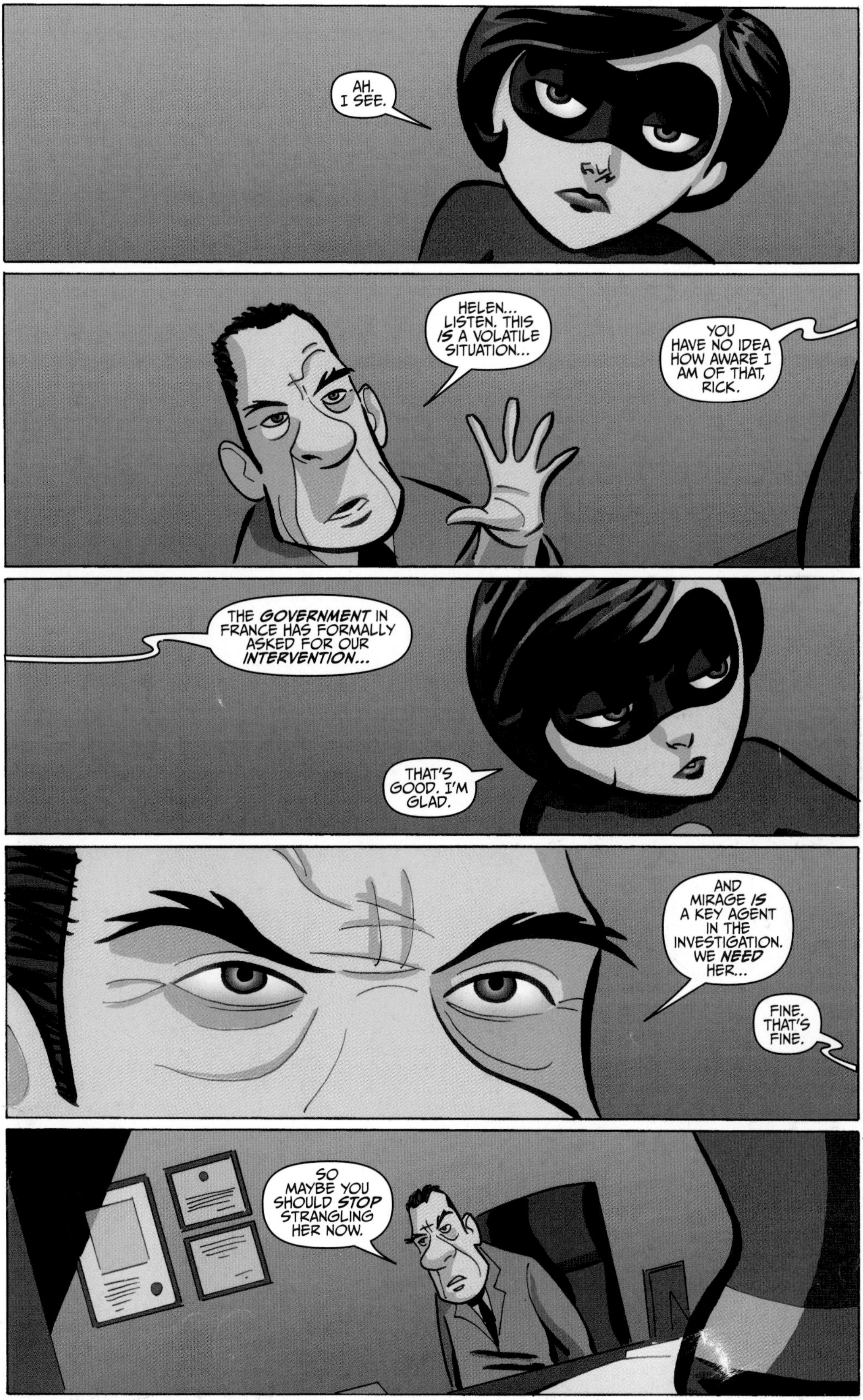
AH. I SEE.
HELEN... LISTEN. THIS *IS* A VOLATILE SITUATION...
YOU HAVE NO IDEA HOW AWARE I AM OF THAT, RICK.
THE *GOVERNMENT* IN FRANCE HAS FORMALLY ASKED FOR OUR *INTERVENTION*...
THAT'S GOOD. I'M GLAD.
AND MIRAGE *IS* A KEY AGENT IN THE INVESTIGATION. WE *NEED* HER...
FINE. THAT'S FINE.
SO MAYBE YOU SHOULD *STOP* STRANGLING HER NOW.

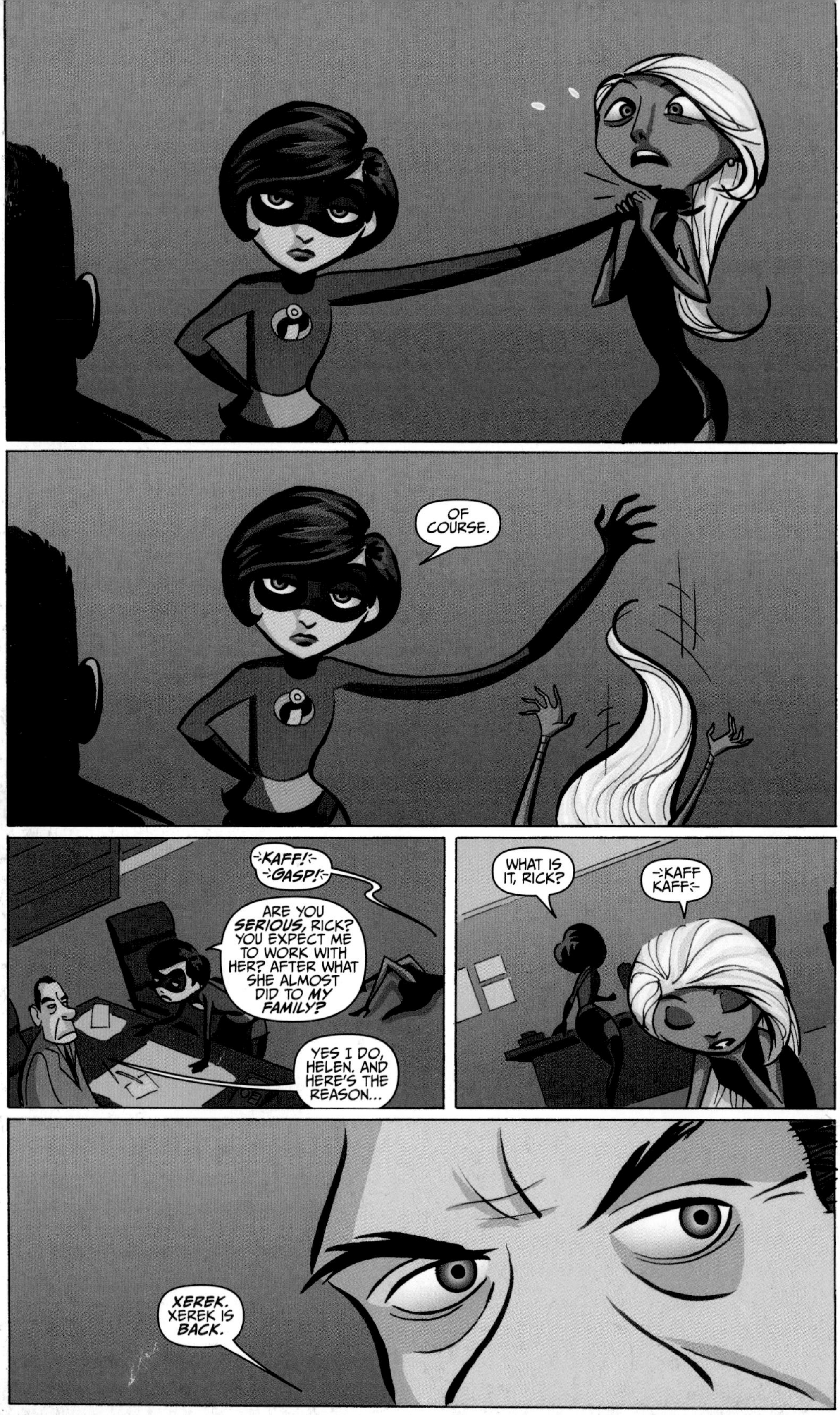
OF COURSE.
-KAFF!- -GASP!-
ARE YOU SERIOUS, RICK? YOU EXPECT ME TO WORK WITH HER? AFTER WHAT SHE ALMOST DID TO MY FAMILY?
YES I DO, HELEN. AND HERE'S THE REASON...
WHAT IS IT, RICK?
-KAFF KAFF-
XEREK. XEREK IS BACK.

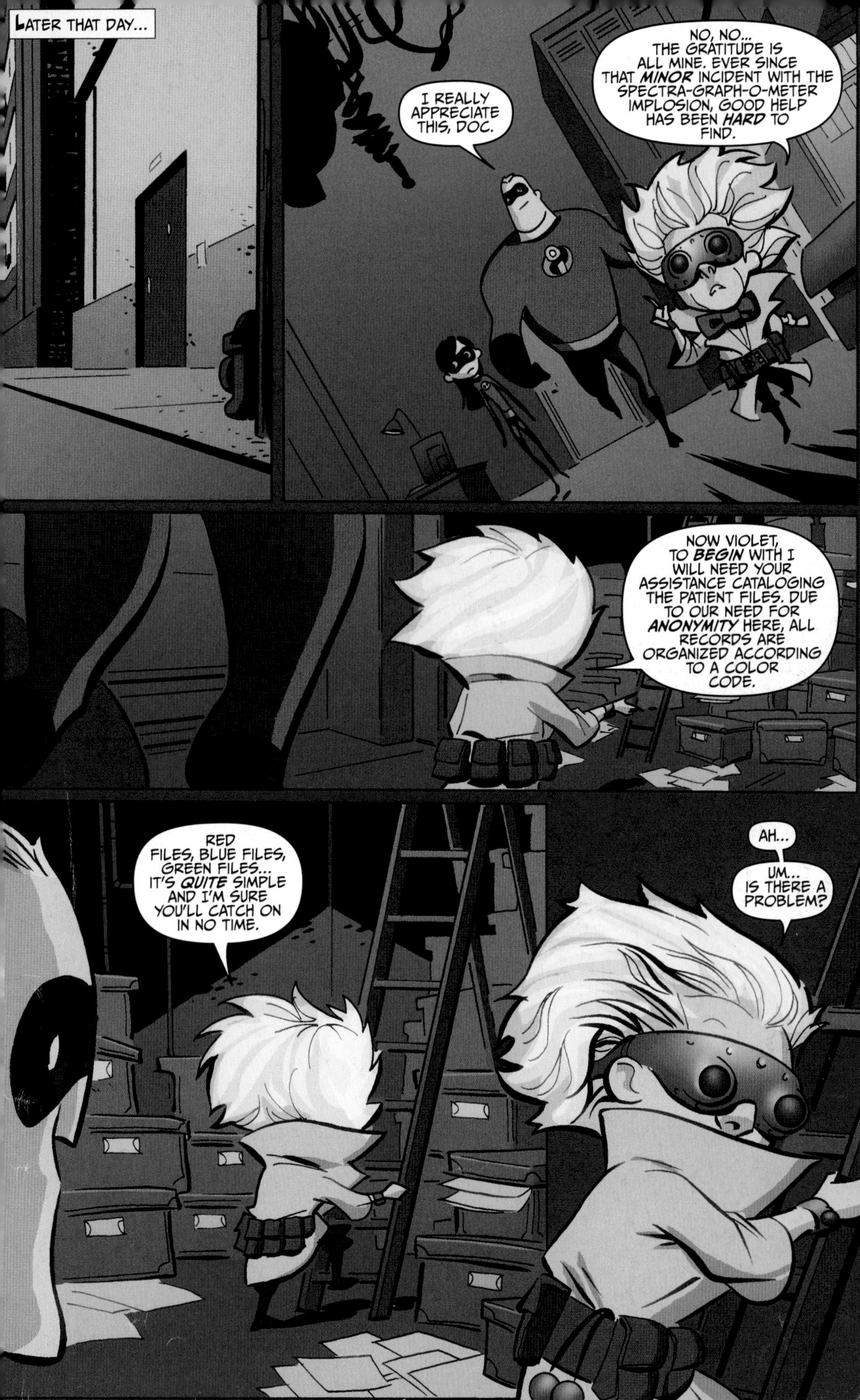

LATER THAT DAY...
I REALLY APPRECIATE THIS, DOC.
NO, NO... THE GRATITUDE IS ALL MINE. EVER SINCE THAT MINOR INCIDENT WITH THE SPECTRA-GRAPH-O-METER IMPLOSION, GOOD HELP HAS BEEN HARD TO FIND.
NOW VIOLET, TO BEGIN WITH I WILL NEED YOUR ASSISTANCE CATALOGING THE PATIENT FILES. DUE TO OUR NEED FOR ANONYMITY HERE, ALL RECORDS ARE ORGANIZED ACCORDING TO A COLOR CODE.
RED FILES, BLUE FILES, GREEN FILES... IT'S QUITE SIMPLE AND I'M SURE YOU'LL CATCH ON IN NO TIME.
AH...
UM... IS THERE A PROBLEM?

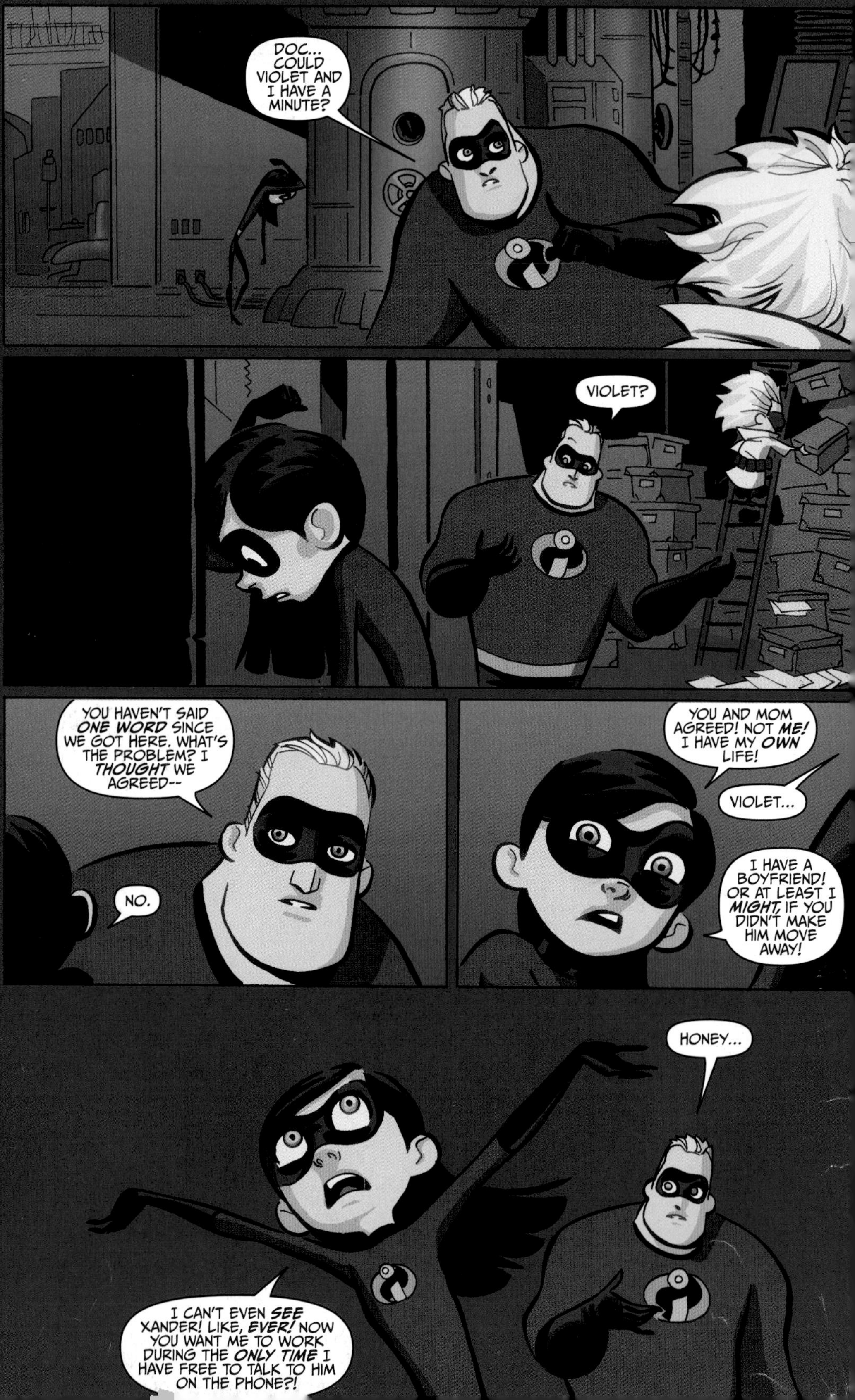
DOC... COULD VIOLET AND I HAVE A MINUTE?
VIOLET?
YOU HAVEN'T SAID ONE WORD SINCE WE GOT HERE. WHAT'S THE PROBLEM? I THOUGHT WE AGREED--
NO.
YOU AND MOM AGREED! NOT ME! I HAVE MY OWN LIFE!
VIOLET...
I HAVE A BOYFRIEND! OR AT LEAST I MIGHT, IF YOU DIDN'T MAKE HIM MOVE AWAY!
HONEY...
I CAN'T EVEN SEE XANDER! LIKE, EVER! NOW YOU WANT ME TO WORK DURING THE ONLY TIME I HAVE FREE TO TALK TO HIM ON THE PHONE?!

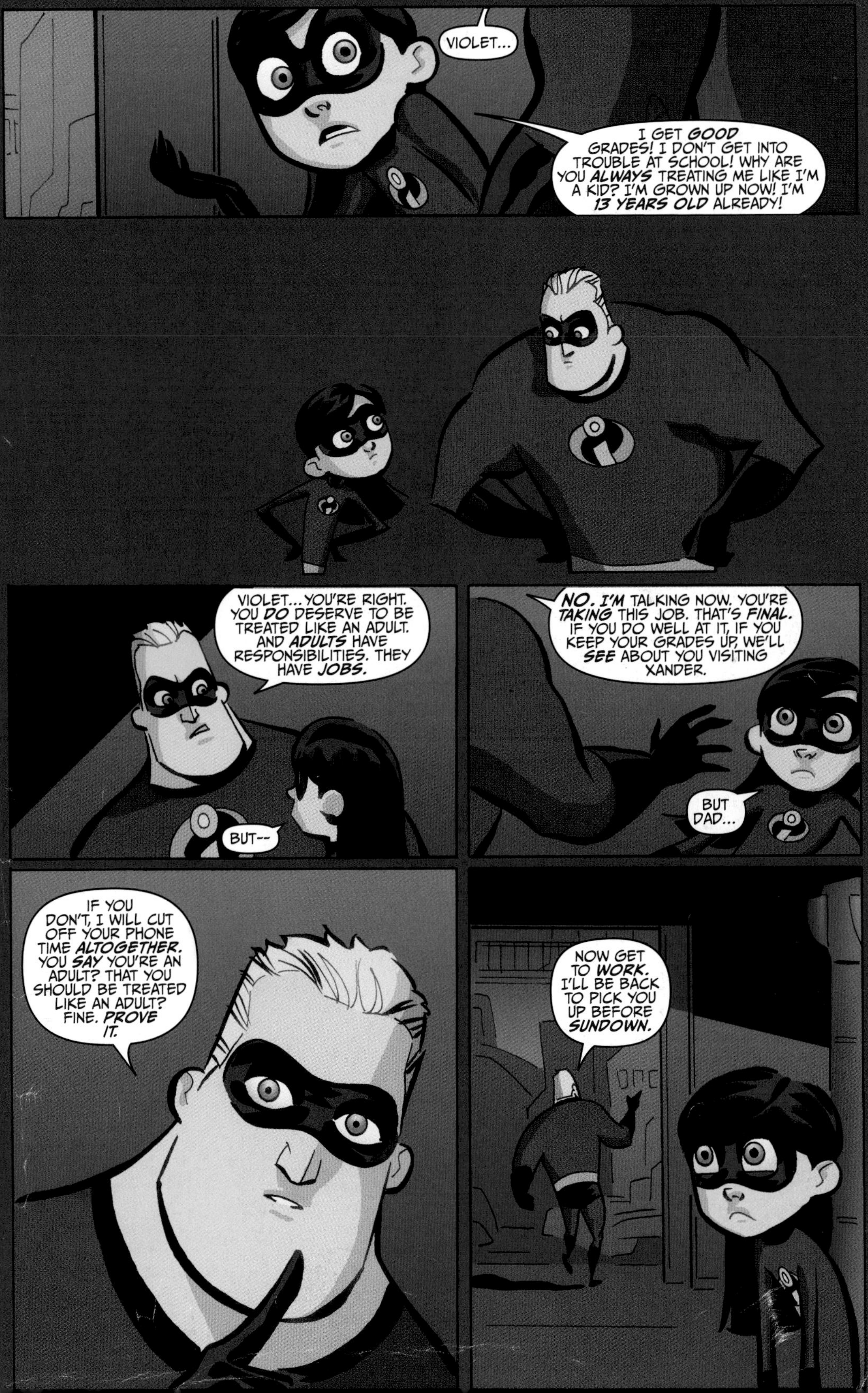
VIOLET...
I GET GOOD GRADES! I DON'T GET INTO TROUBLE AT SCHOOL! WHY ARE YOU ALWAYS TREATING ME LIKE I'M A KID? I'M GROWN UP NOW! I'M 13 YEARS OLD ALREADY!
VIOLET... YOU'RE RIGHT. YOU DO DESERVE TO BE TREATED LIKE AN ADULT. AND ADULTS HAVE RESPONSIBILITIES. THEY HAVE JOBS.
BUT--
NO. I'M TALKING NOW. YOU'RE TAKING THIS JOB. THAT'S FINAL. IF YOU DO WELL AT IT, IF YOU KEEP YOUR GRADES UP, WE'LL SEE ABOUT YOU VISITING XANDER.
BUT DAD...
IF YOU DON'T, I WILL CUT OFF YOUR PHONE TIME ALTOGETHER. YOU SAY YOU'RE AN ADULT? THAT YOU SHOULD BE TREATED LIKE AN ADULT? FINE. PROVE IT.
NOW GET TO WORK. I'LL BE BACK TO PICK YOU UP BEFORE SUNDOWN.

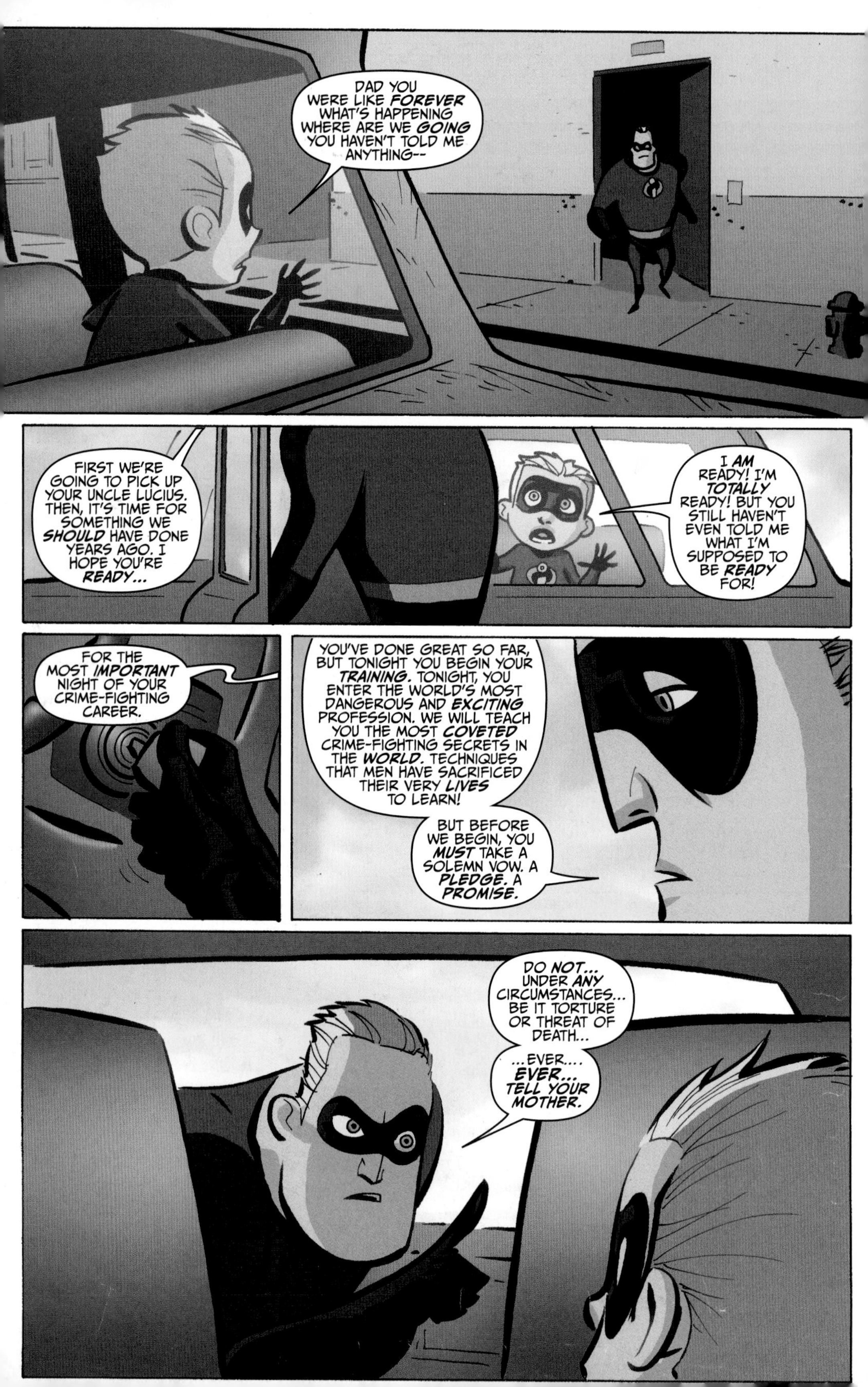
DAD YOU WERE LIKE FOREVER WHAT'S HAPPENING WHERE ARE WE GOING YOU HAVEN'T TOLD ME ANYTHING--
FIRST WE'RE GOING TO PICK UP YOUR UNCLE LUCIUS. THEN, IT'S TIME FOR SOMETHING WE SHOULD HAVE DONE YEARS AGO. I HOPE YOU'RE READY...
I AM READY! I'M TOTALLY READY! BUT YOU STILL HAVEN'T EVEN TOLD ME WHAT I'M SUPPOSED TO BE READY FOR!
FOR THE MOST IMPORTANT NIGHT OF YOUR CRIME-FIGHTING CAREER.
YOU'VE DONE GREAT SO FAR, BUT TONIGHT YOU BEGIN YOUR TRAINING. TONIGHT, YOU ENTER THE WORLD'S MOST DANGEROUS AND EXCITING PROFESSION. WE WILL TEACH YOU THE MOST COVETED CRIME-FIGHTING SECRETS IN THE WORLD. TECHNIQUES THAT MEN HAVE SACRIFICED THEIR VERY LIVES TO LEARN!
BUT BEFORE WE BEGIN, YOU MUST TAKE A SOLEMN VOW. A PLEDGE. A PROMISE.
DO NOT... UNDER ANY CIRCUMSTANCES... BE IT TORTURE OR THREAT OF DEATH...
...EVER.... EVER... TELL YOUR MOTHER.

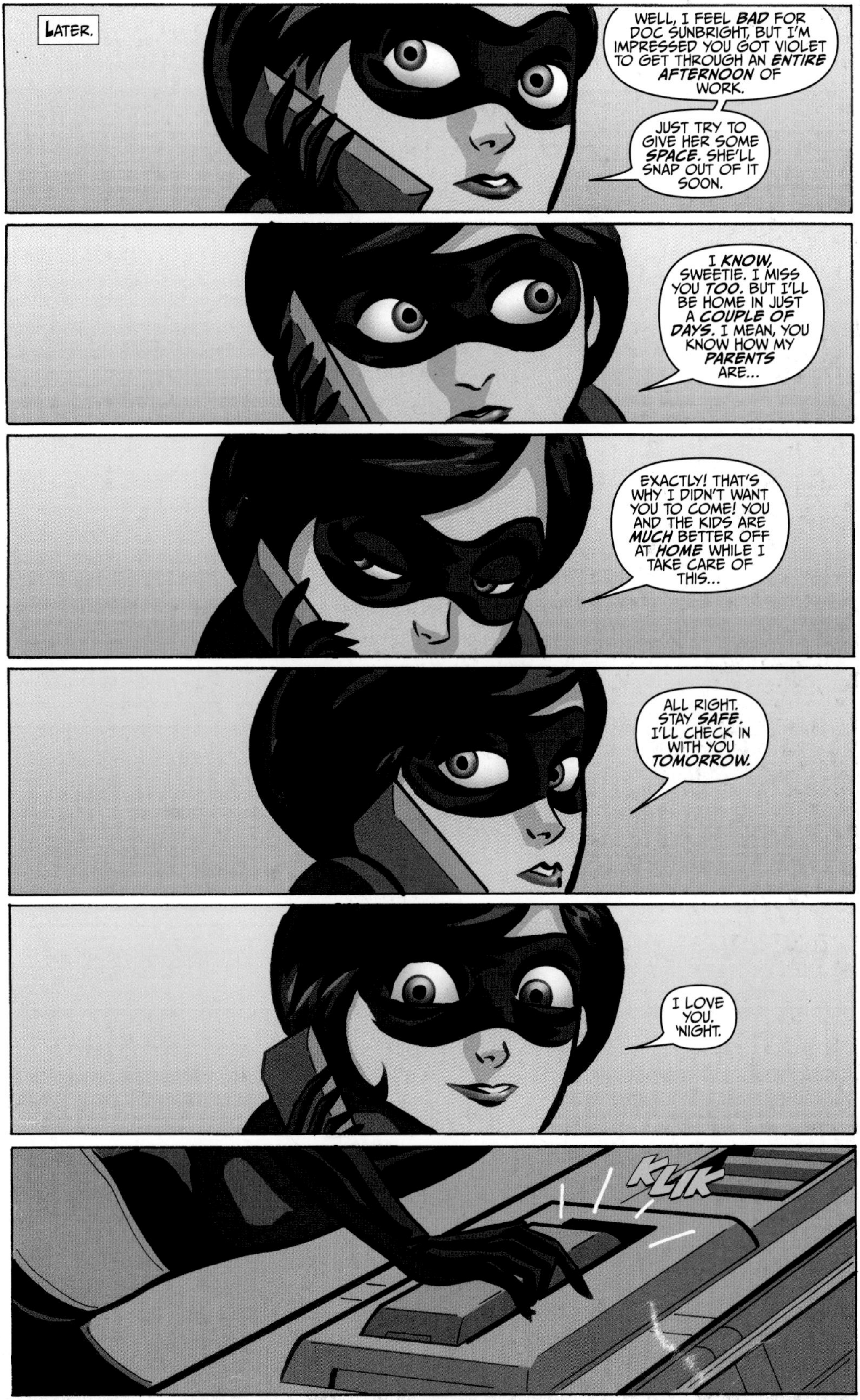
LATER.
WELL, I FEEL BAD FOR DOC SUNBRIGHT, BUT I'M IMPRESSED YOU GOT VIOLET TO GET THROUGH AN ENTIRE AFTERNOON OF WORK.
JUST TRY TO GIVE HER SOME SPACE. SHE'LL SNAP OUT OF IT SOON.
I KNOW, SWEETIE. I MISS YOU TOO. BUT I'LL BE HOME IN JUST A COUPLE OF DAYS. I MEAN, YOU KNOW HOW MY PARENTS ARE...
EXACTLY! THAT'S WHY I DIDN'T WANT YOU TO COME! YOU AND THE KIDS ARE MUCH BETTER OFF AT HOME WHILE I TAKE CARE OF THIS...
ALL RIGHT. STAY SAFE. I'LL CHECK IN WITH YOU TOMORROW.
I LOVE YOU. 'NIGHT.
KLIK

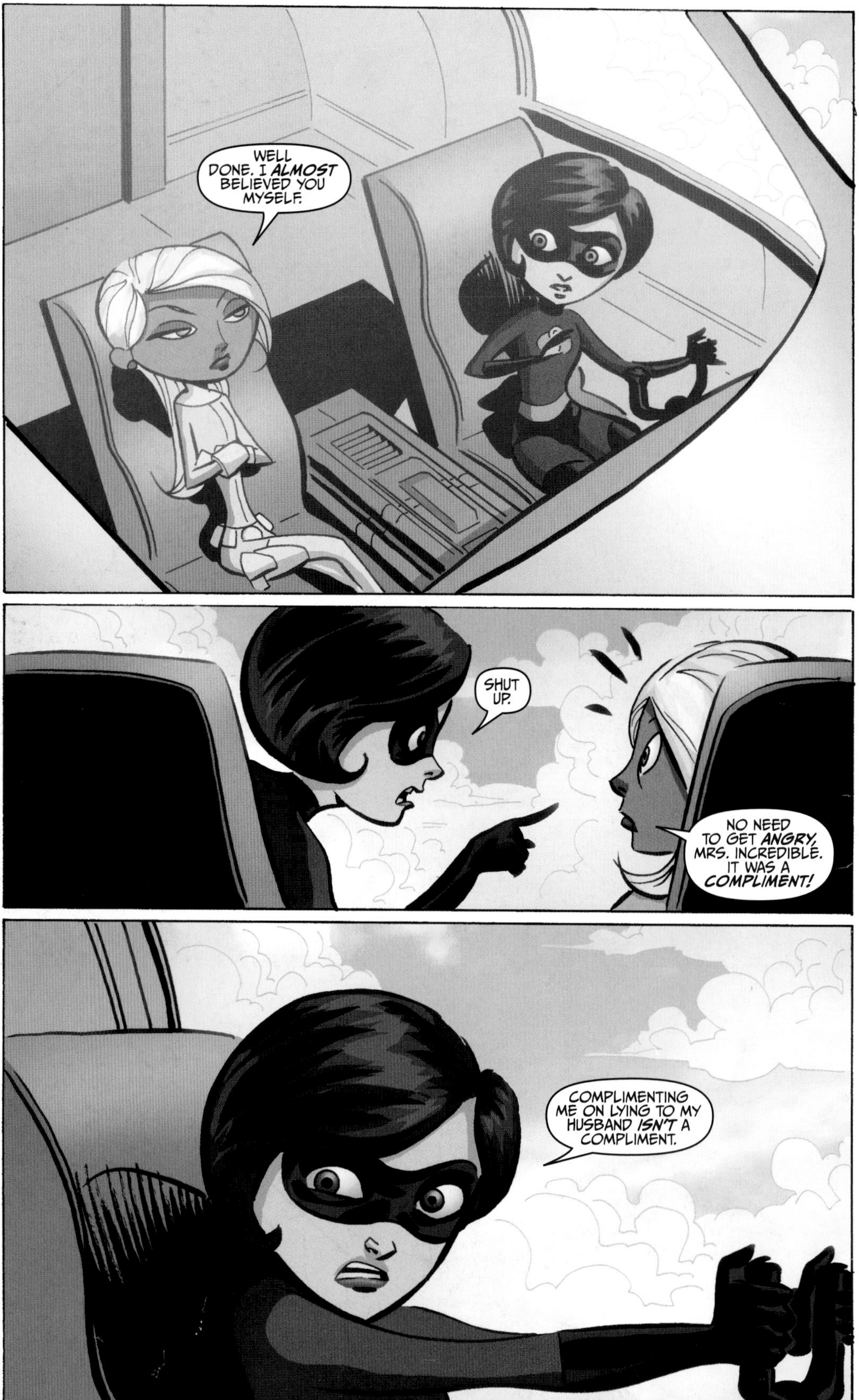
WELL DONE. I ALMOST BELIEVED YOU MYSELF.
SHUT UP.
NO NEED TO GET ANGRY, MRS. INCREDIBLE. IT WAS A COMPLIMENT!
COMPLIMENTING ME ON LYING TO MY HUSBAND ISN'T A COMPLIMENT.

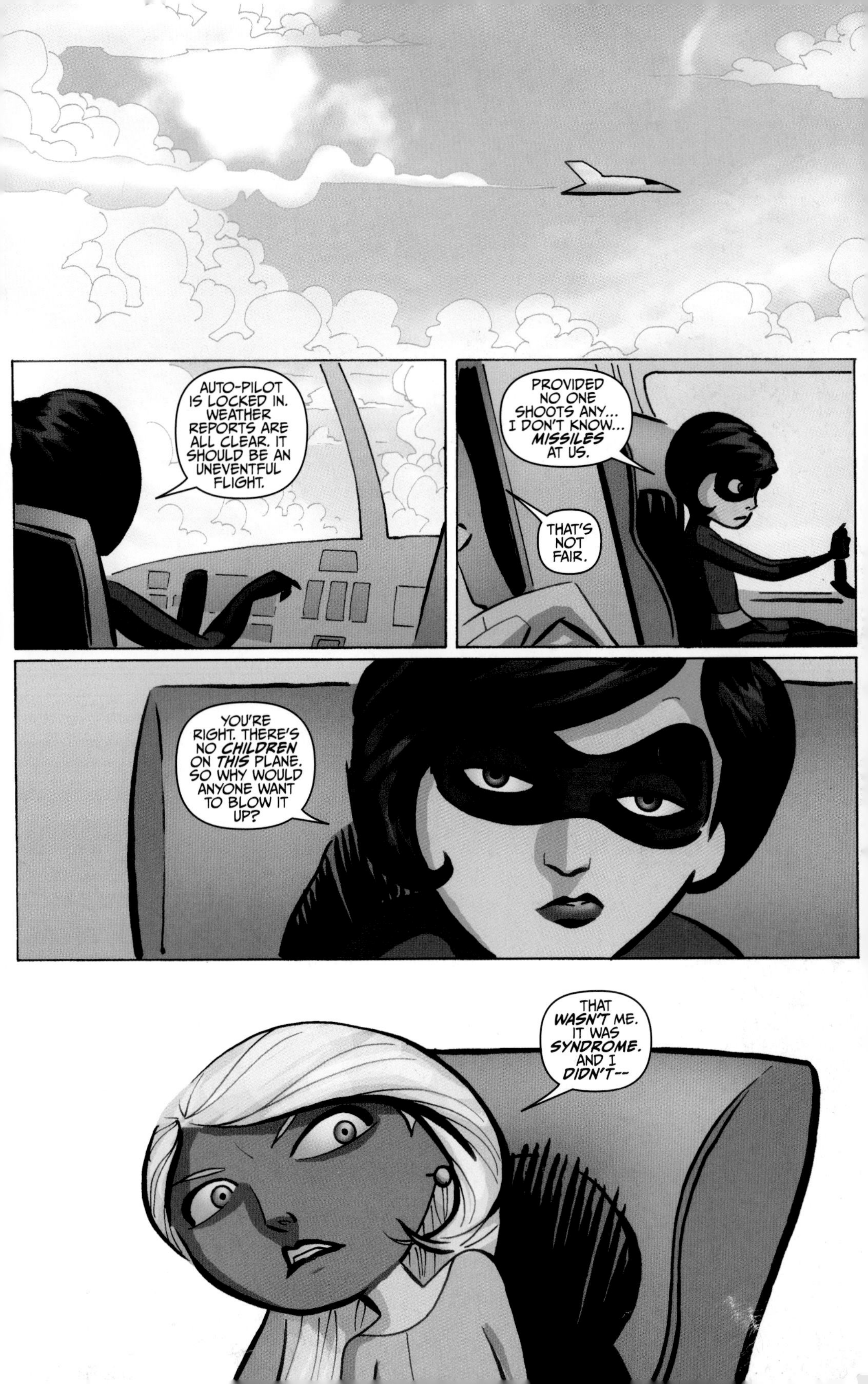
AUTO-PILOT IS LOCKED IN. WEATHER REPORTS ARE ALL CLEAR. IT SHOULD BE AN UNEVENTFUL FLIGHT.
PROVIDED NO ONE SHOOTS ANY... I DON'T KNOW... MISSILES AT US.
THAT'S NOT FAIR.
YOU'RE RIGHT. THERE'S NO CHILDREN ON THIS PLANE. SO WHY WOULD ANYONE WANT TO BLOW IT UP?
THAT WASN'T ME. IT WAS SYNDROME. AND I DIDN'T--

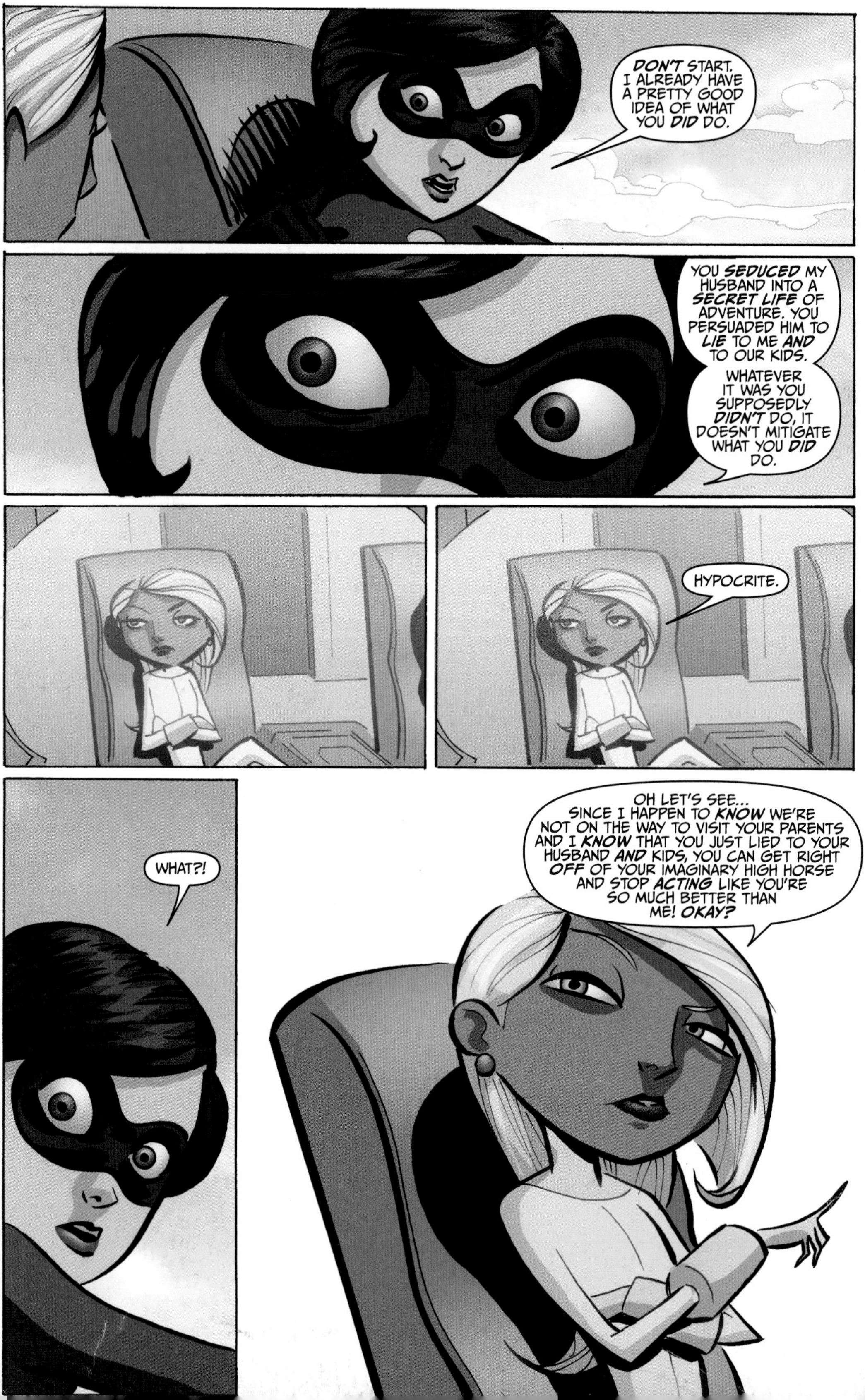
DON'T START. I ALREADY HAVE A PRETTY GOOD IDEA OF WHAT YOU DID DO.
YOU SEDUCED MY HUSBAND INTO A SECRET LIFE OF ADVENTURE. YOU PERSUADED HIM TO LIE TO ME AND TO OUR KIDS.
WHATEVER IT WAS YOU SUPPOSEDLY DIDN'T DO, IT DOESN'T MITIGATE WHAT YOU DID DO.
HYPOCRITE.
WHAT?!
OH LET'S SEE... SINCE I HAPPEN TO KNOW WE'RE NOT ON THE WAY TO VISIT YOUR PARENTS AND I KNOW THAT YOU JUST LIED TO YOUR HUSBAND AND KIDS, YOU CAN GET RIGHT OFF OF YOUR IMAGINARY HIGH HORSE AND STOP ACTING LIKE YOU'RE SO MUCH BETTER THAN ME! OKAY?

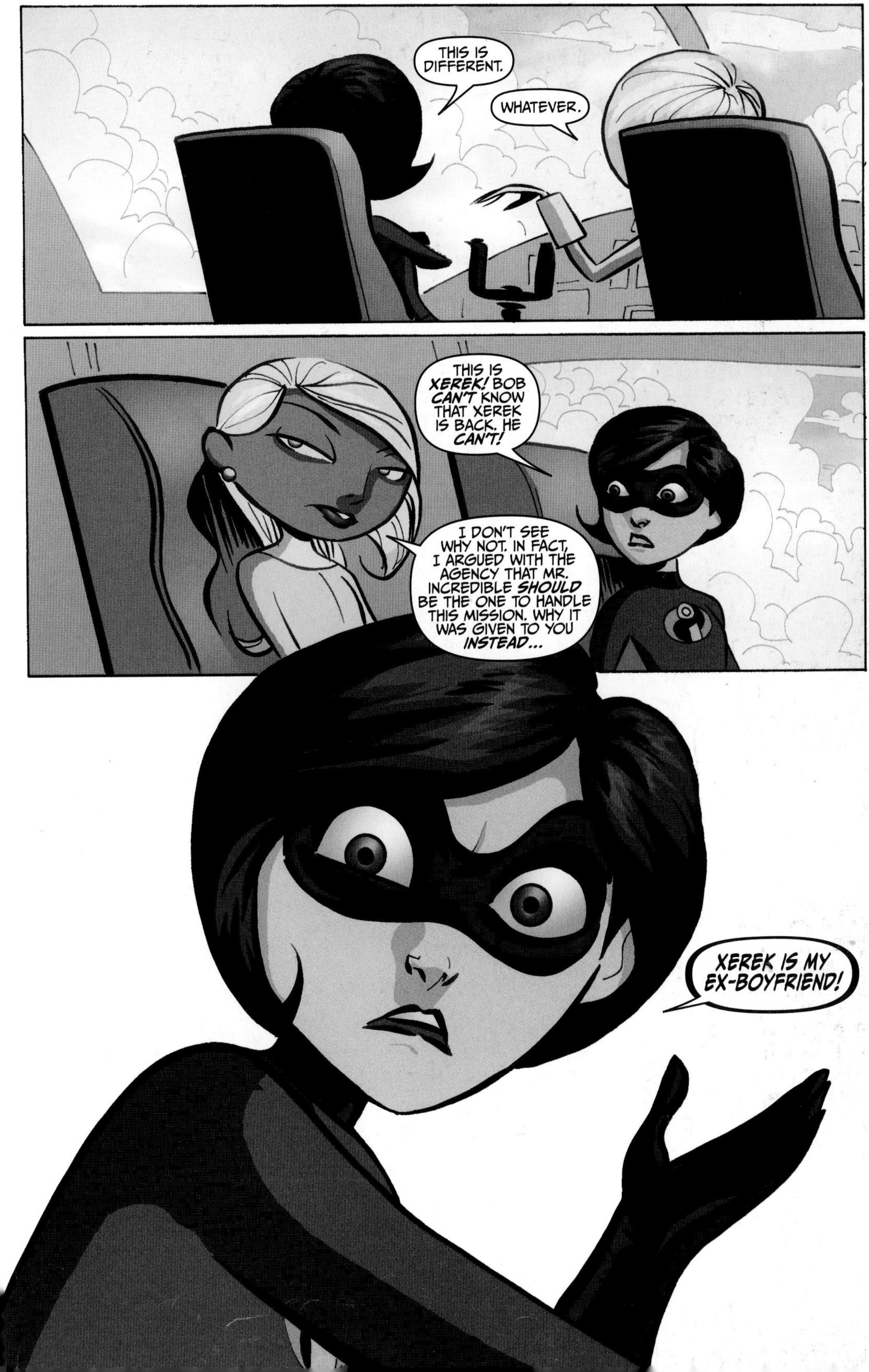
THIS IS DIFFERENT.
WHATEVER.
THIS IS XEREK! BOB CAN'T KNOW THAT XEREK IS BACK. HE CAN'T!
I DON'T SEE WHY NOT. IN FACT, I ARGUED WITH THE AGENCY THAT MR. INCREDIBLE SHOULD BE THE ONE TO HANDLE THIS MISSION. WHY IT WAS GIVEN TO YOU INSTEAD...
XEREK IS MY EX-BOYFRIEND!

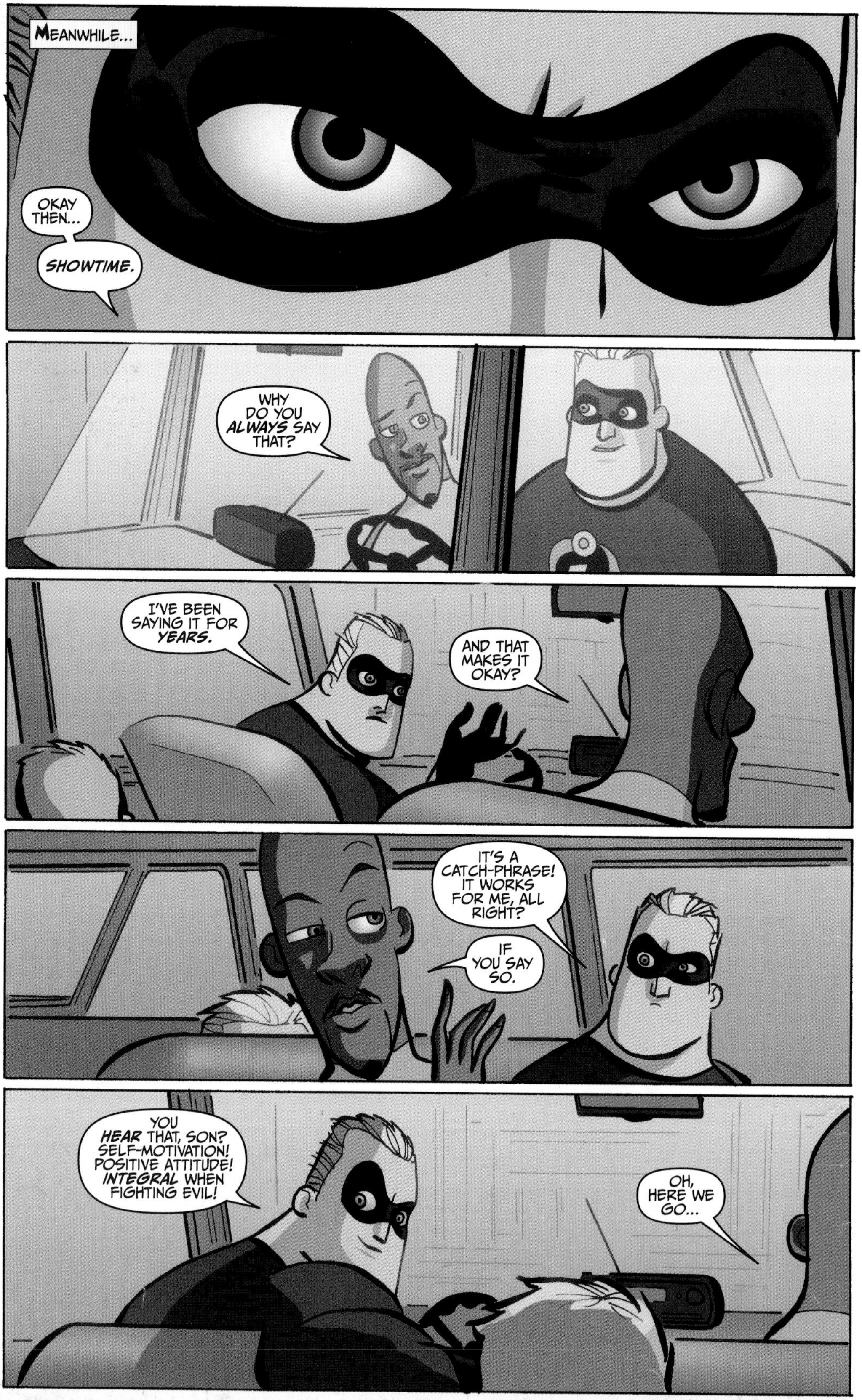
MEANWHILE...
OKAY THEN...
SHOWTIME.
WHY DO YOU ALWAYS SAY THAT?
I'VE BEEN SAYING IT FOR YEARS.
AND THAT MAKES IT OKAY?
IT'S A CATCH-PHRASE! IT WORKS FOR ME, ALL RIGHT?
IF YOU SAY SO.
YOU HEAR THAT, SON? SELF-MOTIVATION! POSITIVE ATTITUDE! INTEGRAL WHEN FIGHTING EVIL!
OH, HERE WE GO...

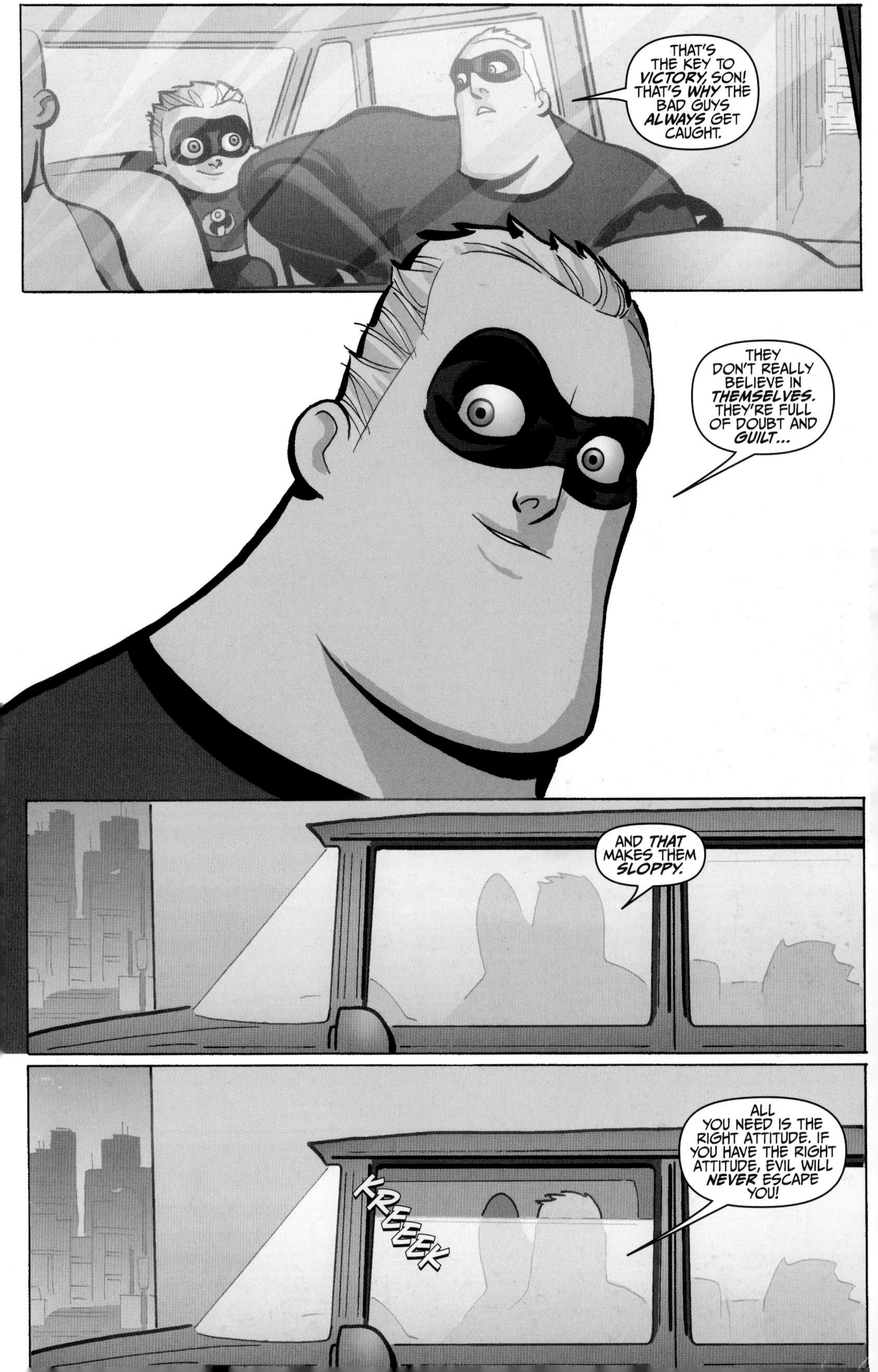
THAT'S THE KEY TO VICTORY, SON! THAT'S WHY THE BAD GUYS ALWAYS GET CAUGHT.
THEY DON'T REALLY BELIEVE IN THEMSELVES. THEY'RE FULL OF DOUBT AND GUILT...
AND THAT MAKES THEM SLOPPY.
KREEEK
ALL YOU NEED IS THE RIGHT ATTITUDE. IF YOU HAVE THE RIGHT ATTITUDE, EVIL WILL NEVER ESCAPE YOU!

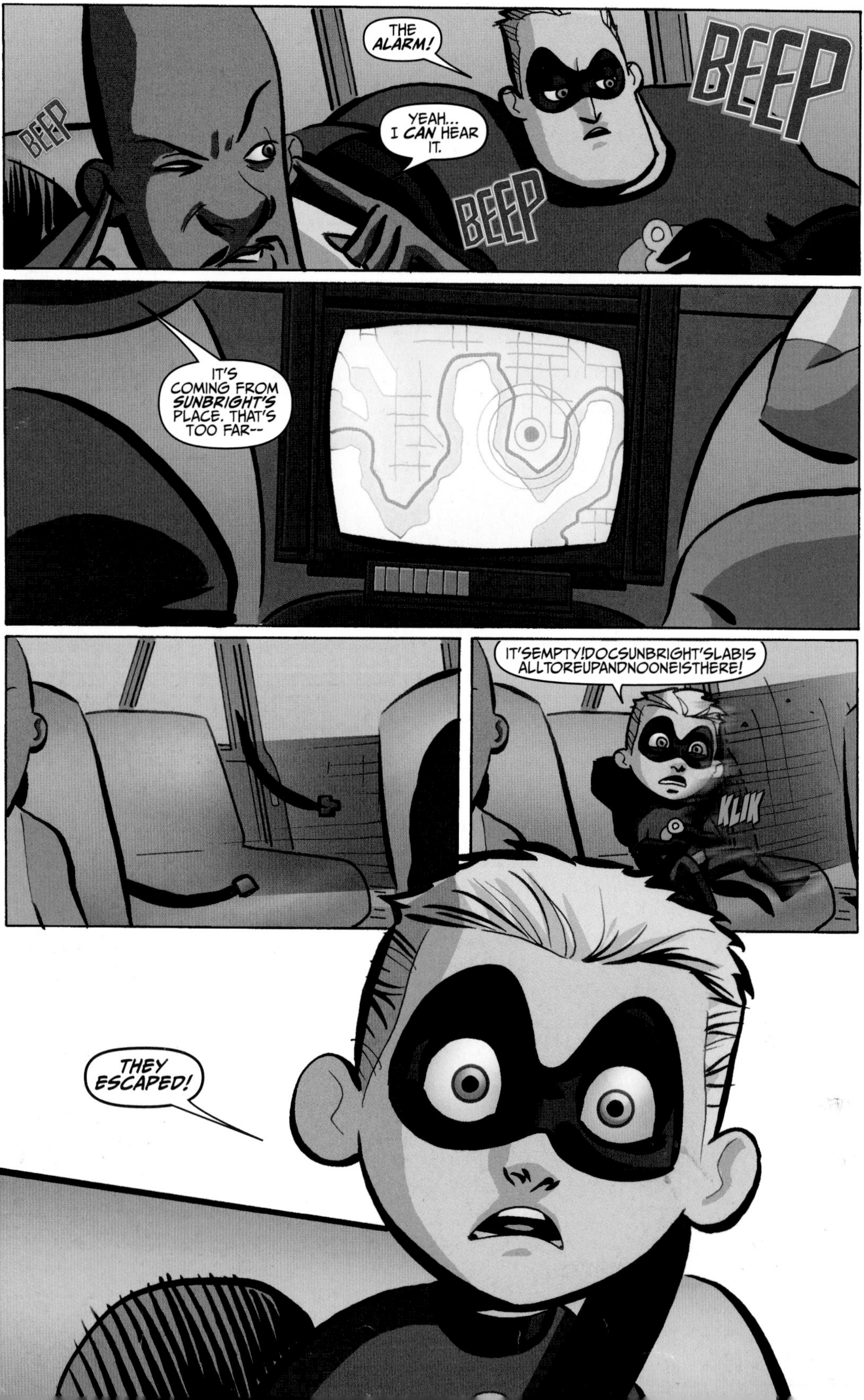
BEEP
THE ALARM!
YEAH... I CAN HEAR IT.
BEEP
BEEP
IT'S COMING FROM SUNBRIGHT'S PLACE. THAT'S TOO FAR--
IT'SEMPTY!DOCSUNBRIGHT'SLABIS ALLTOREUPANDNOONEISTHERE!
KLIK
THEY ESCAPED!

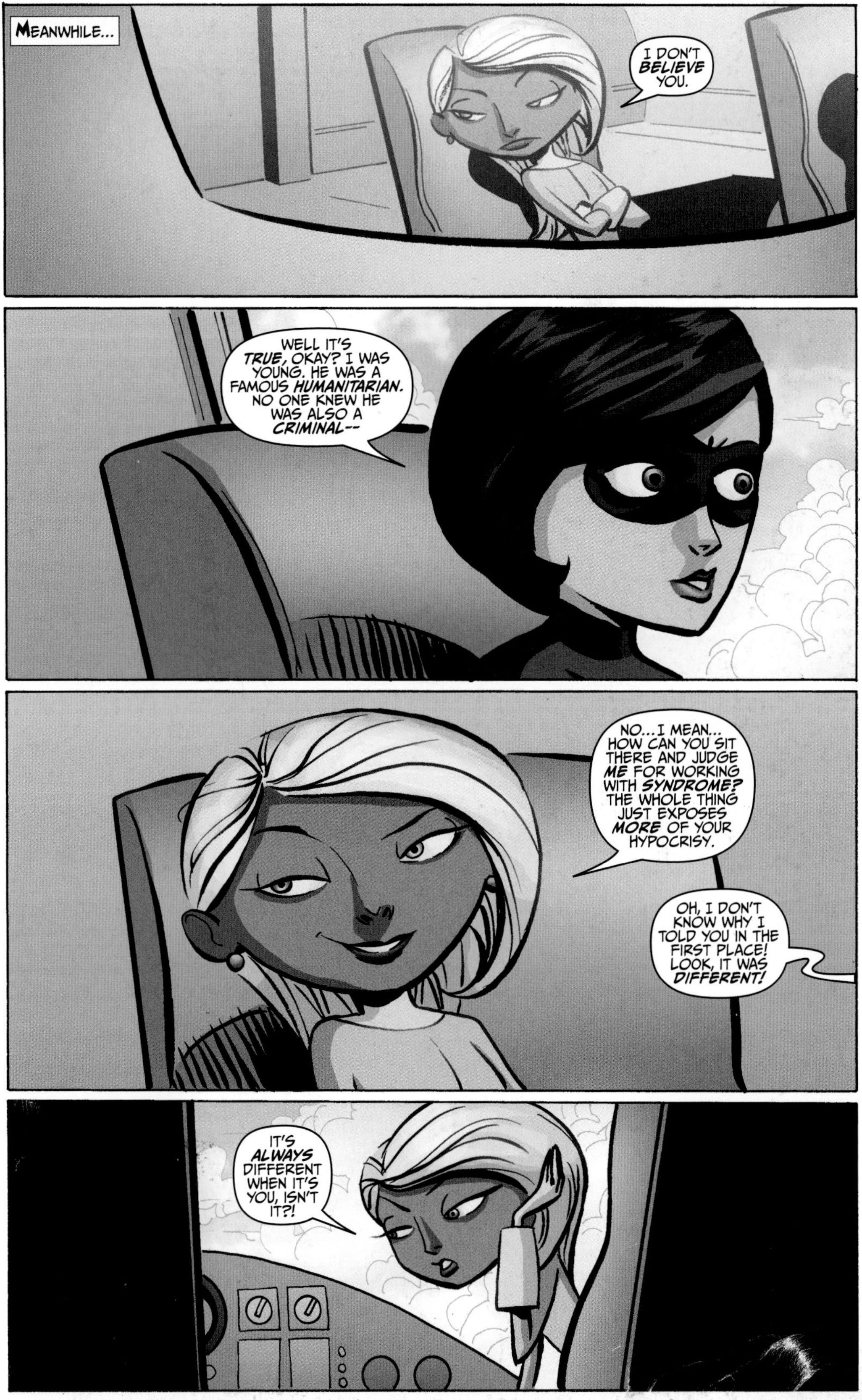
MEANWHILE...
I DON'T BELIEVE YOU.
WELL IT'S TRUE, OKAY? I WAS YOUNG. HE WAS A FAMOUS HUMANITARIAN. NO ONE KNEW HE WAS ALSO A CRIMINAL--
NO...I MEAN... HOW CAN YOU SIT THERE AND JUDGE ME FOR WORKING WITH SYNDROME? THE WHOLE THING JUST EXPOSES MORE OF YOUR HYPOCRISY.
OH, I DON'T KNOW WHY I TOLD YOU IN THE FIRST PLACE! LOOK, IT WAS DIFFERENT!
IT'S ALWAYS DIFFERENT WHEN IT'S YOU, ISN'T IT?!

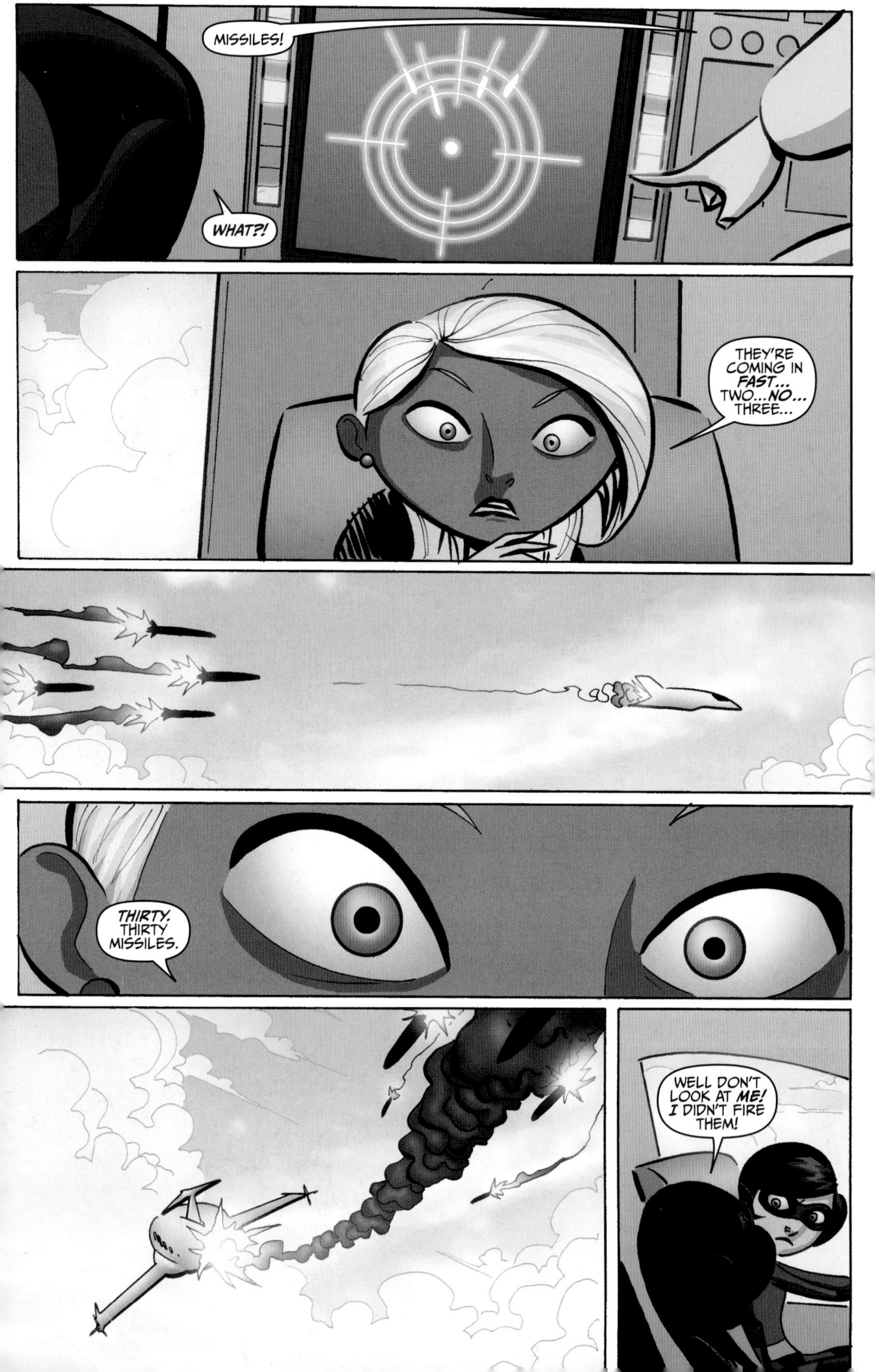
MISSILES!
WHAT?!
THEY'RE COMING IN FAST... TWO...NO... THREE...
THIRTY. THIRTY MISSILES.
WELL DON'T LOOK AT ME! I DIDN'T FIRE THEM!

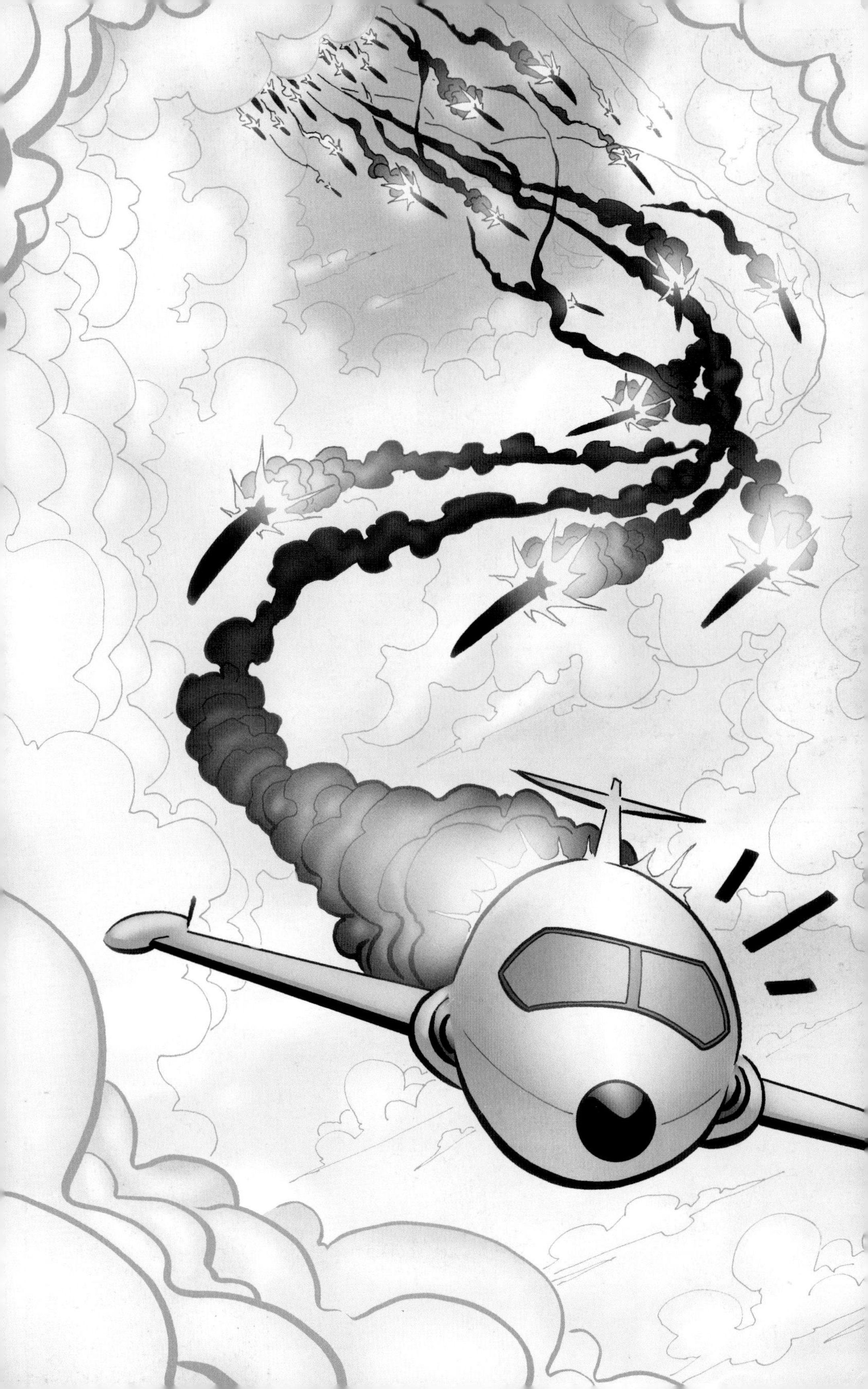

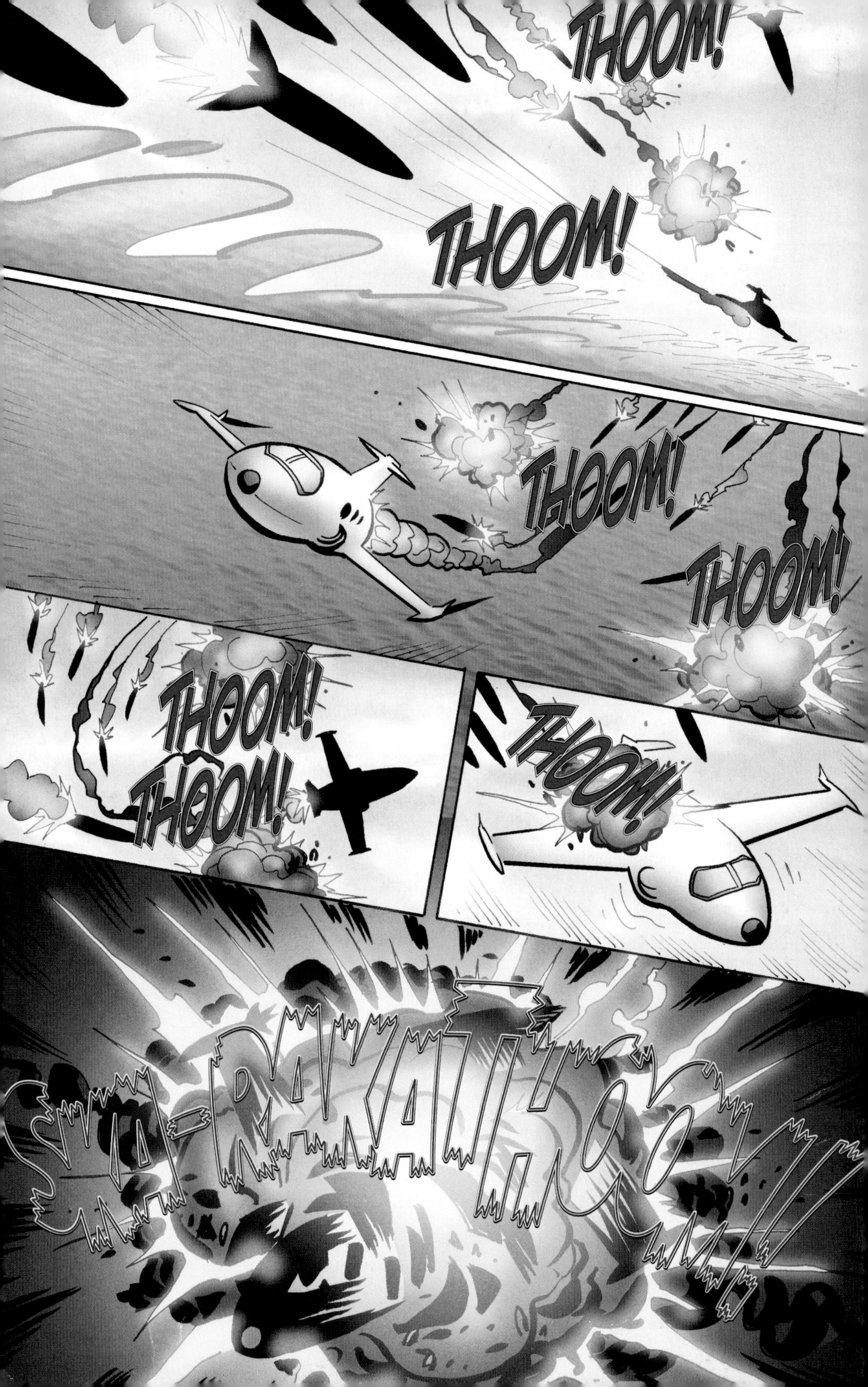
THOOM!
THOOM!
THOOM!
THOOM!
THOOM!
THOOM!
THOOM!
SKA-KAWHOOM!!

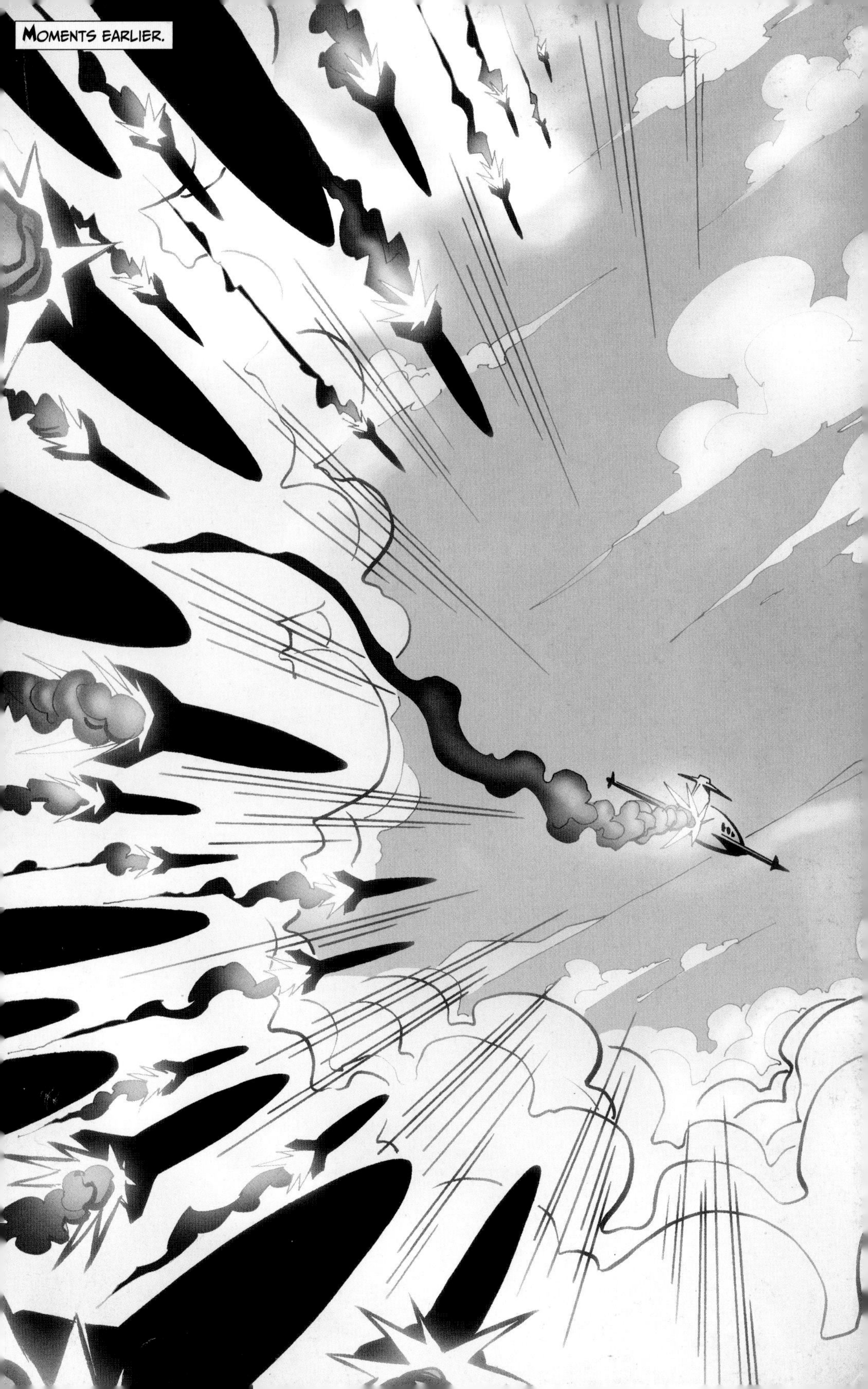
Moments earlier.

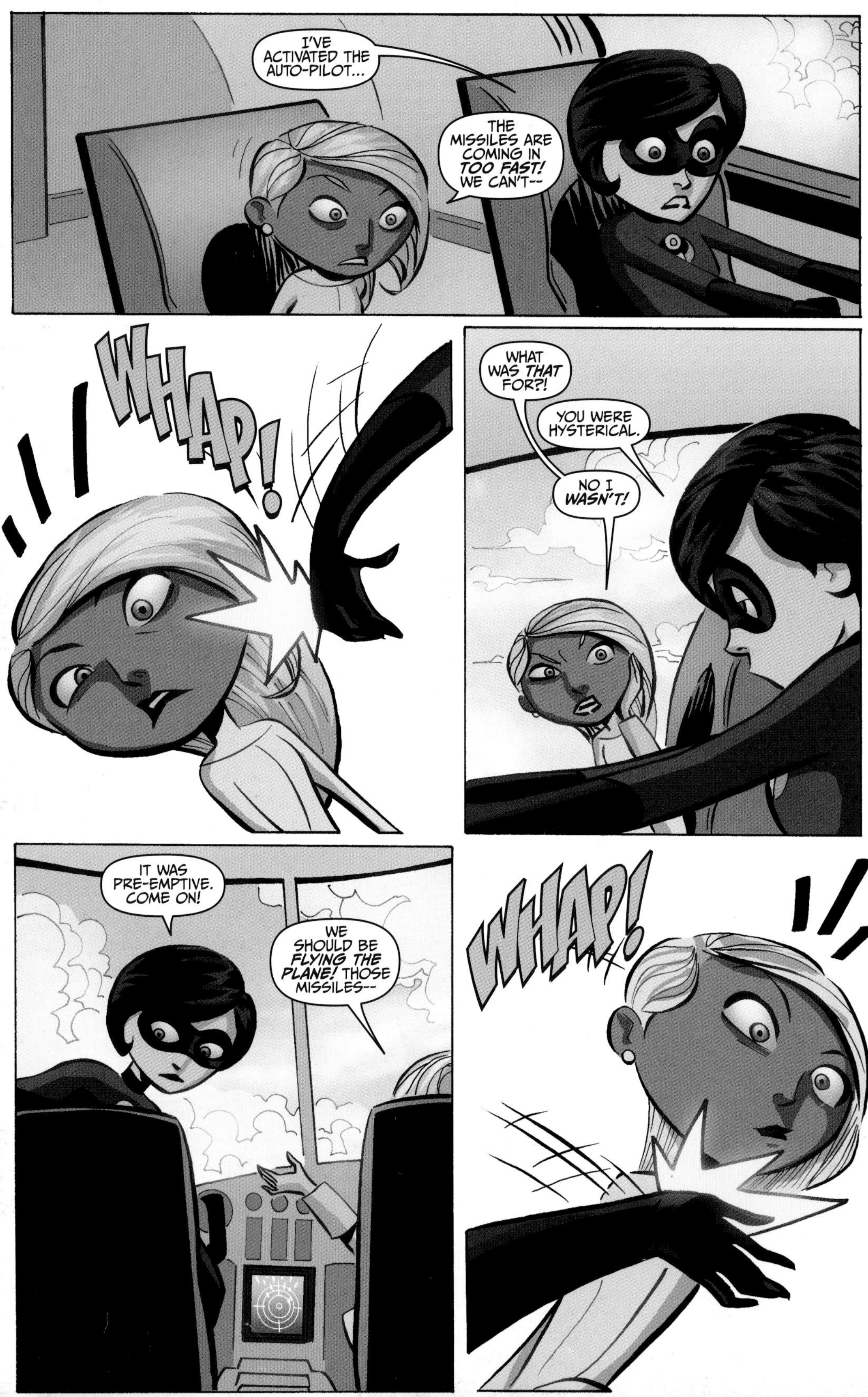
I'VE ACTIVATED THE AUTO-PILOT...
THE MISSILES ARE COMING IN *TOO FAST!* WE CAN'T--
WHAP!
WHAT WAS *THAT* FOR?!
YOU WERE HYSTERICAL.
NO I *WASN'T!*
IT WAS PRE-EMPTIVE. COME ON!
WE SHOULD BE *FLYING THE PLANE!* THOSE MISSILES--
WHAP!

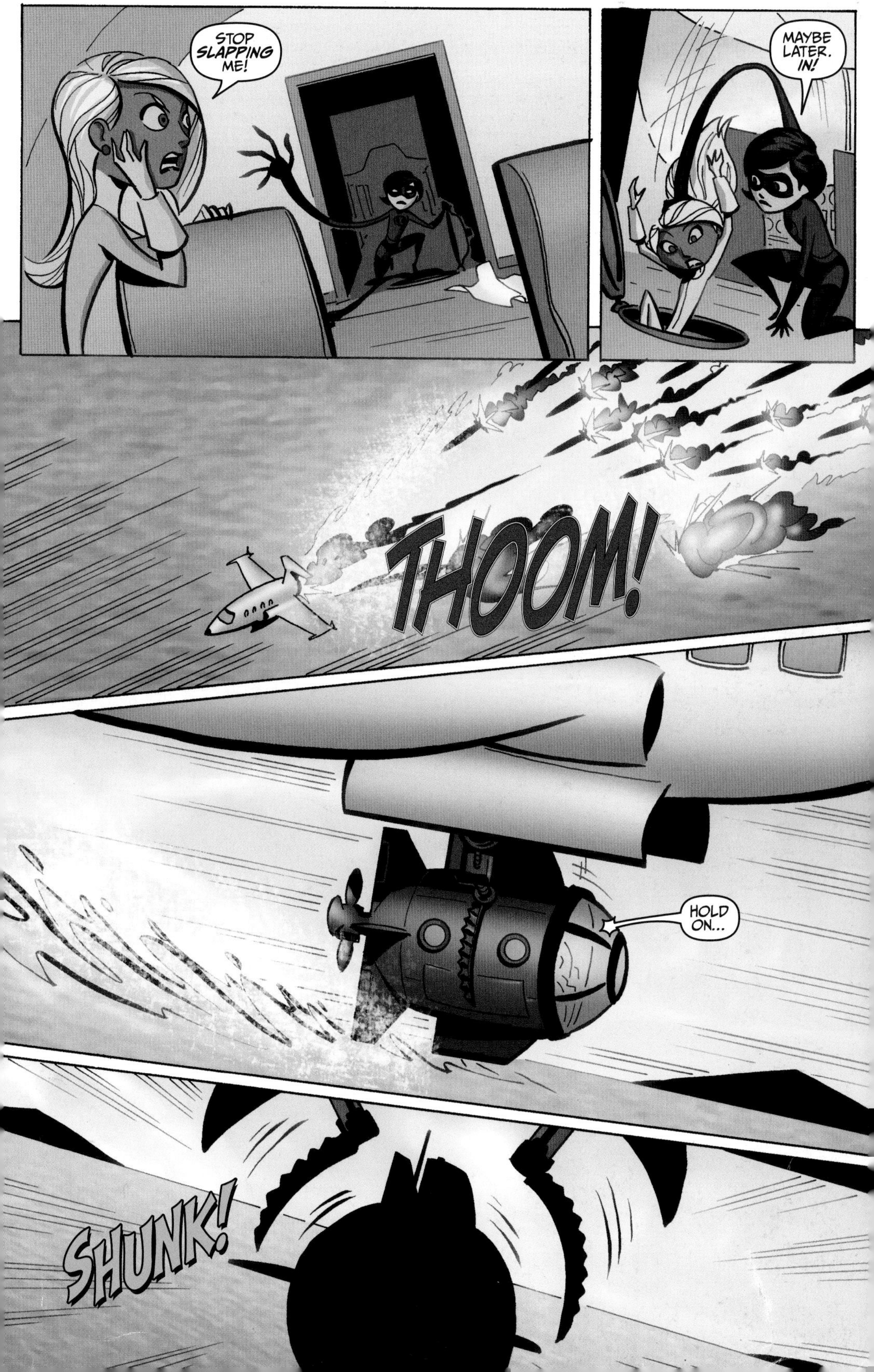
STOP SLAPPING ME!
MAYBE LATER. IN!
THOOM!
HOLD ON...
SHUNK!

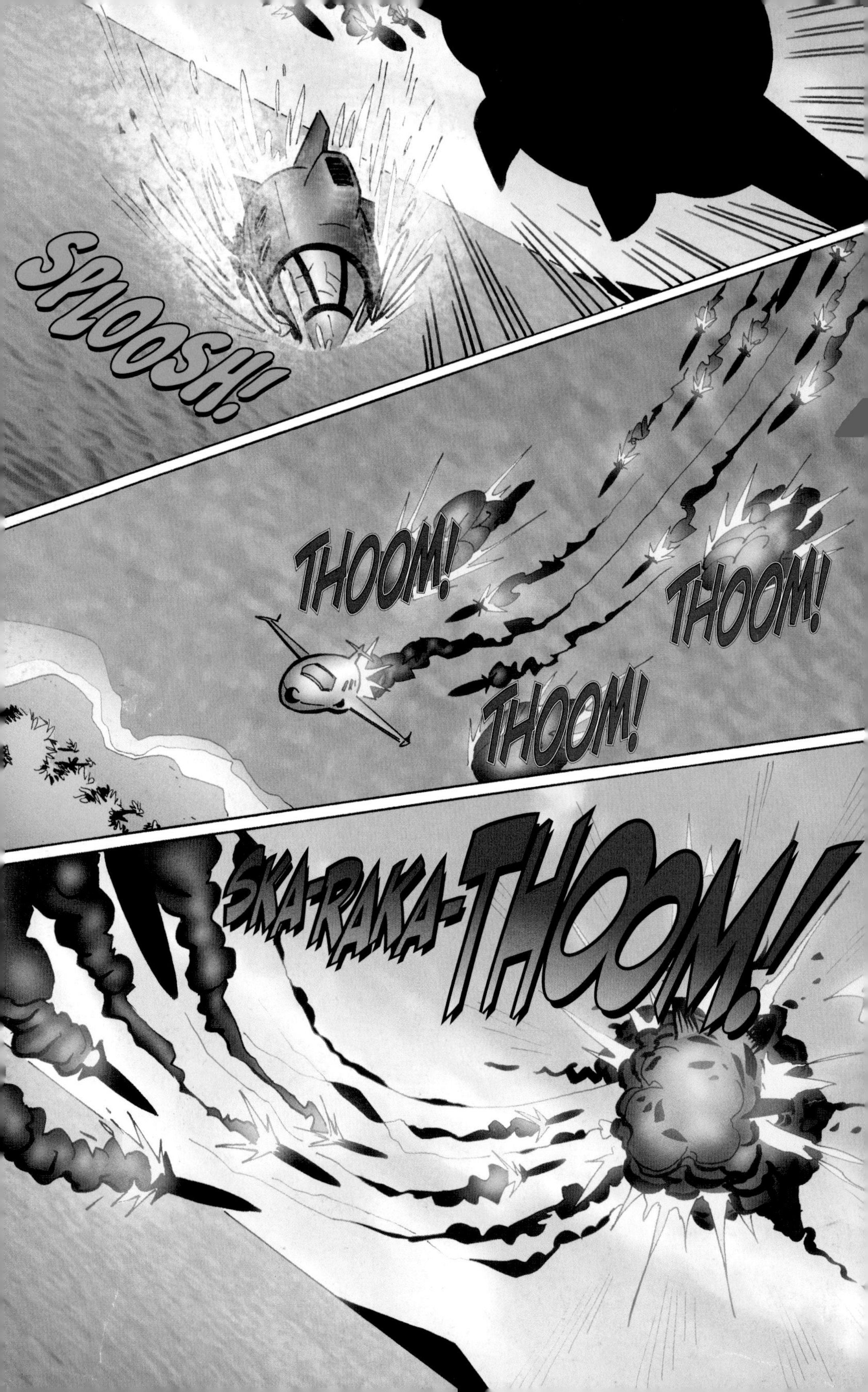
SPLOOSH!!
THOOM!
THOOM!
THOOM!
SKA-RAKA-THOOM!!

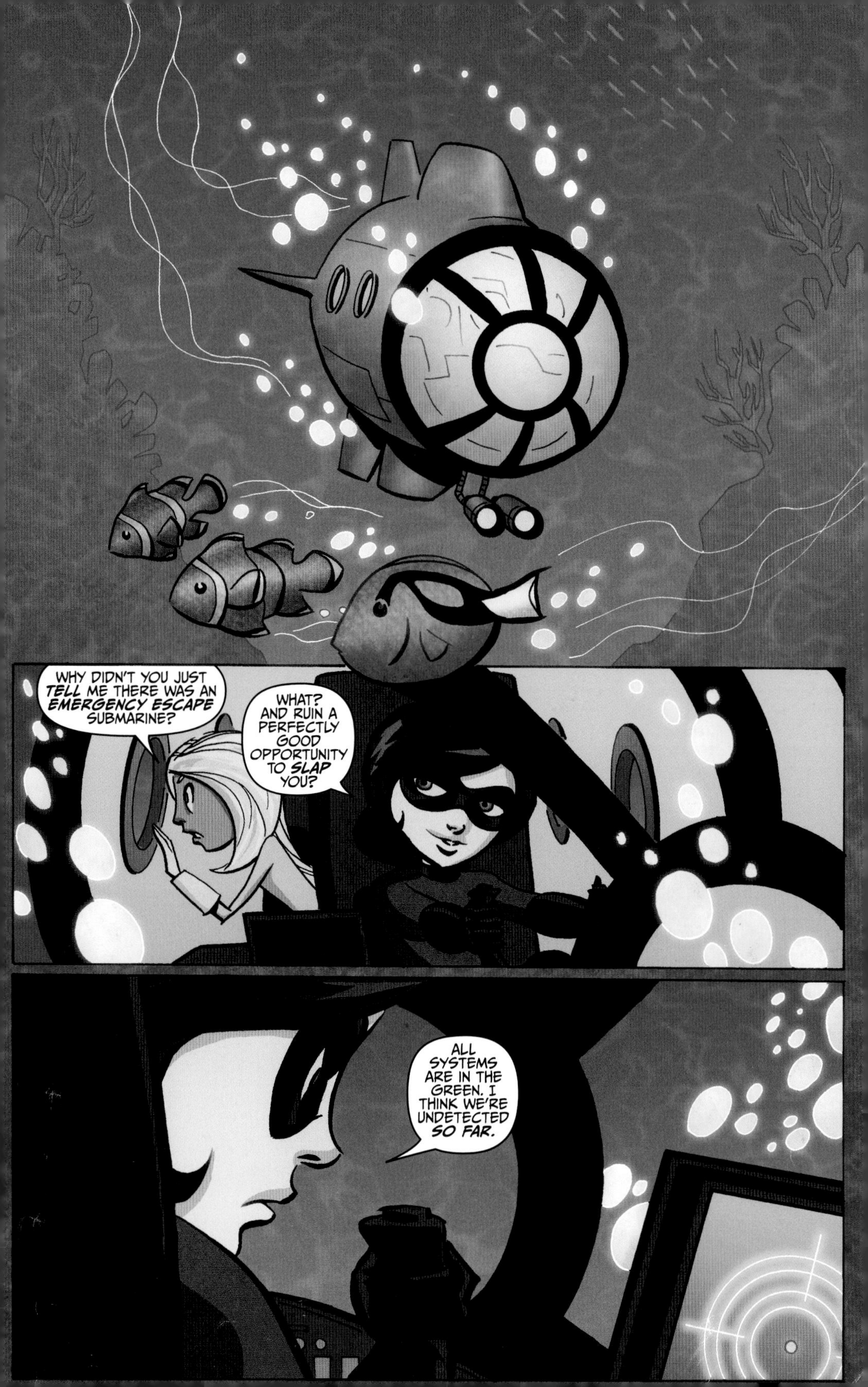
WHY DIDN'T YOU JUST TELL ME THERE WAS AN EMERGENCY ESCAPE SUBMARINE?
WHAT? AND RUIN A PERFECTLY GOOD OPPORTUNITY TO SLAP YOU?
ALL SYSTEMS ARE IN THE GREEN. I THINK WE'RE UNDETECTED SO FAR.

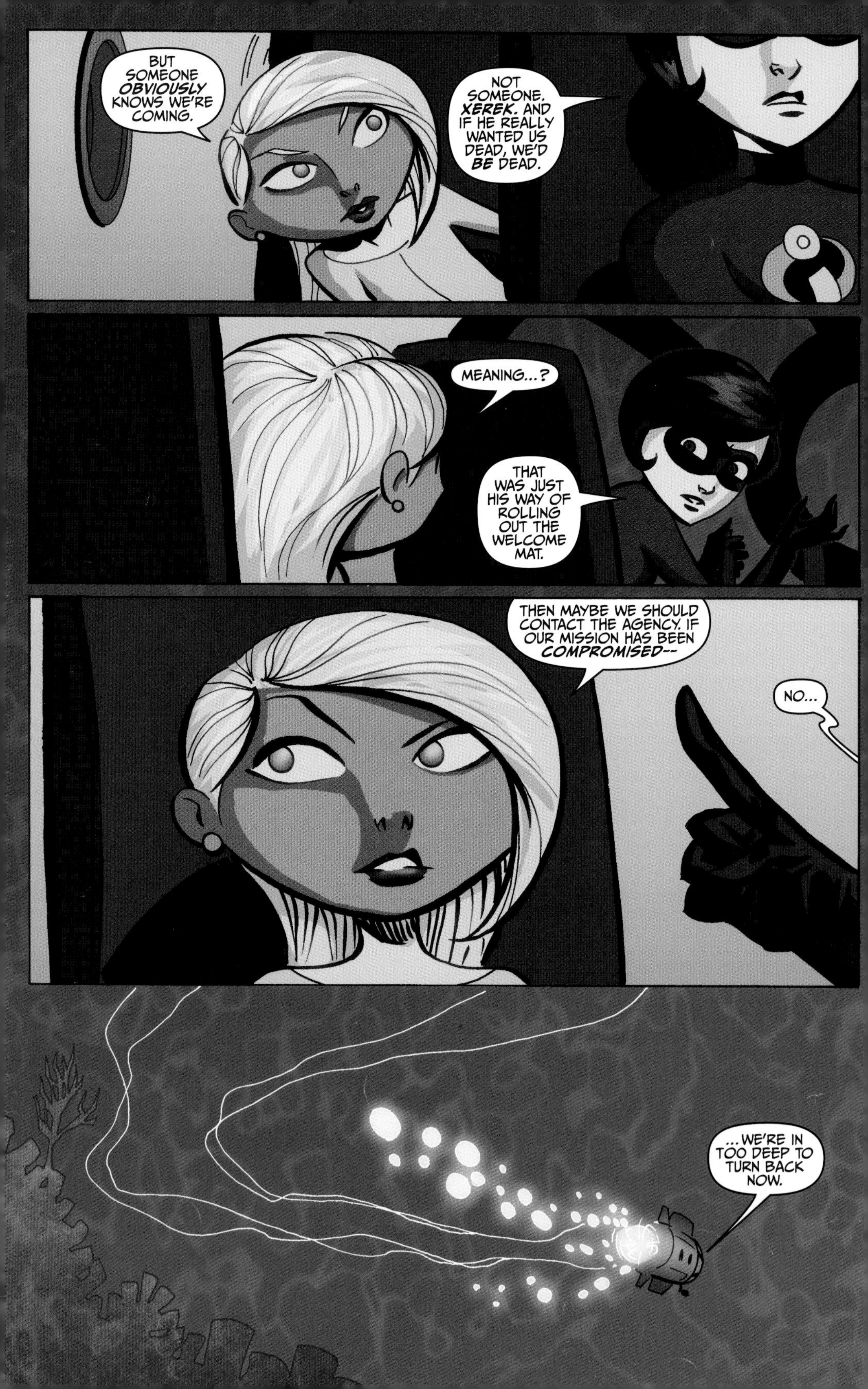
BUT SOMEONE OBVIOUSLY KNOWS WE'RE COMING.
NOT SOMEONE. XEREK. AND IF HE REALLY WANTED US DEAD, WE'D BE DEAD.
MEANING...?
THAT WAS JUST HIS WAY OF ROLLING OUT THE WELCOME MAT.
THEN MAYBE WE SHOULD CONTACT THE AGENCY. IF OUR MISSION HAS BEEN COMPROMISED--
NO...
...WE'RE IN TOO DEEP TO TURN BACK NOW.

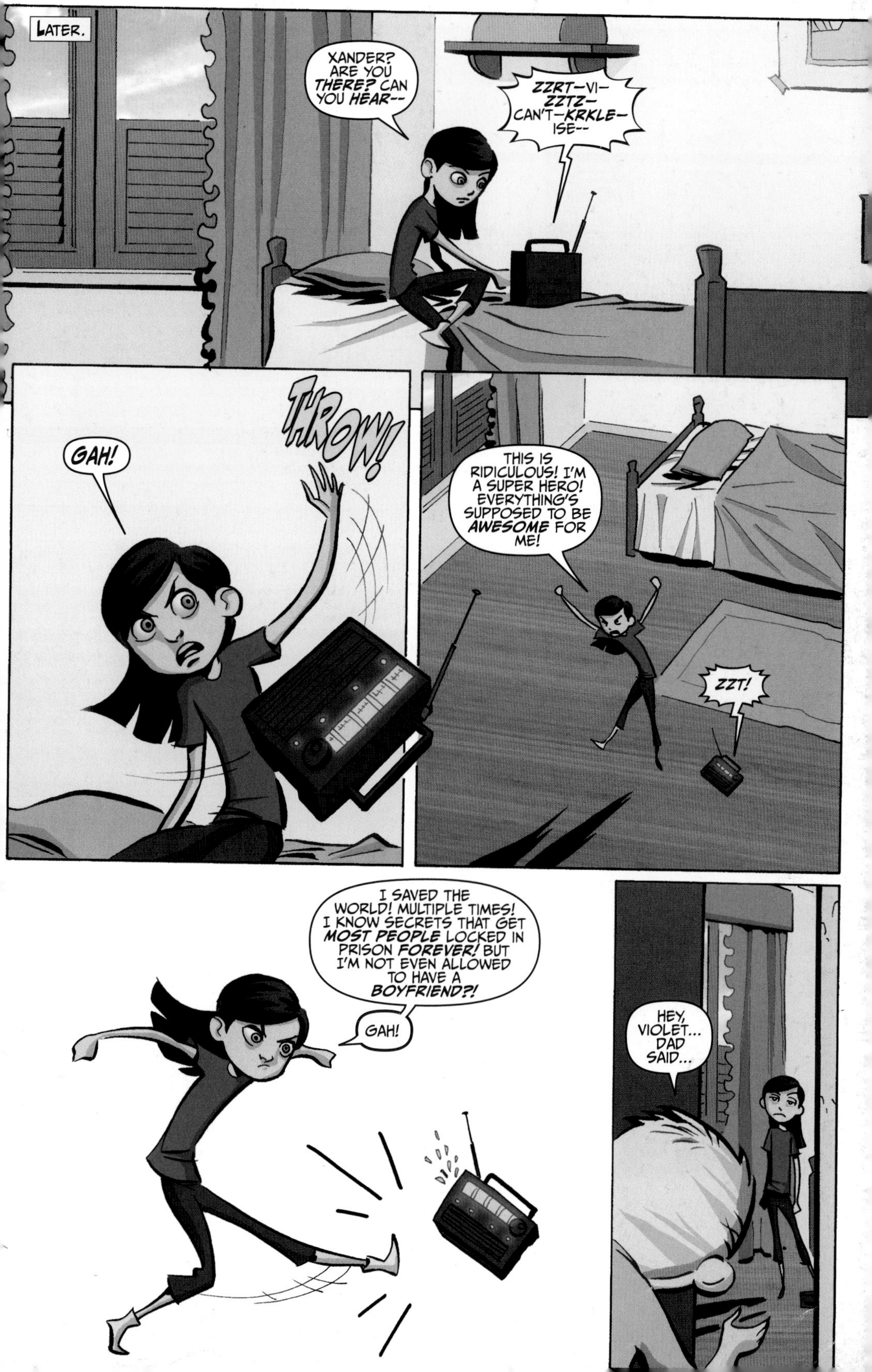
LATER.
XANDER? ARE YOU THERE? CAN YOU HEAR--
ZZRT—VI—ZZTZ—CAN'T—KRKLE—ISE--
THROW!
GAH!
THIS IS RIDICULOUS! I'M A SUPER HERO! EVERYTHING'S SUPPOSED TO BE AWESOME FOR ME!
ZZT!
I SAVED THE WORLD! MULTIPLE TIMES! I KNOW SECRETS THAT GET MOST PEOPLE LOCKED IN PRISON FOREVER! BUT I'M NOT EVEN ALLOWED TO HAVE A BOYFRIEND?!
GAH!
HEY, VIOLET... DAD SAID...

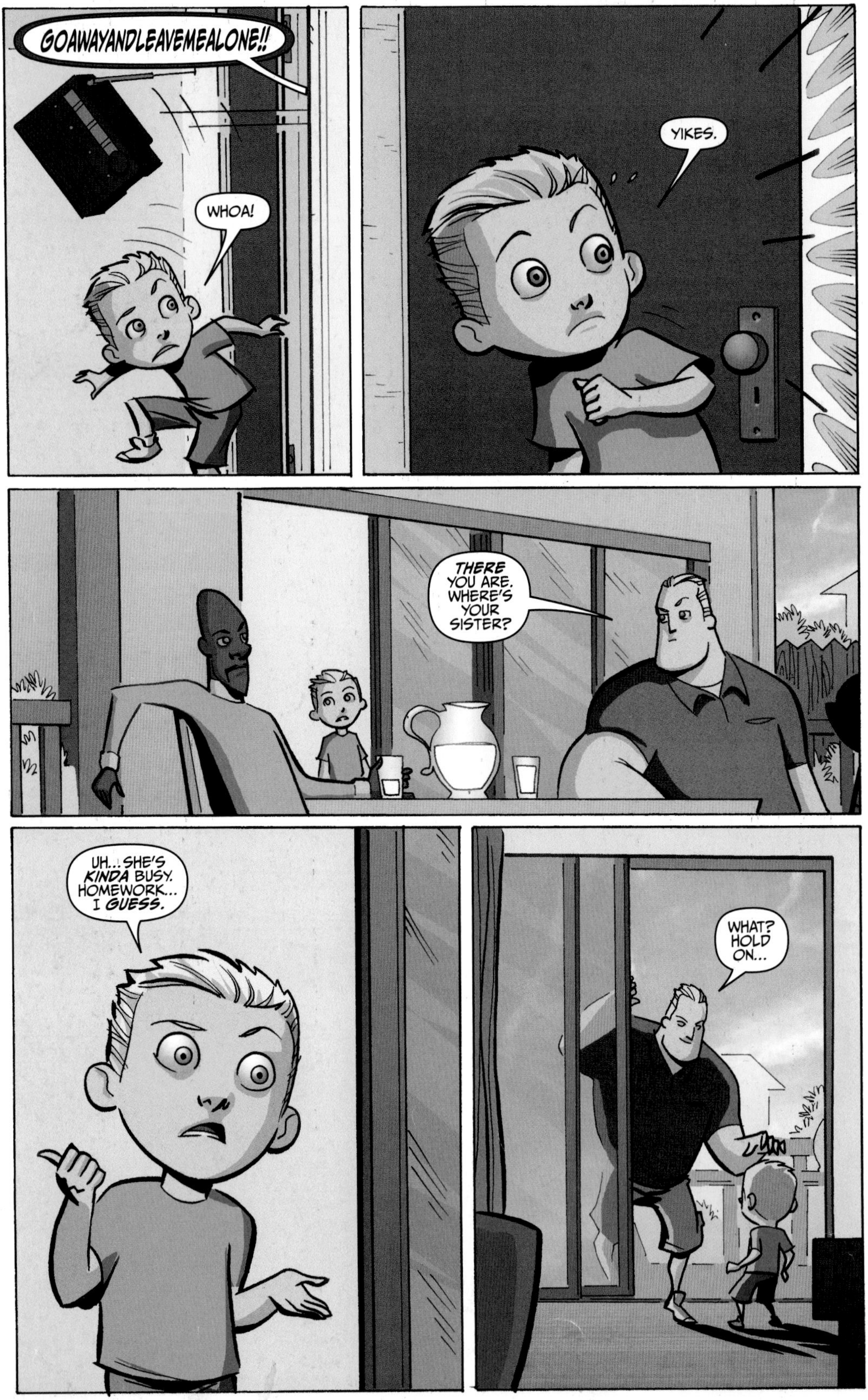
GOAWAYANDLEAVEMEALONE!!
WHOA!
YIKES.
THERE YOU ARE. WHERE'S YOUR SISTER?
UH... SHE'S KINDA BUSY. HOMEWORK... I GUESS.
WHAT? HOLD ON...

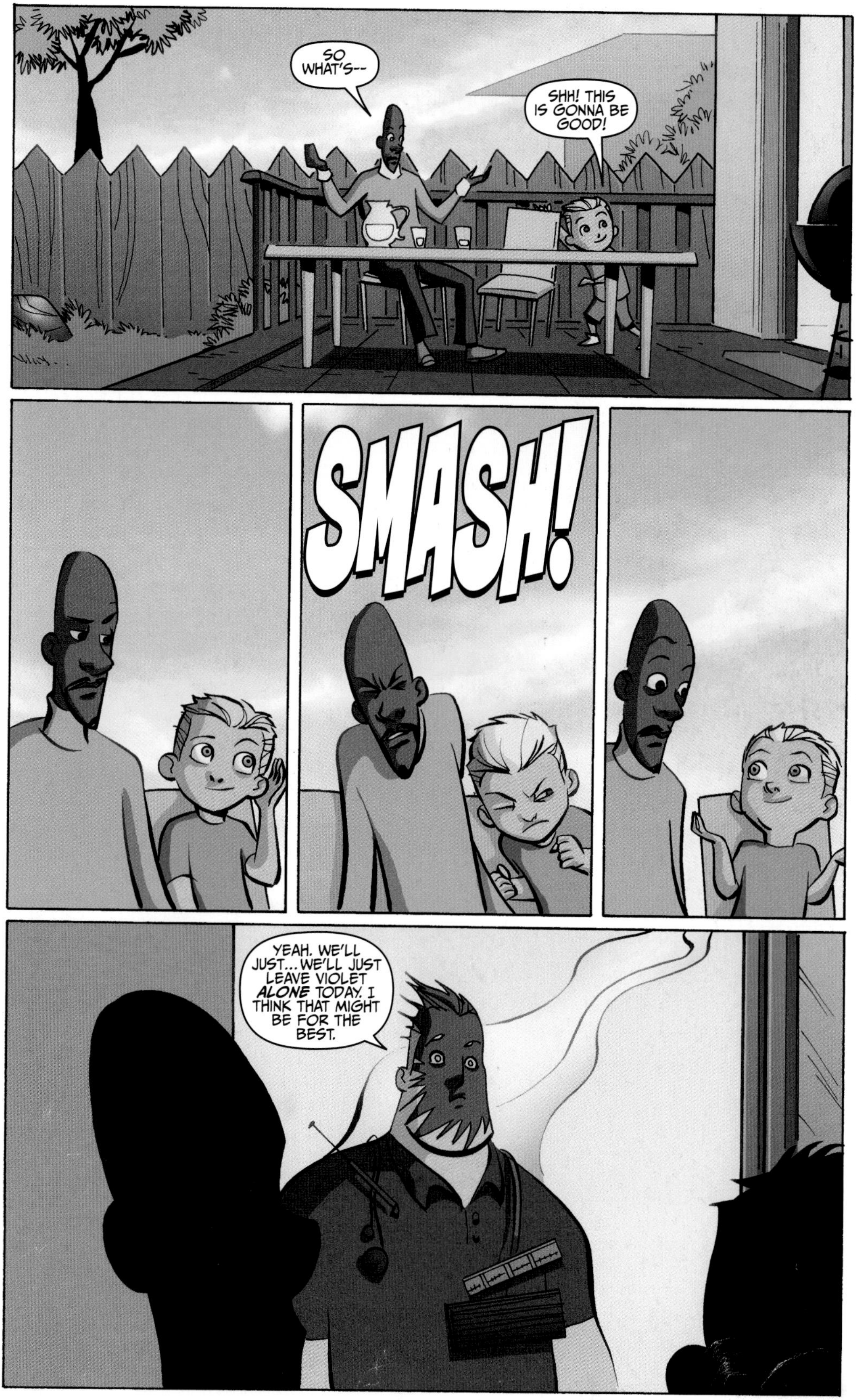
SO WHAT'S--
SHH! THIS IS GONNA BE GOOD!
SMASH!
YEAH. WE'LL JUST... WE'LL JUST LEAVE VIOLET ALONE TODAY. I THINK THAT MIGHT BE FOR THE BEST.

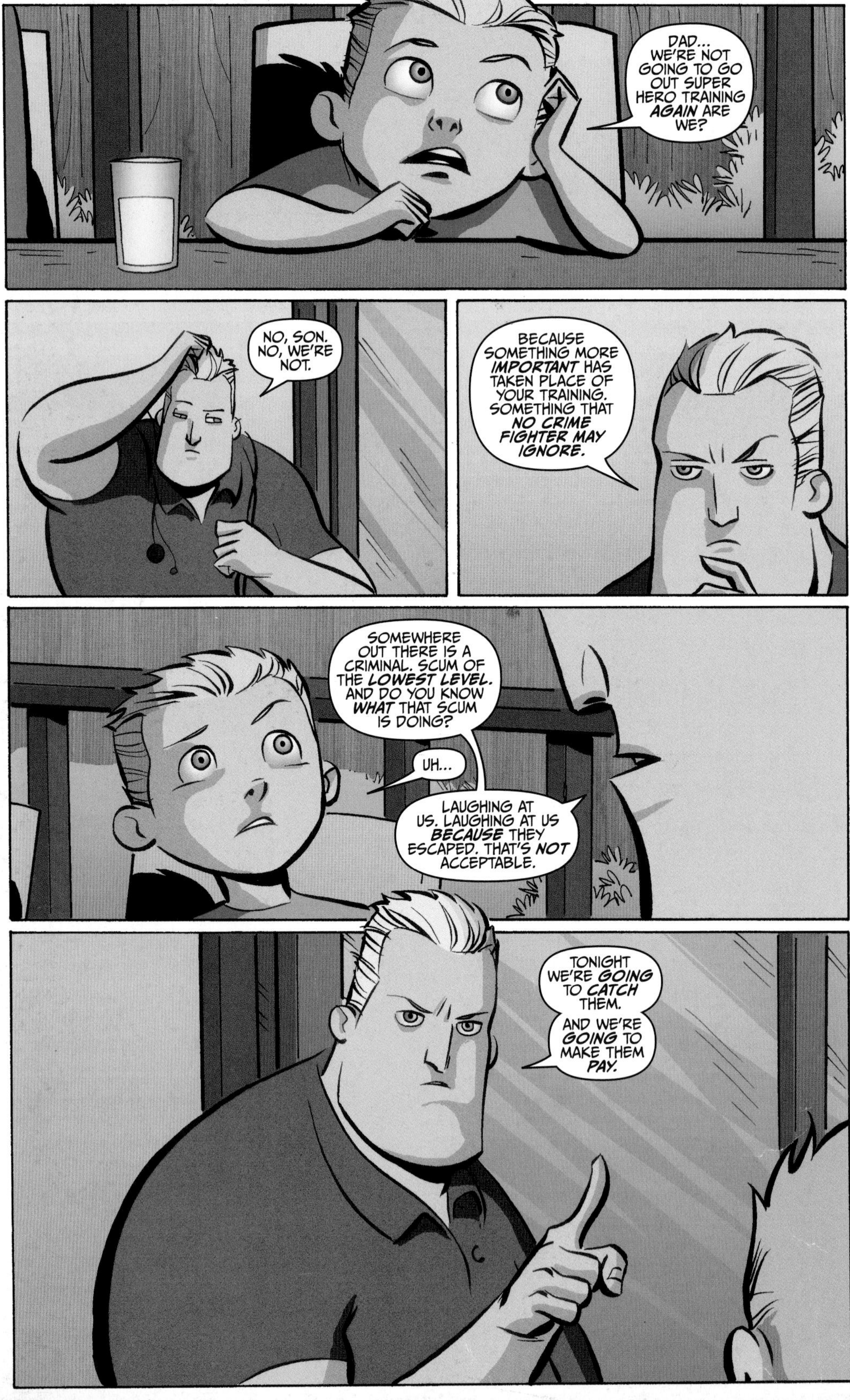
DAD... WE'RE NOT GOING TO GO OUT SUPER HERO TRAINING AGAIN ARE WE?
NO, SON. NO, WE'RE NOT.
BECAUSE SOMETHING MORE IMPORTANT HAS TAKEN PLACE OF YOUR TRAINING. SOMETHING THAT NO CRIME FIGHTER MAY IGNORE.
SOMEWHERE OUT THERE IS A CRIMINAL. SCUM OF THE LOWEST LEVEL. AND DO YOU KNOW WHAT THAT SCUM IS DOING?
UH...
LAUGHING AT US. LAUGHING AT US BECAUSE THEY ESCAPED. THAT'S NOT ACCEPTABLE.
TONIGHT WE'RE GOING TO CATCH THEM.
AND WE'RE GOING TO MAKE THEM PAY.

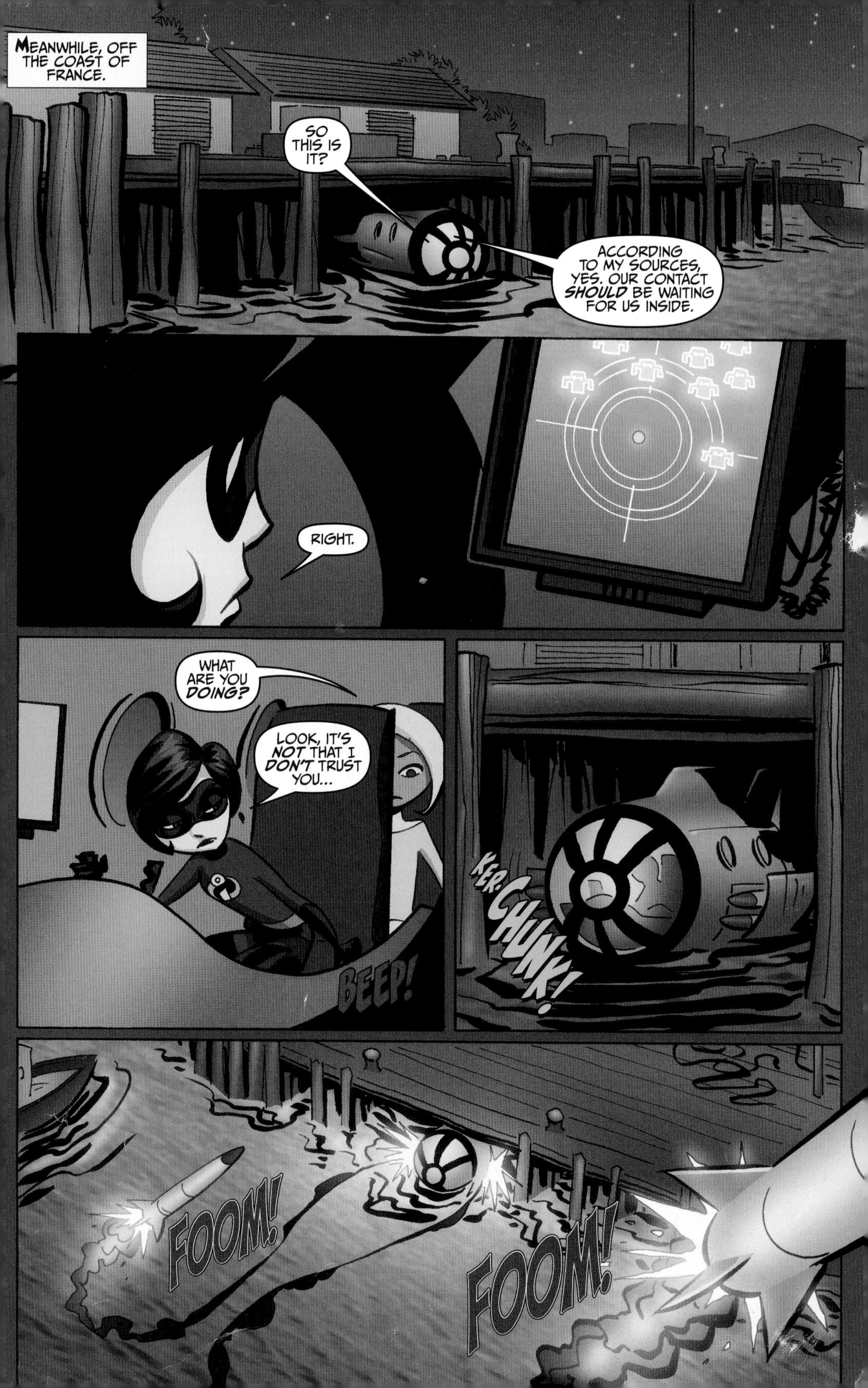
MEANWHILE, OFF THE COAST OF FRANCE.
SO THIS IS IT?
ACCORDING TO MY SOURCES, YES. OUR CONTACT SHOULD BE WAITING FOR US INSIDE.
RIGHT.
WHAT ARE YOU DOING?
LOOK, IT'S NOT THAT I DON'T TRUST YOU...
BEEP!
KER-CHUNK!
FOOM!
FOOM!

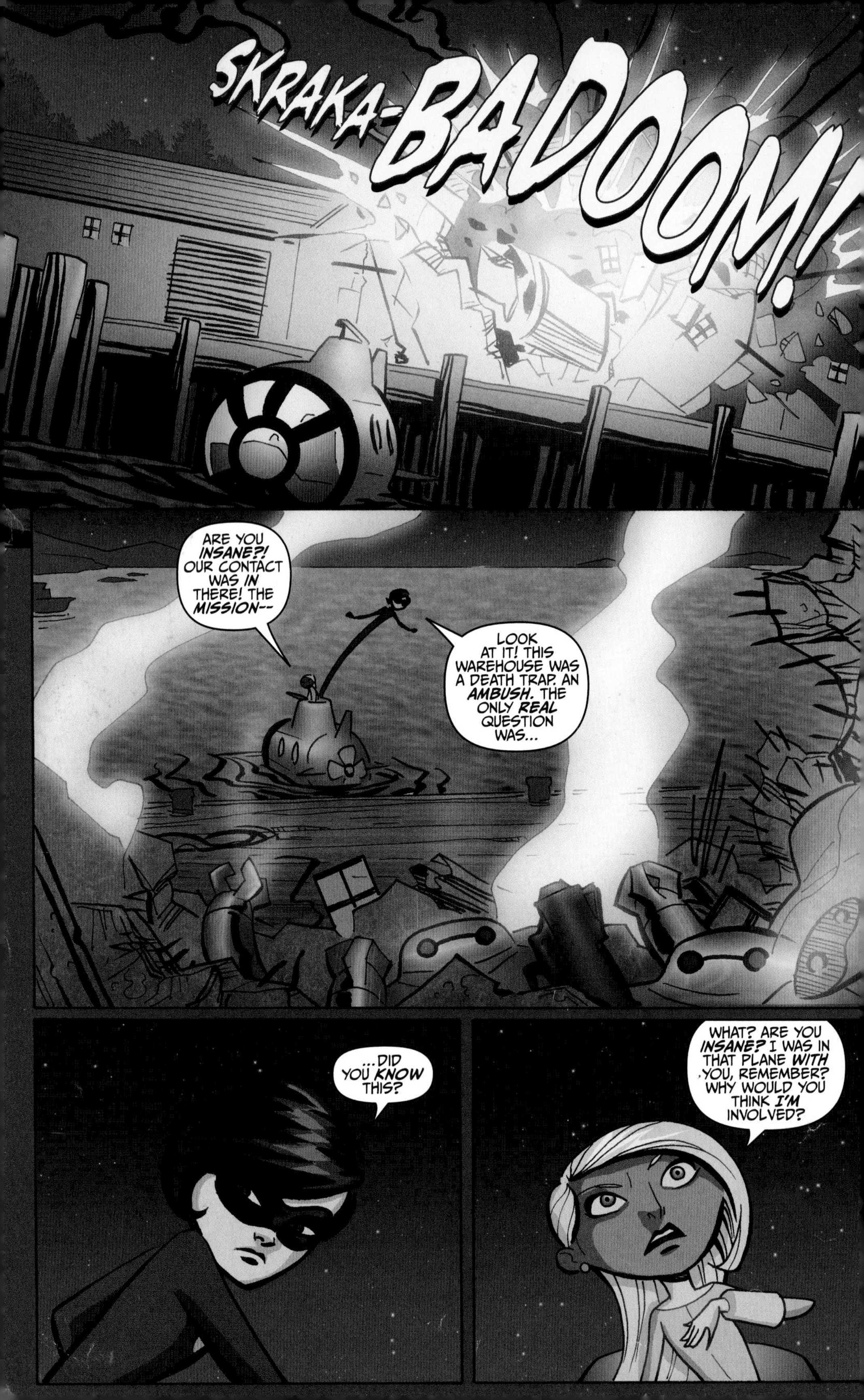
SKRAKA-BADOOM!!
ARE YOU INSANE?! OUR CONTACT WAS IN THERE! THE MISSION--
LOOK AT IT! THIS WAREHOUSE WAS A DEATH TRAP. AN AMBUSH. THE ONLY REAL QUESTION WAS...
...DID YOU KNOW THIS?
WHAT? ARE YOU INSANE? I WAS IN THAT PLANE WITH YOU, REMEMBER? WHY WOULD YOU THINK I'M INVOLVED?

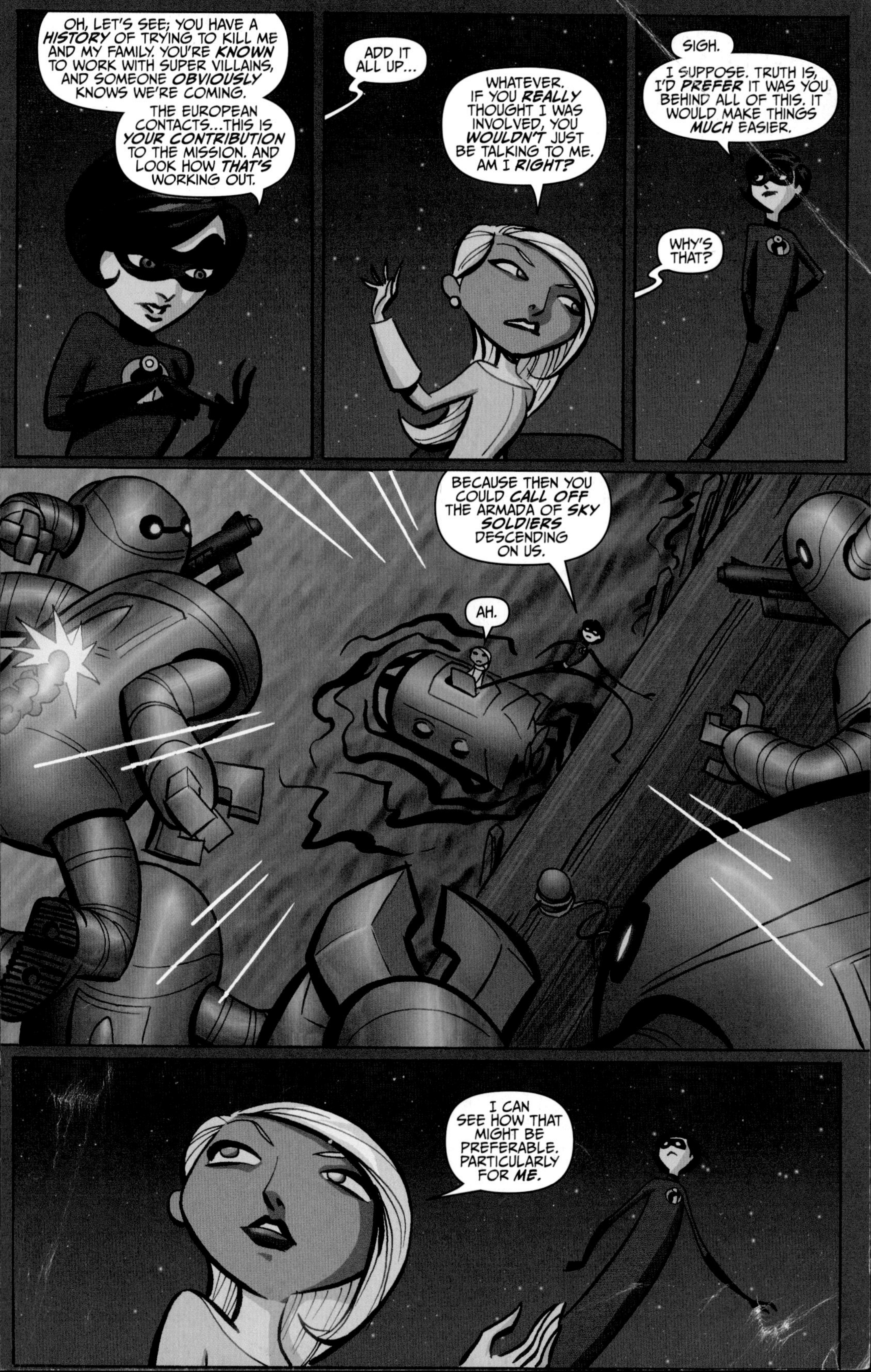
OH, LET'S SEE; YOU HAVE A HISTORY OF TRYING TO KILL ME AND MY FAMILY. YOU'RE KNOWN TO WORK WITH SUPER VILLAINS, AND SOMEONE OBVIOUSLY KNOWS WE'RE COMING.
THE EUROPEAN CONTACTS...THIS IS YOUR CONTRIBUTION TO THE MISSION. AND LOOK HOW THAT'S WORKING OUT.
ADD IT ALL UP...
WHATEVER. IF YOU REALLY THOUGHT I WAS INVOLVED, YOU WOULDN'T JUST BE TALKING TO ME. AM I RIGHT?
SIGH.
I SUPPOSE. TRUTH IS, I'D PREFER IT WAS YOU BEHIND ALL OF THIS. IT WOULD MAKE THINGS MUCH EASIER.
WHY'S THAT?
BECAUSE THEN YOU COULD CALL OFF THE ARMADA OF SKY SOLDIERS DESCENDING ON US.
AH.
I CAN SEE HOW THAT MIGHT BE PREFERABLE. PARTICULARLY FOR ME.

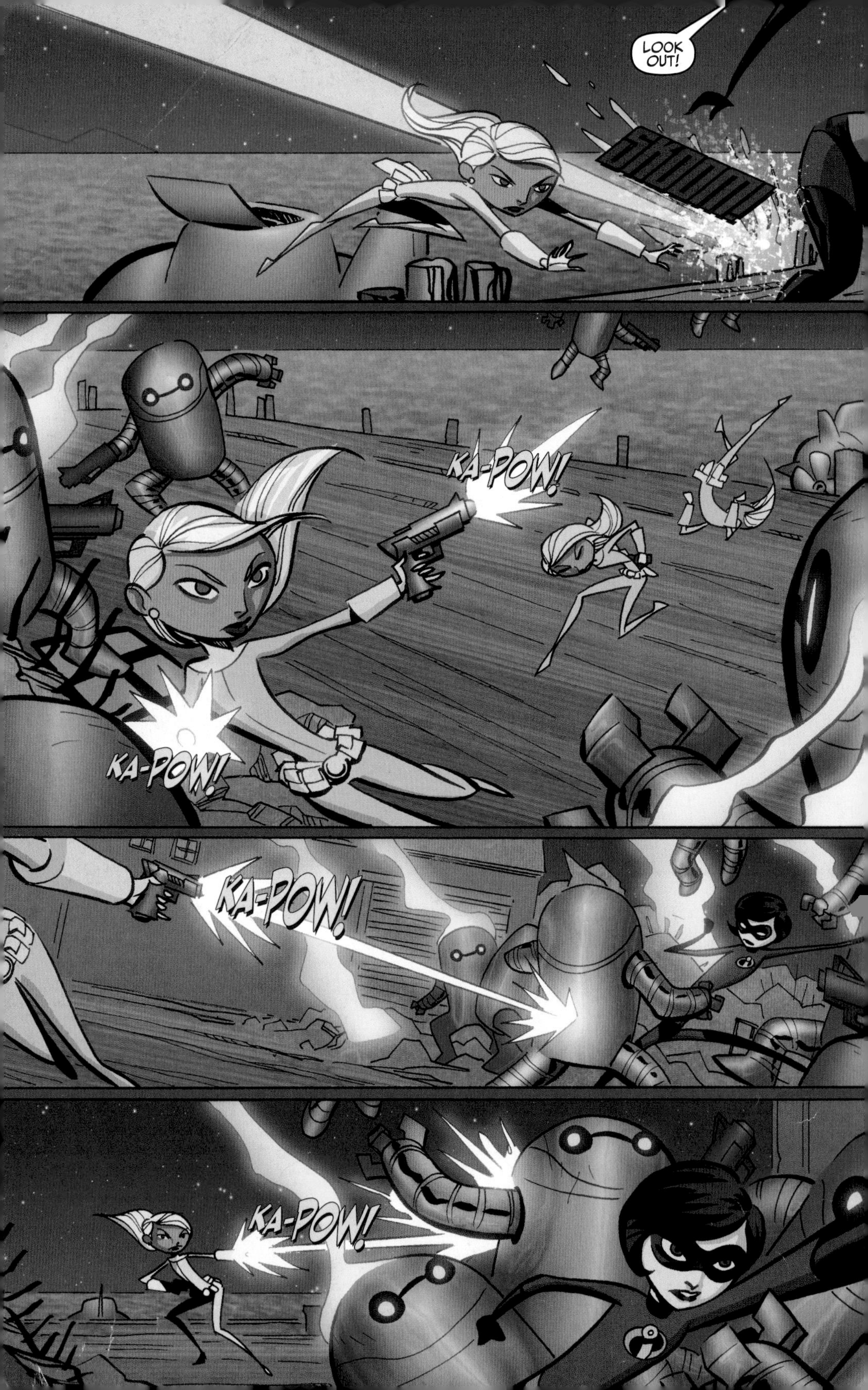
LOOK OUT!
KA-POW!
KA-POW!
KA-POW!
KA-POW!

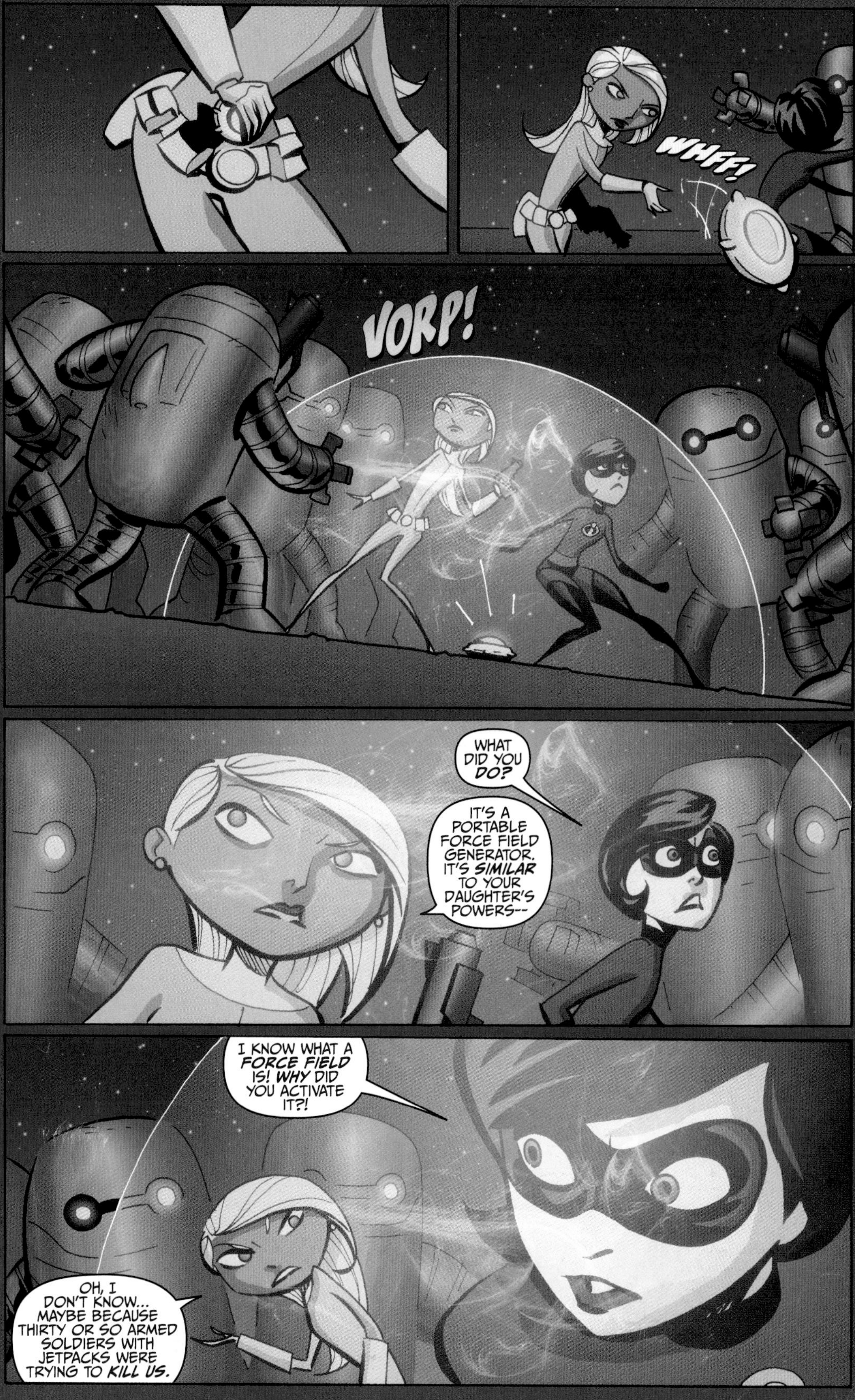
WHFF!
VORP!
WHAT DID YOU *DO?*
IT'S A PORTABLE FORCE FIELD GENERATOR. IT'S *SIMILAR* TO YOUR DAUGHTER'S POWERS--
I KNOW WHAT A *FORCE FIELD* IS! *WHY* DID YOU ACTIVATE IT?!
OH, I DON'T KNOW... MAYBE BECAUSE THIRTY OR SO ARMED SOLDIERS WITH JETPACKS WERE TRYING TO *KILL US.*

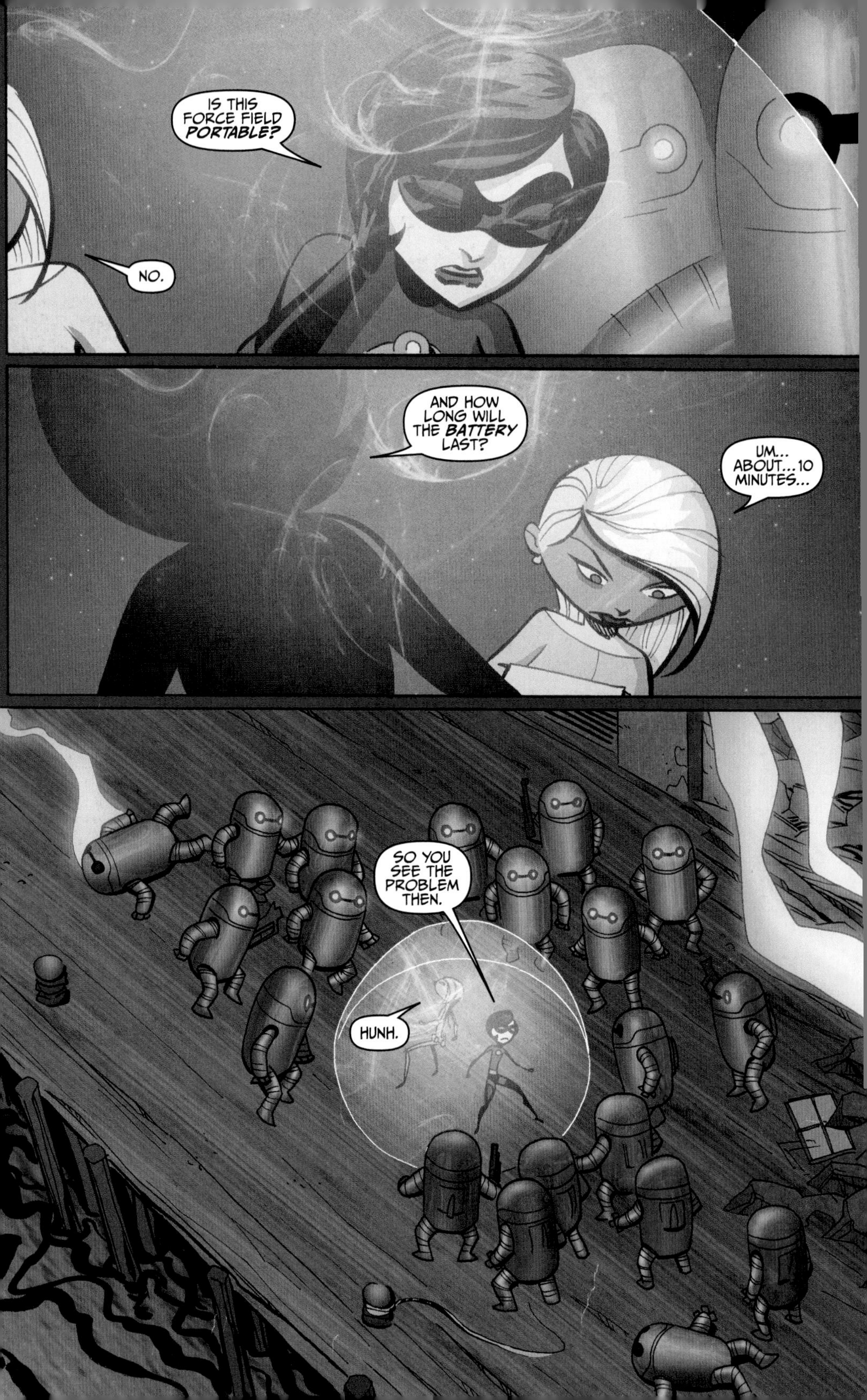
IS THIS FORCE FIELD PORTABLE?
NO.
AND HOW LONG WILL THE BATTERY LAST?
UM... ABOUT...10 MINUTES...
SO YOU SEE THE PROBLEM THEN.
HUNH.

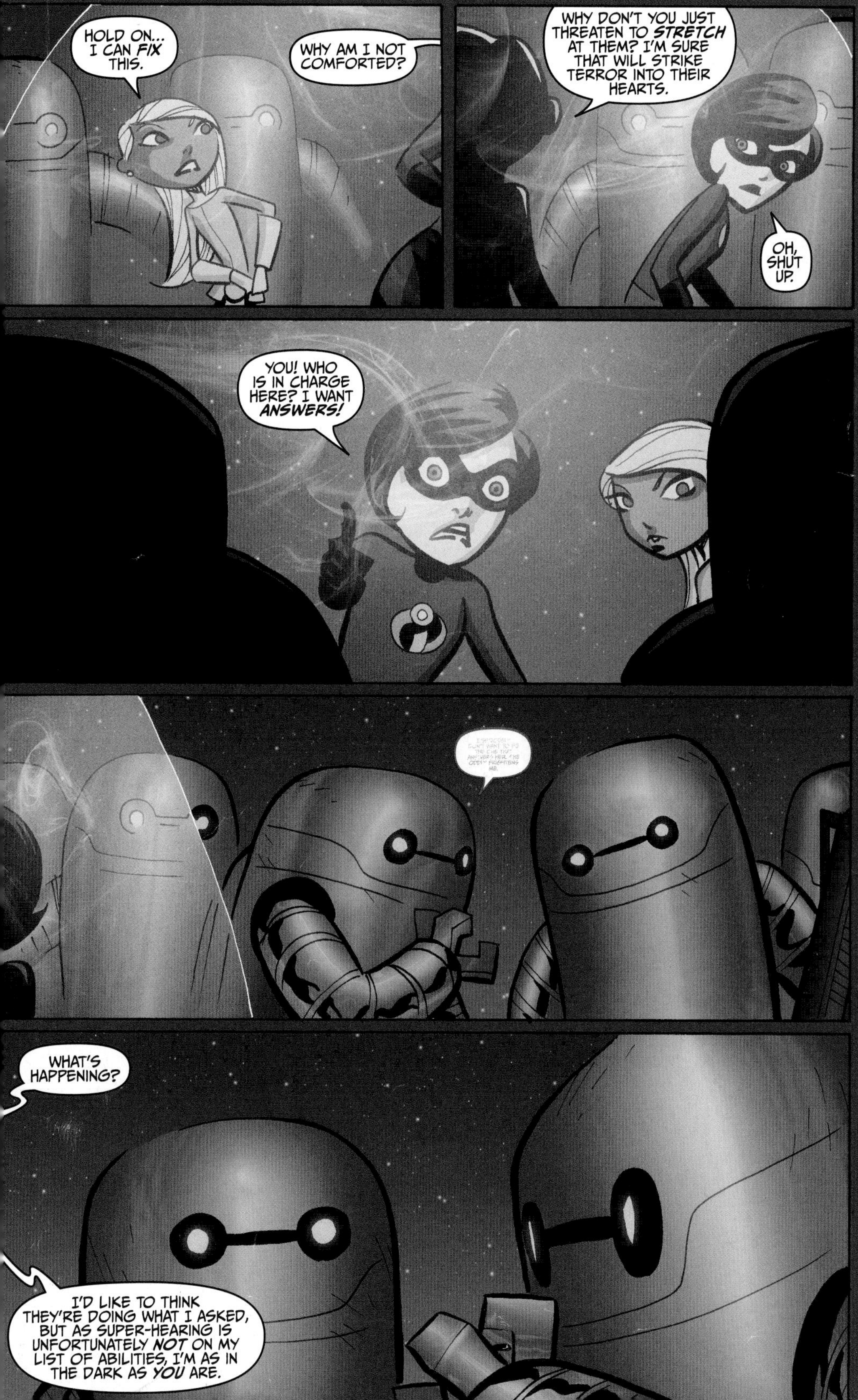
HOLD ON... I CAN FIX THIS.
WHY AM I NOT COMFORTED?
WHY DON'T YOU JUST THREATEN TO STRETCH AT THEM? I'M SURE THAT WILL STRIKE TERROR INTO THEIR HEARTS.
OH, SHUT UP.
YOU! WHO IS IN CHARGE HERE? I WANT ANSWERS!
WHAT'S HAPPENING?
I'D LIKE TO THINK THEY'RE DOING WHAT I ASKED, BUT AS SUPER-HEARING IS UNFORTUNATELY NOT ON MY LIST OF ABILITIES, I'M AS IN THE DARK AS YOU ARE.

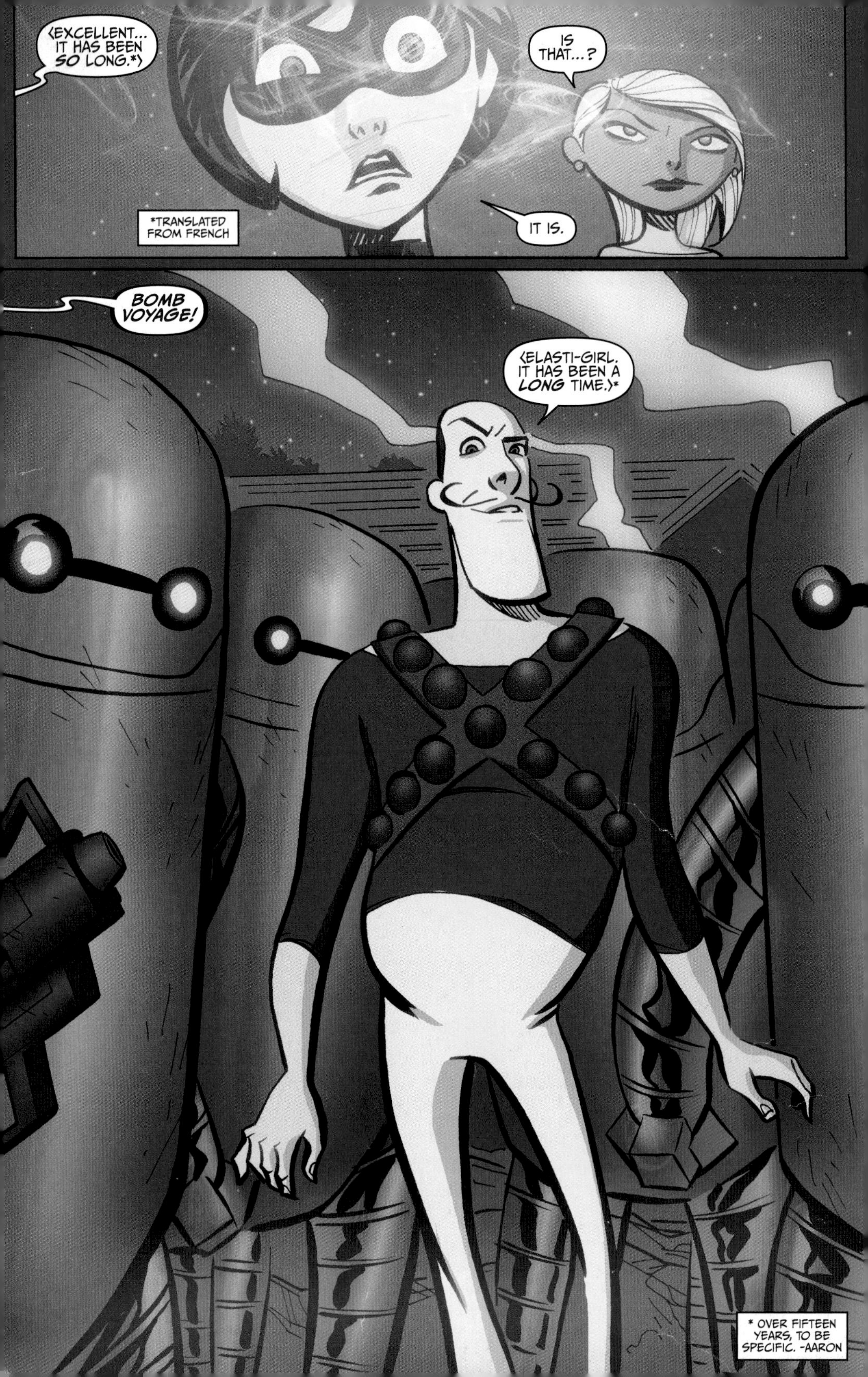
‹EXCELLENT... IT HAS BEEN SO LONG.*›
IS THAT...?
*TRANSLATED FROM FRENCH
IT IS.
BOMB VOYAGE!
‹ELASTI-GIRL. IT HAS BEEN A LONG TIME.›*
* OVER FIFTEEN YEARS, TO BE SPECIFIC. -AARON

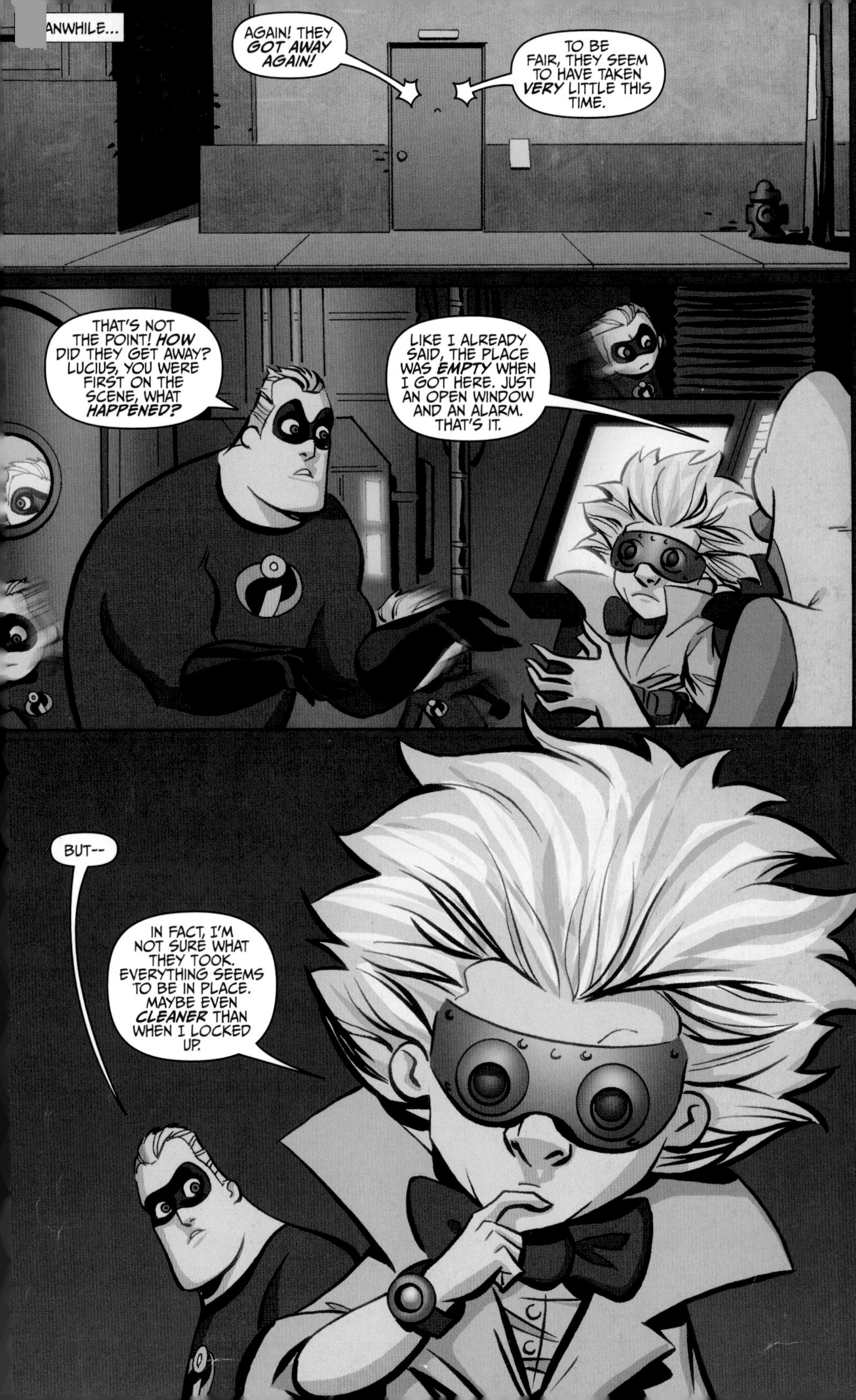
ANWHILE...
AGAIN! THEY GOT AWAY AGAIN!
TO BE FAIR, THEY SEEM TO HAVE TAKEN VERY LITTLE THIS TIME.
THAT'S NOT THE POINT! HOW DID THEY GET AWAY? LUCIUS, YOU WERE FIRST ON THE SCENE, WHAT HAPPENED?
LIKE I ALREADY SAID, THE PLACE WAS EMPTY WHEN I GOT HERE. JUST AN OPEN WINDOW AND AN ALARM. THAT'S IT.
BUT--
IN FACT, I'M NOT SURE WHAT THEY TOOK. EVERYTHING SEEMS TO BE IN PLACE. MAYBE EVEN CLEANER THAN WHEN I LOCKED UP.

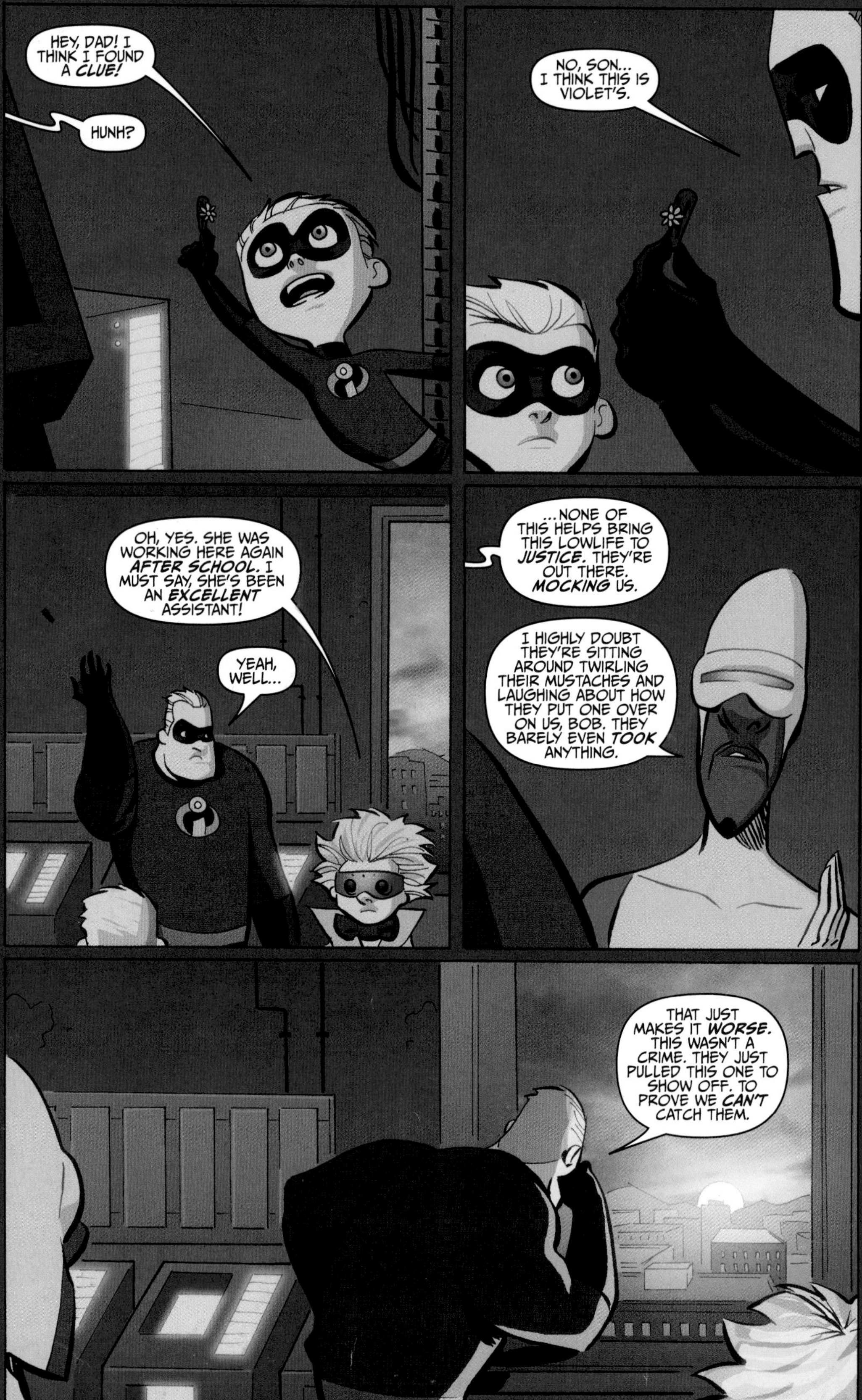
HEY, DAD! I THINK I FOUND A CLUE!
HUNH?
NO, SON... I THINK THIS IS VIOLET'S.
OH, YES. SHE WAS WORKING HERE AGAIN AFTER SCHOOL. I MUST SAY, SHE'S BEEN AN EXCELLENT ASSISTANT!
YEAH, WELL...
...NONE OF THIS HELPS BRING THIS LOWLIFE TO JUSTICE. THEY'RE OUT THERE. MOCKING US.
I HIGHLY DOUBT THEY'RE SITTING AROUND TWIRLING THEIR MUSTACHES AND LAUGHING ABOUT HOW THEY PUT ONE OVER ON US, BOB. THEY BARELY EVEN TOOK ANYTHING.
THAT JUST MAKES IT WORSE. THIS WASN'T A CRIME. THEY JUST PULLED THIS ONE TO SHOW OFF. TO PROVE WE CAN'T CATCH THEM.

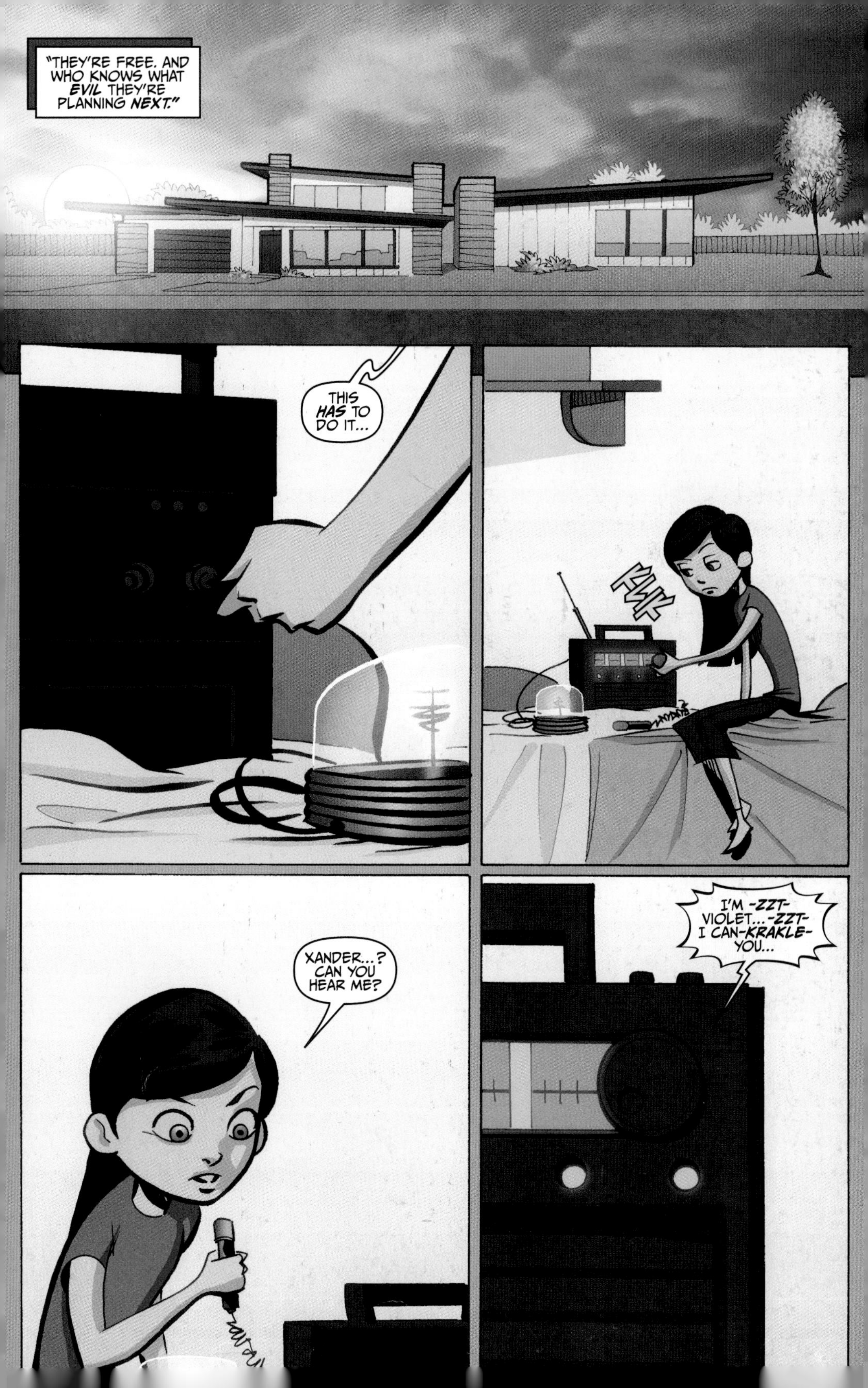
"THEY'RE FREE. AND WHO KNOWS WHAT EVIL THEY'RE PLANNING NEXT."
THIS HAS TO DO IT...
KWIK
XANDER...? CAN YOU HEAR ME?
I'M -ZZT- VIOLET...-ZZT- I CAN-KRAKLE- YOU...

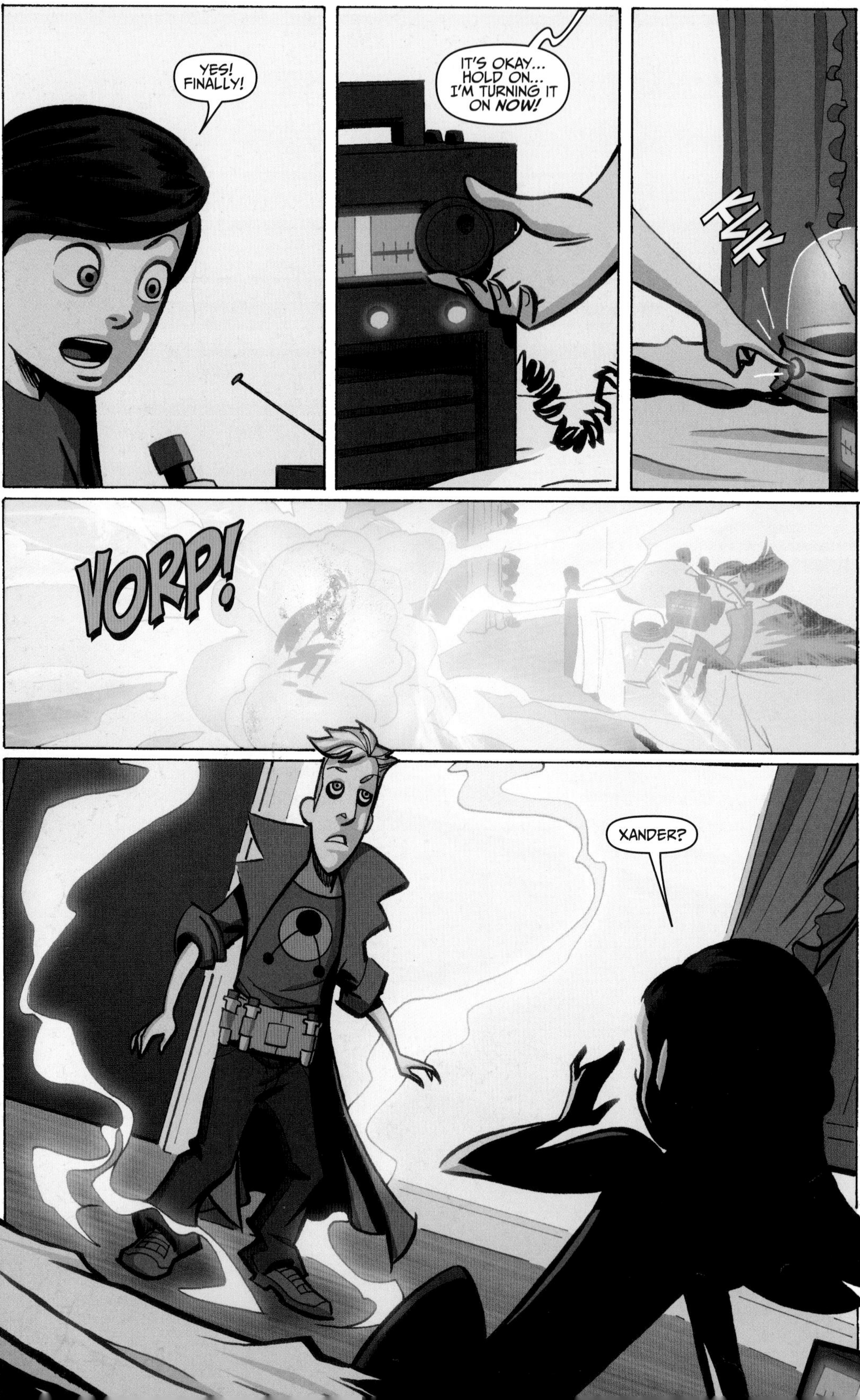
YES! FINALLY!
IT'S OKAY... HOLD ON... I'M TURNING IT ON NOW!
KLIK
VORP!
XANDER?

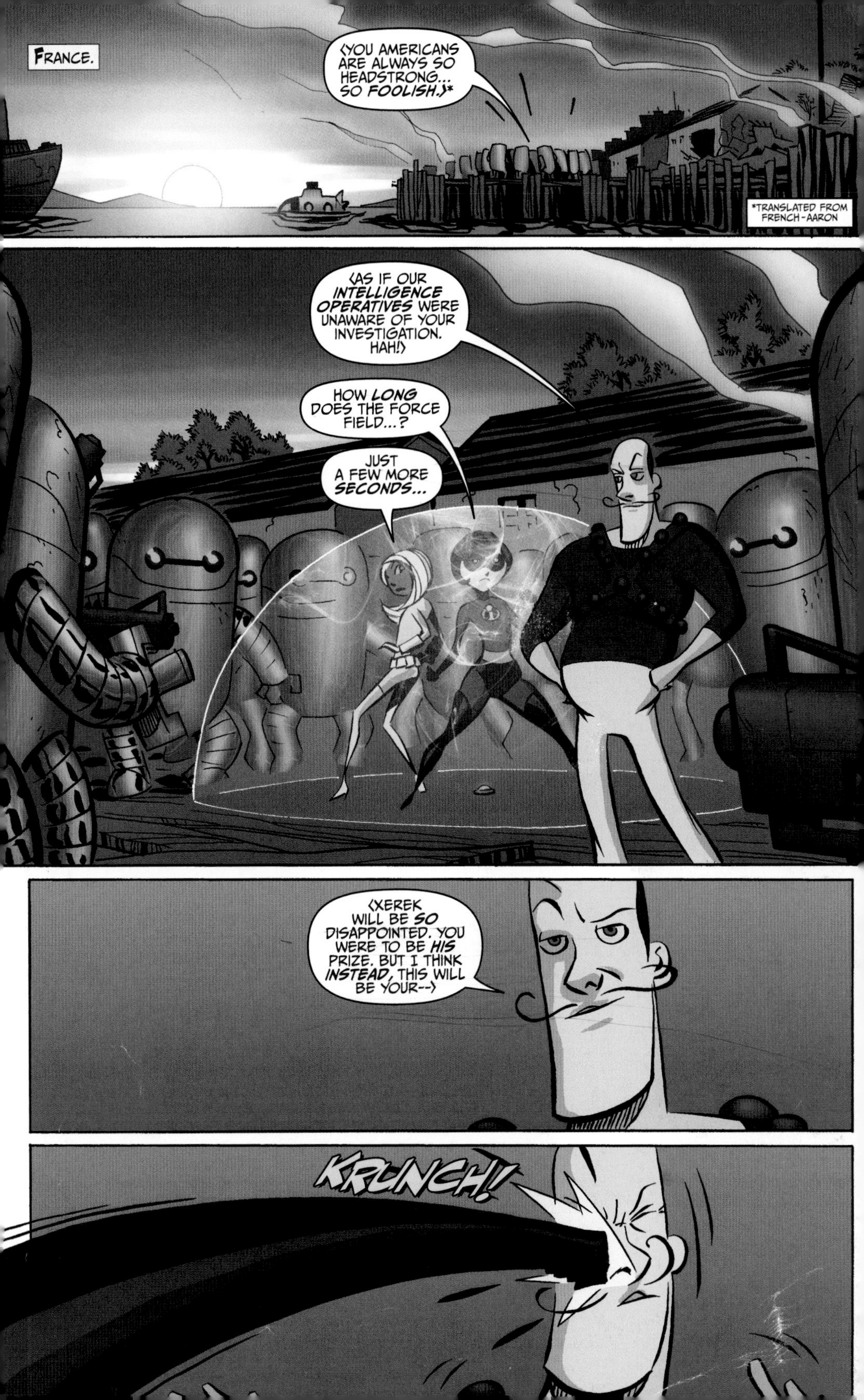
FRANCE.
‹YOU AMERICANS ARE ALWAYS SO HEADSTRONG... SO FOOLISH.›*
*TRANSLATED FROM FRENCH -AARON
‹AS IF OUR INTELLIGENCE OPERATIVES WERE UNAWARE OF YOUR INVESTIGATION. HAH!›
HOW LONG DOES THE FORCE FIELD...?
JUST A FEW MORE SECONDS...
‹XEREK WILL BE SO DISAPPOINTED. YOU WERE TO BE HIS PRIZE. BUT I THINK INSTEAD, THIS WILL BE YOUR--›
KRUNCH!

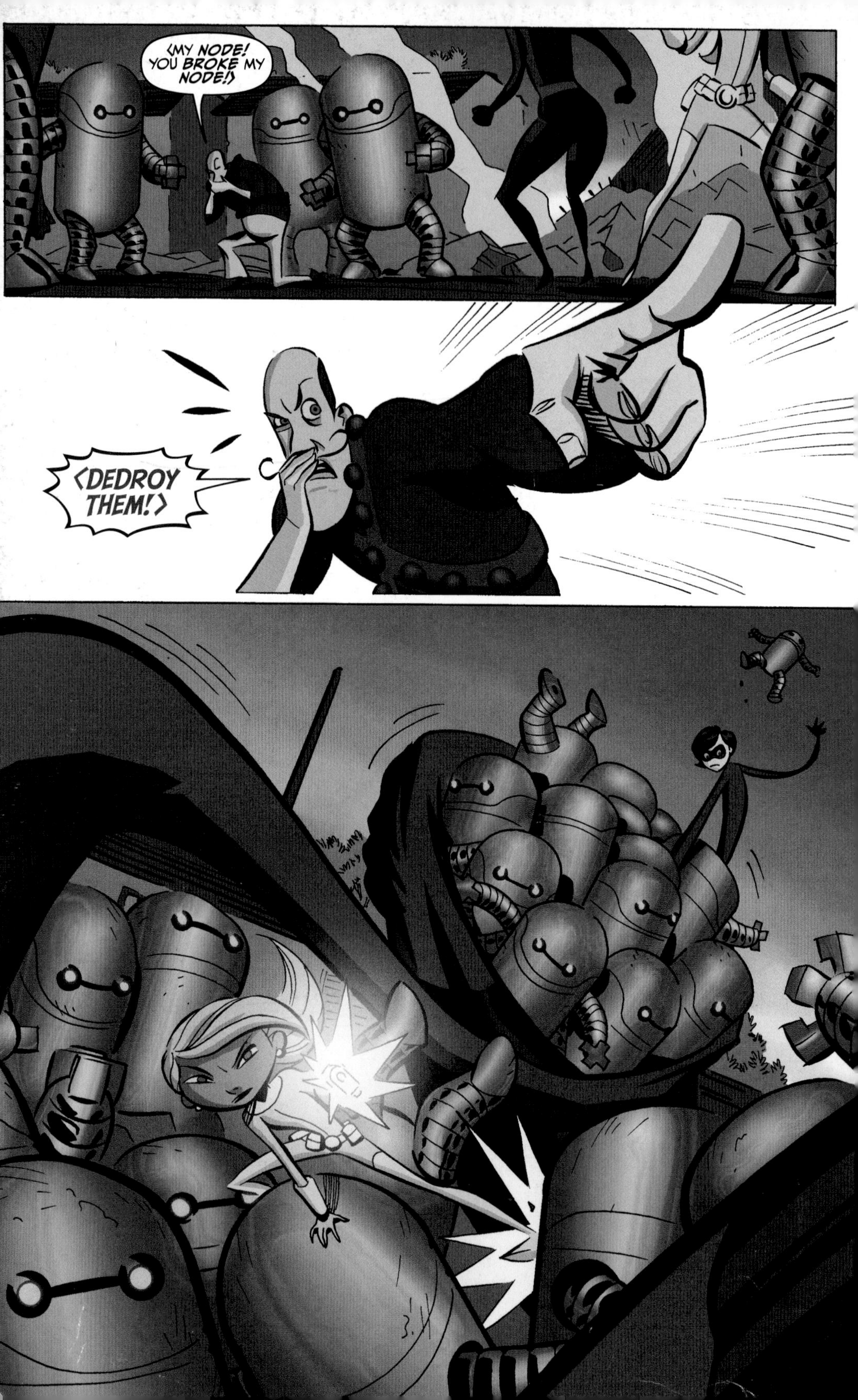

<MY NODE! YOU BROKE MY NODE!>
<DEDROY THEM!>

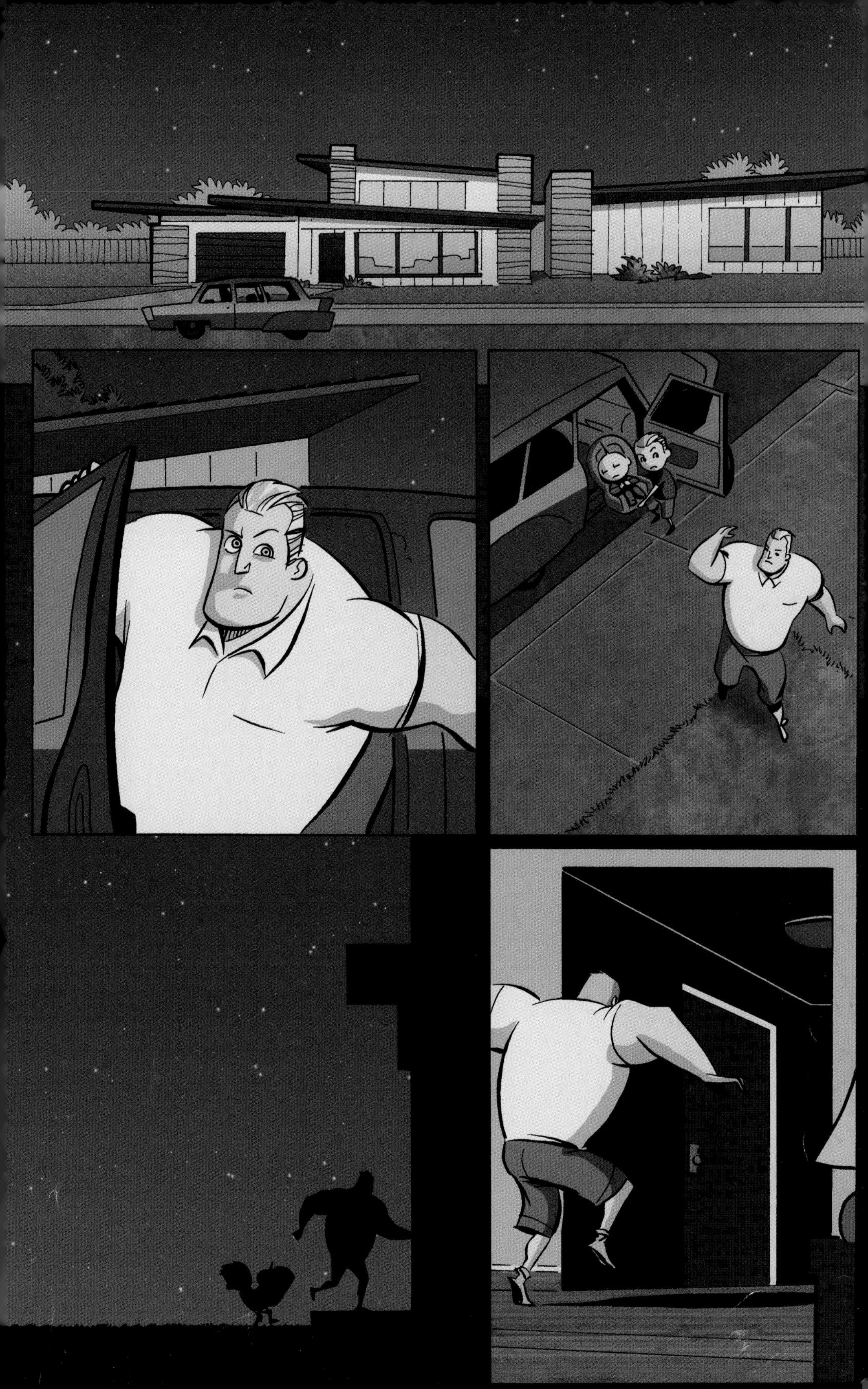

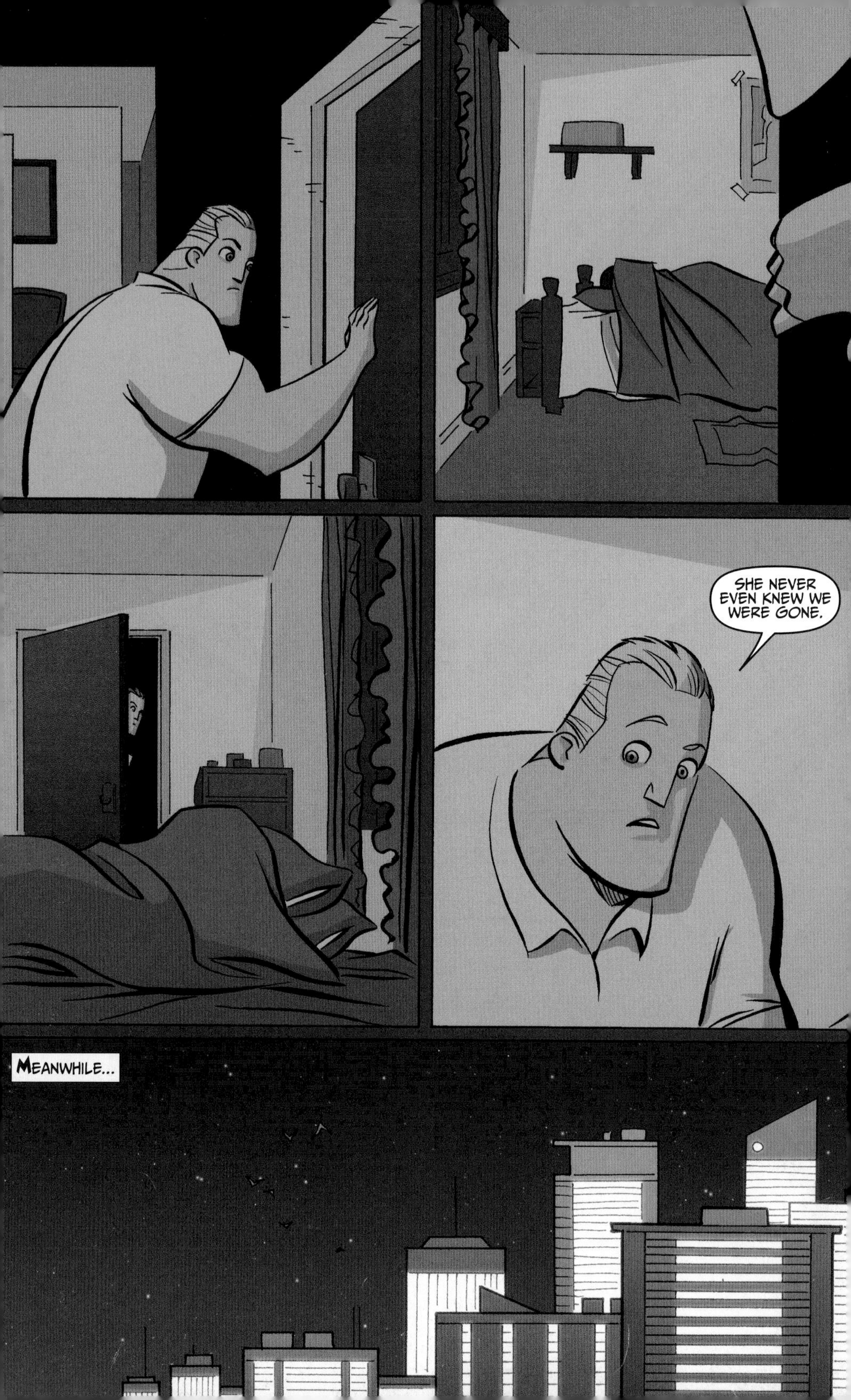
SHE NEVER EVEN KNEW WE WERE GONE.
MEANWHILE...

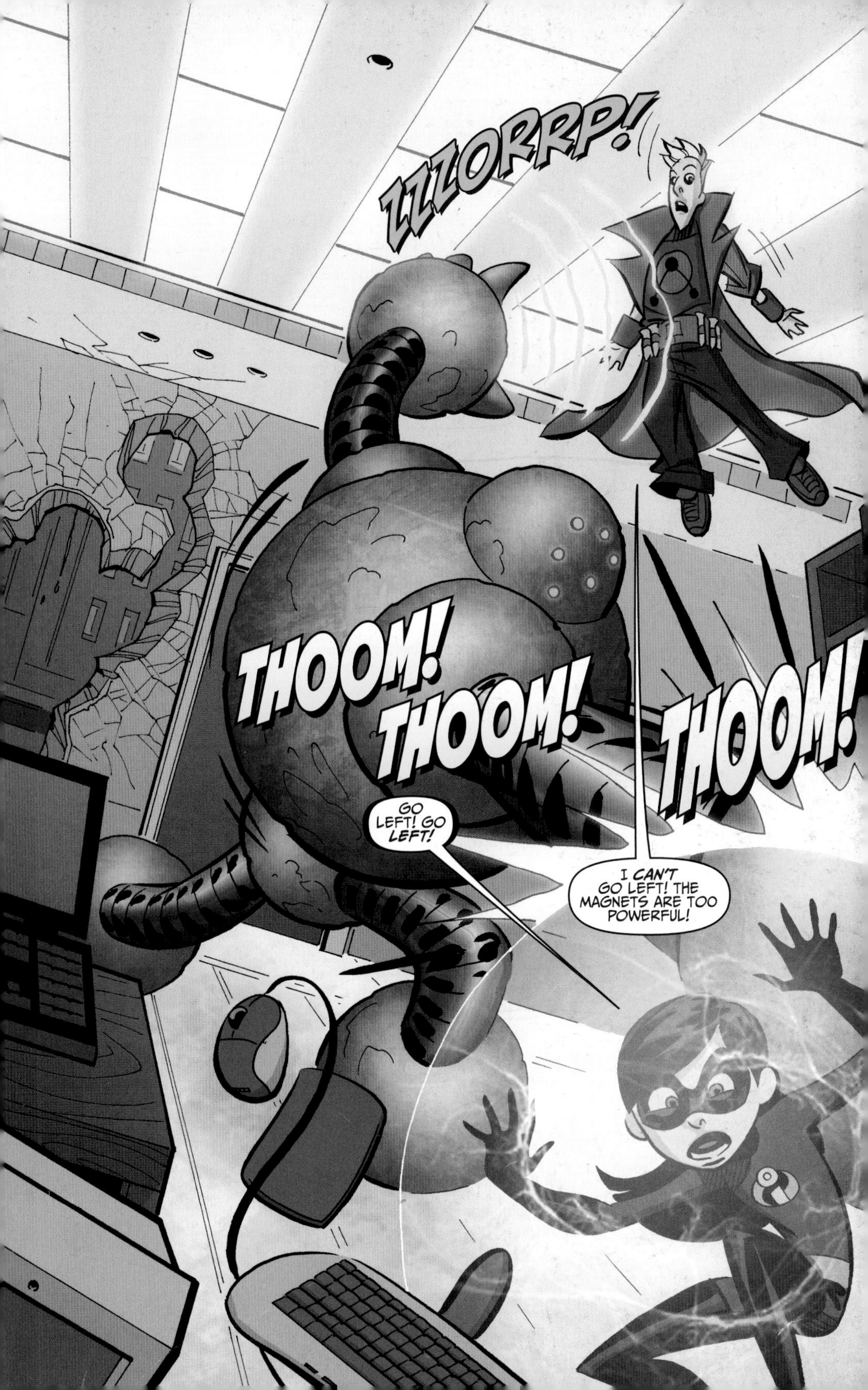
ZZZORRRP!
THOOM! THOOM!
THOOM!
GO LEFT! GO LEFT!
I CAN'T GO LEFT! THE MAGNETS ARE TOO POWERFUL!

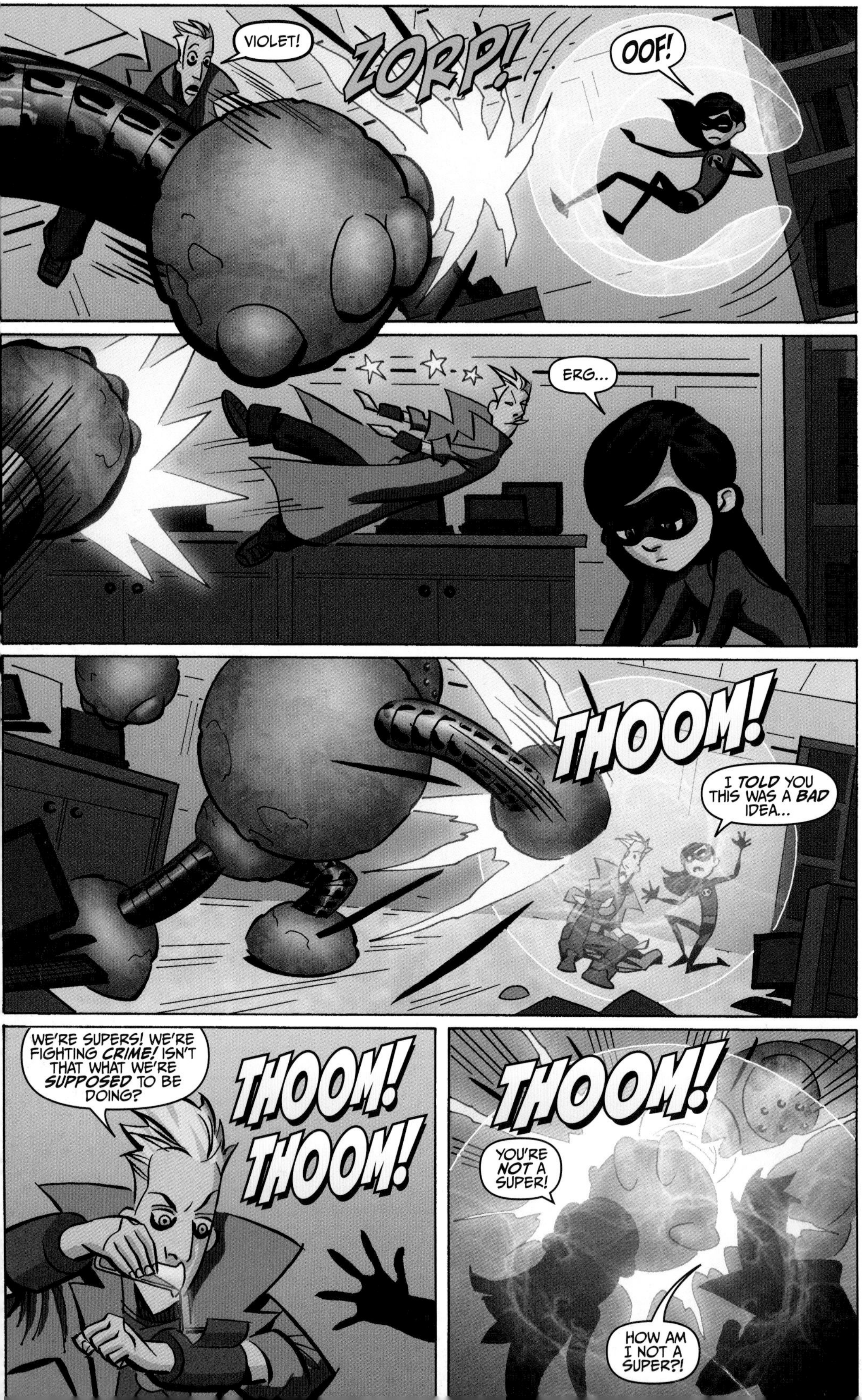
VIOLET!
ZORP!
OOF!
ERG...
THOOM!
I *TOLD* YOU THIS WAS A *BAD* IDEA...
WE'RE SUPERS! WE'RE FIGHTING *CRIME!* ISN'T THAT WHAT WE'RE *SUPPOSED* TO BE DOING?
THOOM! THOOM!
THOOM!
YOU'RE *NOT* A SUPER!
HOW AM I NOT A SUPER?!

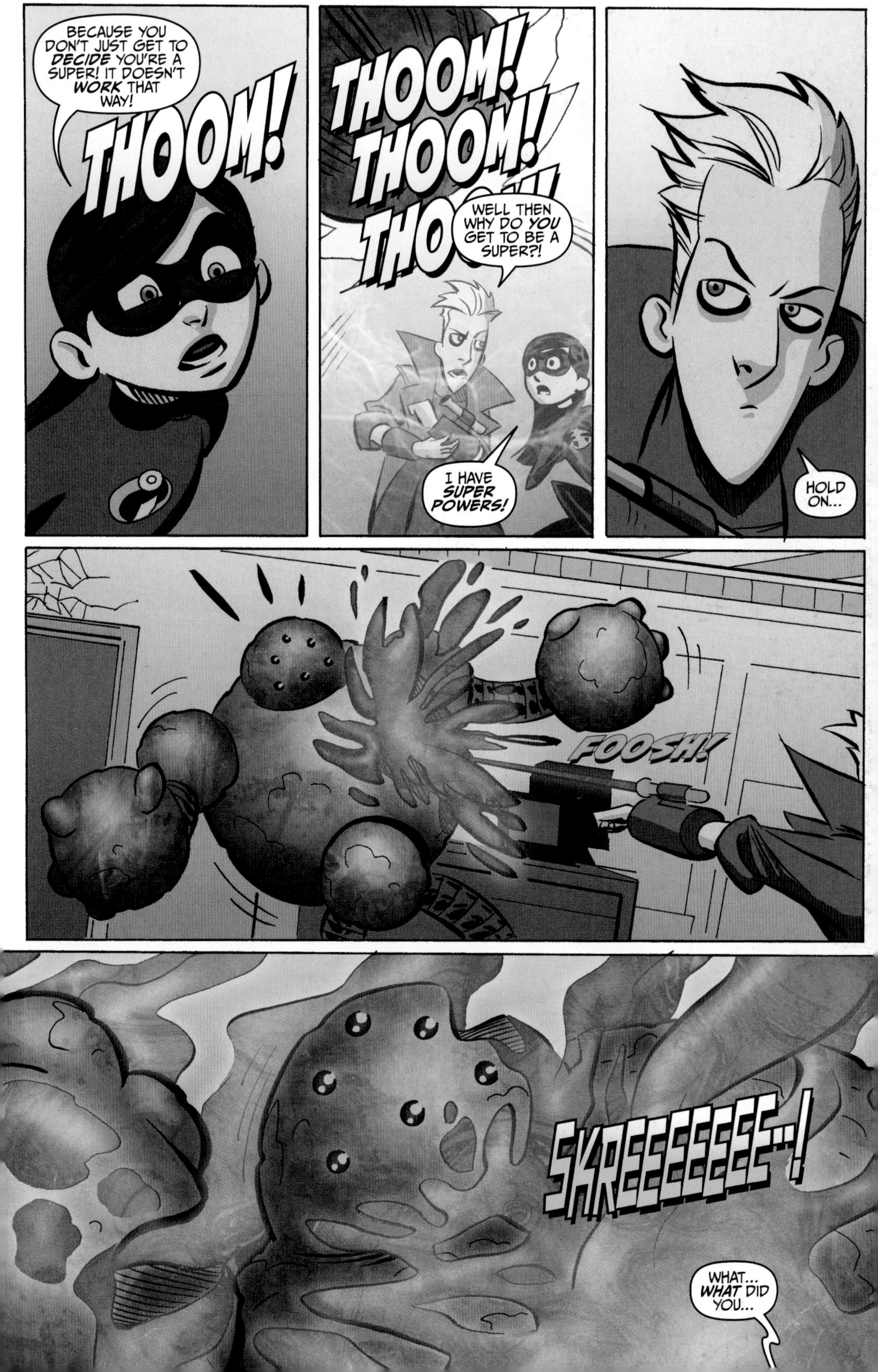
BECAUSE YOU DON'T JUST GET TO *DECIDE* YOU'RE A SUPER! IT DOESN'T *WORK* THAT WAY!
THOOM!
THOOM! THOOM! THOO...
WELL THEN WHY DO *YOU* GET TO BE A SUPER?!
I HAVE *SUPER POWERS!*
HOLD ON...
FOOSH!
SKREEEEEEEE--!
WHAT... *WHAT* DID YOU...

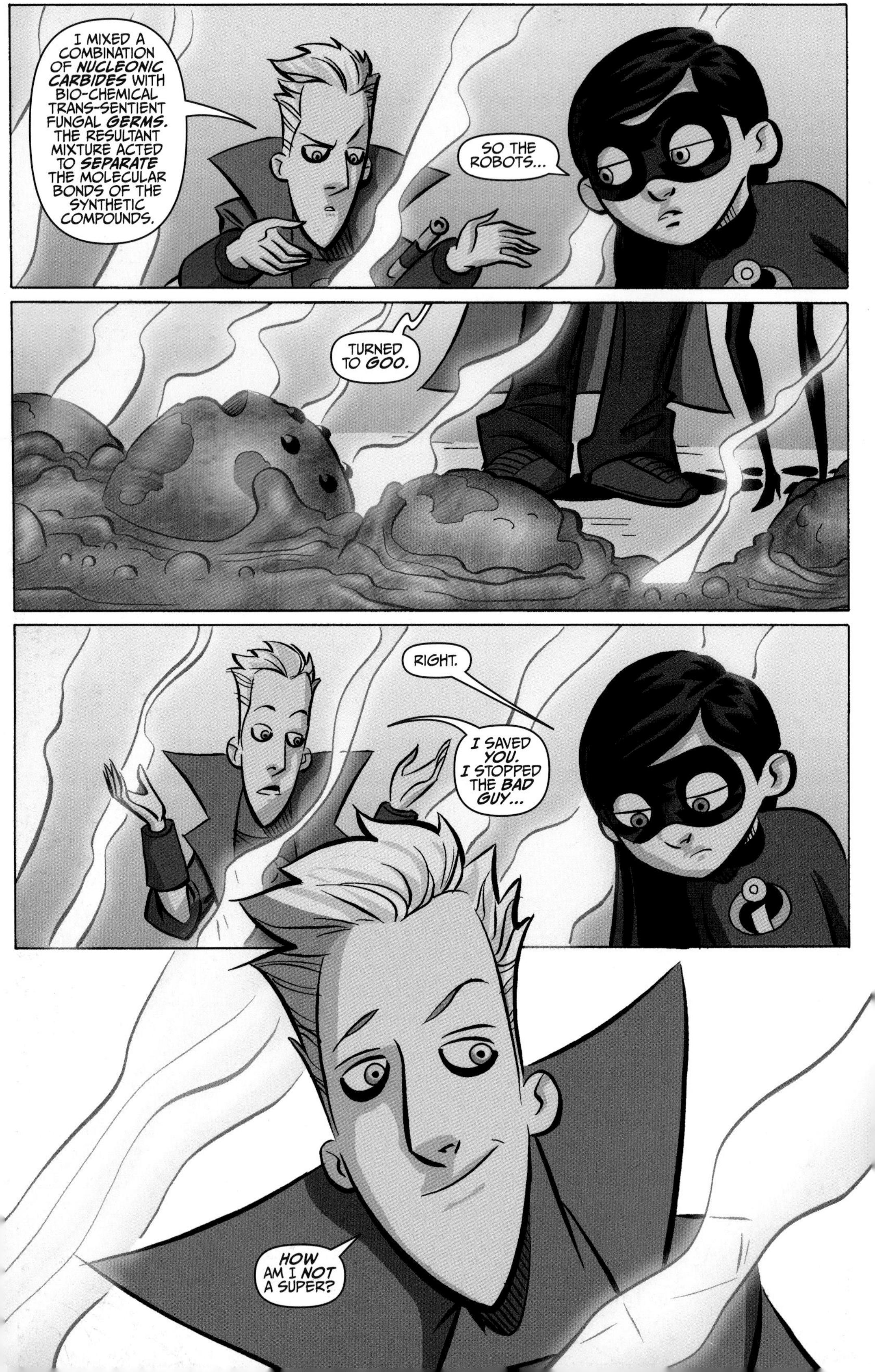
I MIXED A COMBINATION OF NUCLEONIC CARBIDES WITH BIO-CHEMICAL TRANS-SENTIENT FUNGAL GERMS. THE RESULTANT MIXTURE ACTED TO SEPARATE THE MOLECULAR BONDS OF THE SYNTHETIC COMPOUNDS.
SO THE ROBOTS...
TURNED TO GOO.
RIGHT.
I SAVED YOU. I STOPPED THE BAD GUY...
HOW AM I NOT A SUPER?

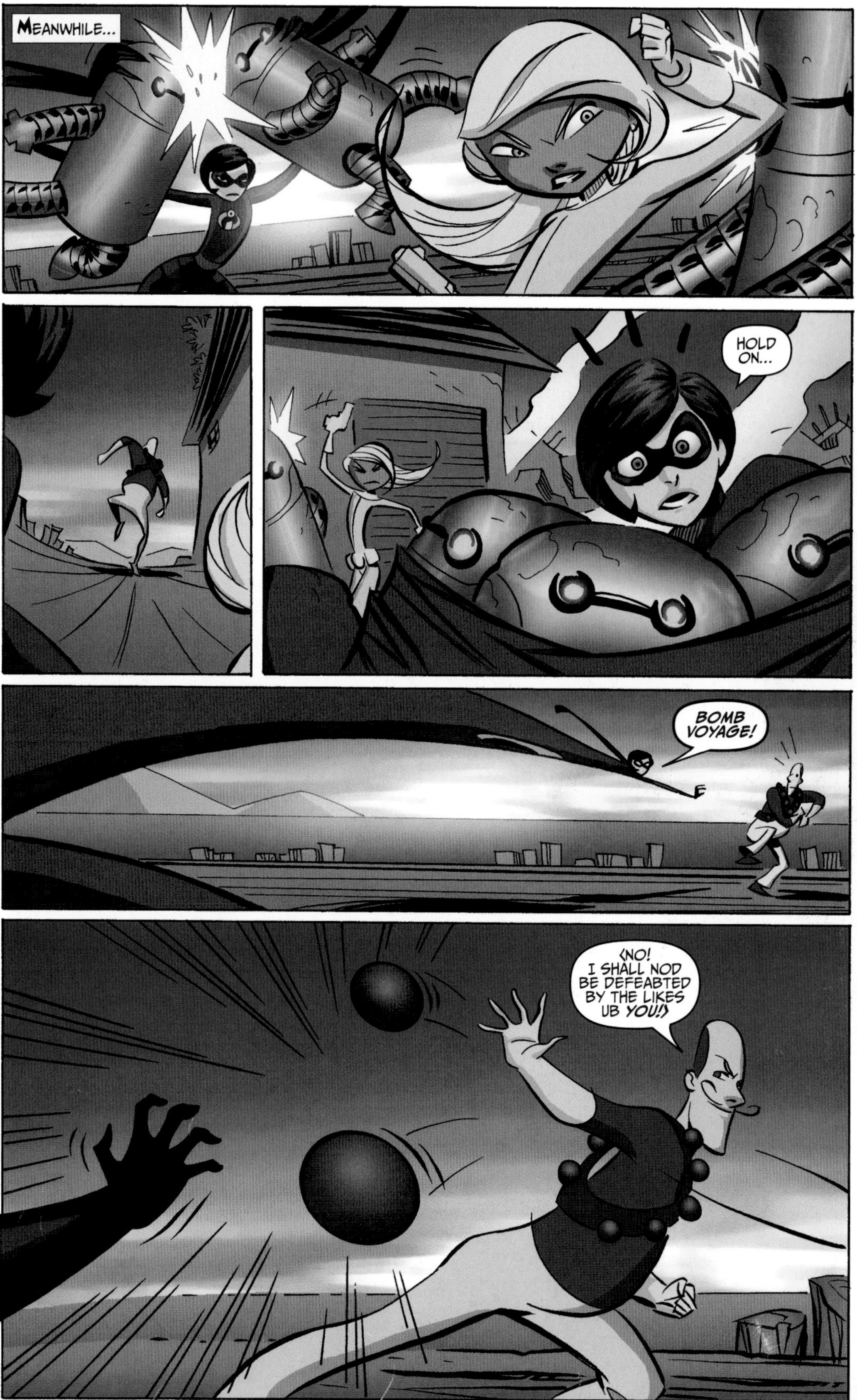

MEANWHILE...
HOLD ON...
BOMB VOYAGE!
‹NO! I SHALL NOD BE DEFEABTED BY THE LIKES UB YOU!›

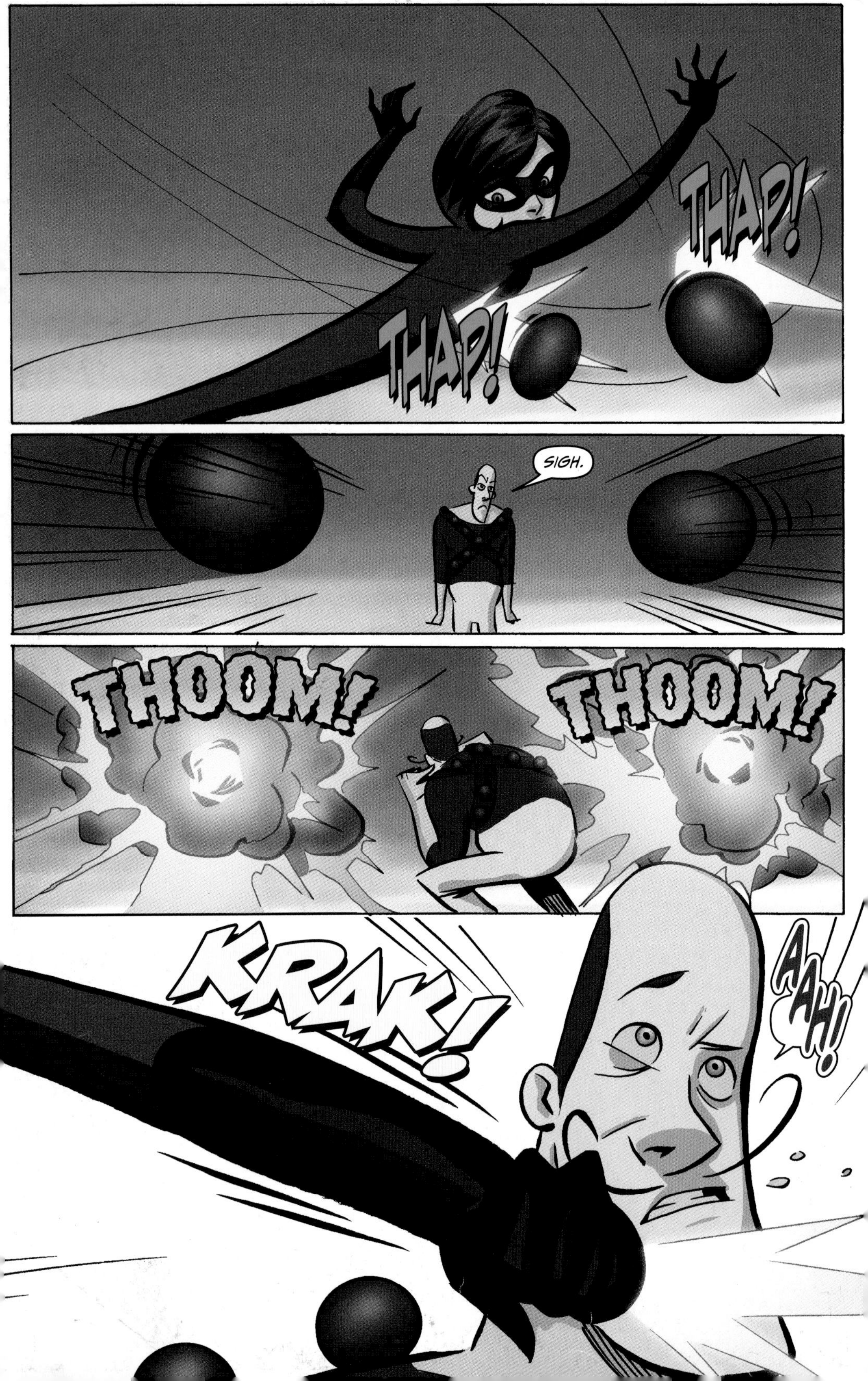
THAP!
THAP!
SIGH.
THOOM!
THOOM!
KRAK!
AAH!

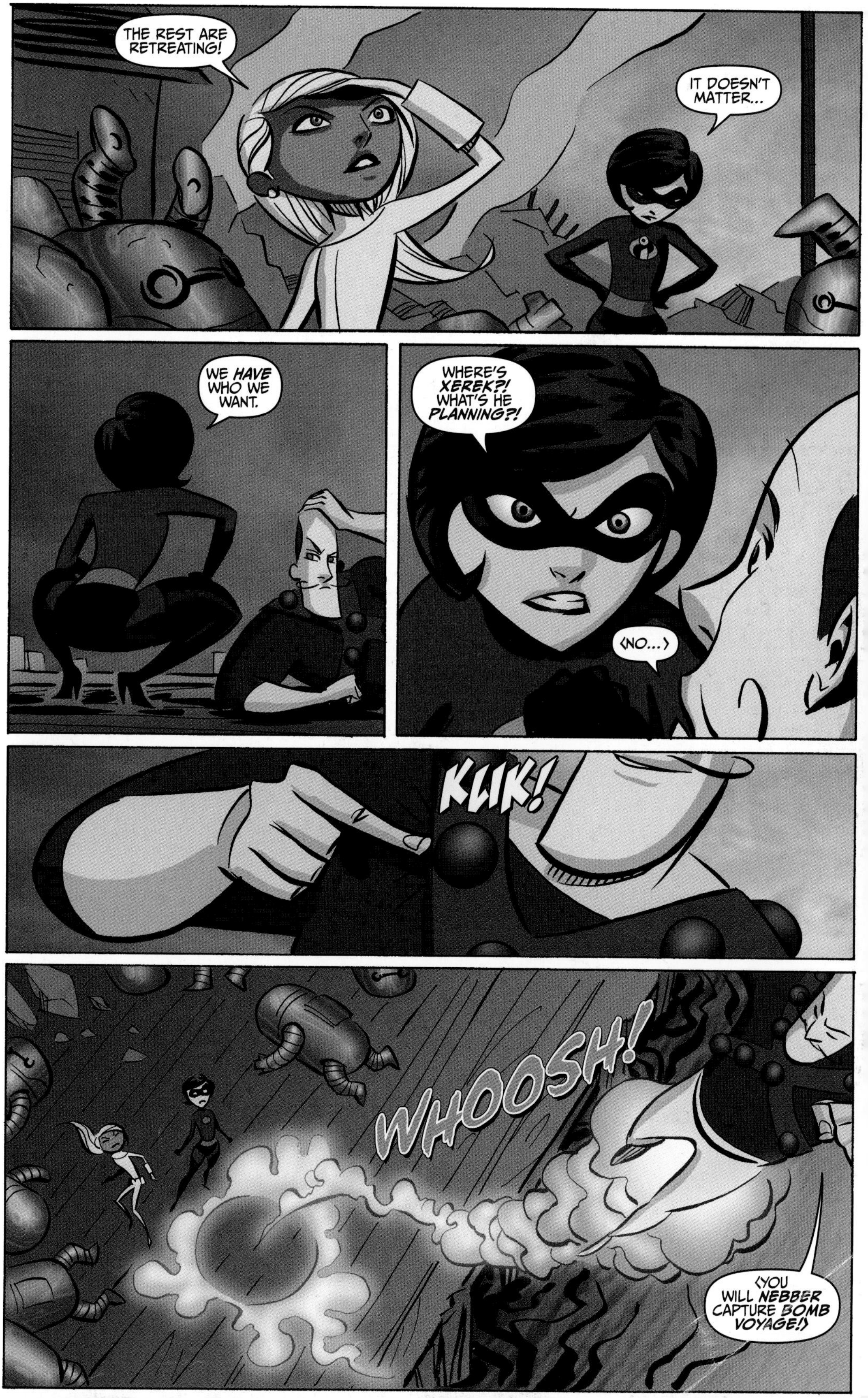
THE REST ARE RETREATING!
IT DOESN'T MATTER...
WE HAVE WHO WE WANT.
WHERE'S XEREK?! WHAT'S HE PLANNING?!
⟨NO...⟩
KLIK!
WHOOSH!
⟨YOU WILL NEBBER CAPTURE BOMB VOYAGE!⟩

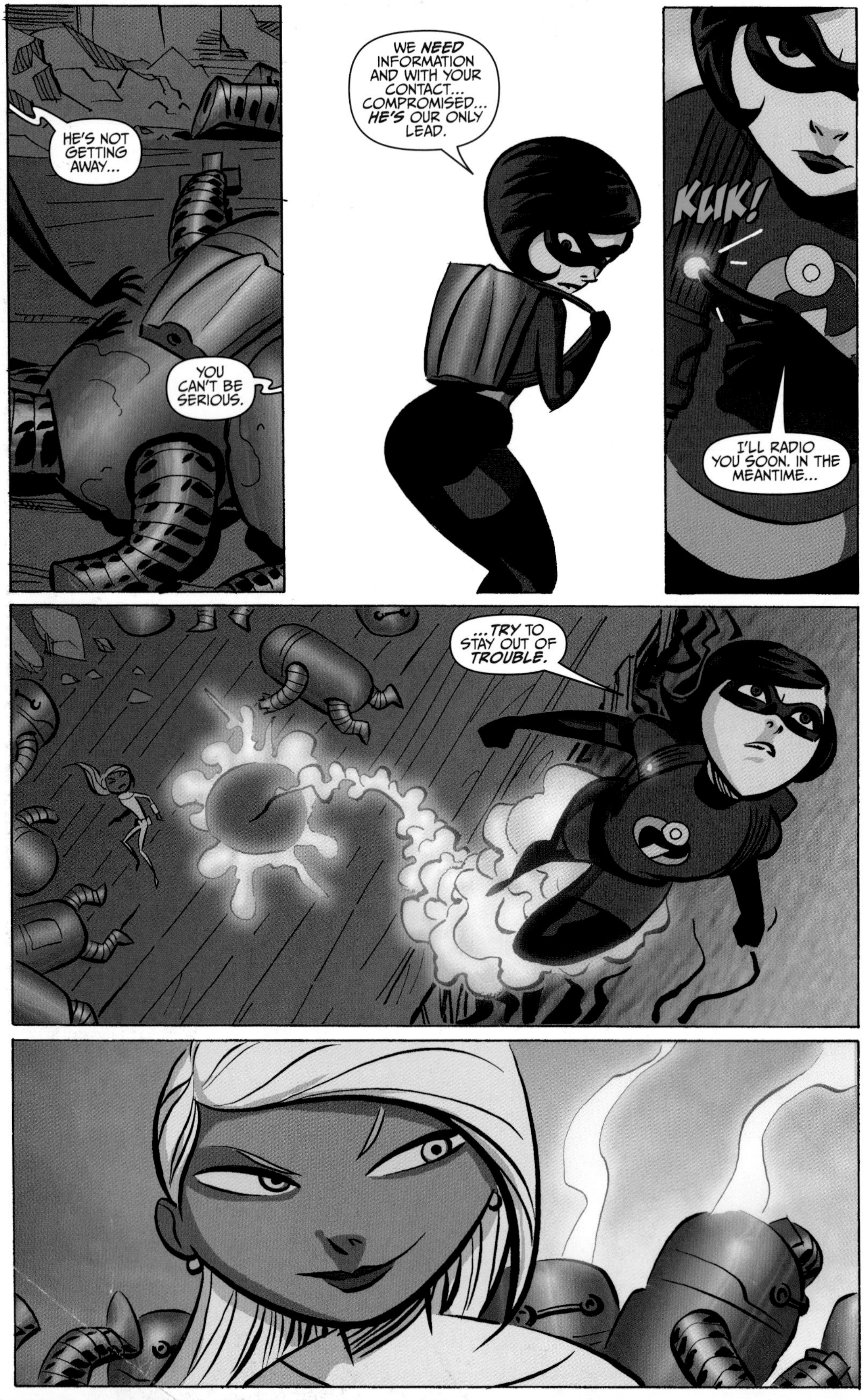
HE'S NOT GETTING AWAY...
YOU CAN'T BE SERIOUS.
WE NEED INFORMATION AND WITH YOUR CONTACT... COMPROMISED... HE'S OUR ONLY LEAD.
KLIK!
I'LL RADIO YOU SOON. IN THE MEANTIME...
...TRY TO STAY OUT OF TROUBLE.

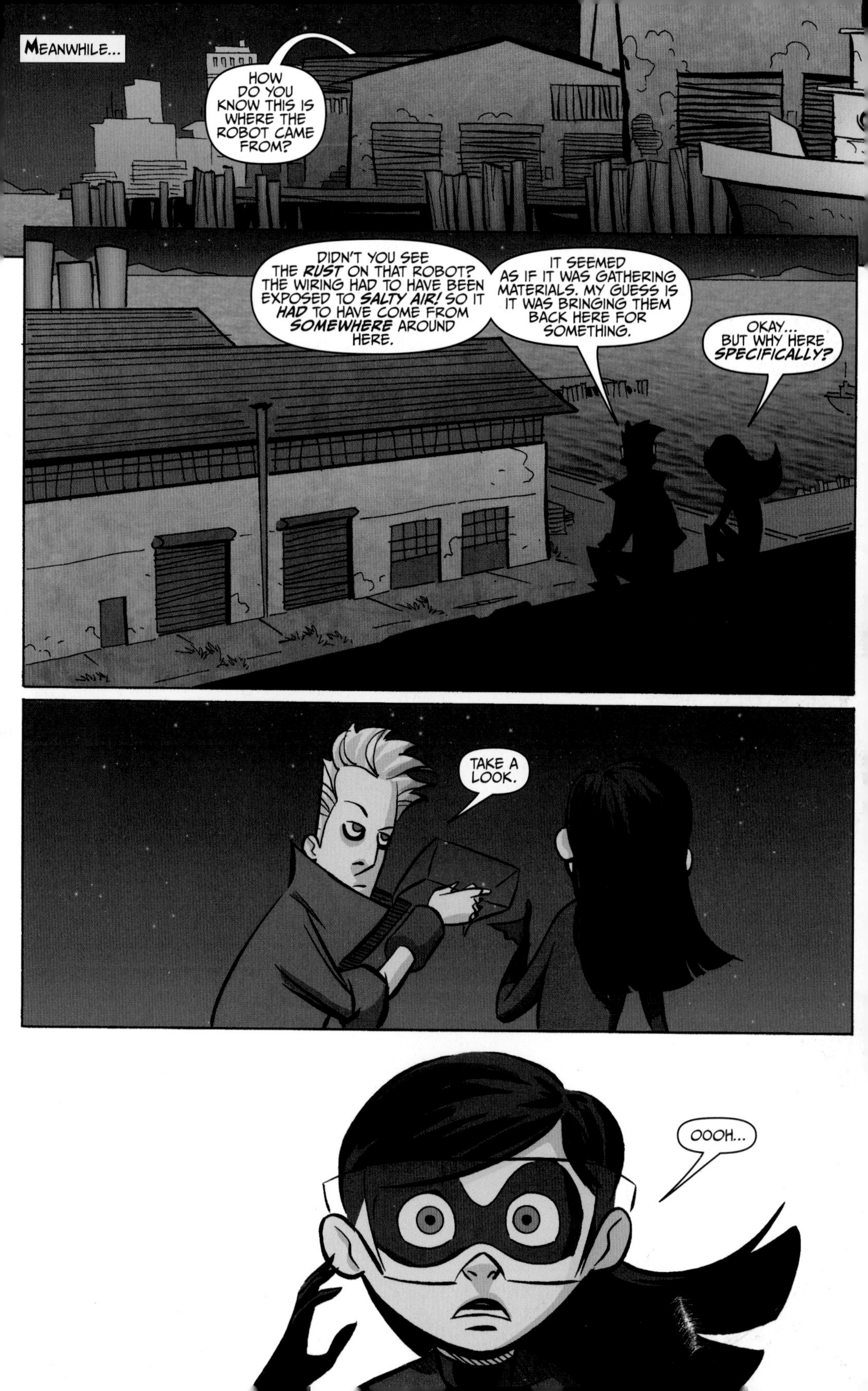
MEANWHILE...
HOW DO YOU KNOW THIS IS WHERE THE ROBOT CAME FROM?
DIDN'T YOU SEE THE RUST ON THAT ROBOT? THE WIRING HAD TO HAVE BEEN EXPOSED TO SALTY AIR! SO IT HAD TO HAVE COME FROM SOMEWHERE AROUND HERE.
IT SEEMED AS IF IT WAS GATHERING MATERIALS. MY GUESS IS IT WAS BRINGING THEM BACK HERE FOR SOMETHING.
OKAY... BUT WHY HERE SPECIFICALLY?
TAKE A LOOK.
OOOH...

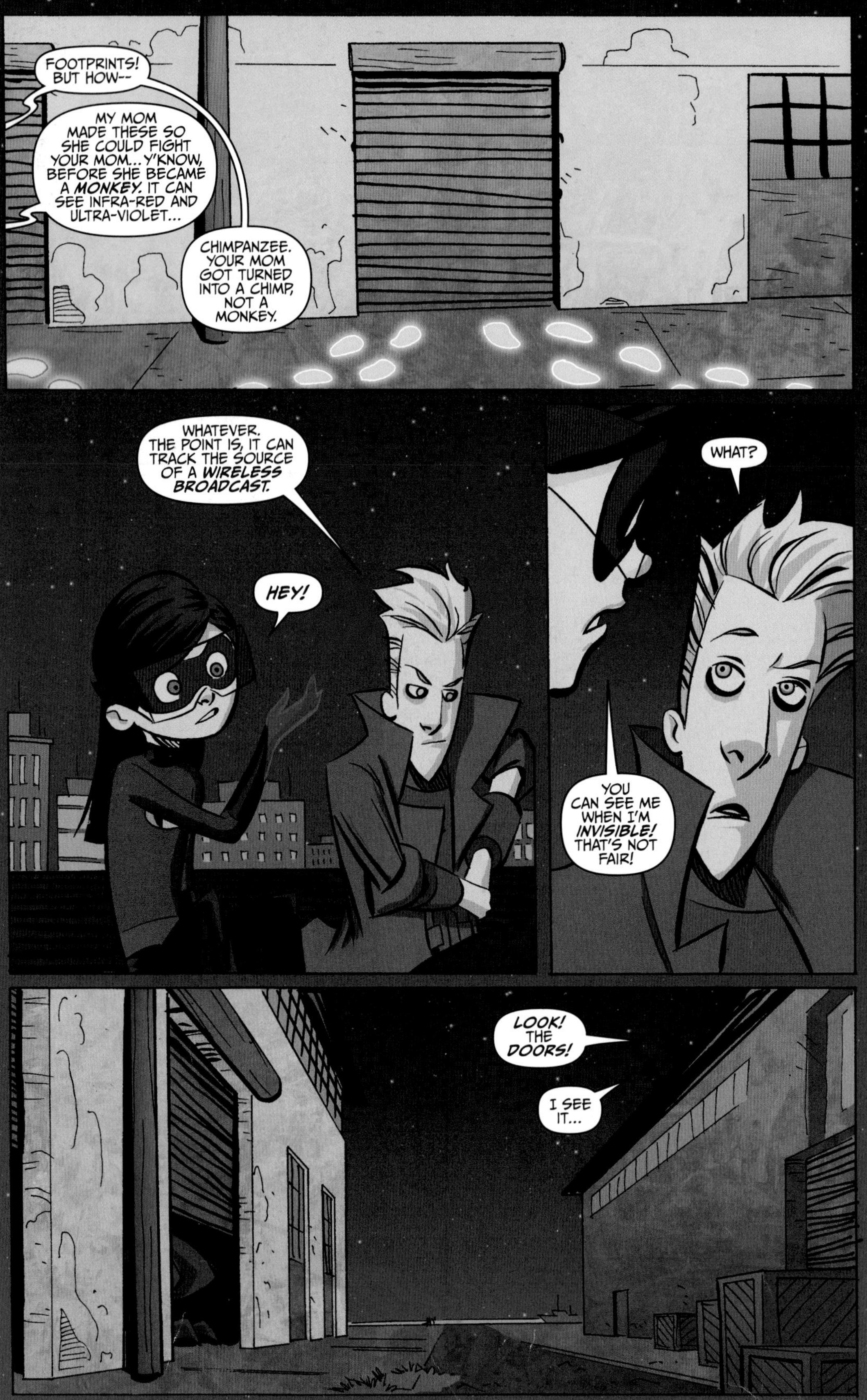
FOOTPRINTS! BUT HOW--
MY MOM MADE THESE SO SHE COULD FIGHT YOUR MOM... Y'KNOW, BEFORE SHE BECAME A MONKEY. IT CAN SEE INFRA-RED AND ULTRA-VIOLET...
CHIMPANZEE. YOUR MOM GOT TURNED INTO A CHIMP, NOT A MONKEY.
WHATEVER. THE POINT IS, IT CAN TRACK THE SOURCE OF A WIRELESS BROADCAST.
HEY!
WHAT?
YOU CAN SEE ME WHEN I'M INVISIBLE! THAT'S NOT FAIR!
LOOK! THE DOORS!
I SEE IT...

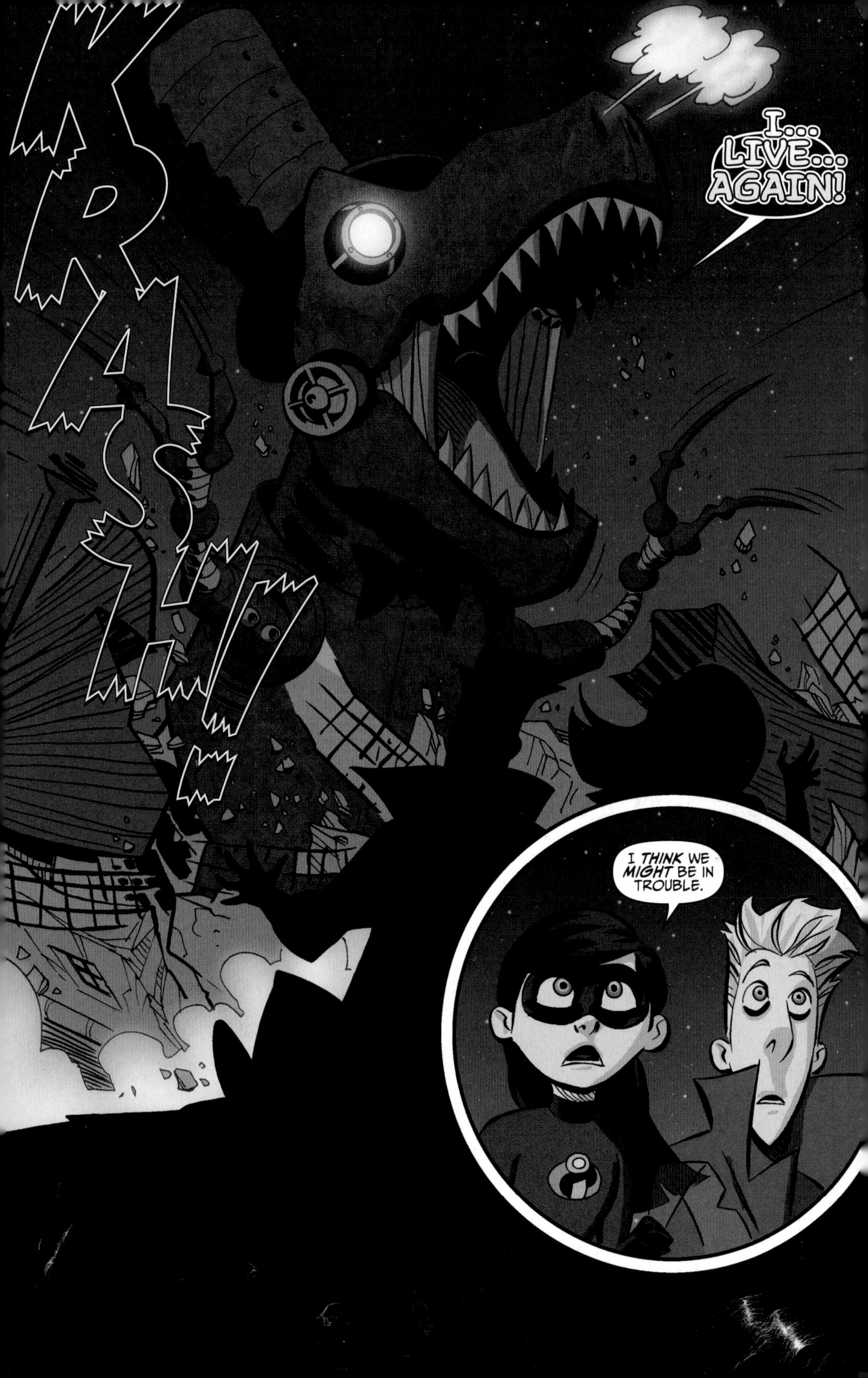
KRASSH!!
I... LIVE... AGAIN!
I THINK WE MIGHT BE IN TROUBLE.

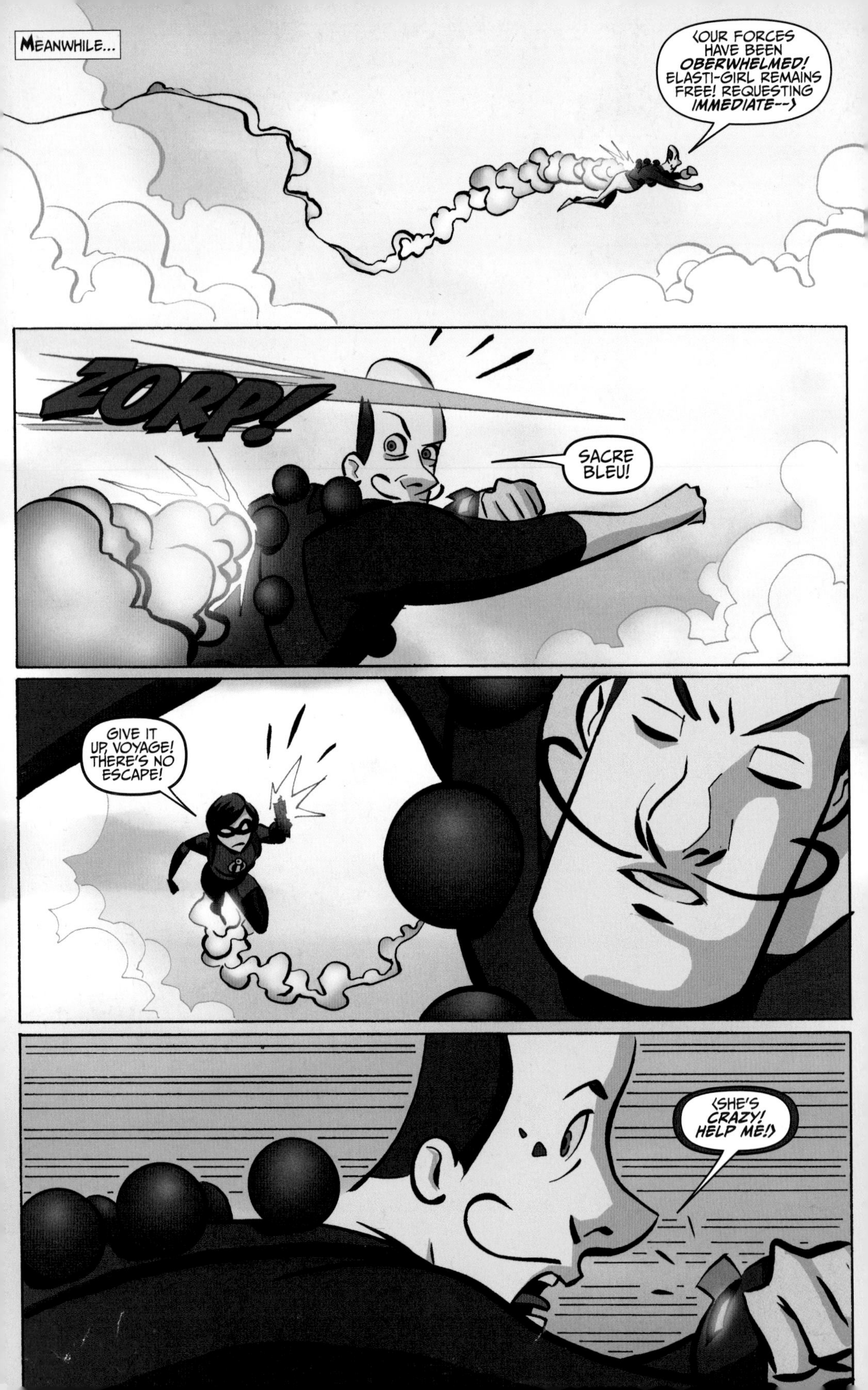
MEANWHILE...
‹OUR FORCES HAVE BEEN OBERWHELMED! ELASTI-GIRL REMAINS FREE! REQUESTING IMMEDIATE--›
ZORP!
SACRE BLEU!
GIVE IT UP, VOYAGE! THERE'S NO ESCAPE!
‹SHE'S CRAZY! HELP ME!›

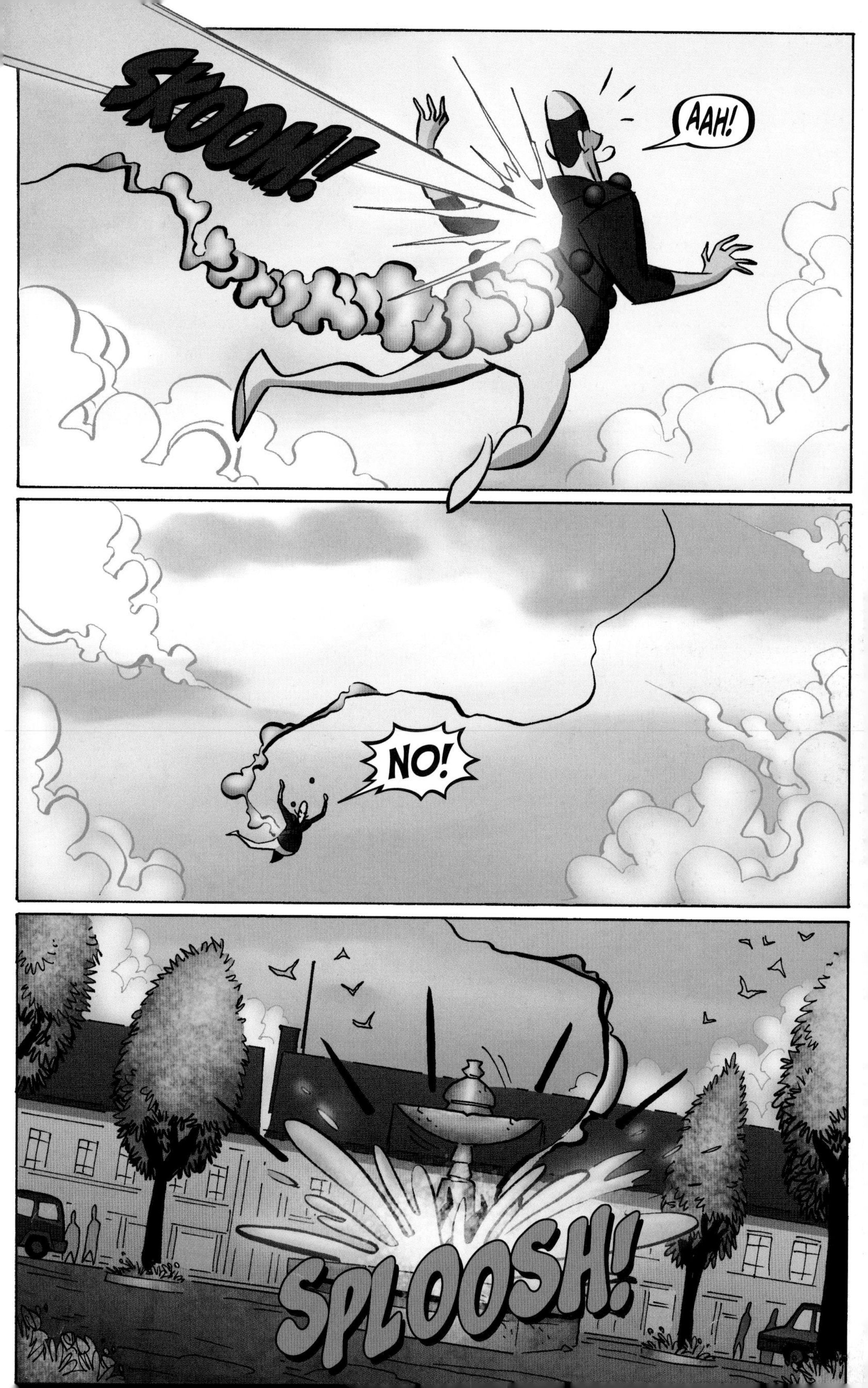
SKOOM!
AAH!
NO!
SPLOOSH!

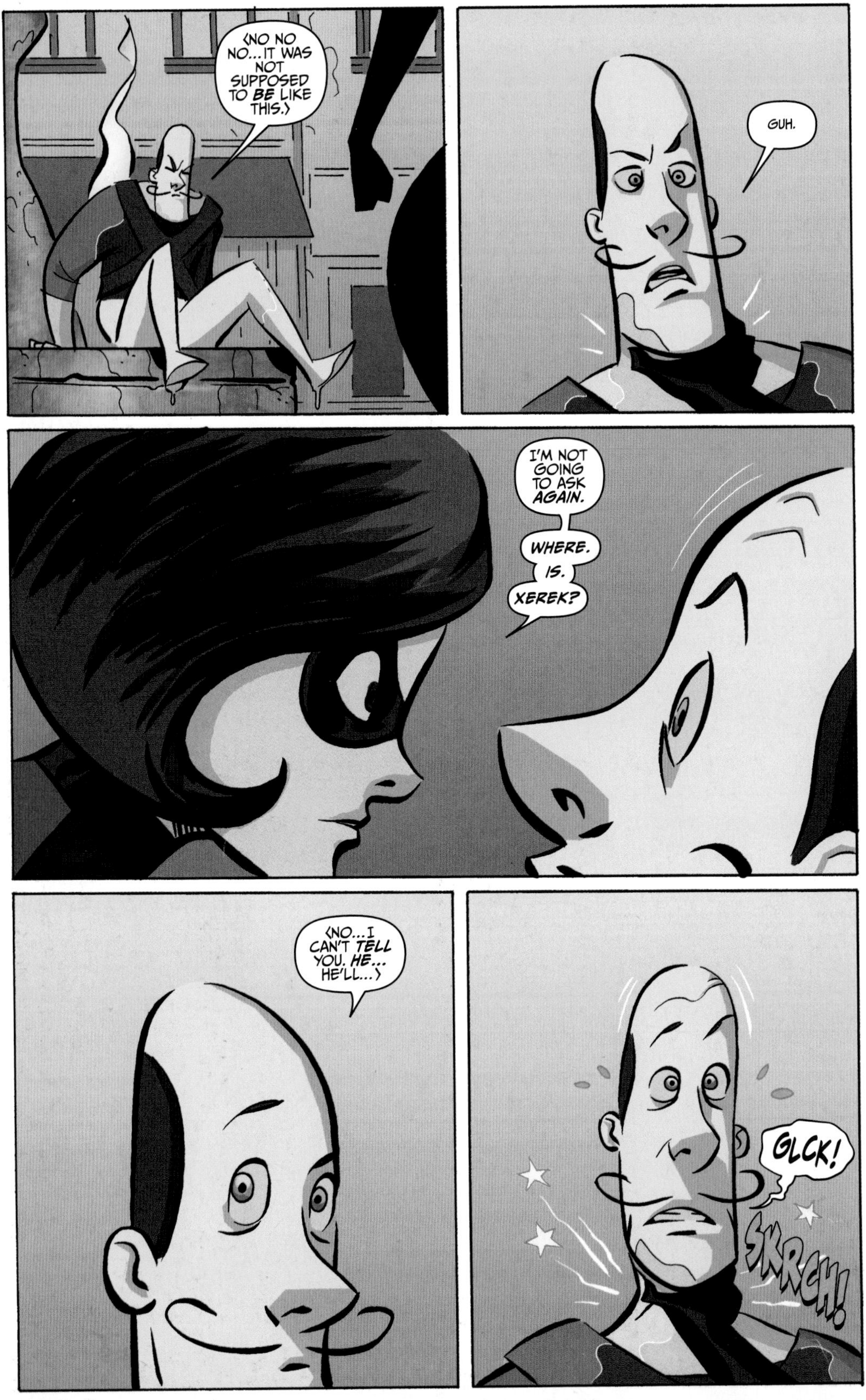

⟨NO NO NO...IT WAS NOT SUPPOSED TO BE LIKE THIS.⟩
GUH.
I'M NOT GOING TO ASK AGAIN.
WHERE. IS. XEREK?
⟨NO...I CAN'T TELL YOU. HE... HE'LL...⟩
GLCK!
SKRCH!

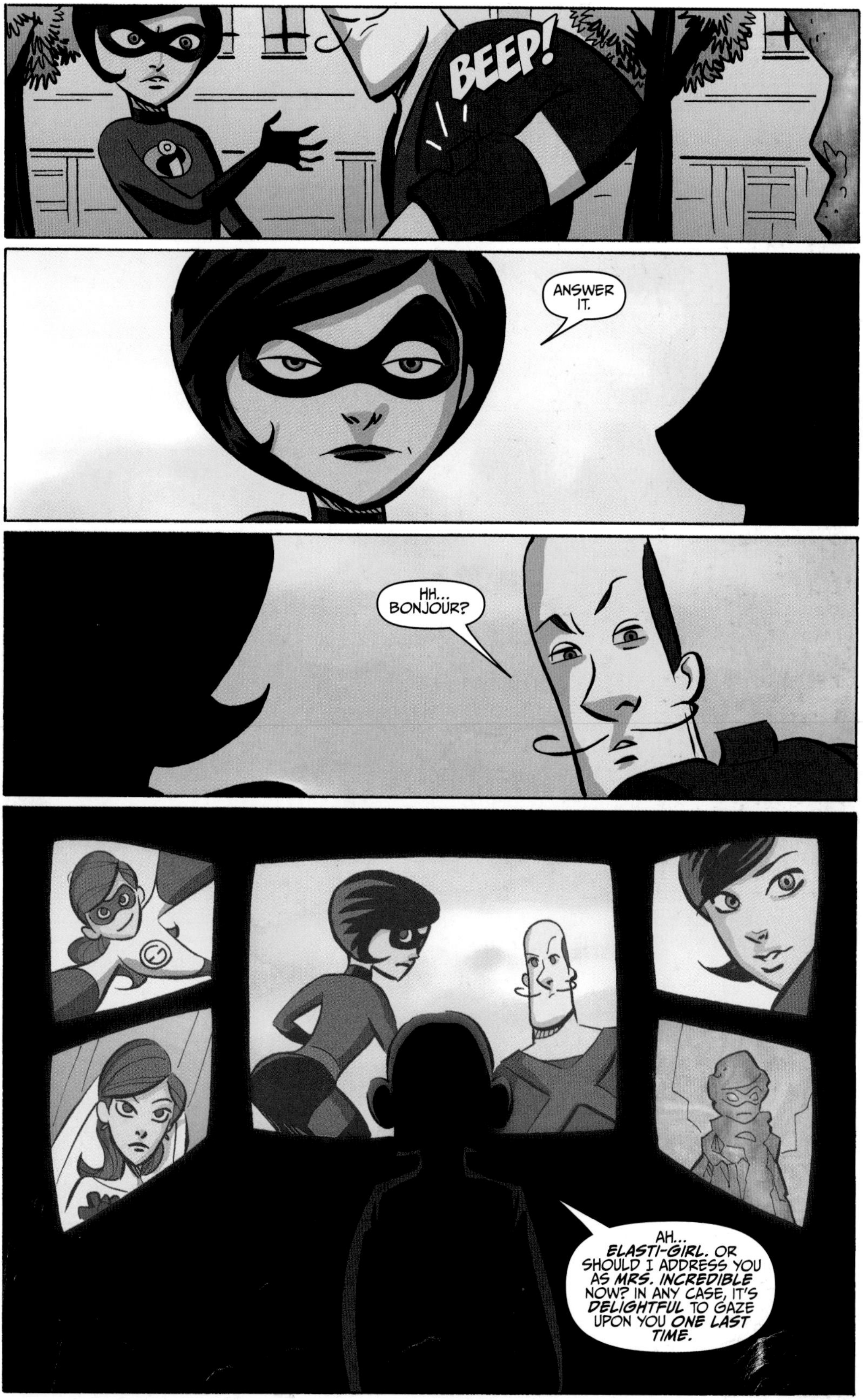
BEEP!
ANSWER IT.
HH... BONJOUR?
AH... ELASTI-GIRL. OR SHOULD I ADDRESS YOU AS MRS. INCREDIBLE NOW? IN ANY CASE, IT'S DELIGHTFUL TO GAZE UPON YOU ONE LAST TIME.

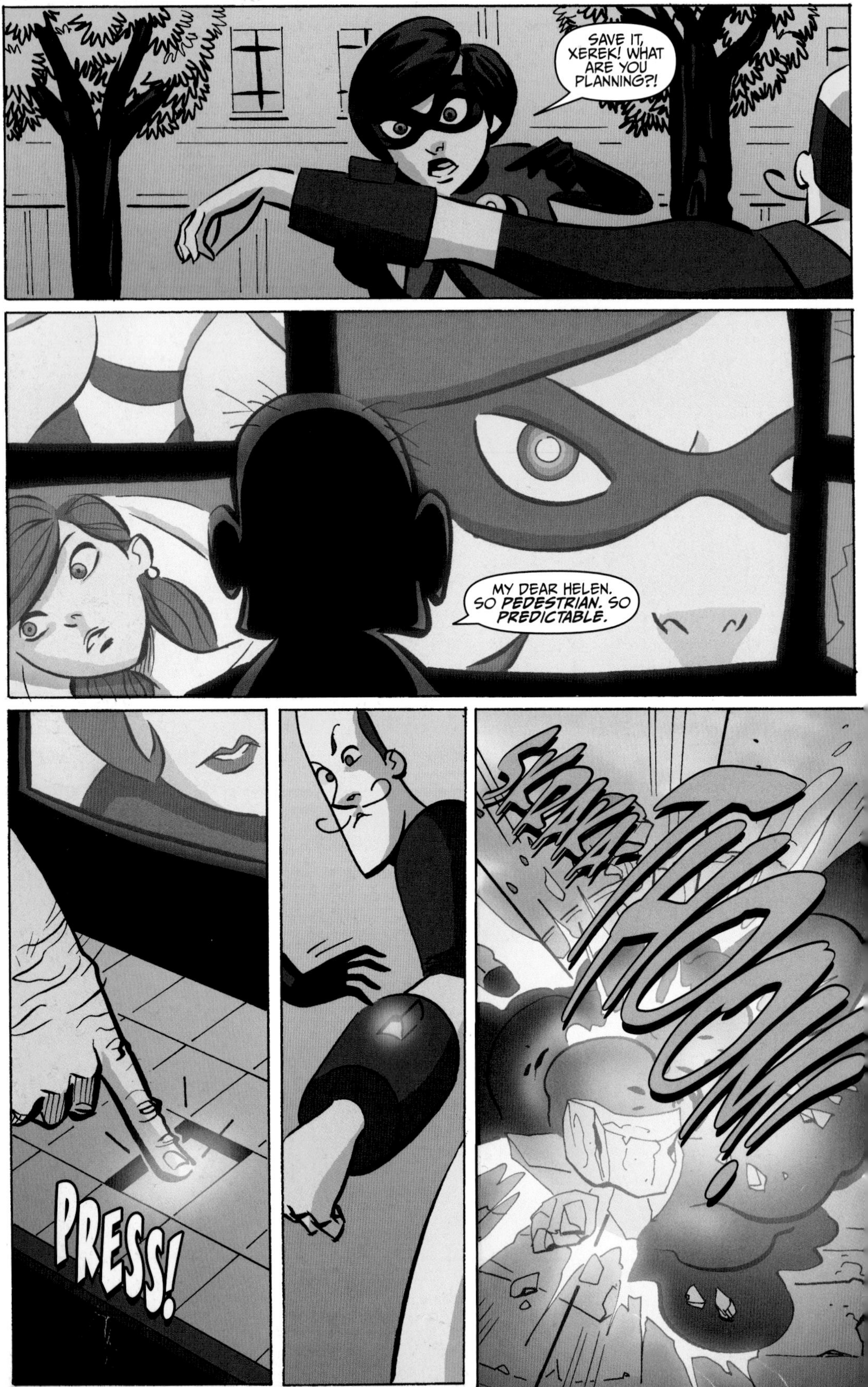
SAVE IT, XEREK! WHAT ARE YOU PLANNING?!
MY DEAR HELEN. SO *PEDESTRIAN*. SO *PREDICTABLE*.
PRESS!
SKRAKA
THOOM!

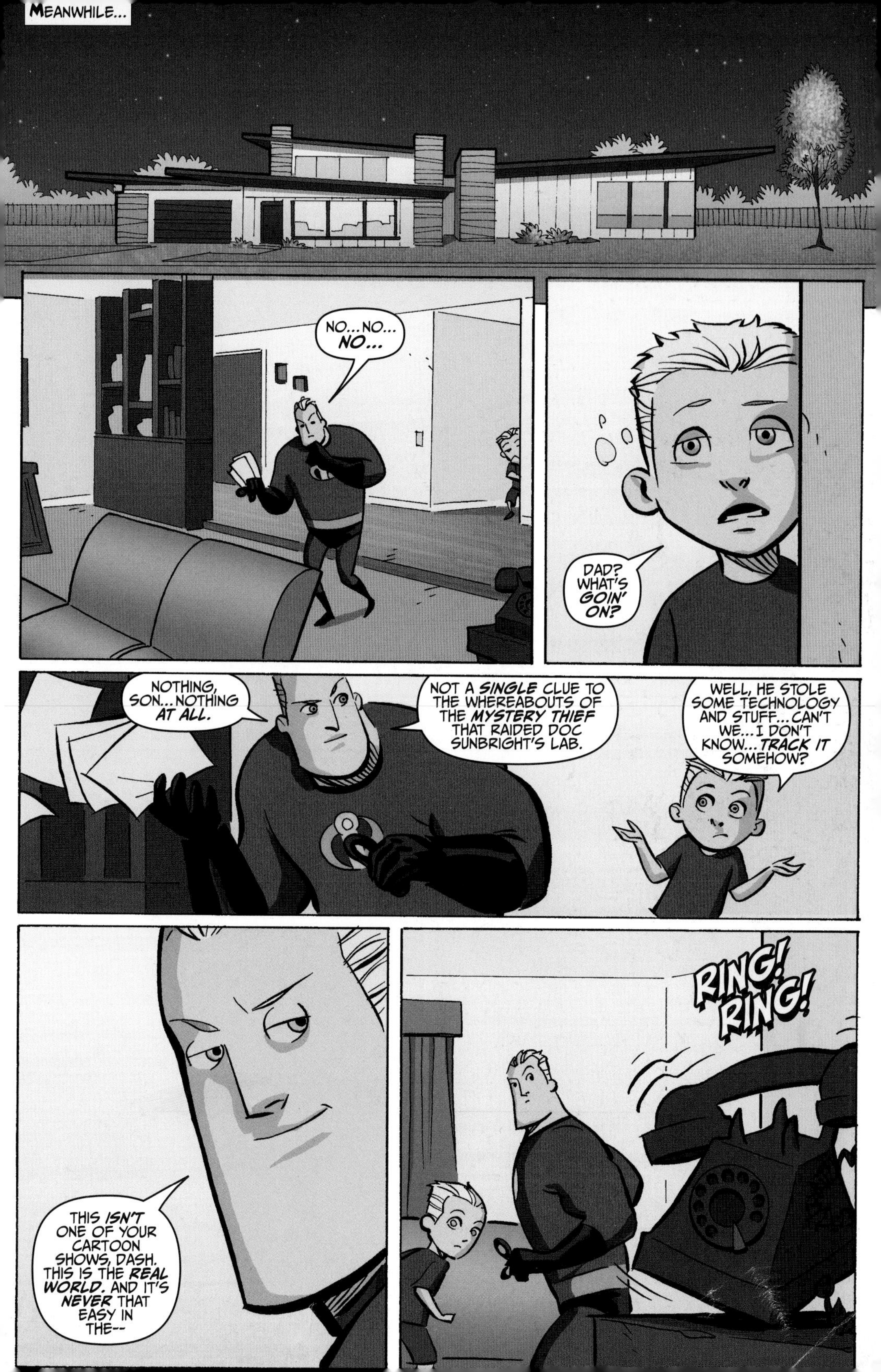
MEANWHILE...
NO...NO... NO...
DAD? WHAT'S GOIN' ON?
NOTHING, SON...NOTHING AT ALL.
NOT A SINGLE CLUE TO THE WHEREABOUTS OF THE MYSTERY THIEF THAT RAIDED DOC SUNBRIGHT'S LAB.
WELL, HE STOLE SOME TECHNOLOGY AND STUFF...CAN'T WE...I DON'T KNOW...TRACK IT SOMEHOW?
THIS ISN'T ONE OF YOUR CARTOON SHOWS, DASH. THIS IS THE REAL WORLD. AND IT'S NEVER THAT EASY IN THE--
RING! RING!

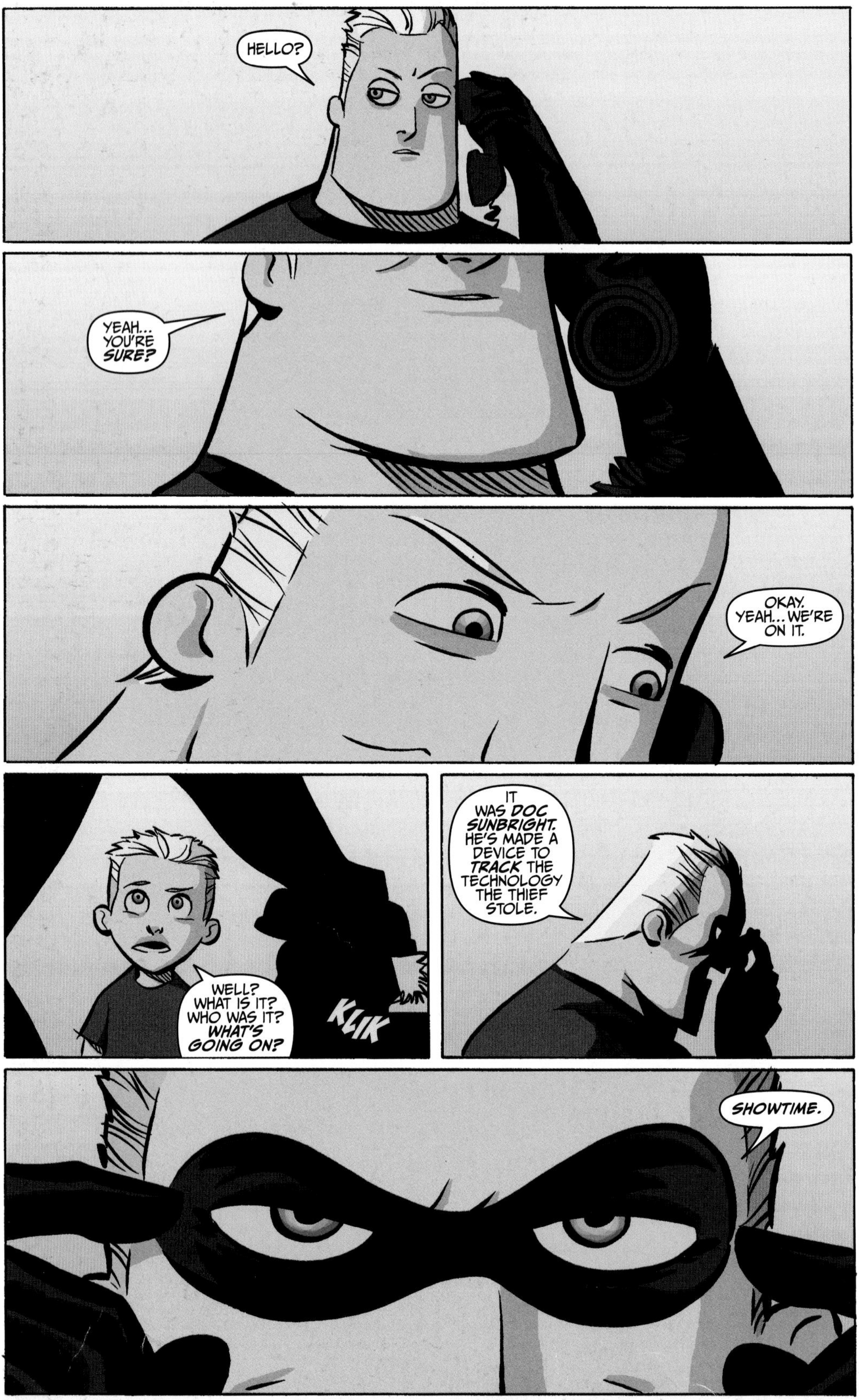
HELLO?
YEAH... YOU'RE SURE?
OKAY. YEAH... WE'RE ON IT.
WELL? WHAT IS IT? WHO WAS IT? WHAT'S GOING ON?
KLIK
IT WAS DOC SUNBRIGHT. HE'S MADE A DEVICE TO TRACK THE TECHNOLOGY THE THIEF STOLE.
SHOWTIME.

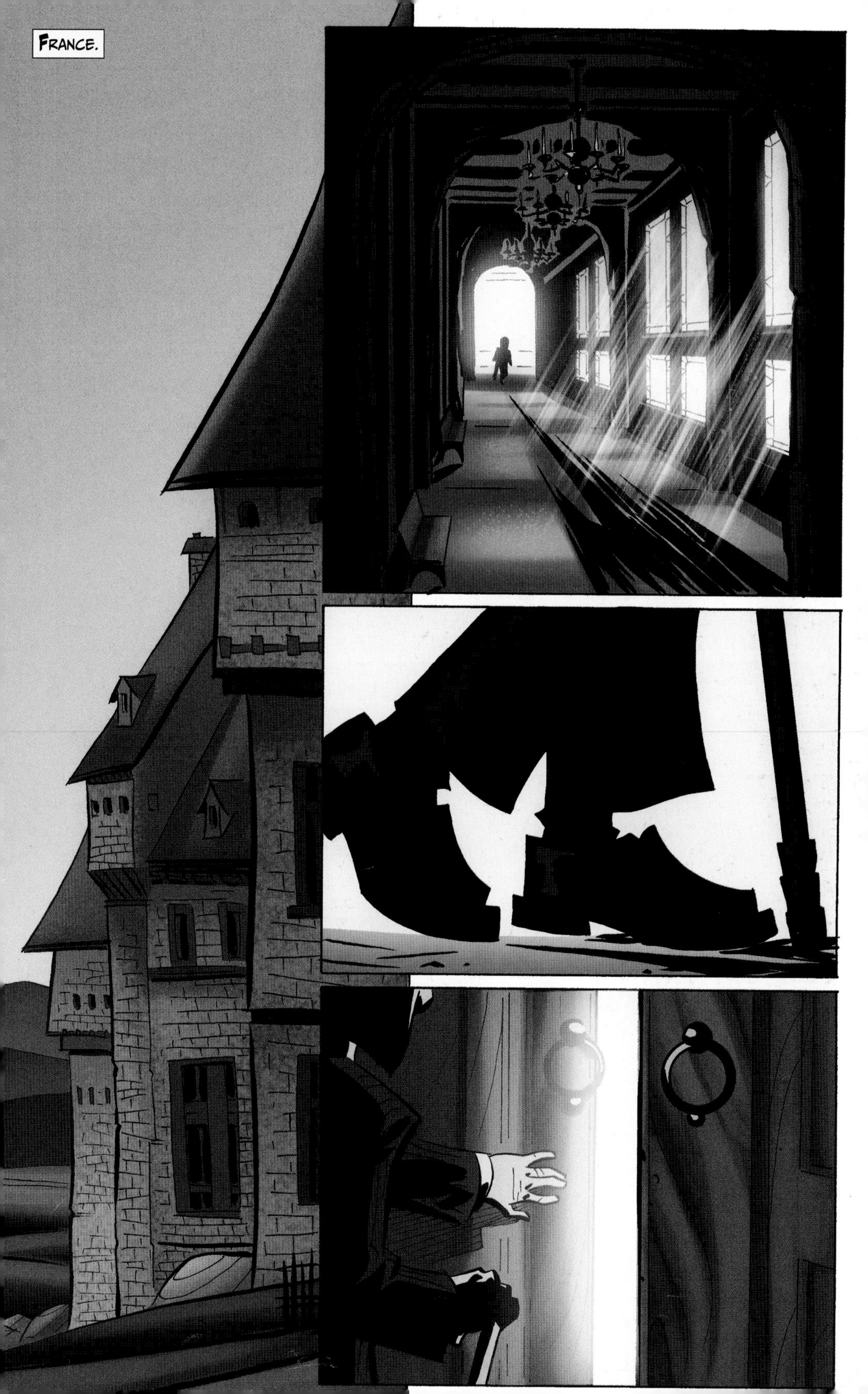
FRANCE.

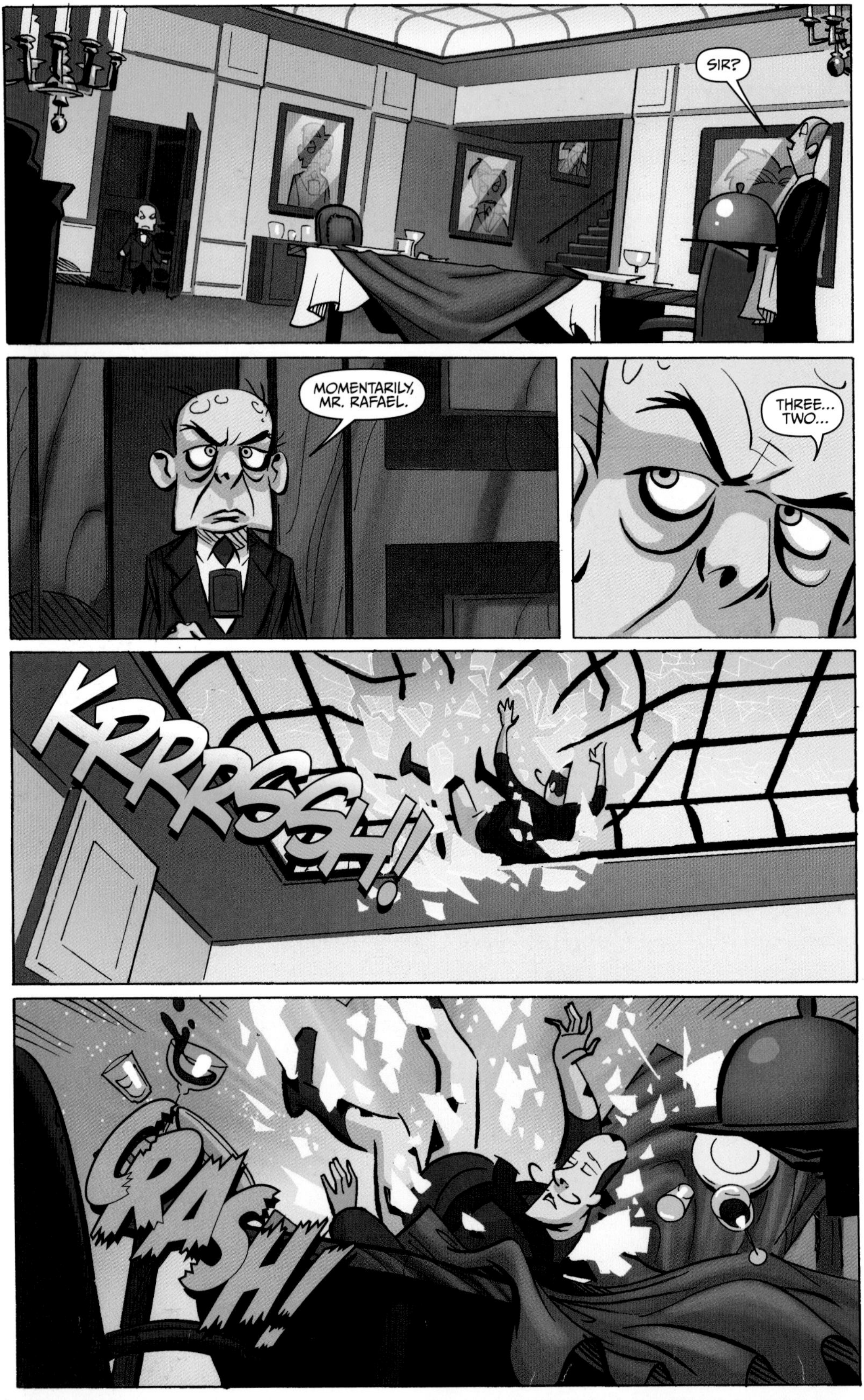
SIR?
MOMENTARILY, MR. RAFAEL.
THREE... TWO...
KRRRSSH!!
CRASH!

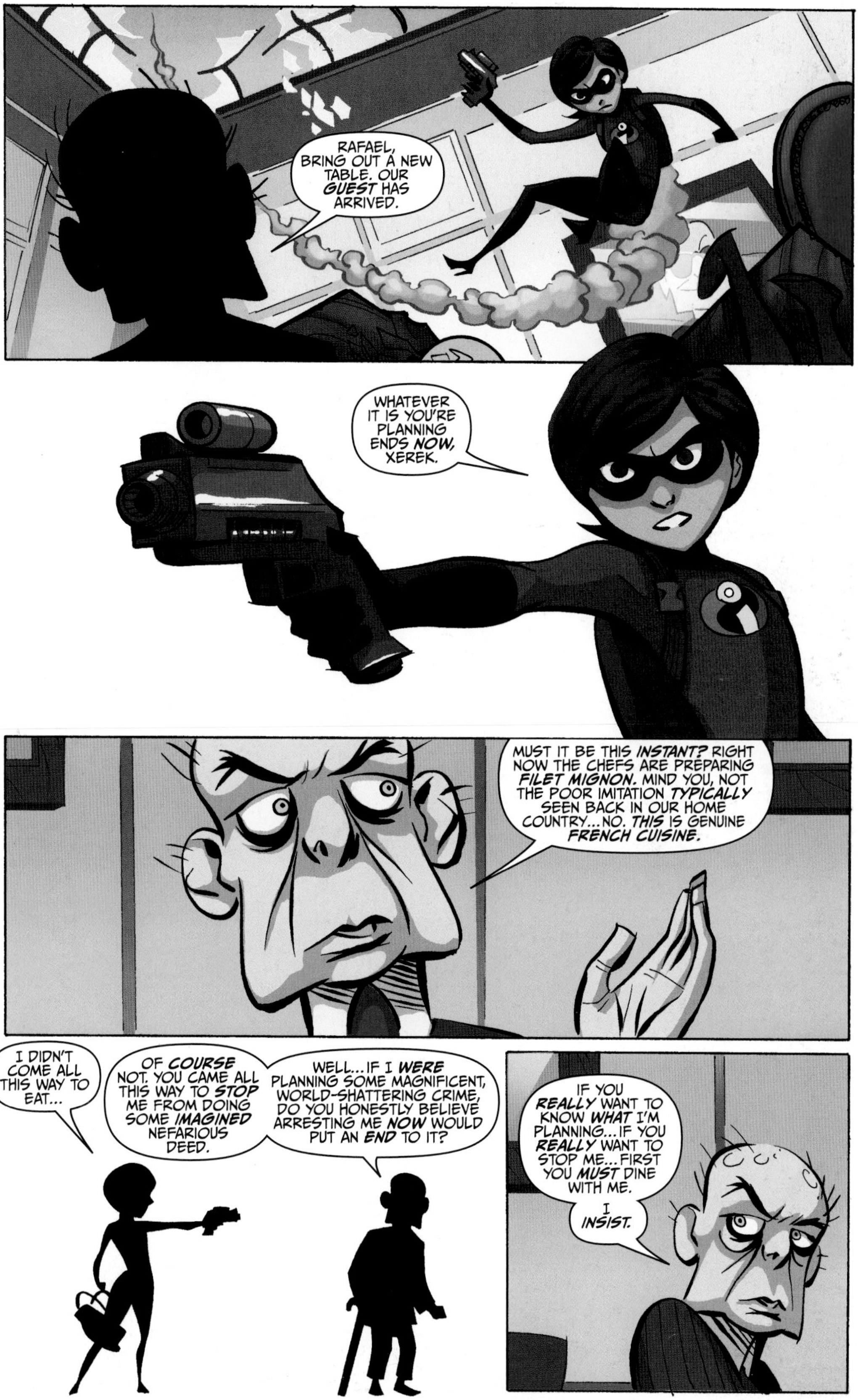
RAFAEL, BRING OUT A NEW TABLE. OUR GUEST HAS ARRIVED.
WHATEVER IT IS YOU'RE PLANNING ENDS NOW, XEREK.
MUST IT BE THIS INSTANT? RIGHT NOW THE CHEFS ARE PREPARING FILET MIGNON. MIND YOU, NOT THE POOR IMITATION TYPICALLY SEEN BACK IN OUR HOME COUNTRY...NO. THIS IS GENUINE FRENCH CUISINE.
I DIDN'T COME ALL THIS WAY TO EAT...
OF COURSE NOT. YOU CAME ALL THIS WAY TO STOP ME FROM DOING SOME IMAGINED NEFARIOUS DEED.
WELL...IF I WERE PLANNING SOME MAGNIFICENT, WORLD-SHATTERING CRIME, DO YOU HONESTLY BELIEVE ARRESTING ME NOW WOULD PUT AN END TO IT?
IF YOU REALLY WANT TO KNOW WHAT I'M PLANNING...IF YOU REALLY WANT TO STOP ME...FIRST YOU MUST DINE WITH ME.
I INSIST.

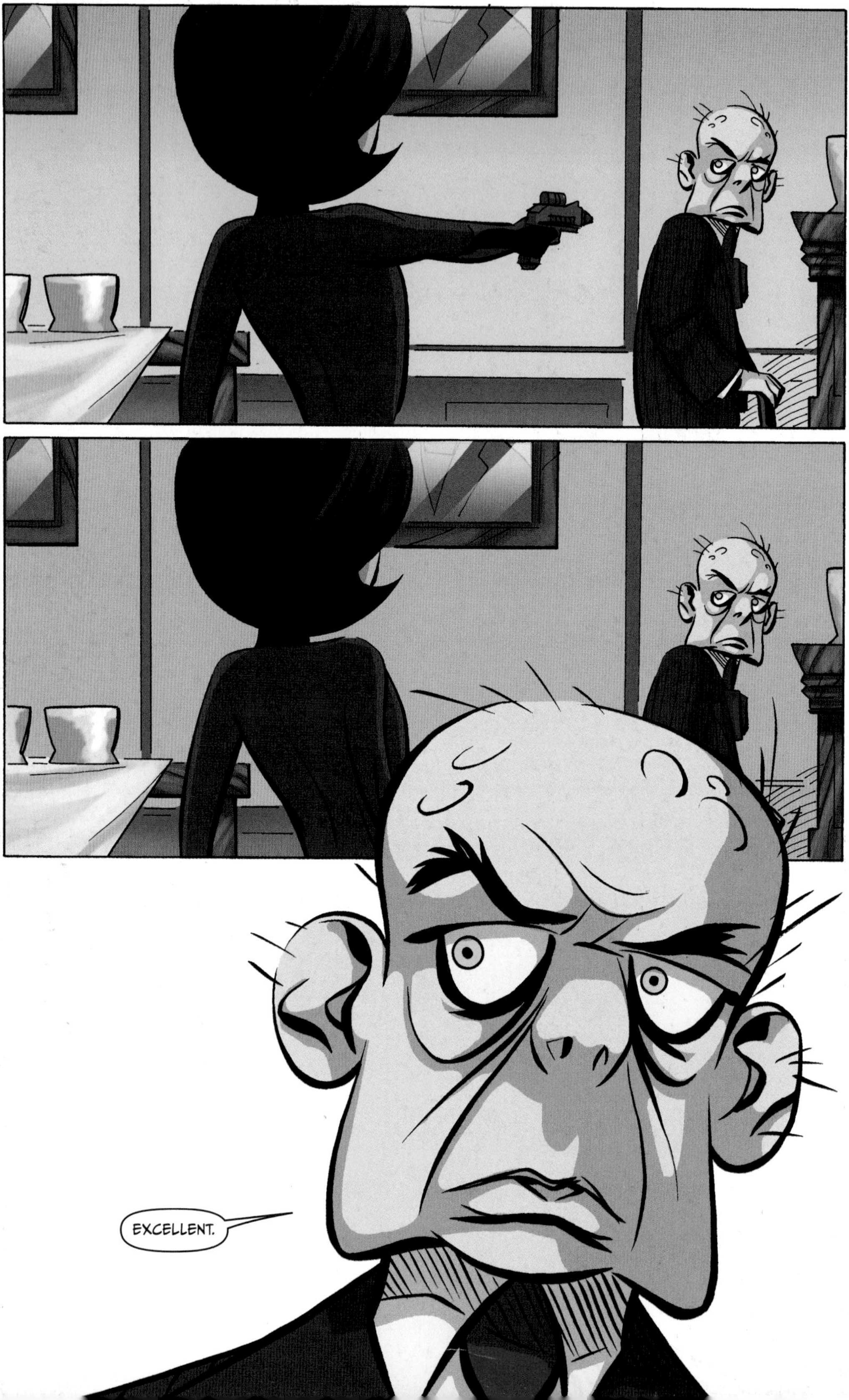
EXCELLENT.

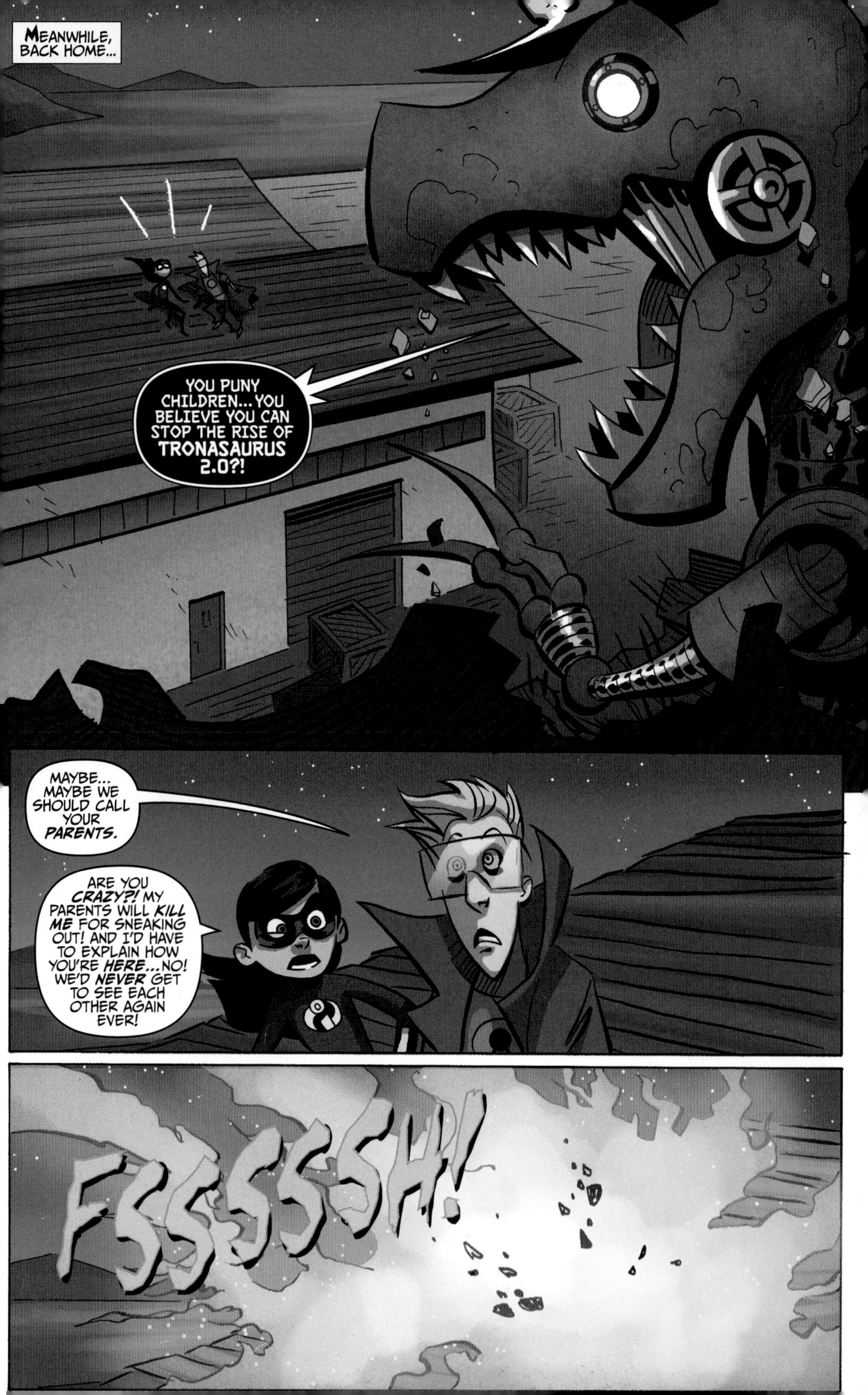
MEANWHILE, BACK HOME...
YOU PUNY CHILDREN...YOU BELIEVE YOU CAN STOP THE RISE OF TRONASAURUS 2.0?!
MAYBE... MAYBE WE SHOULD CALL YOUR PARENTS.
ARE YOU CRAZY?! MY PARENTS WILL KILL ME FOR SNEAKING OUT! AND I'D HAVE TO EXPLAIN HOW YOU'RE HERE...NO! WE'D NEVER GET TO SEE EACH OTHER AGAIN EVER!
FSSSSSH!

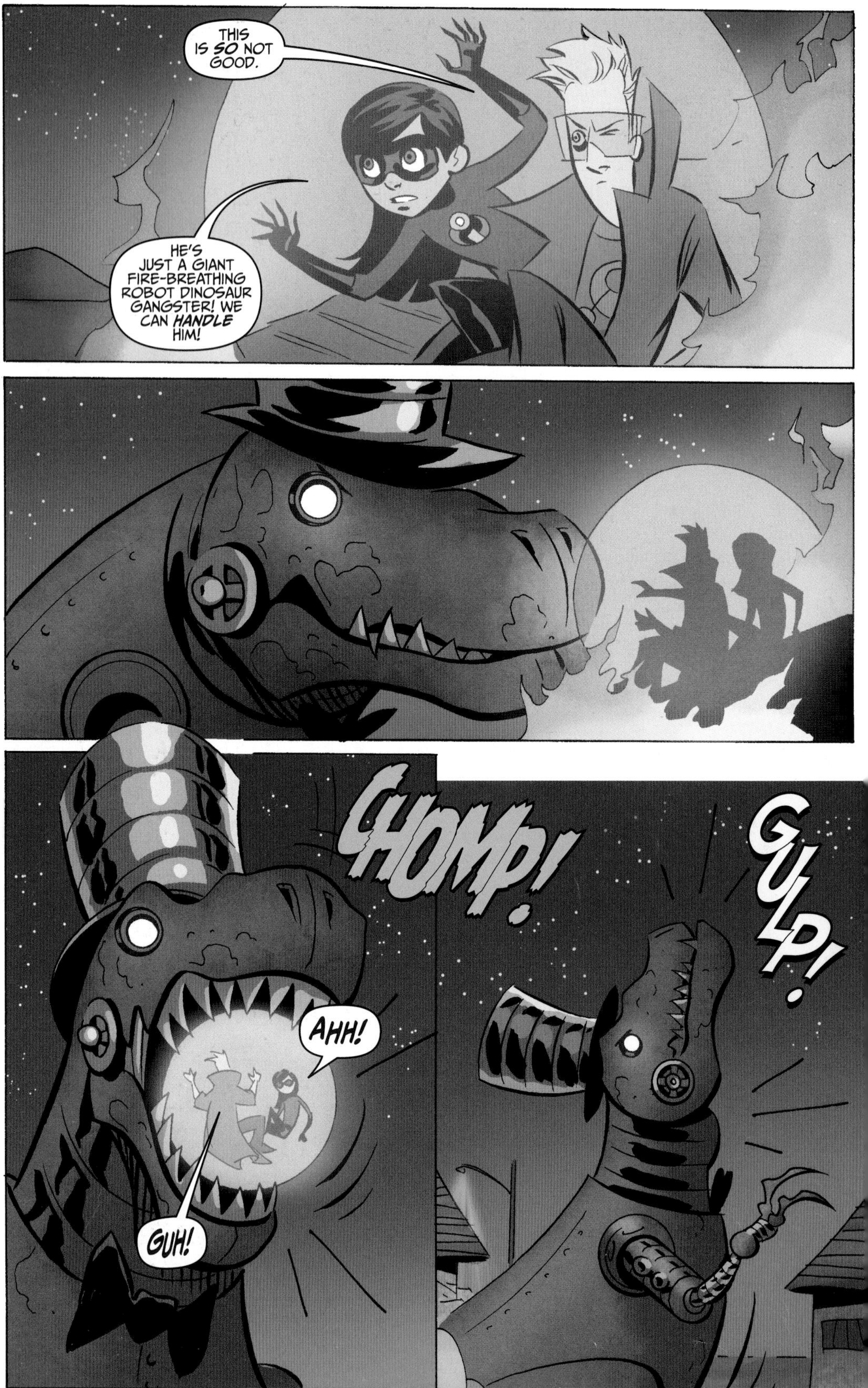
THIS IS SO NOT GOOD.
HE'S JUST A GIANT FIRE-BREATHING ROBOT DINOSAUR GANGSTER! WE CAN HANDLE HIM!
CHOMP!
AHH!
GUH!
GULP!

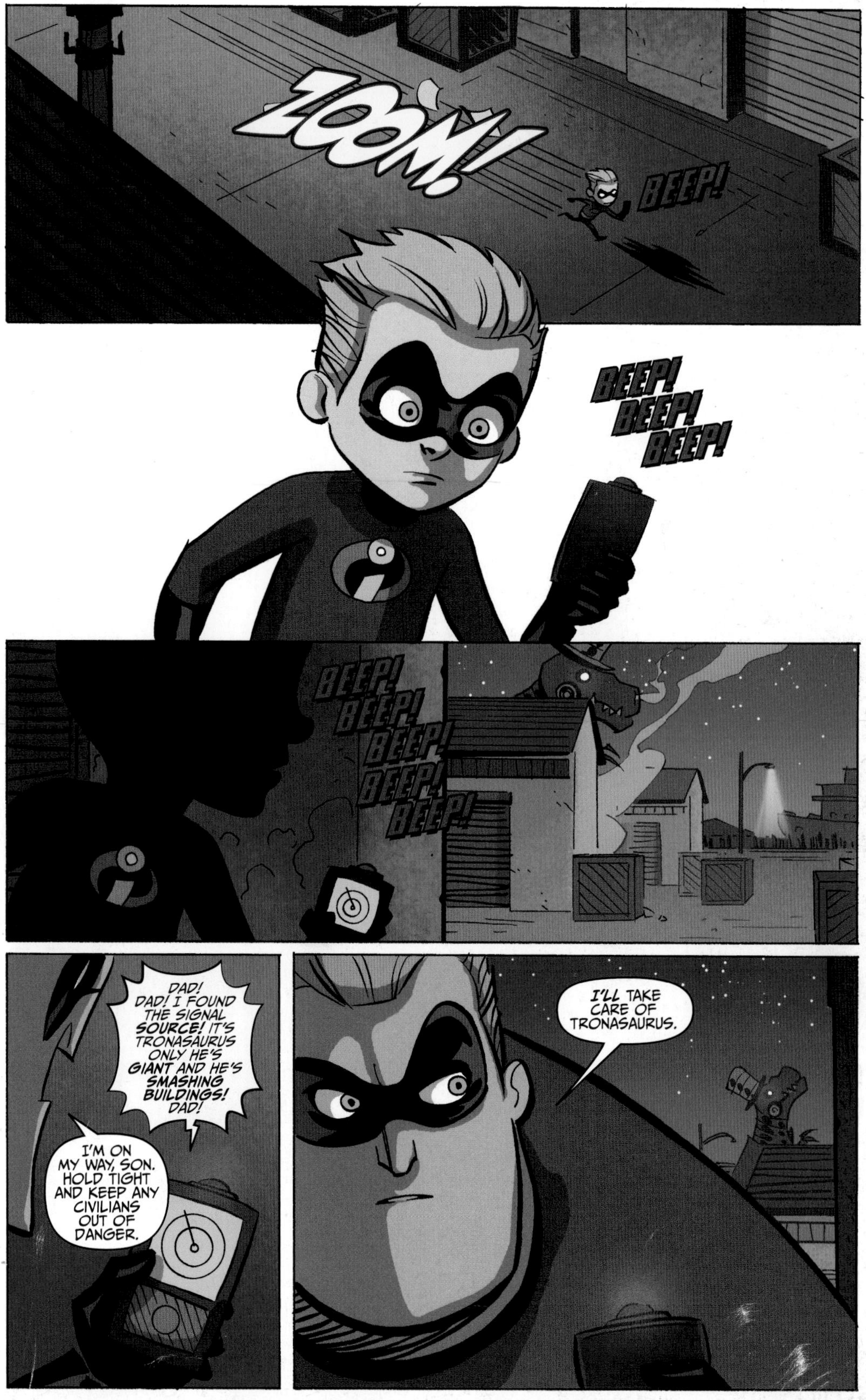
ZOOM!
BEEP!
BEEP! BEEP! BEEP!
BEEP! BEEP! BEEP! BEEP! BEEP!
DAD! DAD! I FOUND THE SIGNAL SOURCE! IT'S TRONASAURUS ONLY HE'S GIANT AND HE'S SMASHING BUILDINGS! DAD!
I'M ON MY WAY, SON. HOLD TIGHT AND KEEP ANY CIVILIANS OUT OF DANGER.
I'LL TAKE CARE OF TRONASAURUS.

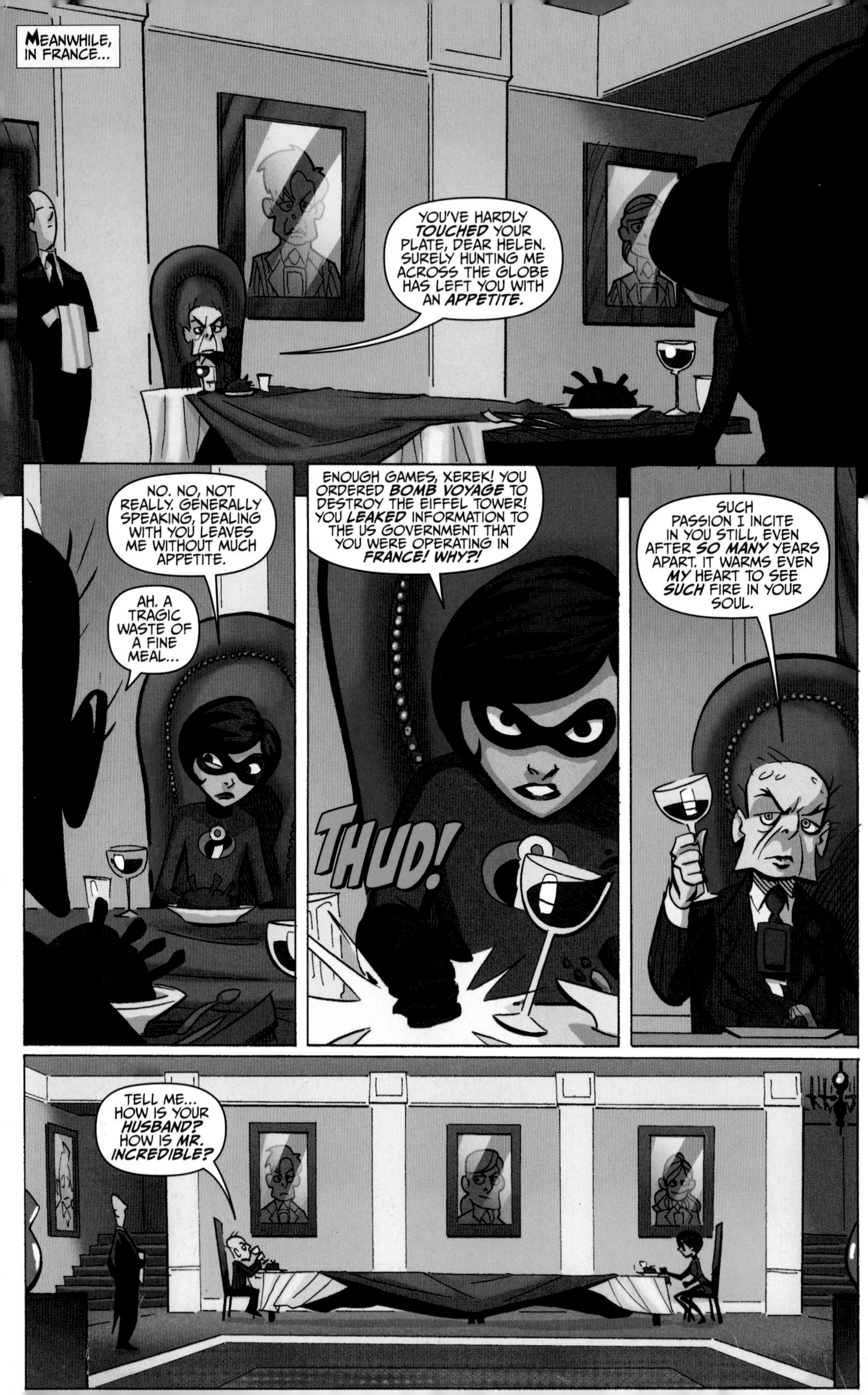
MEANWHILE, IN FRANCE...
YOU'VE HARDLY TOUCHED YOUR PLATE, DEAR HELEN. SURELY HUNTING ME ACROSS THE GLOBE HAS LEFT YOU WITH AN APPETITE.
NO. NO, NOT REALLY. GENERALLY SPEAKING, DEALING WITH YOU LEAVES ME WITHOUT MUCH APPETITE.
AH. A TRAGIC WASTE OF A FINE MEAL...
ENOUGH GAMES, XEREK! YOU ORDERED BOMB VOYAGE TO DESTROY THE EIFFEL TOWER! YOU LEAKED INFORMATION TO THE US GOVERNMENT THAT YOU WERE OPERATING IN FRANCE! WHY?!
THUD!
SUCH PASSION I INCITE IN YOU STILL, EVEN AFTER SO MANY YEARS APART. IT WARMS EVEN MY HEART TO SEE SUCH FIRE IN YOUR SOUL.
TELL ME... HOW IS YOUR HUSBAND? HOW IS MR. INCREDIBLE?

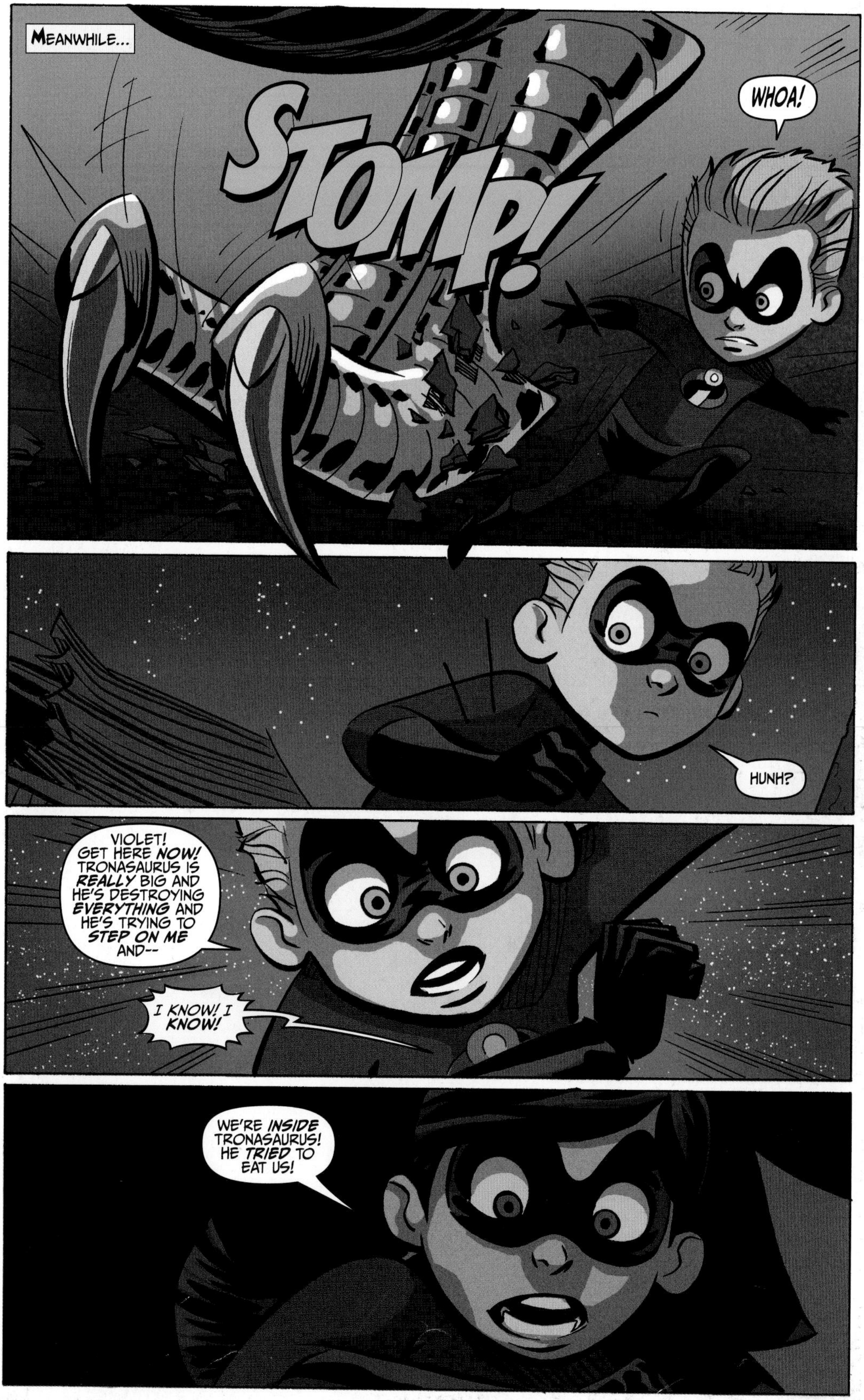
MEANWHILE...
STOMP!
WHOA!
HUNH?
VIOLET! GET HERE NOW! TRONASAURUS IS REALLY BIG AND HE'S DESTROYING EVERYTHING AND HE'S TRYING TO STEP ON ME AND--
I KNOW! I KNOW!
WE'RE INSIDE TRONASAURUS! HE TRIED TO EAT US!

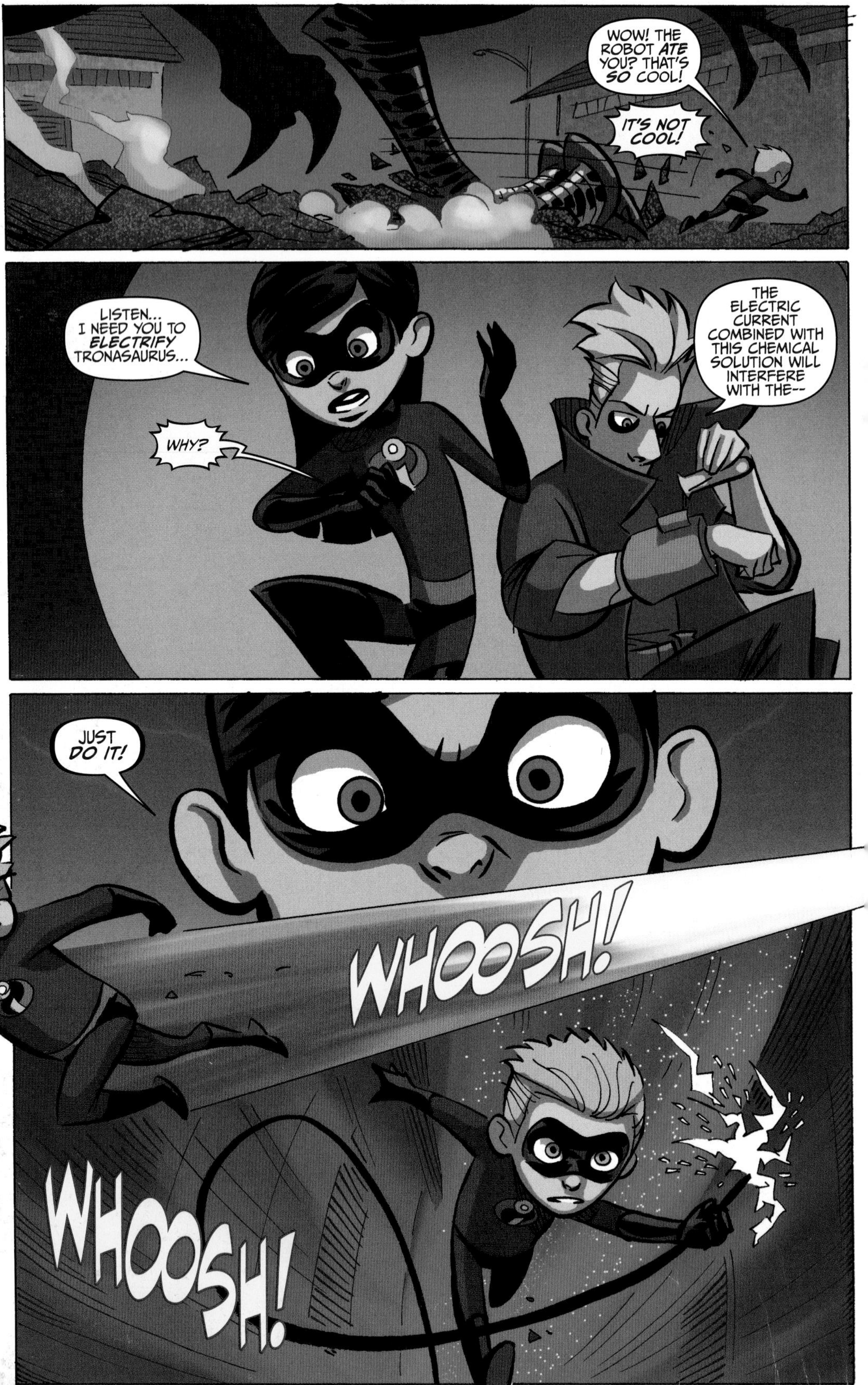
WOW! THE ROBOT ATE YOU? THAT'S SO COOL!
IT'S NOT COOL!
LISTEN... I NEED YOU TO ELECTRIFY TRONASAURUS...
THE ELECTRIC CURRENT COMBINED WITH THIS CHEMICAL SOLUTION WILL INTERFERE WITH THE--
WHY?
JUST DO IT!
WHOOSH!
WHOOSH!

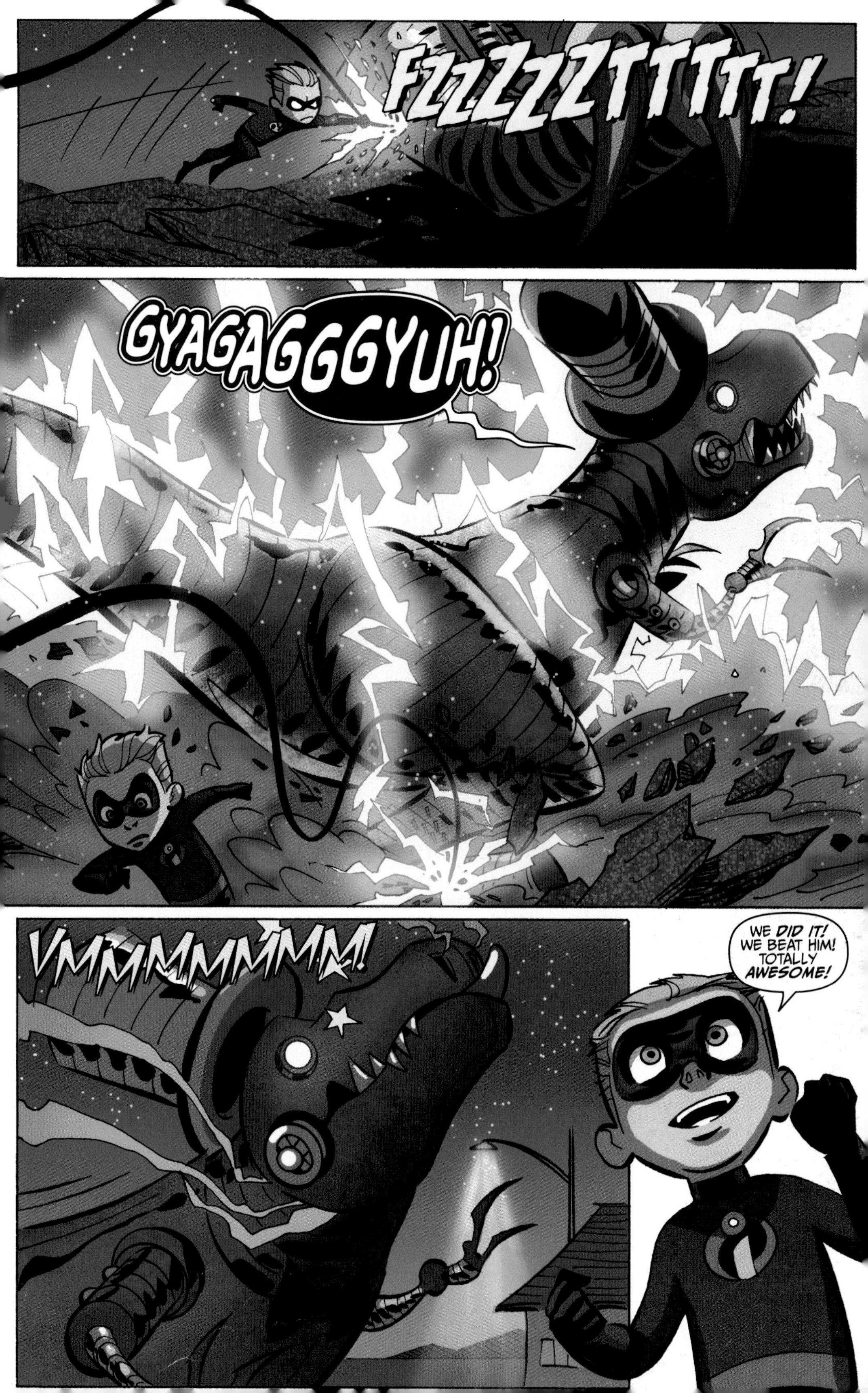
FZZZZZTTTTTT!
GYAGAGGGYUH!
VMMMMMMMM!
WE DID IT! WE BEAT HIM! TOTALLY AWESOME!

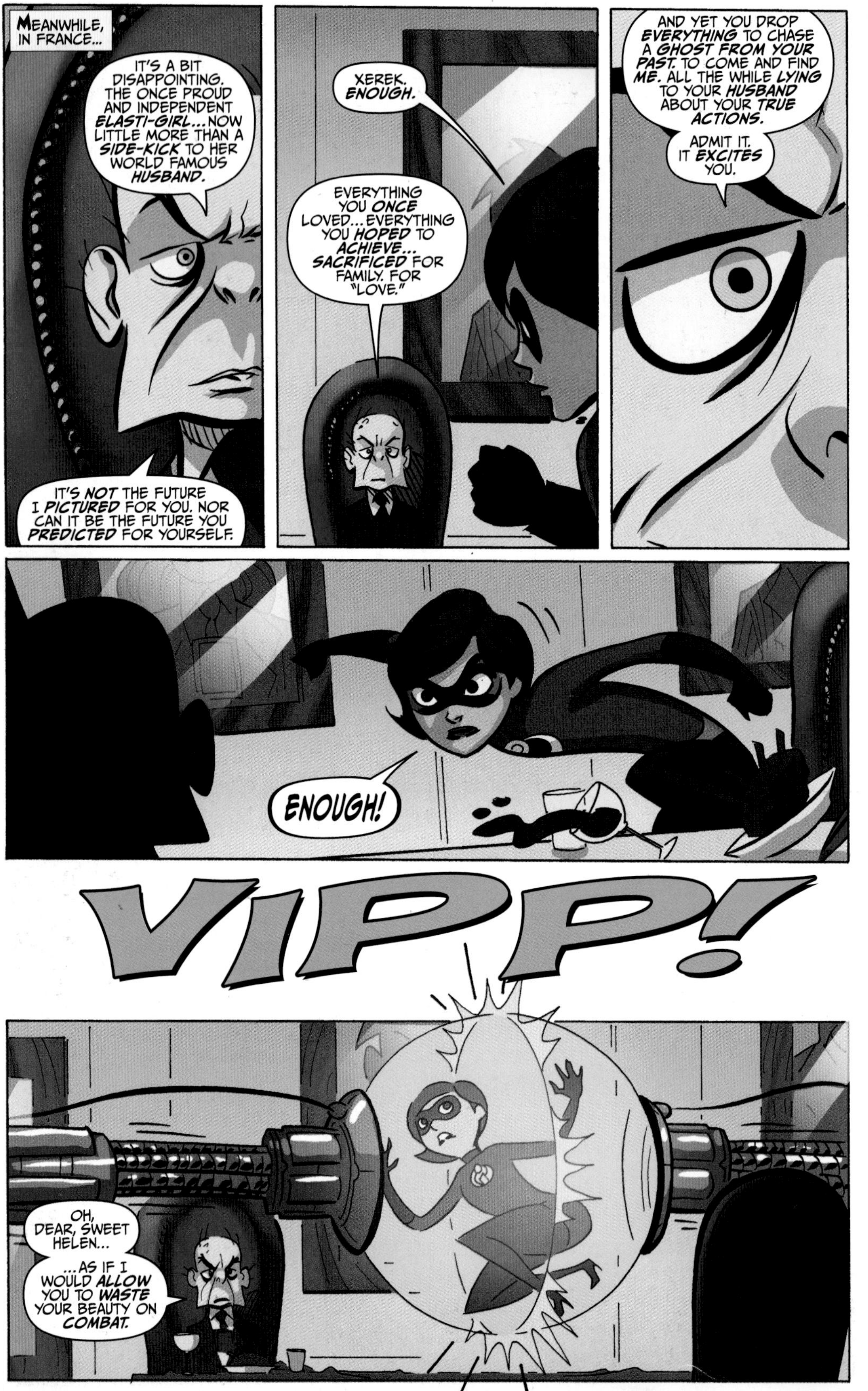
MEANWHILE, IN FRANCE...
IT'S A BIT DISAPPOINTING. THE ONCE PROUD AND INDEPENDENT ELASTI-GIRL... NOW LITTLE MORE THAN A SIDE-KICK TO HER WORLD FAMOUS HUSBAND.
IT'S NOT THE FUTURE I PICTURED FOR YOU. NOR CAN IT BE THE FUTURE YOU PREDICTED FOR YOURSELF.
XEREK. ENOUGH.
EVERYTHING YOU ONCE LOVED... EVERYTHING YOU HOPED TO ACHIEVE... SACRIFICED FOR FAMILY. FOR "LOVE."
AND YET YOU DROP EVERYTHING TO CHASE A GHOST FROM YOUR PAST. TO COME AND FIND ME. ALL THE WHILE LYING TO YOUR HUSBAND ABOUT YOUR TRUE ACTIONS.
ADMIT IT. IT EXCITES YOU.
ENOUGH!
VIPP!
OH, DEAR, SWEET HELEN...
...AS IF I WOULD ALLOW YOU TO WASTE YOUR BEAUTY ON COMBAT.

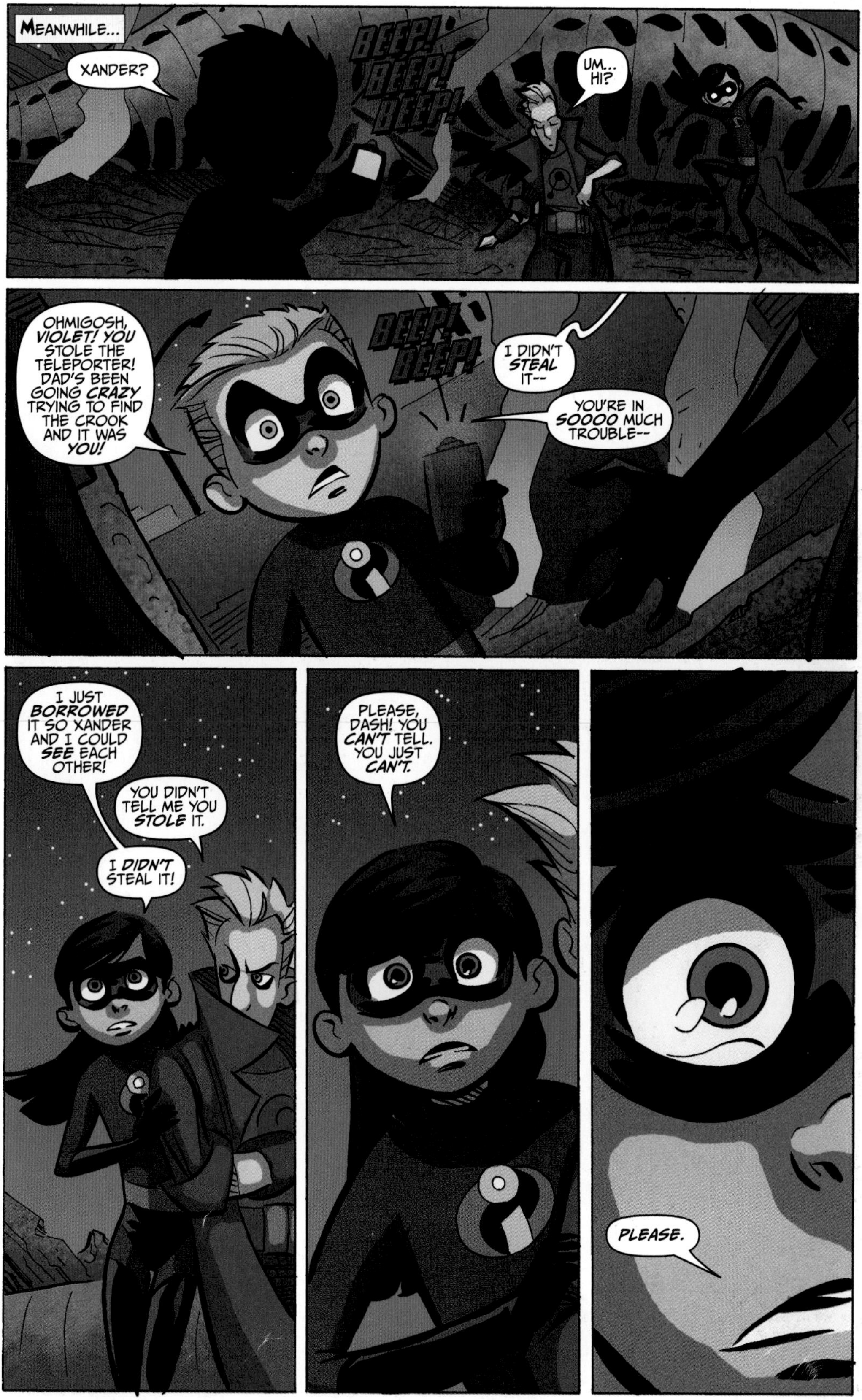
MEANWHILE...
XANDER?
BEEP! BEEP! BEEP!
UM... HI?
OHMIGOSH, VIOLET! YOU STOLE THE TELEPORTER! DAD'S BEEN GOING CRAZY TRYING TO FIND THE CROOK AND IT WAS YOU!
BEEP! BEEP!
I DIDN'T STEAL IT--
YOU'RE IN SOOOO MUCH TROUBLE--
I JUST BORROWED IT SO XANDER AND I COULD SEE EACH OTHER!
YOU DIDN'T TELL ME YOU STOLE IT.
I DIDN'T STEAL IT!
PLEASE, DASH! YOU CAN'T TELL. YOU JUST CAN'T.
PLEASE.

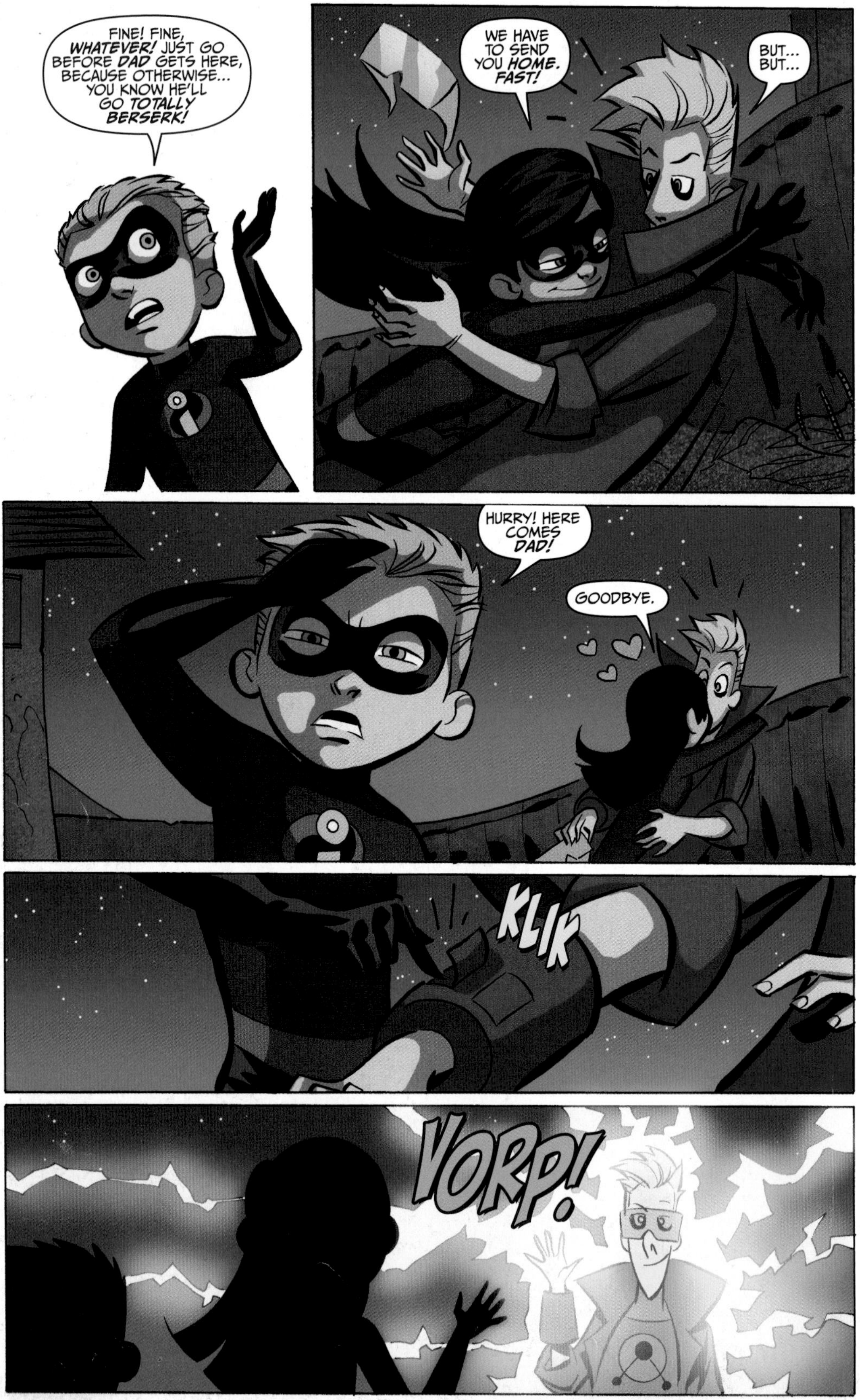
FINE! FINE, WHATEVER! JUST GO BEFORE DAD GETS HERE, BECAUSE OTHERWISE... YOU KNOW HE'LL GO TOTALLY BERSERK!
WE HAVE TO SEND YOU HOME. FAST!
BUT... BUT...
HURRY! HERE COMES DAD!
GOODBYE.
KLIK
VORP!

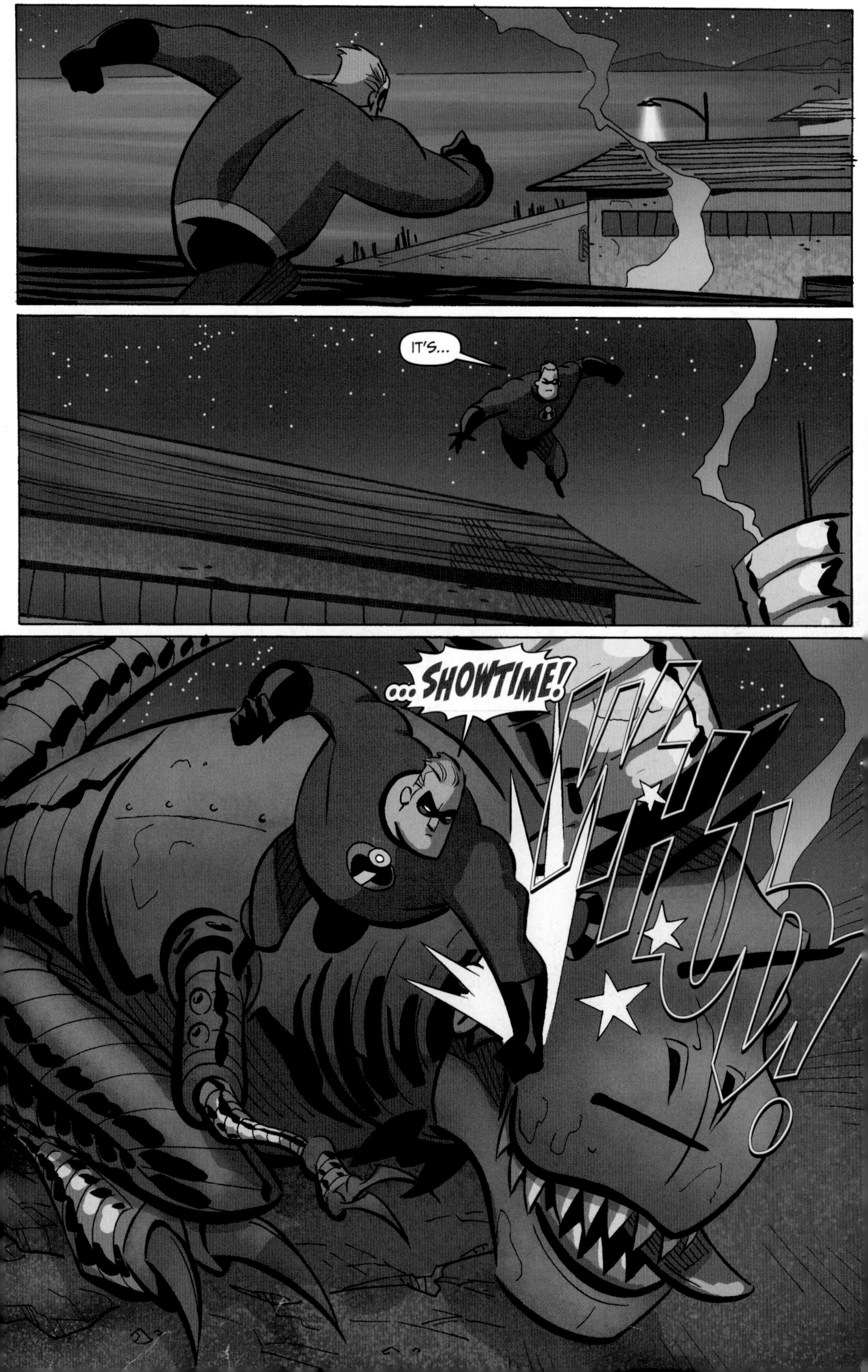
IT'S...
...SHOWTIME!

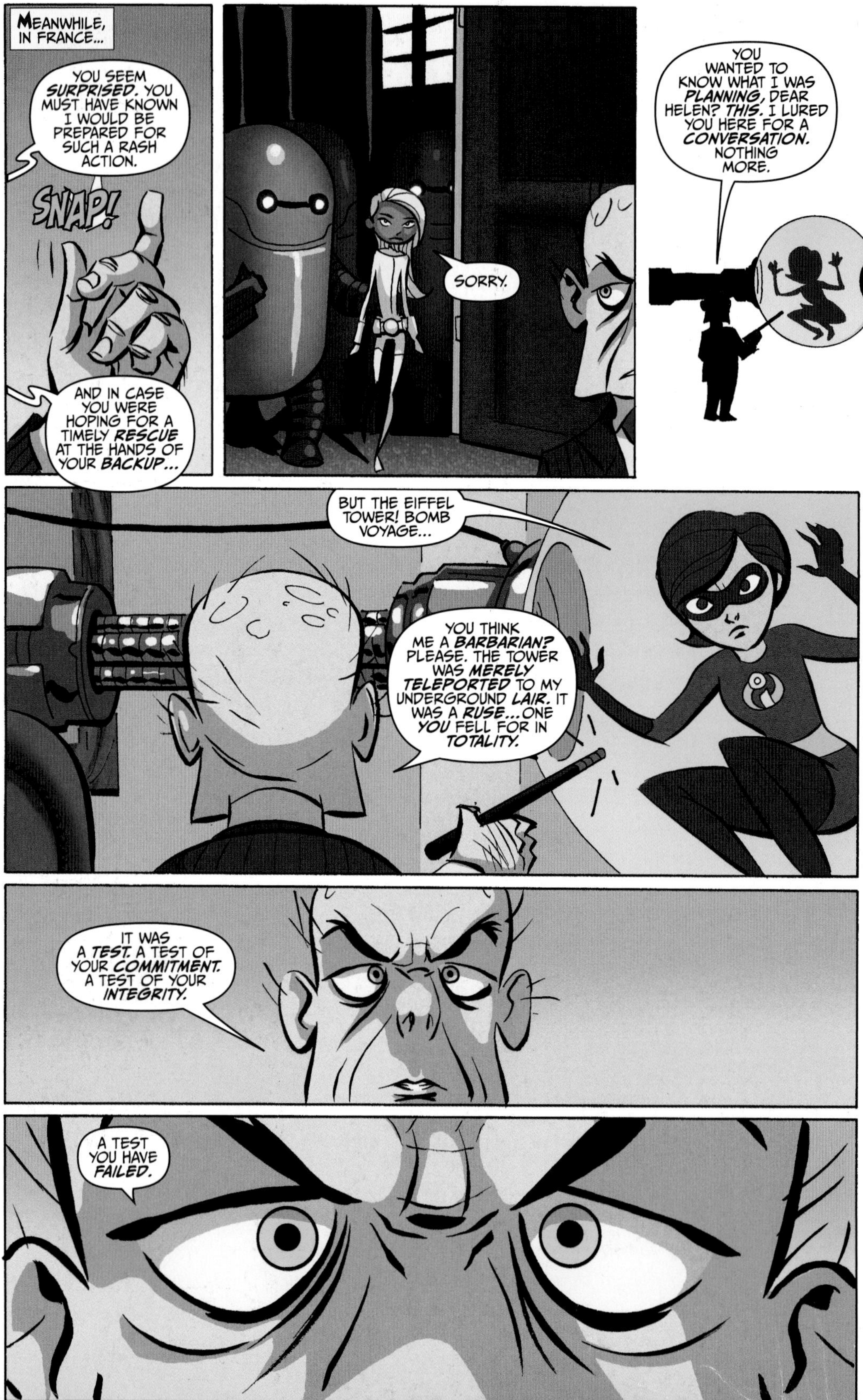
MEANWHILE, IN FRANCE...
YOU SEEM SURPRISED. YOU MUST HAVE KNOWN I WOULD BE PREPARED FOR SUCH A RASH ACTION.
SNAP!
AND IN CASE YOU WERE HOPING FOR A TIMELY RESCUE AT THE HANDS OF YOUR BACKUP...
SORRY.
YOU WANTED TO KNOW WHAT I WAS PLANNING, DEAR HELEN? THIS. I LURED YOU HERE FOR A CONVERSATION. NOTHING MORE.
BUT THE EIFFEL TOWER! BOMB VOYAGE...
YOU THINK ME A BARBARIAN? PLEASE. THE TOWER WAS MERELY TELEPORTED TO MY UNDERGROUND LAIR. IT WAS A RUSE...ONE YOU FELL FOR IN TOTALITY.
IT WAS A TEST. A TEST OF YOUR COMMITMENT. A TEST OF YOUR INTEGRITY.
A TEST YOU HAVE FAILED.

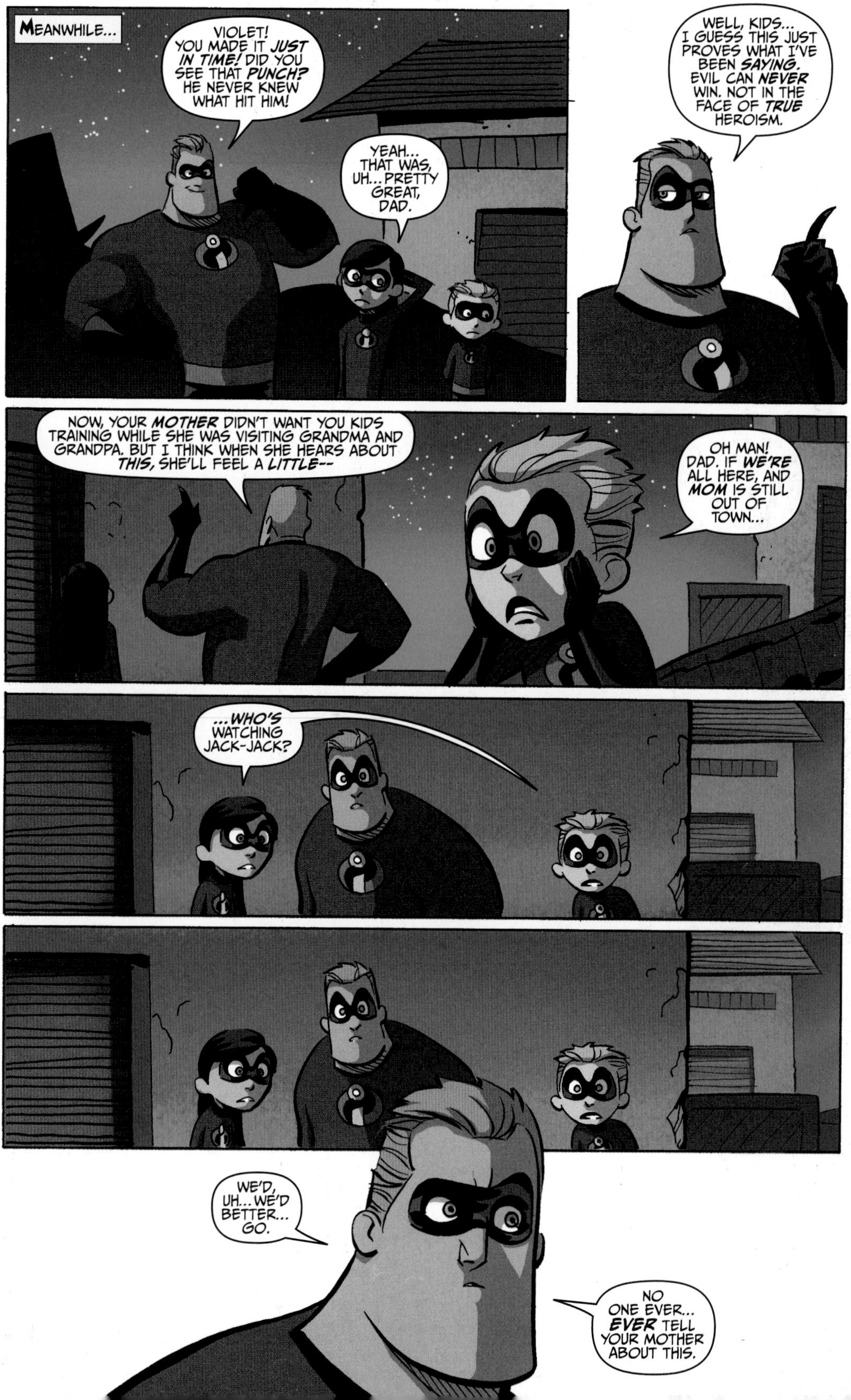
MEANWHILE...
VIOLET! YOU MADE IT JUST IN TIME! DID YOU SEE THAT PUNCH? HE NEVER KNEW WHAT HIT HIM!
YEAH... THAT WAS, UH... PRETTY GREAT, DAD.
WELL, KIDS... I GUESS THIS JUST PROVES WHAT I'VE BEEN SAYING. EVIL CAN NEVER WIN. NOT IN THE FACE OF TRUE HEROISM.
NOW, YOUR MOTHER DIDN'T WANT YOU KIDS TRAINING WHILE SHE WAS VISITING GRANDMA AND GRANDPA. BUT I THINK WHEN SHE HEARS ABOUT THIS, SHE'LL FEEL A LITTLE--
OH MAN! DAD. IF WE'RE ALL HERE, AND MOM IS STILL OUT OF TOWN...
...WHO'S WATCHING JACK-JACK?
WE'D, UH... WE'D BETTER... GO.
NO ONE EVER... EVER TELL YOUR MOTHER ABOUT THIS.

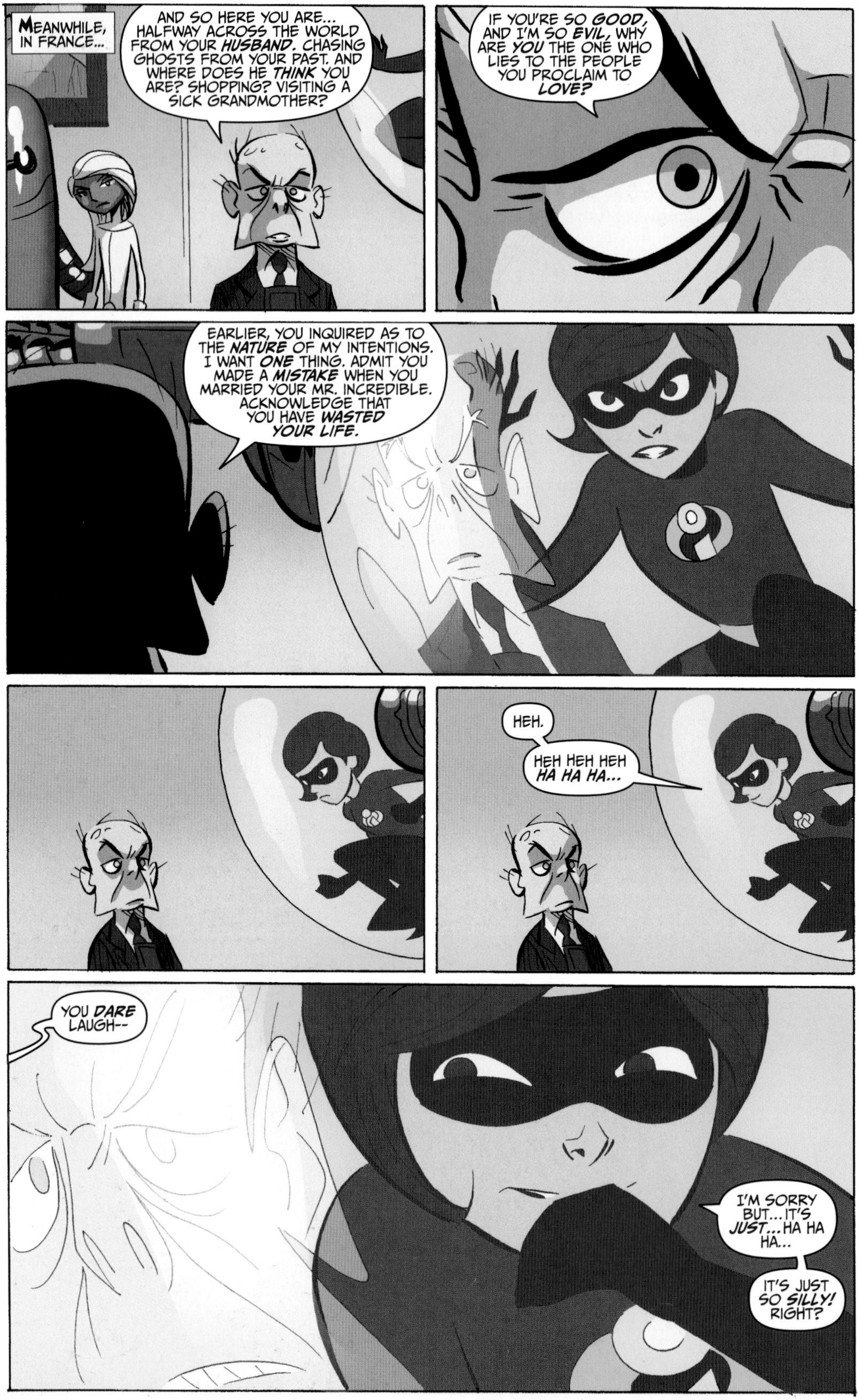
MEANWHILE, IN FRANCE...
AND SO HERE YOU ARE... HALFWAY ACROSS THE WORLD FROM YOUR HUSBAND. CHASING GHOSTS FROM YOUR PAST. AND WHERE DOES HE THINK YOU ARE? SHOPPING? VISITING A SICK GRANDMOTHER?
IF YOU'RE SO GOOD, AND I'M SO EVIL, WHY ARE YOU THE ONE WHO LIES TO THE PEOPLE YOU PROCLAIM TO LOVE?
EARLIER, YOU INQUIRED AS TO THE NATURE OF MY INTENTIONS. I WANT ONE THING. ADMIT YOU MADE A MISTAKE WHEN YOU MARRIED YOUR MR. INCREDIBLE. ACKNOWLEDGE THAT YOU HAVE WASTED YOUR LIFE.
HEH.
HEH HEH HEH HA HA HA...
YOU DARE LAUGH--
I'M SORRY BUT... IT'S JUST... HA HA HA...
IT'S JUST SO SILLY! RIGHT?

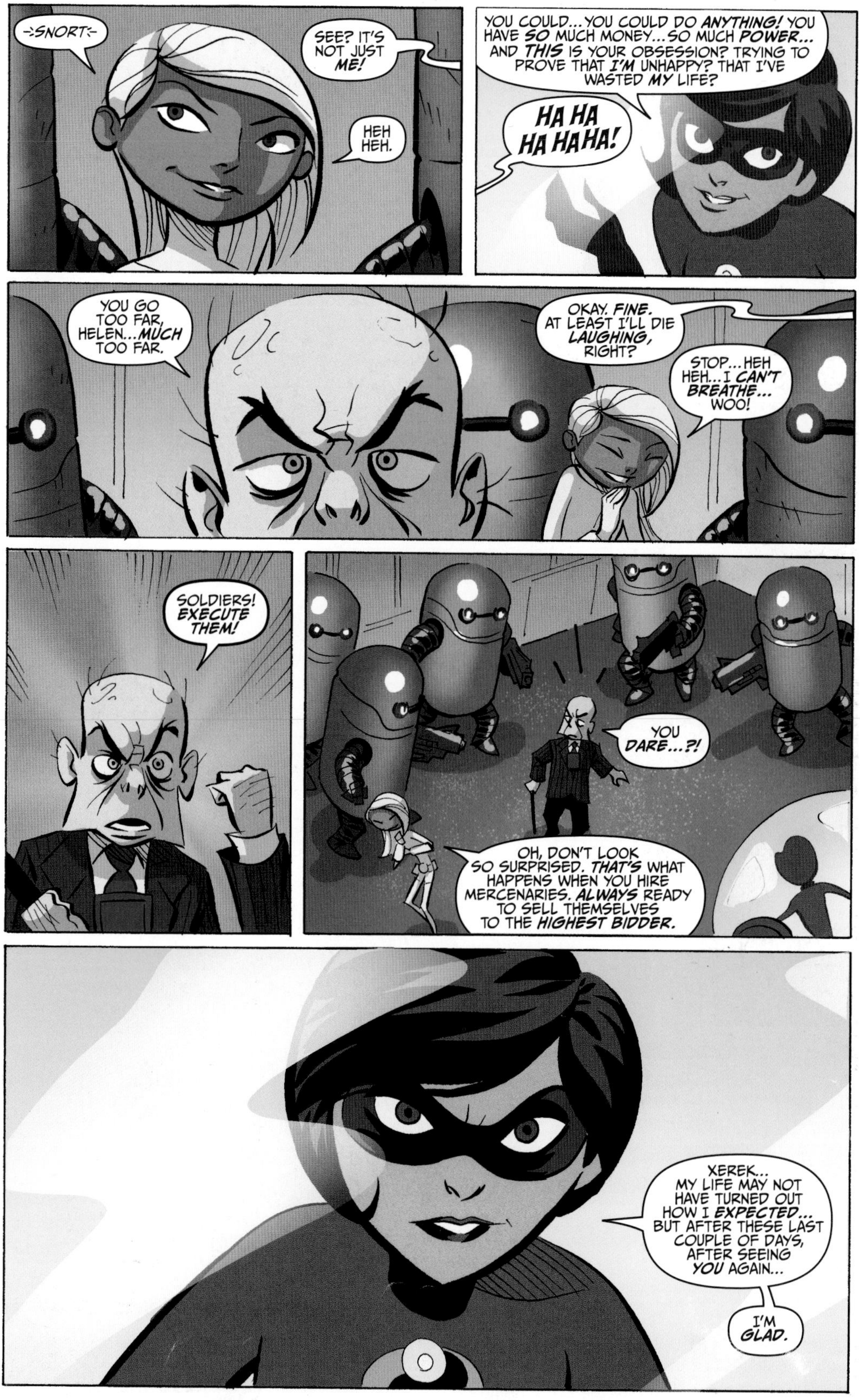

-:-SNORT-:-
SEE? IT'S NOT JUST ME!
HEH HEH.
YOU COULD...YOU COULD DO ANYTHING! YOU HAVE SO MUCH MONEY...SO MUCH POWER... AND THIS IS YOUR OBSESSION? TRYING TO PROVE THAT I'M UNHAPPY? THAT I'VE WASTED MY LIFE?
HA HA HA HAHA!
YOU GO TOO FAR, HELEN...MUCH TOO FAR.
OKAY. FINE. AT LEAST I'LL DIE LAUGHING, RIGHT?
STOP...HEH HEH...I CAN'T BREATHE... WOO!
SOLDIERS! EXECUTE THEM!
YOU DARE...?!
OH, DON'T LOOK SO SURPRISED. THAT'S WHAT HAPPENS WHEN YOU HIRE MERCENARIES. ALWAYS READY TO SELL THEMSELVES TO THE HIGHEST BIDDER.
XEREK... MY LIFE MAY NOT HAVE TURNED OUT HOW I EXPECTED... BUT AFTER THESE LAST COUPLE OF DAYS, AFTER SEEING YOU AGAIN...
I'M GLAD.

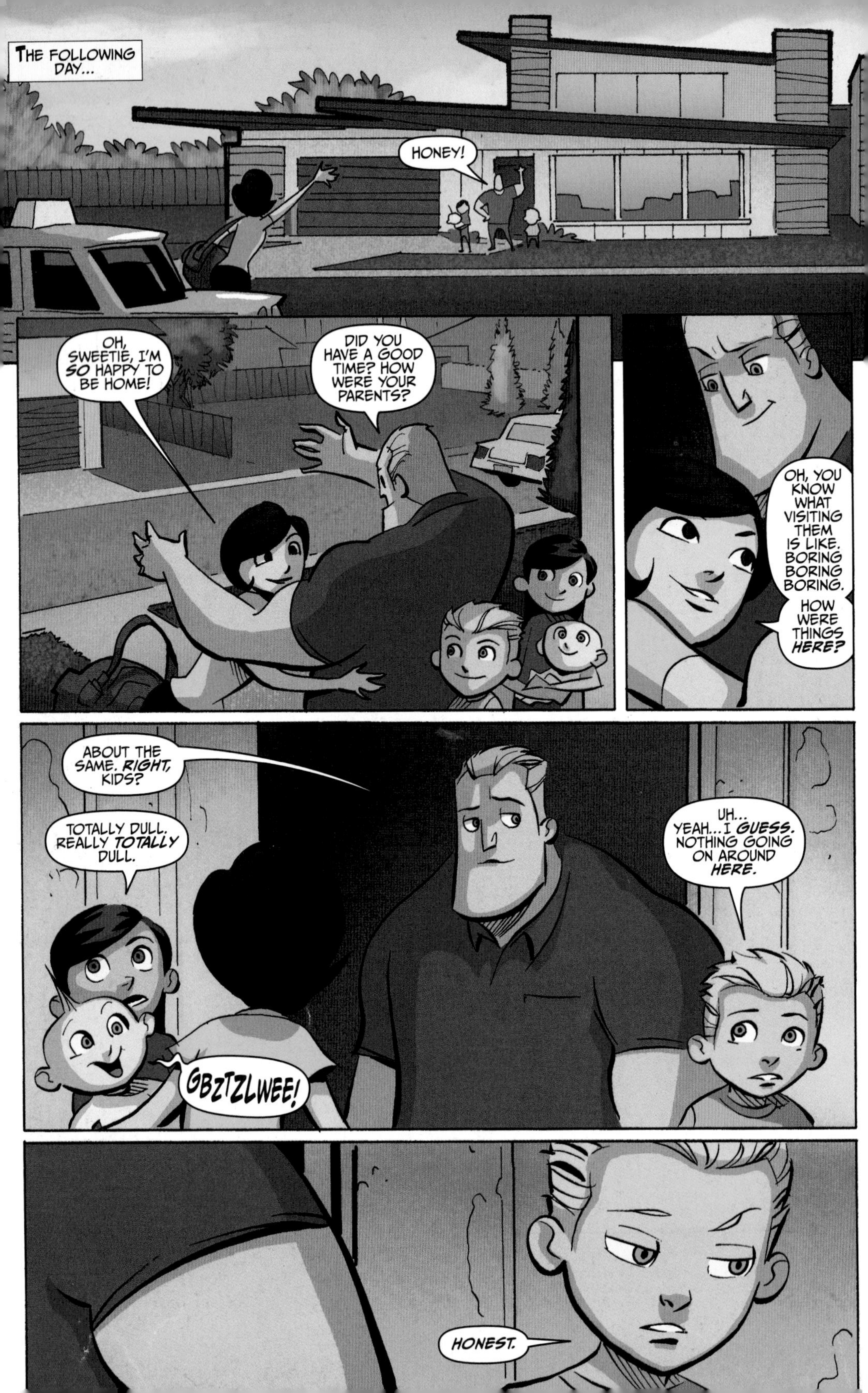
THE FOLLOWING DAY...
HONEY!
OH, SWEETIE, I'M *SO* HAPPY TO BE HOME!
DID YOU HAVE A GOOD TIME? HOW WERE YOUR PARENTS?
OH, YOU KNOW WHAT VISITING THEM IS LIKE. BORING BORING BORING.
HOW WERE THINGS *HERE?*
ABOUT THE SAME. *RIGHT,* KIDS?
TOTALLY DULL. REALLY *TOTALLY* DULL.
UH... YEAH...I *GUESS.* NOTHING GOING ON AROUND *HERE.*
GBZTZLWEE!
HONEST.

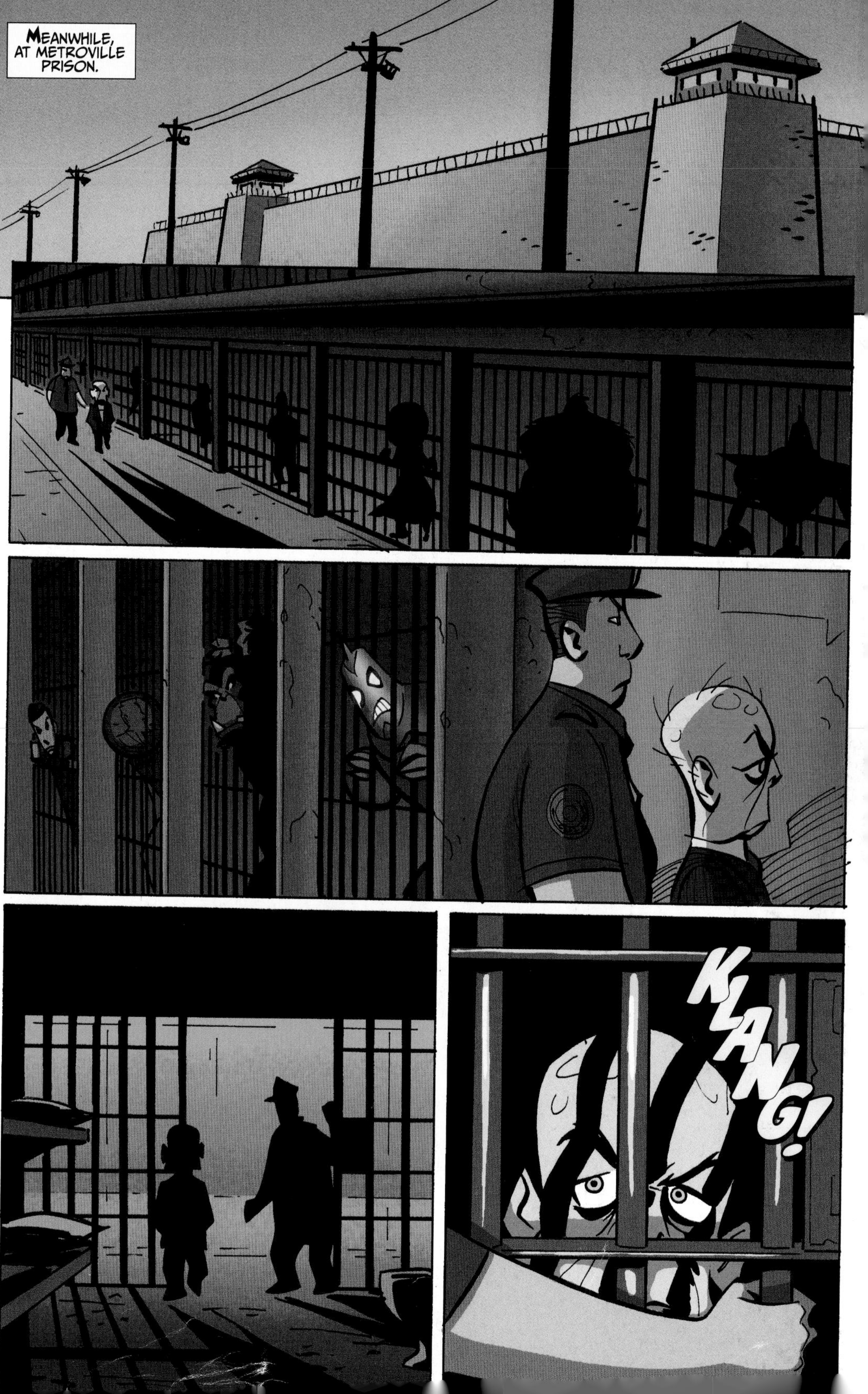
MEANWHILE, AT METROVILLE PRISON.
KLANG!

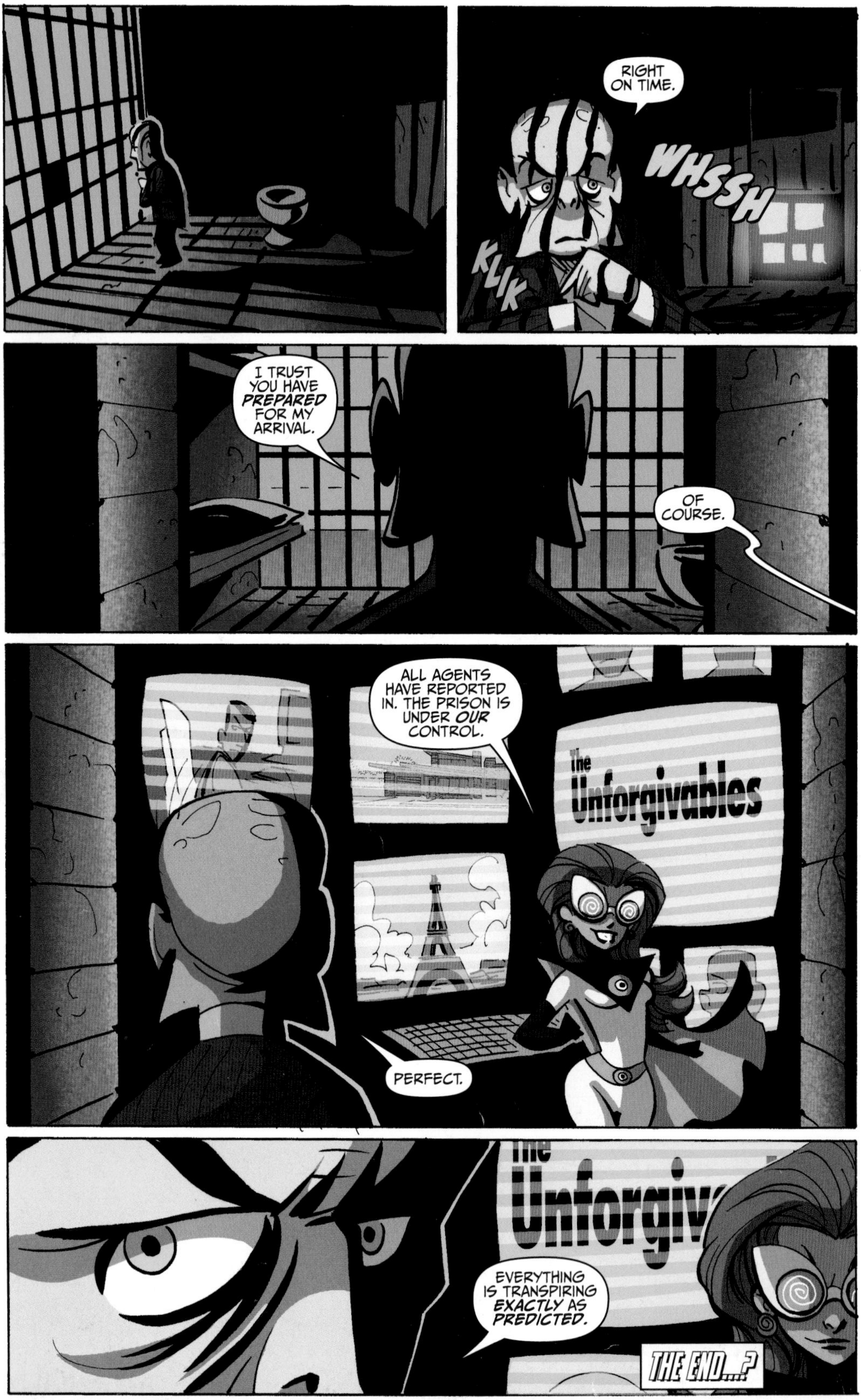
RIGHT ON TIME.
WHSSH
KLIK
I TRUST YOU HAVE *PREPARED* FOR MY ARRIVAL.
OF COURSE.
ALL AGENTS HAVE REPORTED IN. THE PRISON IS UNDER *OUR* CONTROL.
The Unforgivables
PERFECT.
EVERYTHING IS TRANSPIRING *EXACTLY* AS *PREDICTED*.
THE END...?

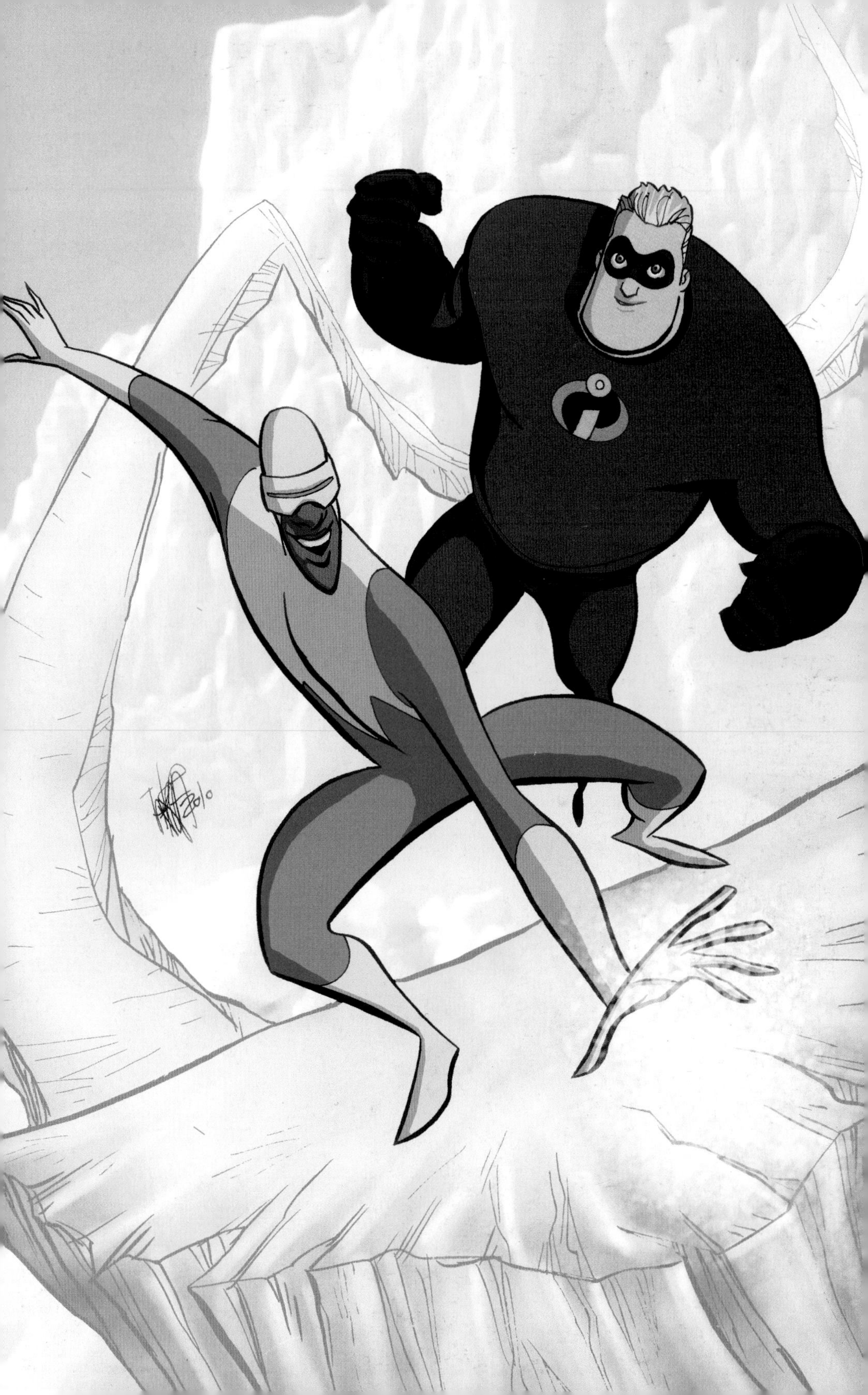

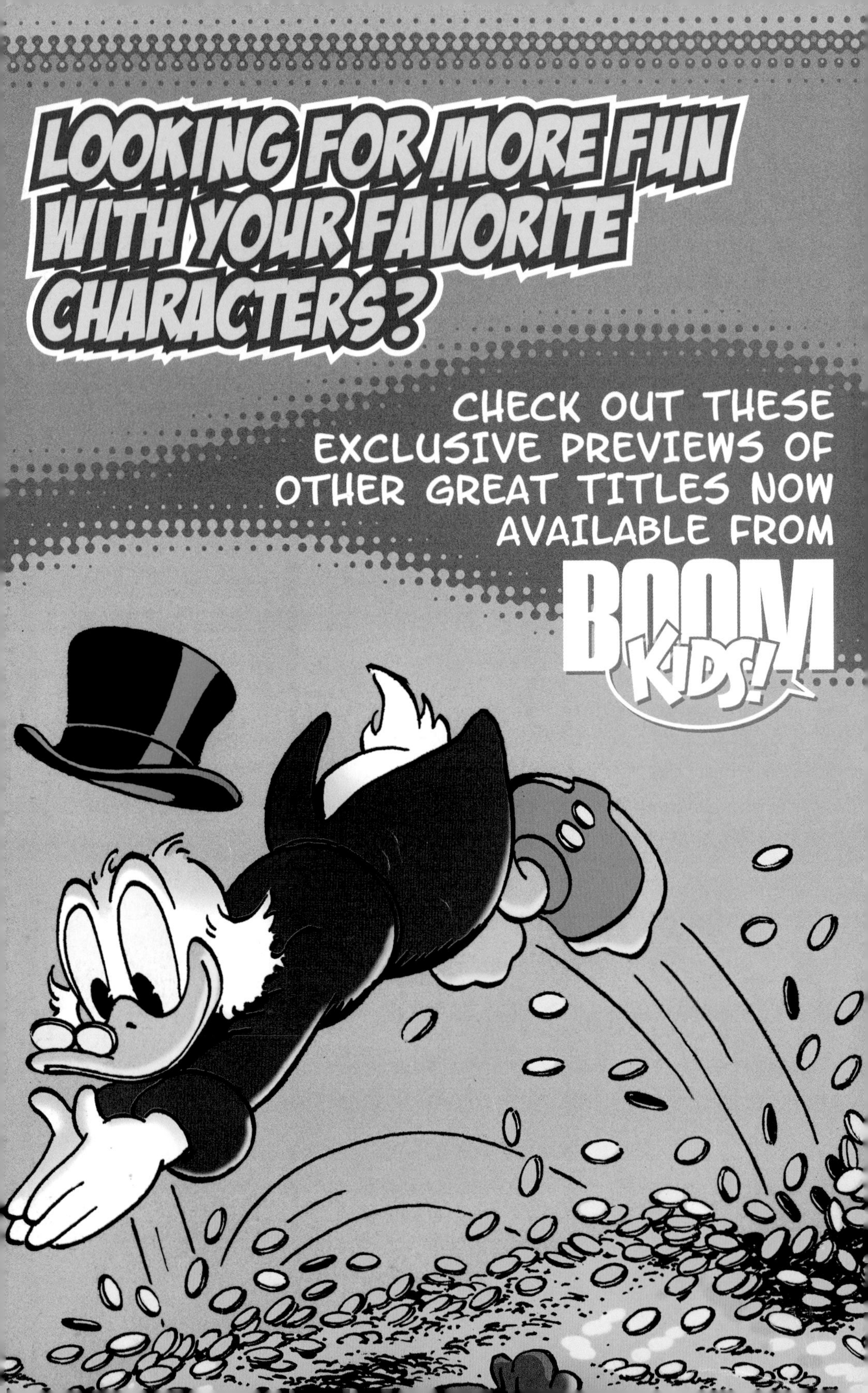
LOOKING FOR MORE FUN WITH YOUR FAVORITE CHARACTERS?
CHECK OUT THESE EXCLUSIVE PREVIEWS OF OTHER GREAT TITLES NOW AVAILABLE FROM
BOOM KIDS!

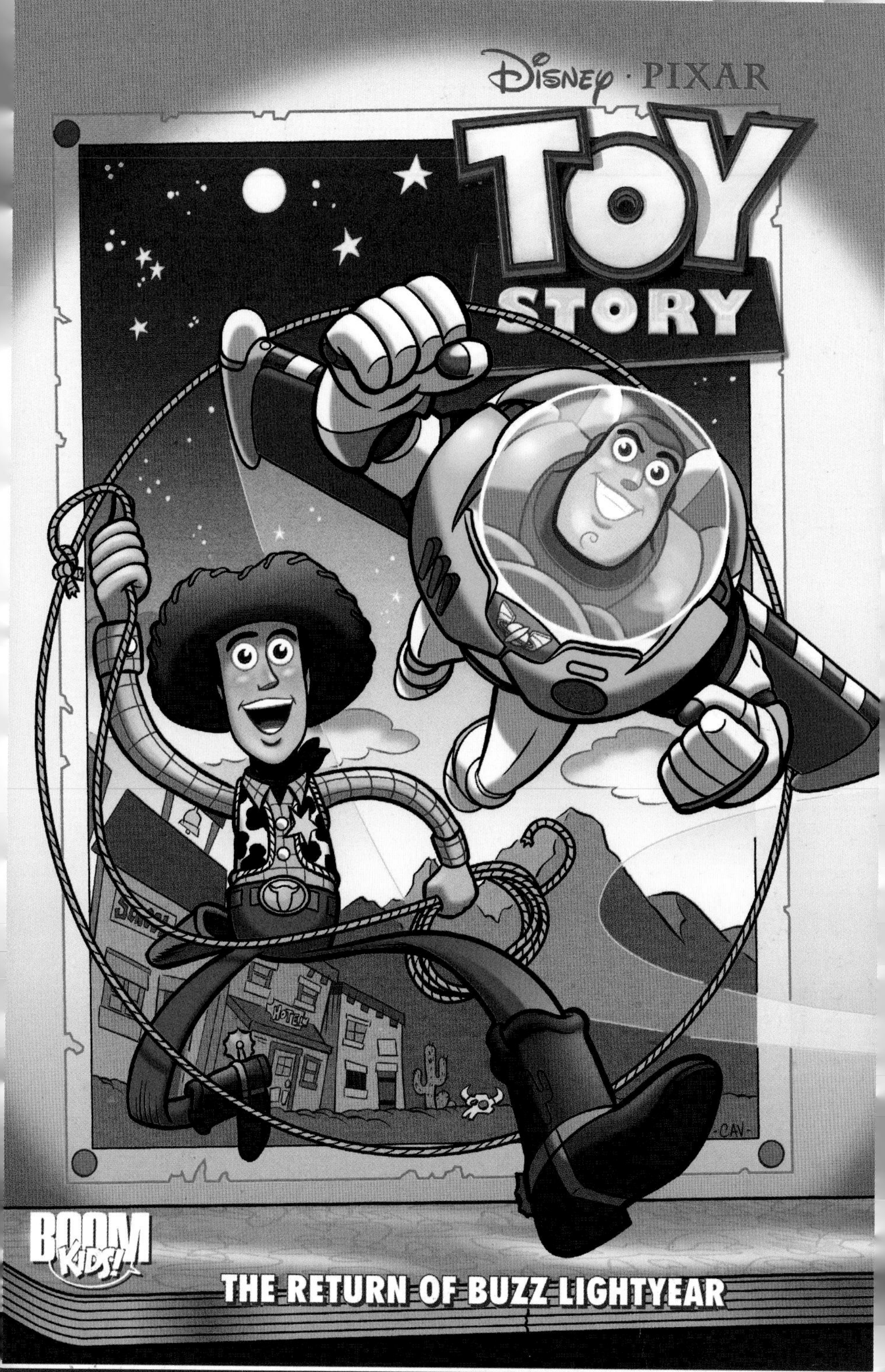

DISNEY · PIXAR
TOY STORY
HOTEL
-CAV-
BOOM KIDS!
THE RETURN OF BUZZ LIGHTYEAR

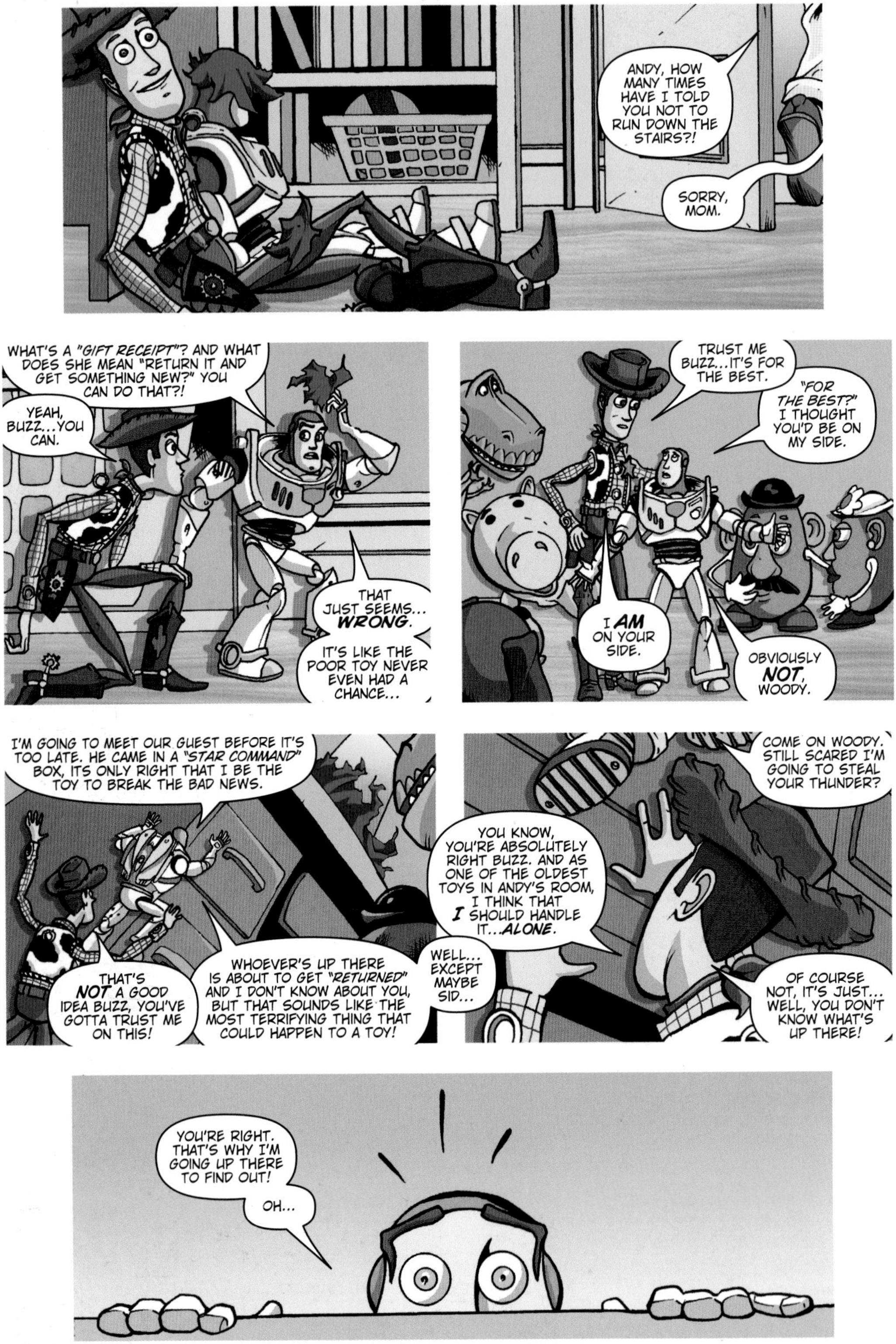
ANDY, HOW MANY TIMES HAVE I TOLD YOU NOT TO RUN DOWN THE STAIRS?!
SORRY, MOM.
WHAT'S A "GIFT RECEIPT"? AND WHAT DOES SHE MEAN "RETURN IT AND GET SOMETHING NEW?" YOU CAN DO THAT?!
YEAH, BUZZ... YOU CAN.
THAT JUST SEEMS... WRONG.
IT'S LIKE THE POOR TOY NEVER EVEN HAD A CHANCE...
TRUST ME BUZZ... IT'S FOR THE BEST.
"FOR THE BEST?" I THOUGHT YOU'D BE ON MY SIDE.
I AM ON YOUR SIDE.
OBVIOUSLY NOT, WOODY.
I'M GOING TO MEET OUR GUEST BEFORE IT'S TOO LATE. HE CAME IN A "STAR COMMAND" BOX, ITS ONLY RIGHT THAT I BE THE TOY TO BREAK THE BAD NEWS.
THAT'S NOT A GOOD IDEA BUZZ, YOU'VE GOTTA TRUST ME ON THIS!
WHOEVER'S UP THERE IS ABOUT TO GET "RETURNED" AND I DON'T KNOW ABOUT YOU, BUT THAT SOUNDS LIKE THE MOST TERRIFYING THING THAT COULD HAPPEN TO A TOY!
WELL... EXCEPT MAYBE SID...
COME ON WOODY. STILL SCARED I'M GOING TO STEAL YOUR THUNDER?
YOU KNOW, YOU'RE ABSOLUTELY RIGHT BUZZ. AND AS ONE OF THE OLDEST TOYS IN ANDY'S ROOM, I THINK THAT I SHOULD HANDLE IT... ALONE.
OF COURSE NOT, IT'S JUST... WELL, YOU DON'T KNOW WHAT'S UP THERE!
YOU'RE RIGHT. THAT'S WHY I'M GOING UP THERE TO FIND OUT!
OH...

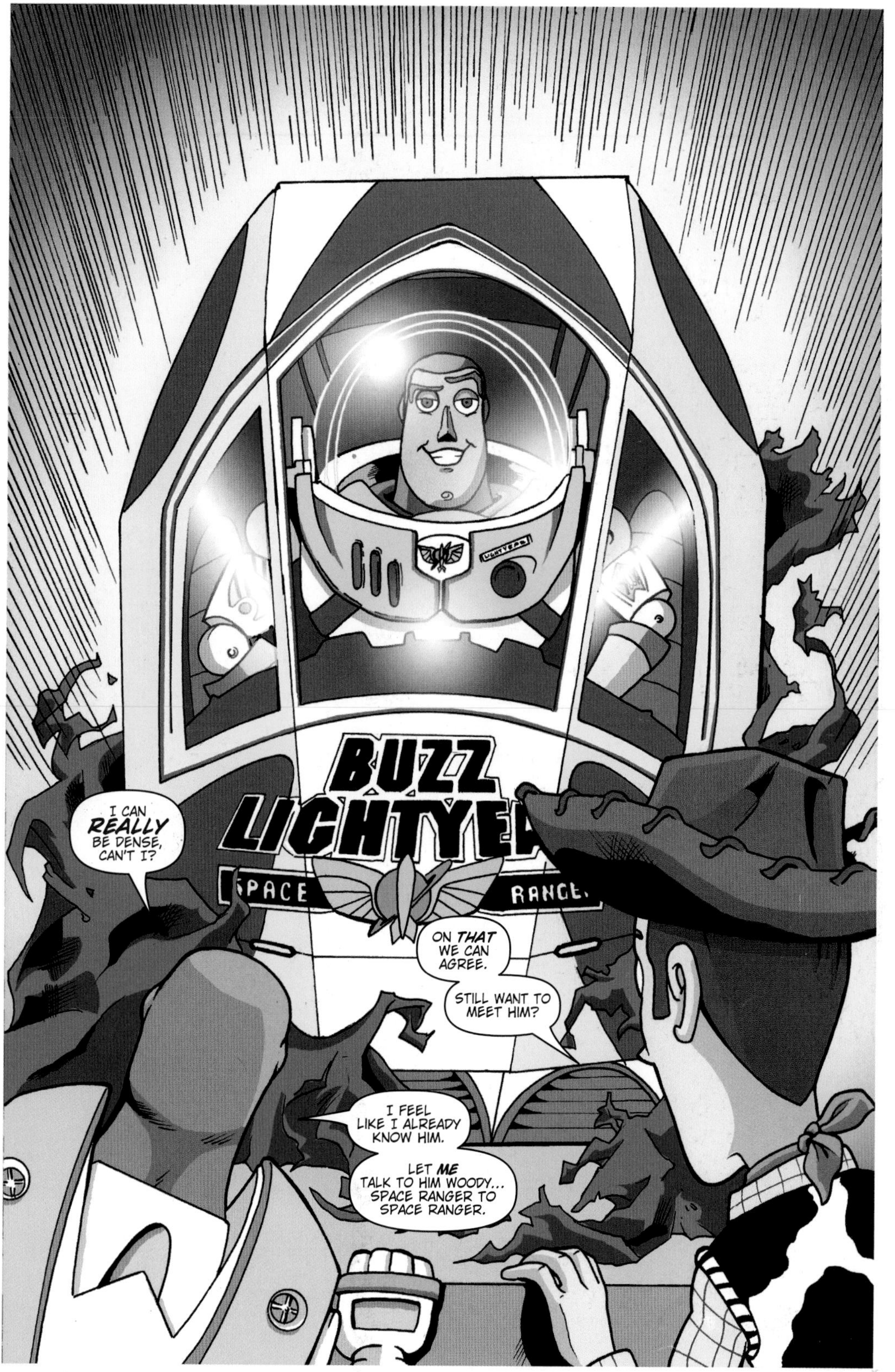
BUZZ
LIGHTYEA
SPACE
RANGE
I CAN REALLY BE DENSE, CAN'T I?
ON THAT WE CAN AGREE.
STILL WANT TO MEET HIM?
I FEEL LIKE I ALREADY KNOW HIM.
LET ME TALK TO HIM WOODY... SPACE RANGER TO SPACE RANGER.

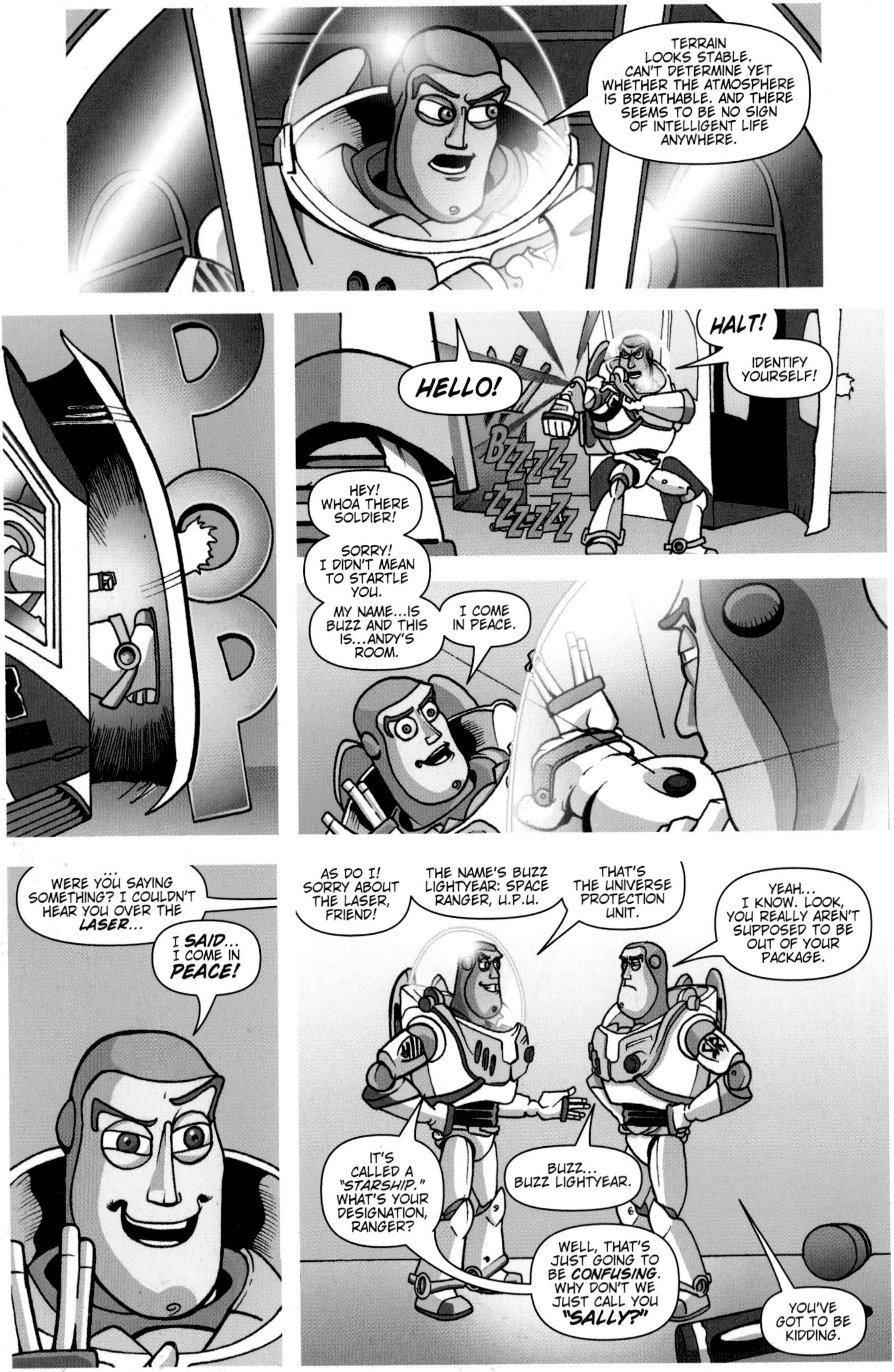
TERRAIN LOOKS STABLE. CAN'T DETERMINE YET WHETHER THE ATMOSPHERE IS BREATHABLE. AND THERE SEEMS TO BE NO SIGN OF INTELLIGENT LIFE ANYWHERE.
POP
HALT!
IDENTIFY YOURSELF!
HELLO!
BZZZZZ ZZZZZZ
HEY! WHOA THERE SOLDIER!
SORRY! I DIDN'T MEAN TO STARTLE YOU.
MY NAME...IS BUZZ AND THIS IS...ANDY'S ROOM.
I COME IN PEACE.
... WERE YOU SAYING SOMETHING? I COULDN'T HEAR YOU OVER THE LASER...
I SAID... I COME IN PEACE!
AS DO I! SORRY ABOUT THE LASER, FRIEND!
THE NAME'S BUZZ LIGHTYEAR: SPACE RANGER, U.P.U.
THAT'S THE UNIVERSE PROTECTION UNIT.
YEAH... I KNOW. LOOK, YOU REALLY AREN'T SUPPOSED TO BE OUT OF YOUR PACKAGE.
IT'S CALLED A "STARSHIP." WHAT'S YOUR DESIGNATION, RANGER?
BUZZ... BUZZ LIGHTYEAR.
WELL, THAT'S JUST GOING TO BE CONFUSING. WHY DON'T WE JUST CALL YOU "SALLY?"
YOU'VE GOT TO BE KIDDING.

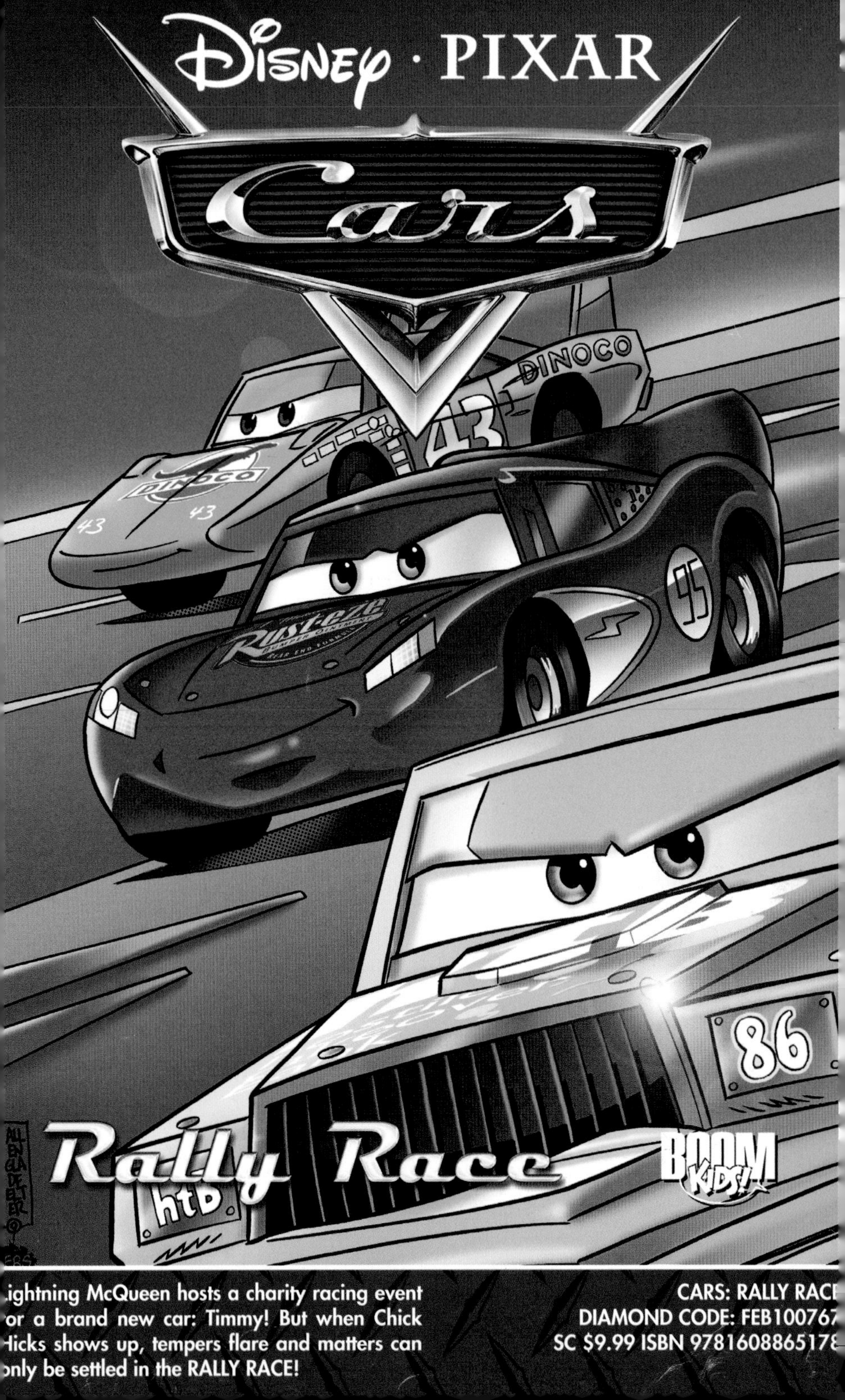

DISNEY · PIXAR
Cars
DINOCO
43
DINOCO
43 43
Rust-eze
95
86
htb
Rally Race
BOOM KIDS!

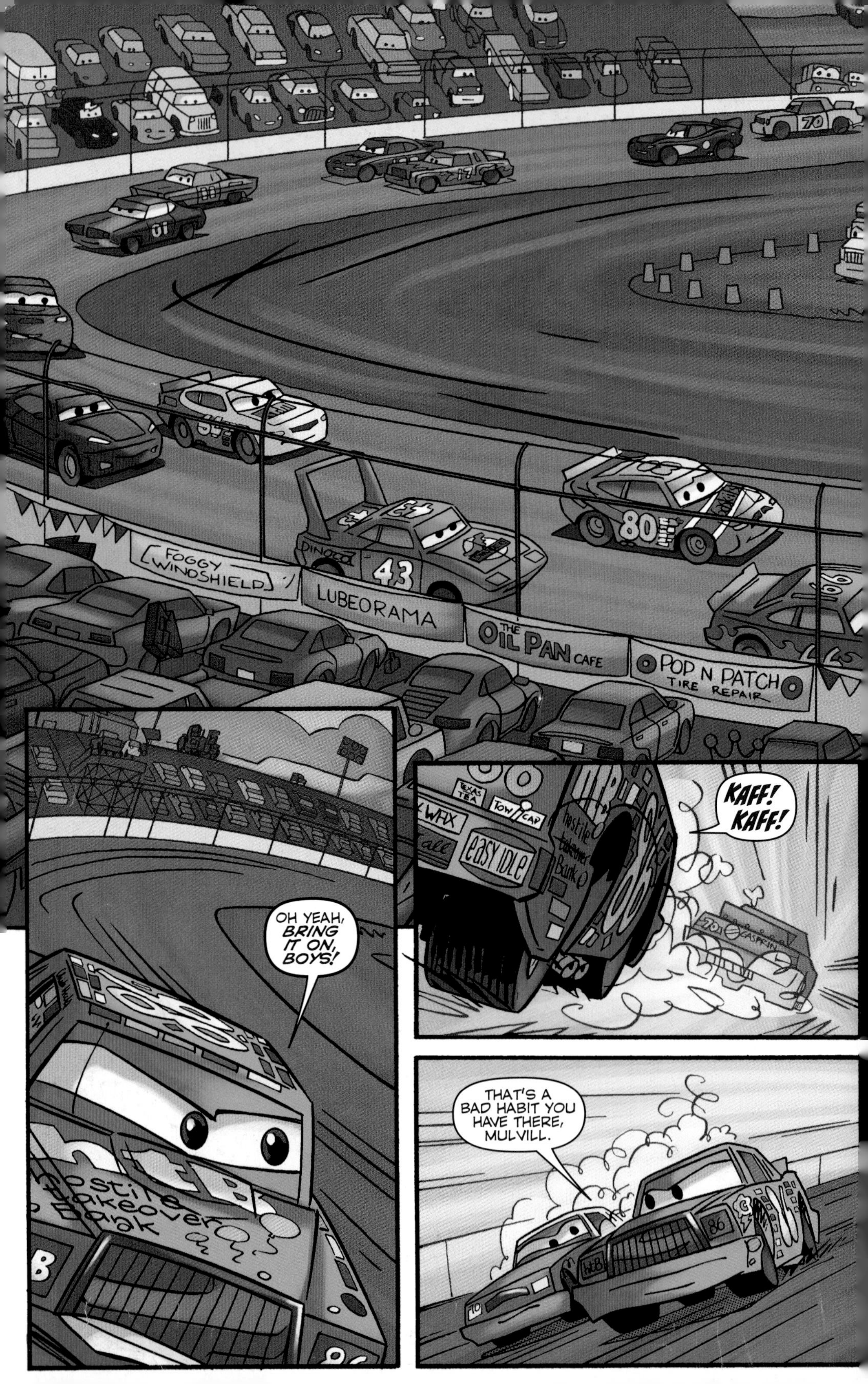
FOGGY WINDSHIELD
LUBEORAMA
THE OIL PAN CAFE
POP N PATCH TIRE REPAIR
DINOCO
43
80
OH YEAH, *BRING IT ON, BOYS!*
TEXAS TEA
TOW CAP
easy IDLE
KAFF! KAFF!
THAT'S A BAD HABIT YOU HAVE THERE, MULVILL.

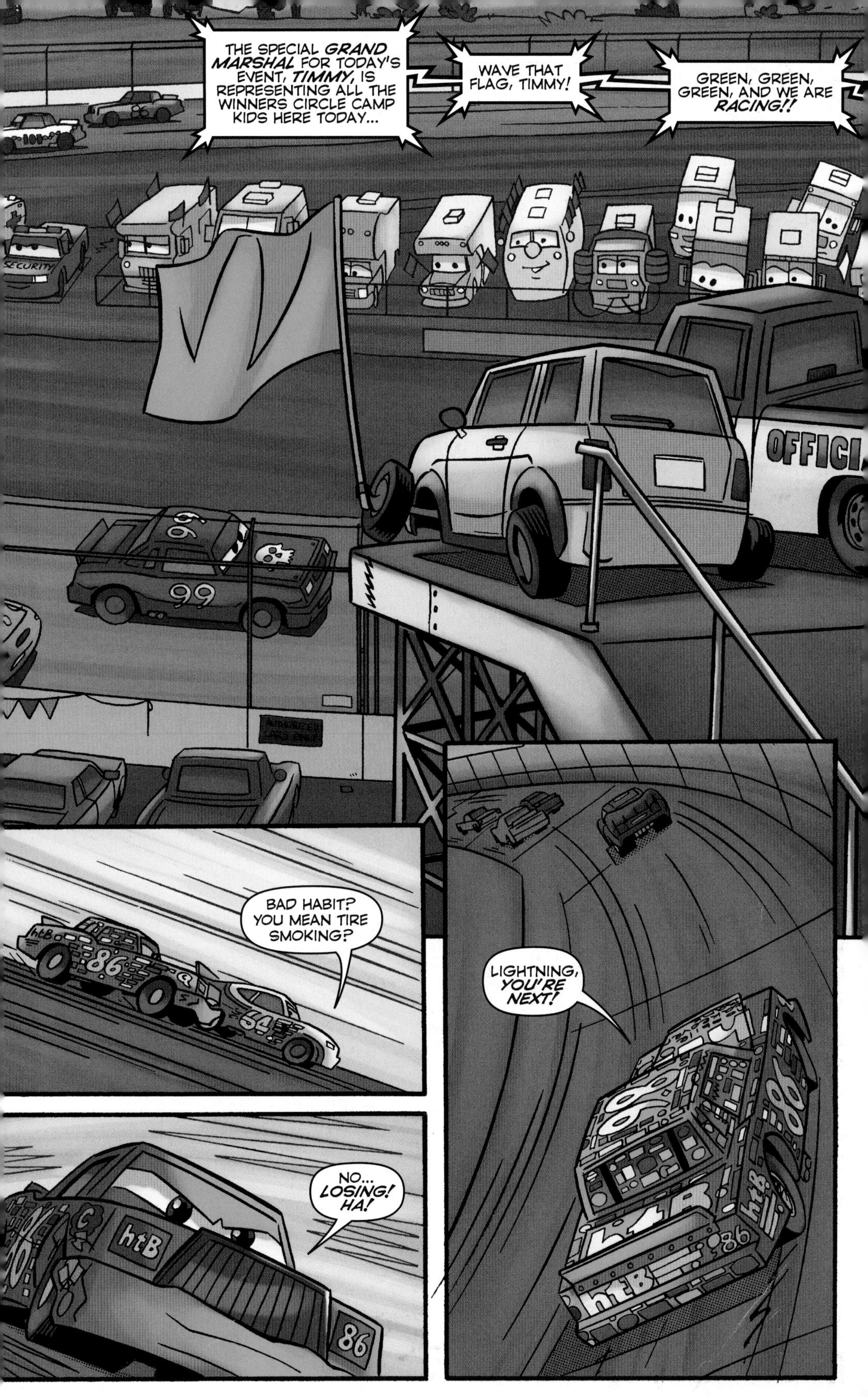
THE SPECIAL GRAND MARSHAL FOR TODAY'S EVENT, TIMMY, IS REPRESENTING ALL THE WINNERS CIRCLE CAMP KIDS HERE TODAY...
WAVE THAT FLAG, TIMMY!
GREEN, GREEN, GREEN, AND WE ARE RACING!!
SECURITY
OFFICI
BAD HABIT? YOU MEAN TIRE SMOKING?
NO... LOSING! HA!
LIGHTNING, YOU'RE NEXT!

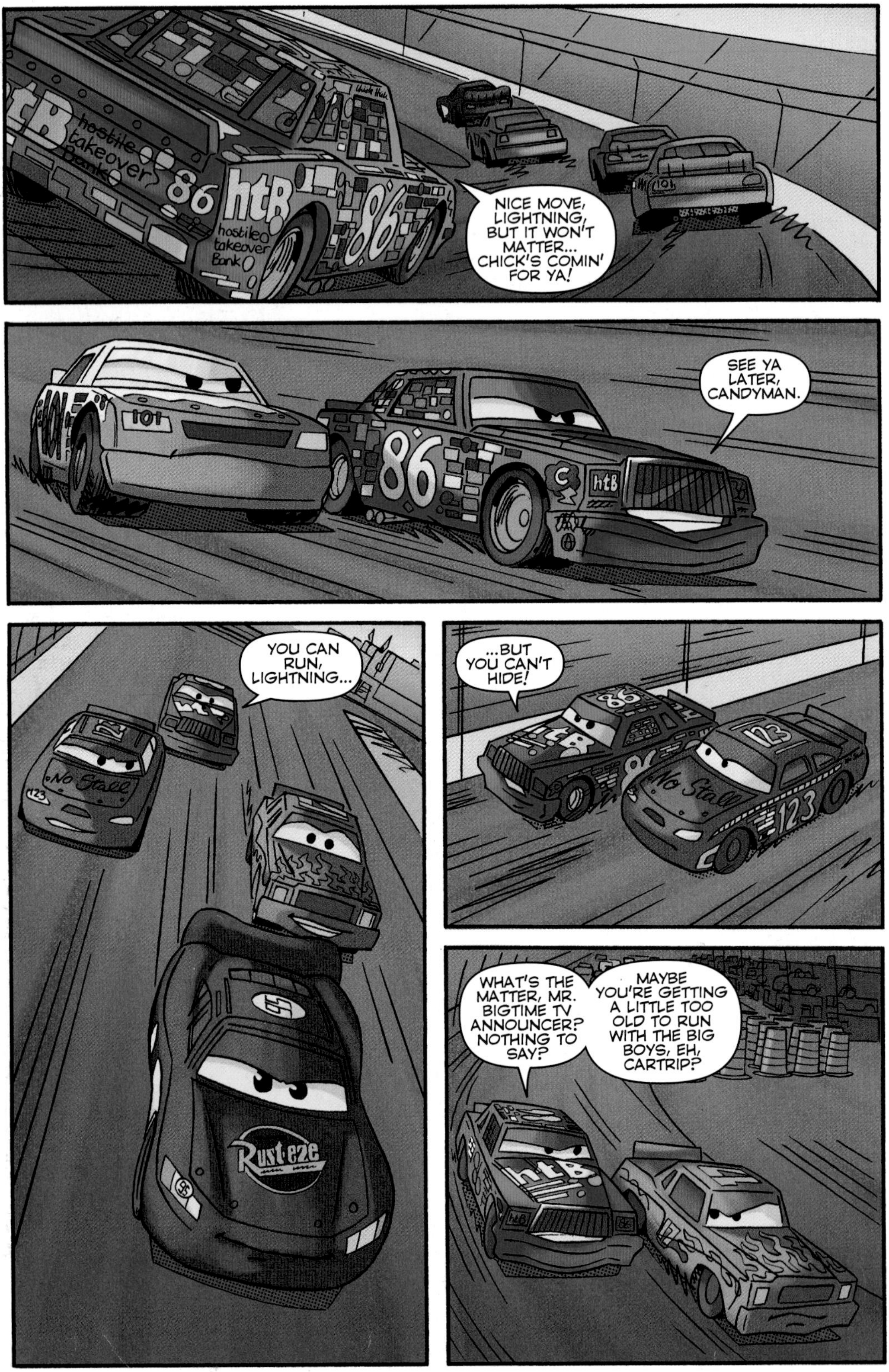
NICE MOVE, LIGHTNING, BUT IT WON'T MATTER... CHICK'S COMIN' FOR YA!
SEE YA LATER, CANDYMAN.
YOU CAN RUN, LIGHTNING...
...BUT YOU CAN'T HIDE!
WHAT'S THE MATTER, MR. BIGTIME TV ANNOUNCER? NOTHING TO SAY?
MAYBE YOU'RE GETTING A LITTLE TOO OLD TO RUN WITH THE BIG BOYS, EH, CARTRIP?

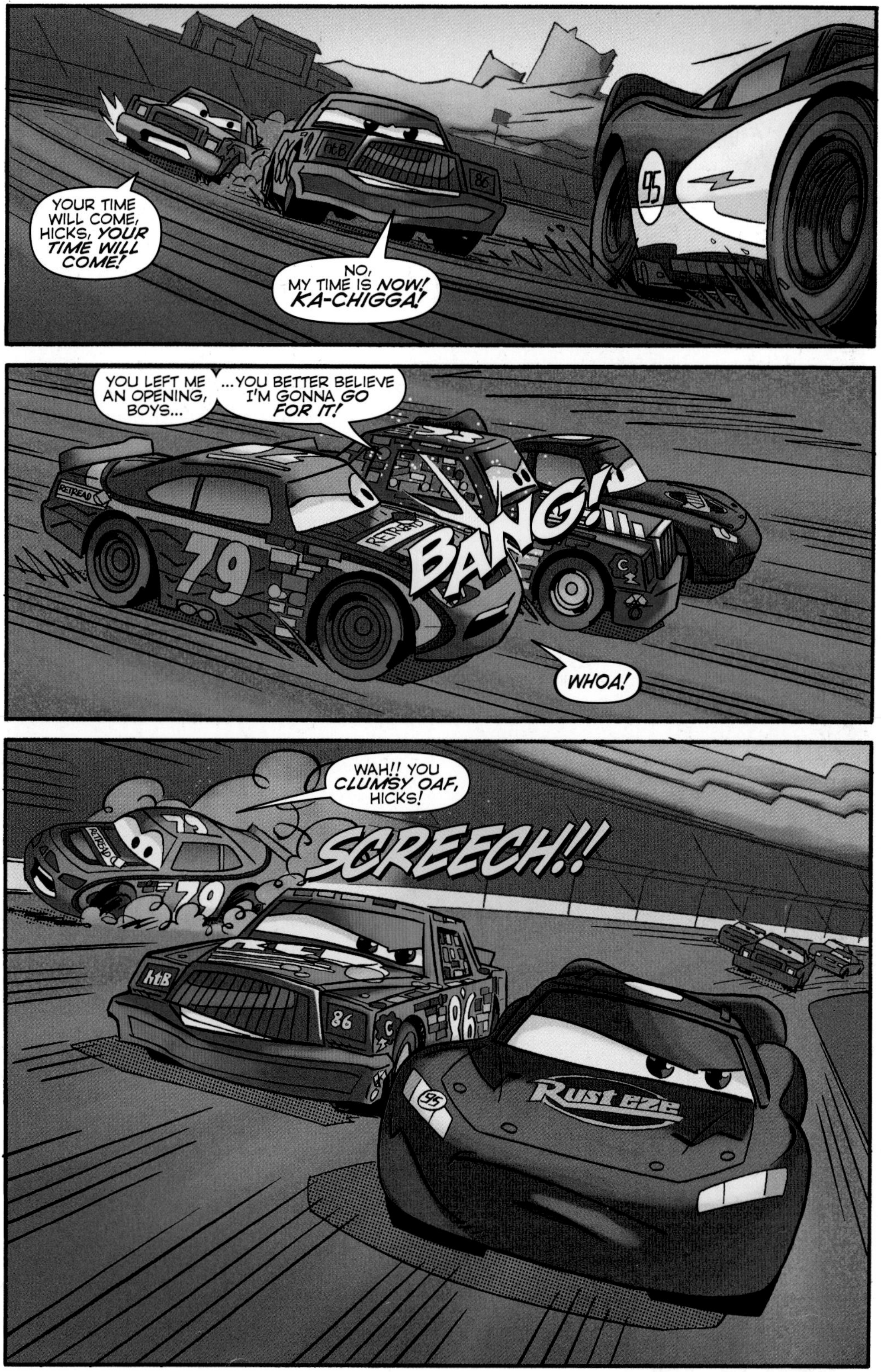
YOUR TIME WILL COME, HICKS, YOUR TIME WILL COME!
NO, MY TIME IS NOW! KA-CHIGGA!
YOU LEFT ME AN OPENING, BOYS...
...YOU BETTER BELIEVE I'M GONNA GO FOR IT!
BANG!
WHOA!
WAH!! YOU CLUMSY OAF, HICKS!
SCREECH!!

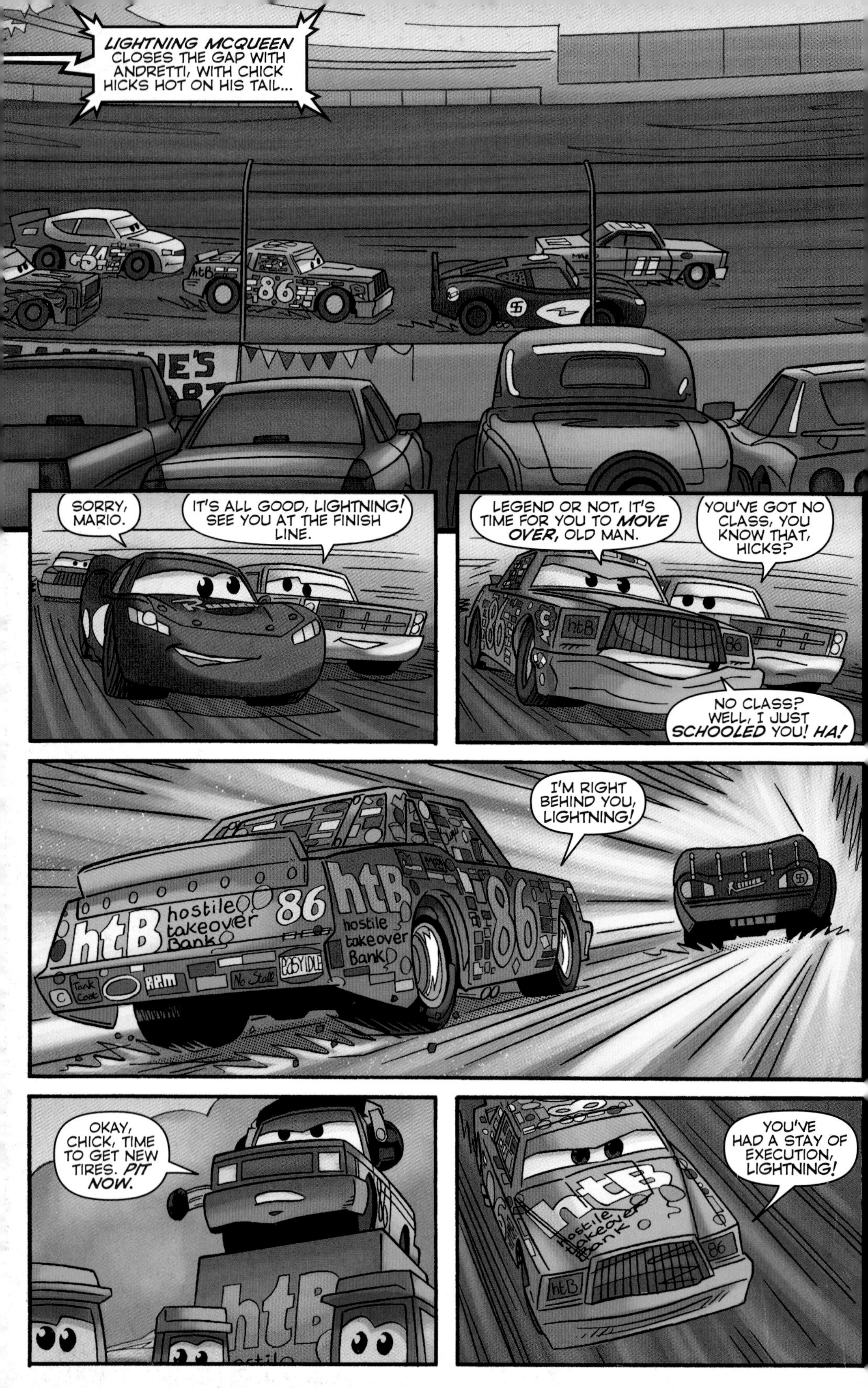
LIGHTNING MCQUEEN CLOSES THE GAP WITH ANDRETTI, WITH CHICK HICKS HOT ON HIS TAIL...
SORRY, MARIO.
IT'S ALL GOOD, LIGHTNING! SEE YOU AT THE FINISH LINE.
LEGEND OR NOT, IT'S TIME FOR YOU TO MOVE OVER, OLD MAN.
YOU'VE GOT NO CLASS, YOU KNOW THAT, HICKS?
NO CLASS? WELL, I JUST SCHOOLED YOU! HA!
I'M RIGHT BEHIND YOU, LIGHTNING!
htB hostile takeover Bank
86
OKAY, CHICK, TIME TO GET NEW TIRES. PIT NOW.
YOU'VE HAD A STAY OF EXECUTION, LIGHTNING!

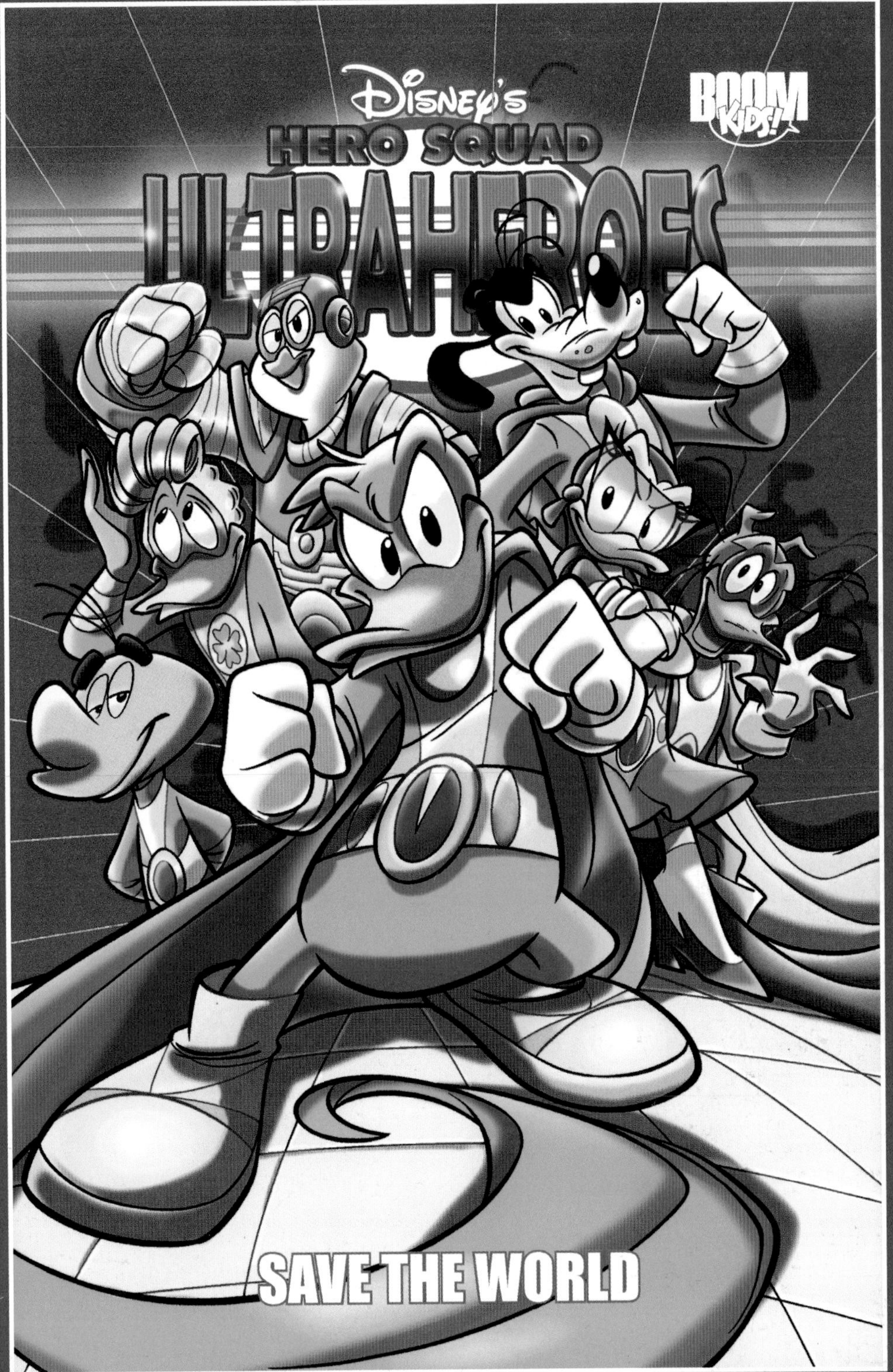
DISNEY'S
HERO SQUAD
ULTRAHEROES
BOOM KIDS!
SAVE THE WORLD

Super Goof, Duck Avenger, Super Daisy, Iron Gus, Cloverleaf, The Red Bat, Eega Beeva and even Mickey Mouse fight to save the planet from Emil Eagle and the Sinister-7!

DISNEY'S HERO SQUAD: ULTRAHEROES
DIAMOND CODE: DEC090746
SC $9.99 ISBN 9781608865437
HC $24.99 ISBN 9781608865529

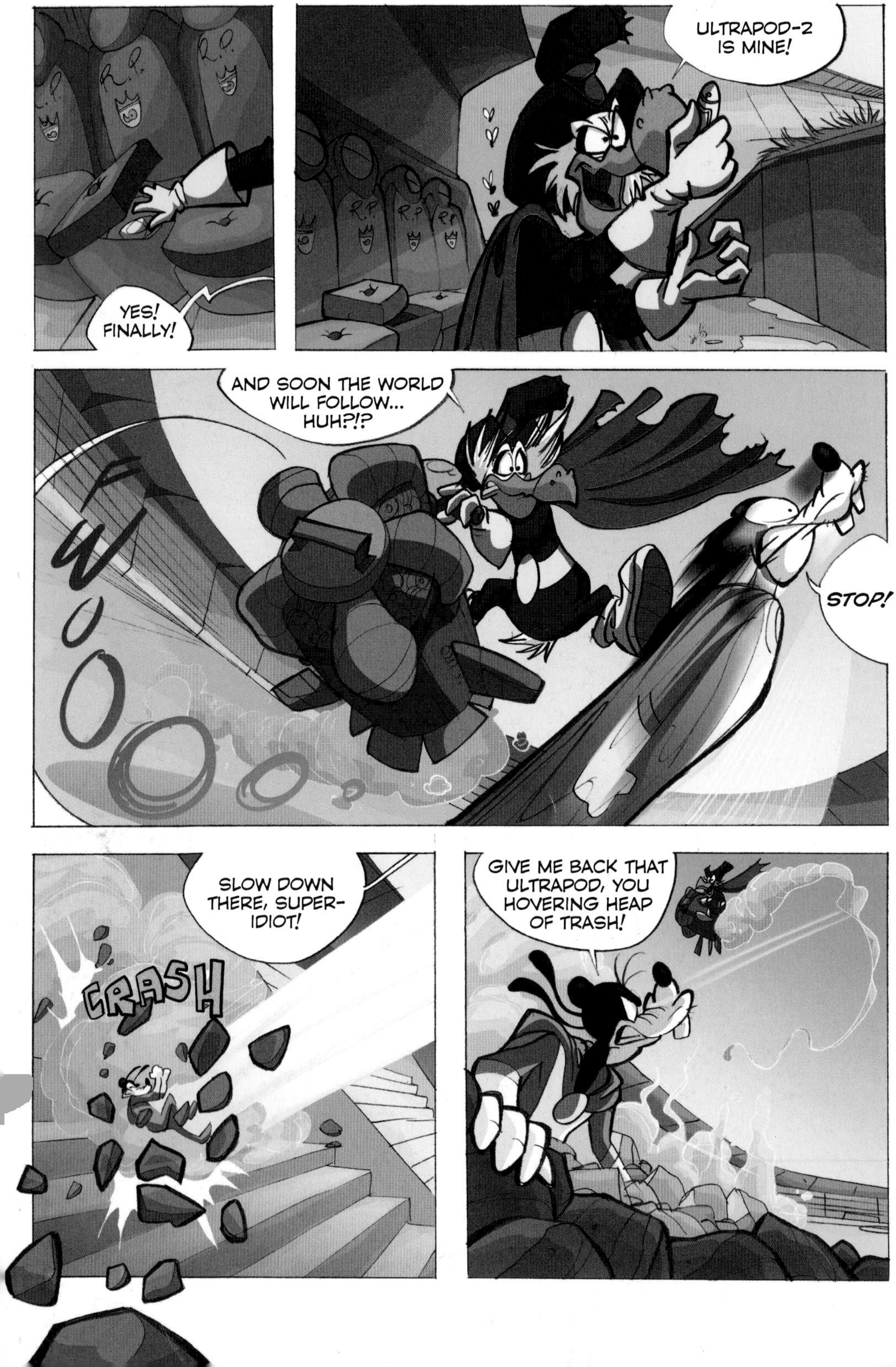
YES! FINALLY!
ULTRAPOD-2 IS MINE!
AND SOON THE WORLD WILL FOLLOW... HUH?!?
STOP!
SLOW DOWN THERE, SUPER-IDIOT!
CRASH
GIVE ME BACK THAT ULTRAPOD, YOU HOVERING HEAP OF TRASH!

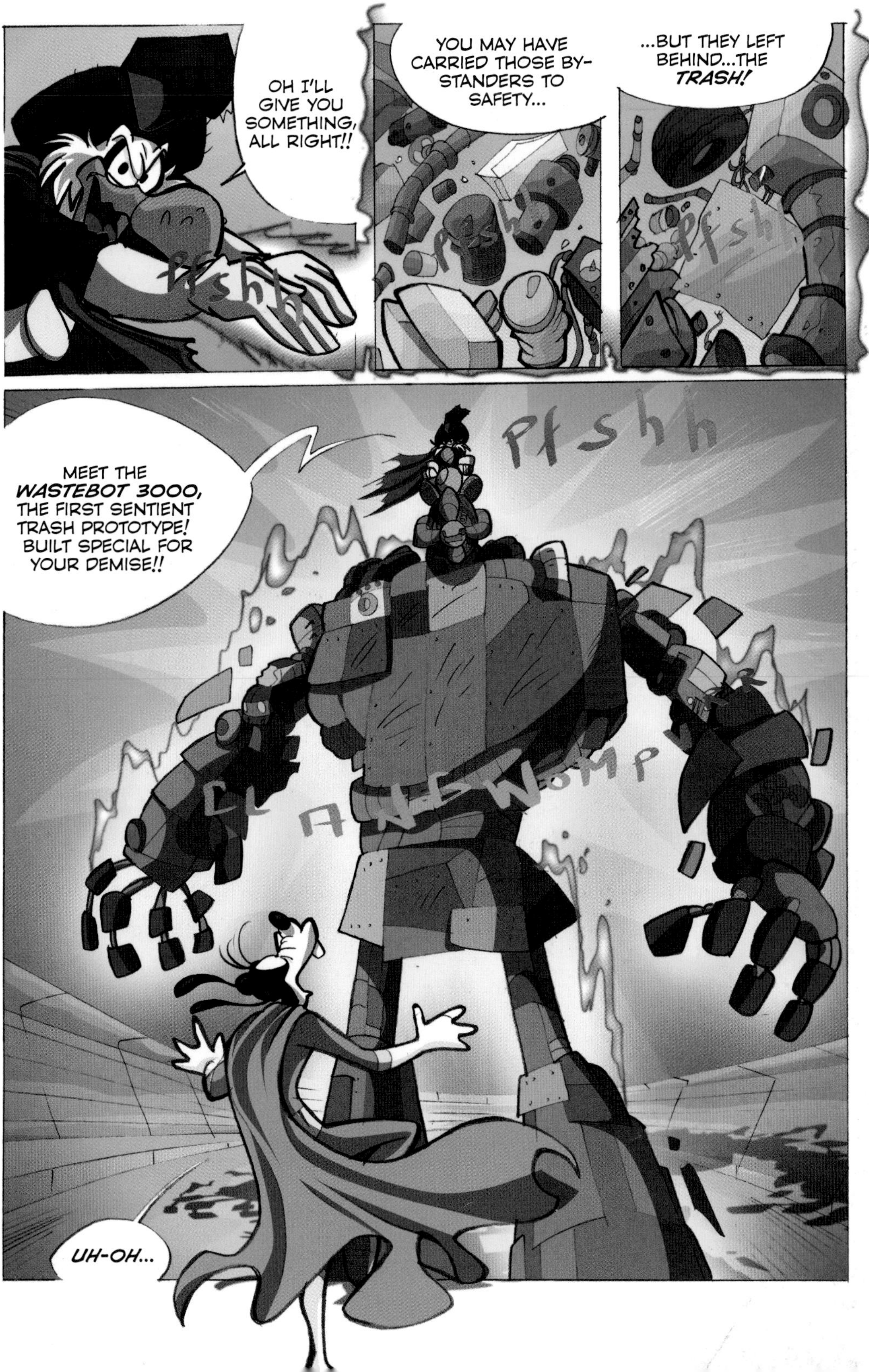
OH I'LL GIVE YOU SOMETHING, ALL RIGHT!!
Pfshh
YOU MAY HAVE CARRIED THOSE BY-STANDERS TO SAFETY...
Pfshh
...BUT THEY LEFT BEHIND...THE *TRASH!*
Pfshh
MEET THE *WASTEBOT 3000,* THE FIRST SENTIENT TRASH PROTOTYPE! BUILT SPECIAL FOR YOUR DEMISE!!
Pfshh
CLANGWOMP
UH-OH...

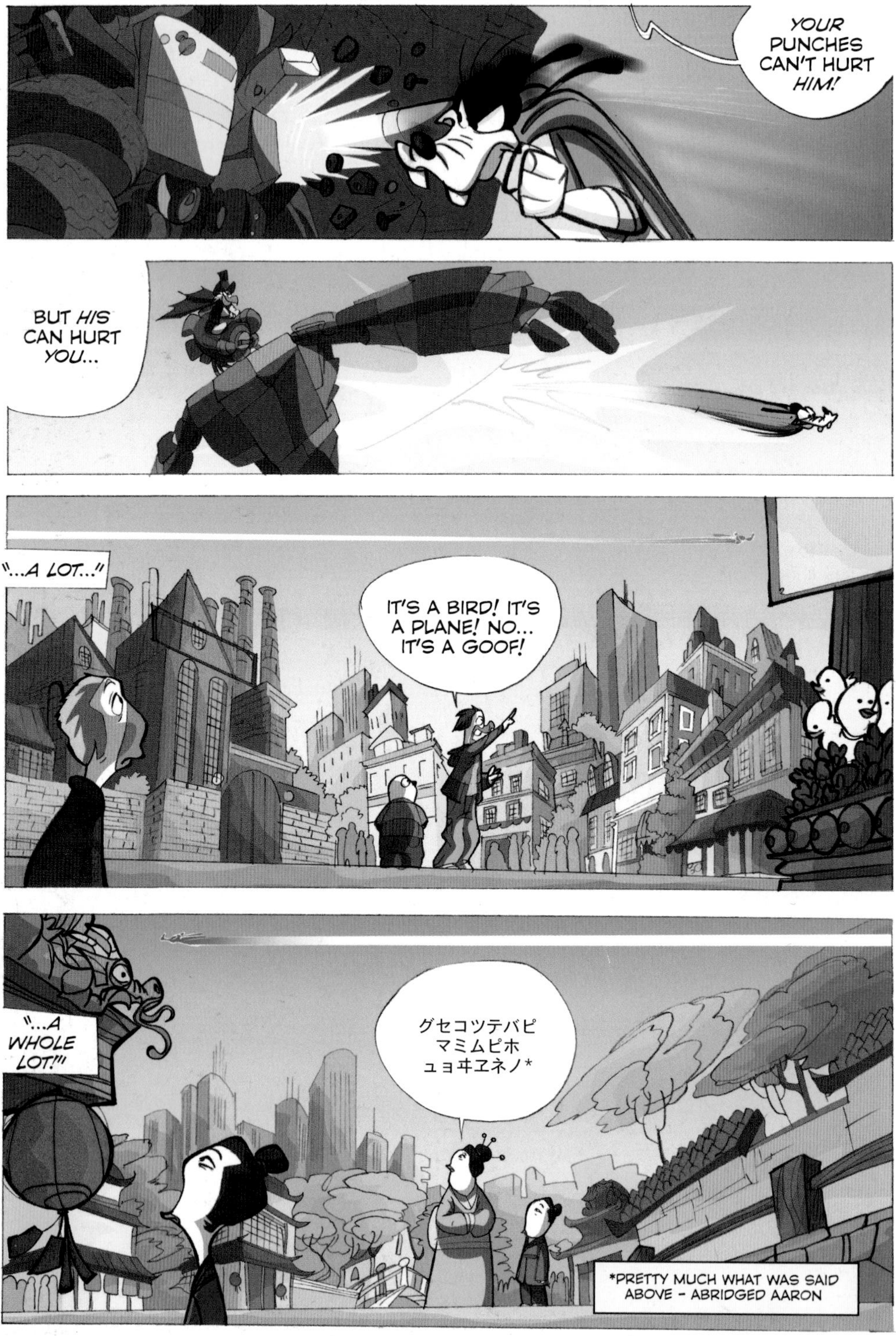
YOUR PUNCHES CAN'T HURT HIM!
BUT HIS CAN HURT YOU...
"...A LOT..."
IT'S A BIRD! IT'S A PLANE! NO... IT'S A GOOF!
"...A WHOLE LOT!"
グセコツテバピ マミムピホ ュョヰヱネノ*
*PRETTY MUCH WHAT WAS SAID ABOVE - ABRIDGED AARON

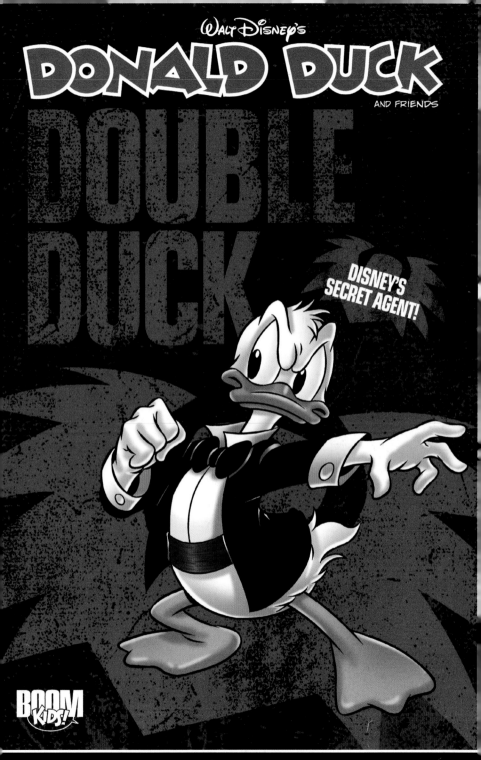

Donald Duck...as a secret agent? Villainous
fiends beware as the world of super-sleuthing
and espionage will never be the same! This is
Donald Duck like you've never seen him!

DONALD DUCK AND FRIENDS: DOUBLE DUCK
DIAMOND CODE: DEC090752
SC $9.99 ISBN 9781608865451
HC $24.99 ISBN 9781608865512

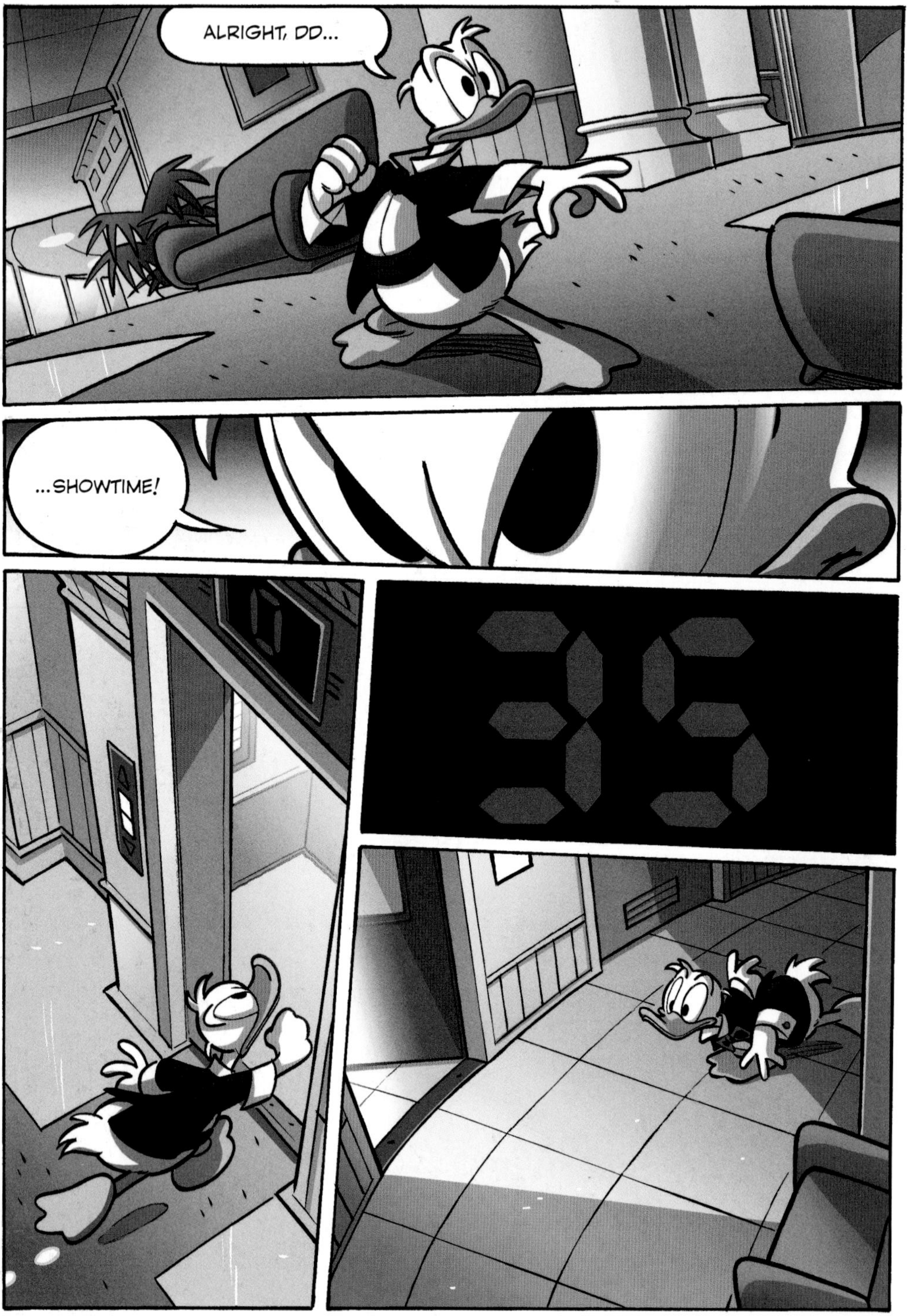
ALRIGHT, DD...
...SHOWTIME!

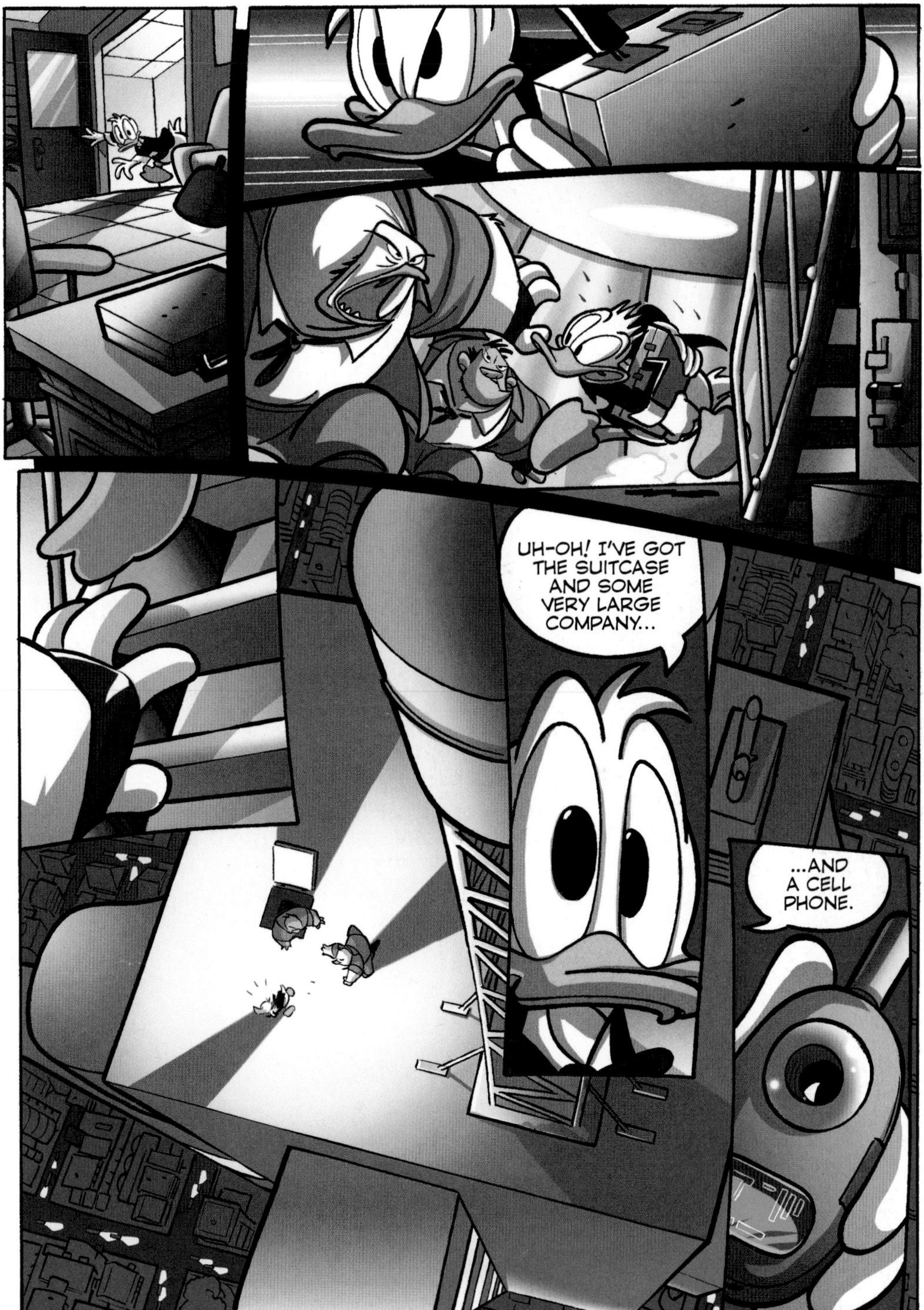
UH-OH! I'VE GOT THE SUITCASE AND SOME VERY LARGE COMPANY...
...AND A CELL PHONE.

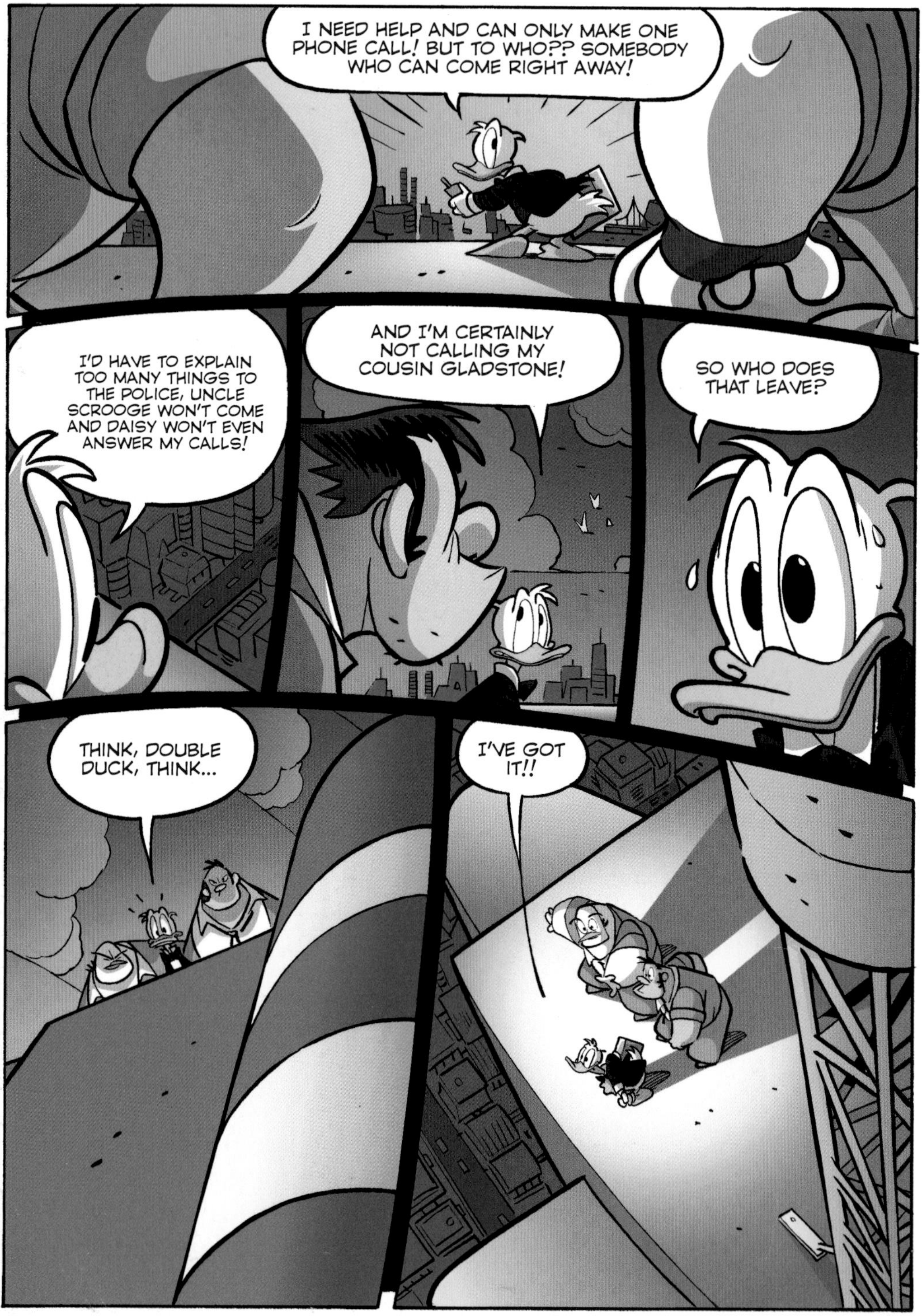
I NEED HELP AND CAN ONLY MAKE ONE PHONE CALL! BUT TO WHO?? SOMEBODY WHO CAN COME RIGHT AWAY!
I'D HAVE TO EXPLAIN TOO MANY THINGS TO THE POLICE, UNCLE SCROOGE WON'T COME AND DAISY WON'T EVEN ANSWER MY CALLS!
AND I'M CERTAINLY NOT CALLING MY COUSIN GLADSTONE!
SO WHO DOES THAT LEAVE?
THINK, DOUBLE DUCK, THINK...
I'VE GOT IT!!

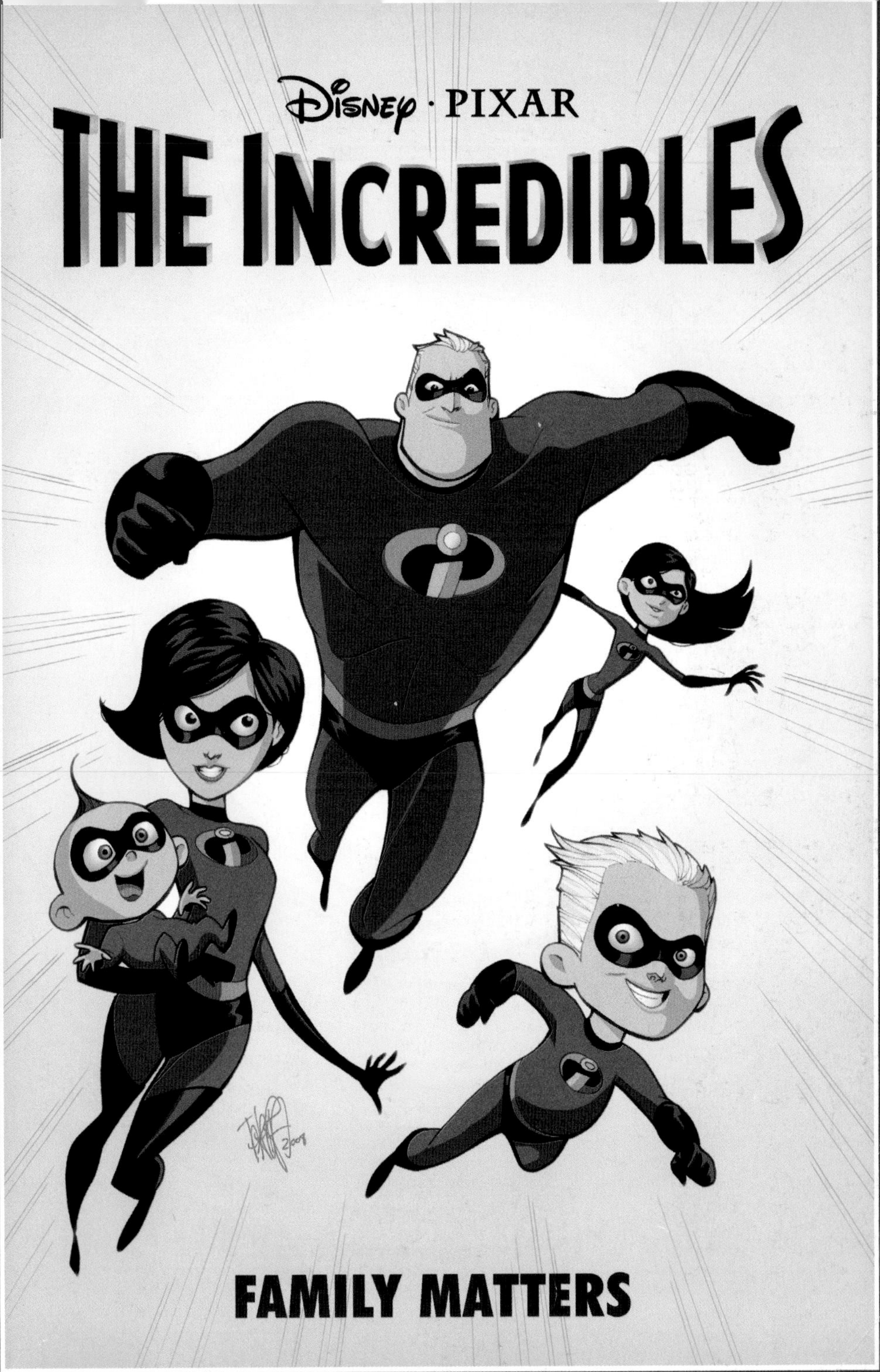
DISNEY · PIXAR
THE INCREDIBLES
FAMILY MATTERS

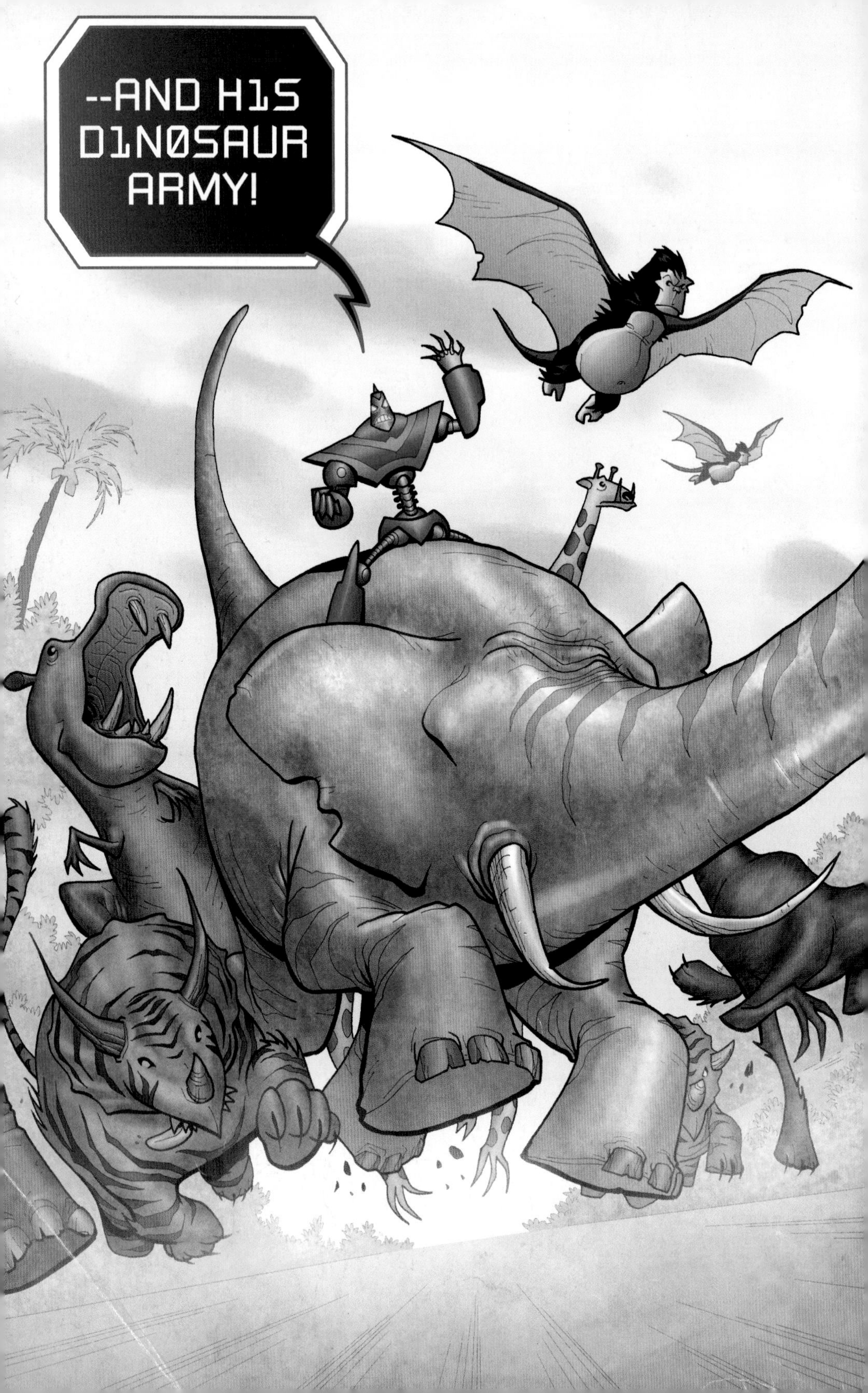
--AND H1S D1N0SAUR ARMY!

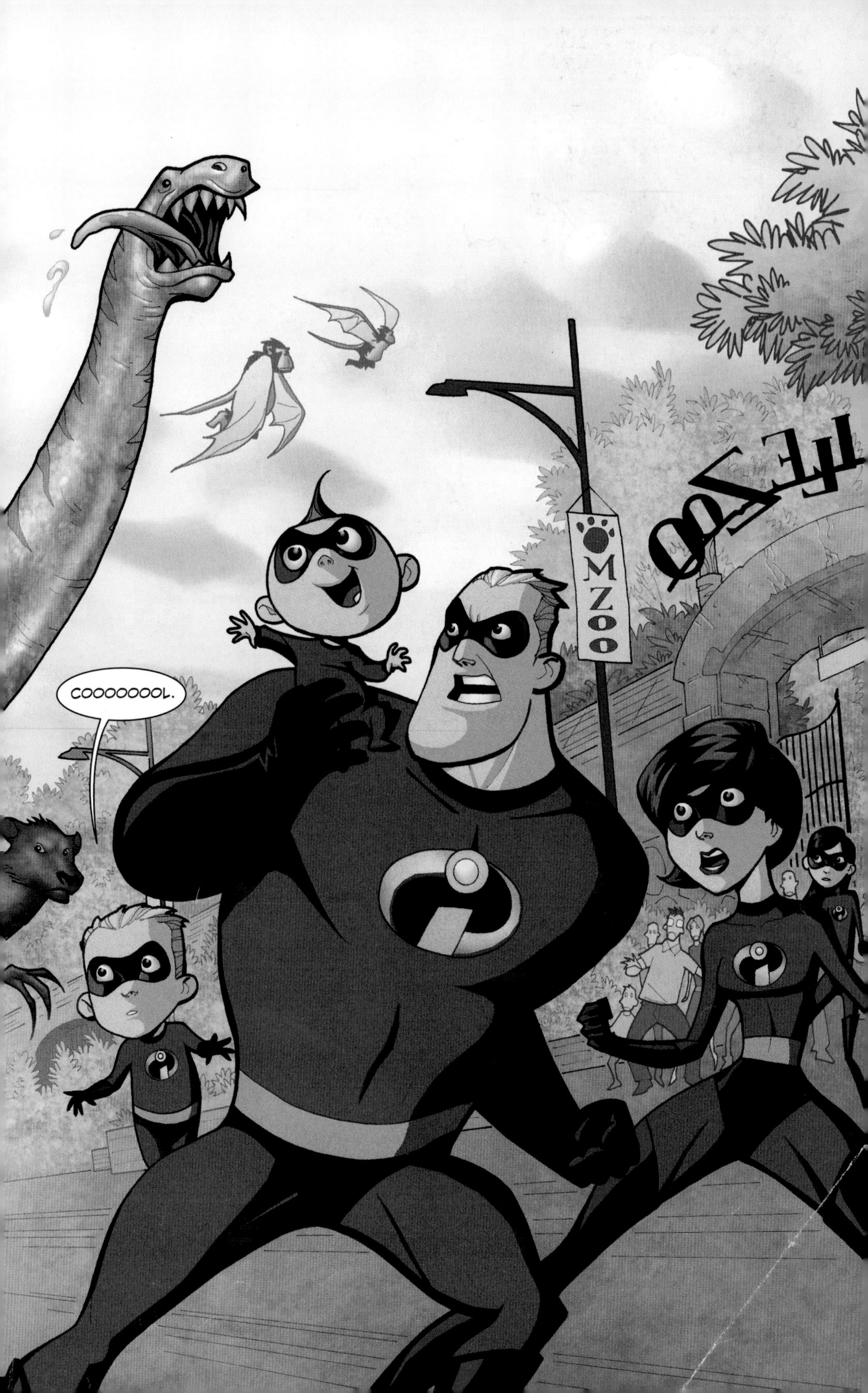
COOOOOOOL.
M ZOO
THE ZOO

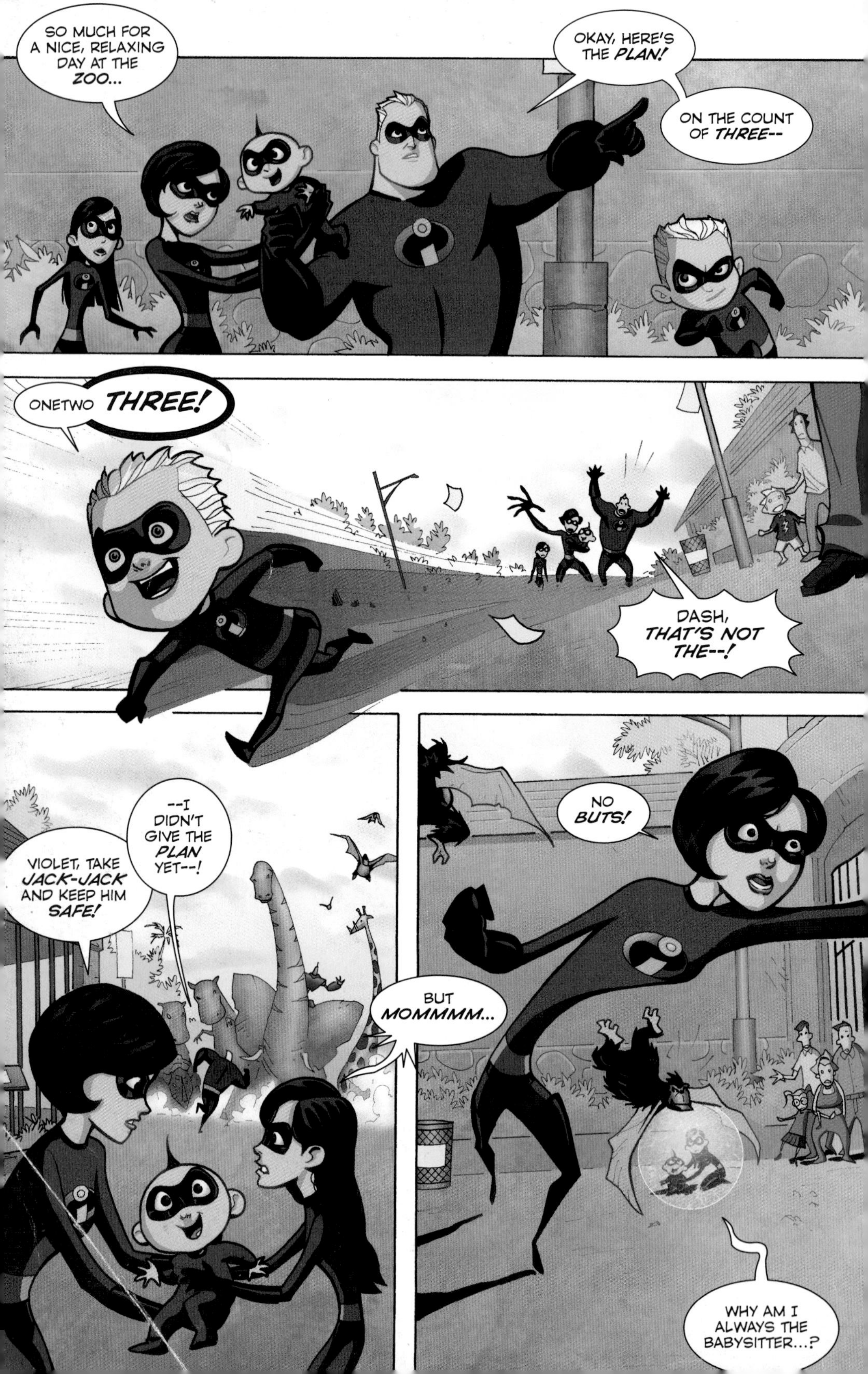
SO MUCH FOR A NICE, RELAXING DAY AT THE *ZOO*...
OKAY, HERE'S THE *PLAN!*
ON THE COUNT OF *THREE*--
ONETWO **THREE!**
DASH, *THAT'S NOT THE*--!
VIOLET, TAKE *JACK-JACK* AND KEEP HIM *SAFE!*
--I DIDN'T GIVE THE *PLAN* YET--!
BUT *MOMMMM*...
NO *BUTS!*
WHY AM I ALWAYS THE BABYSITTER...?

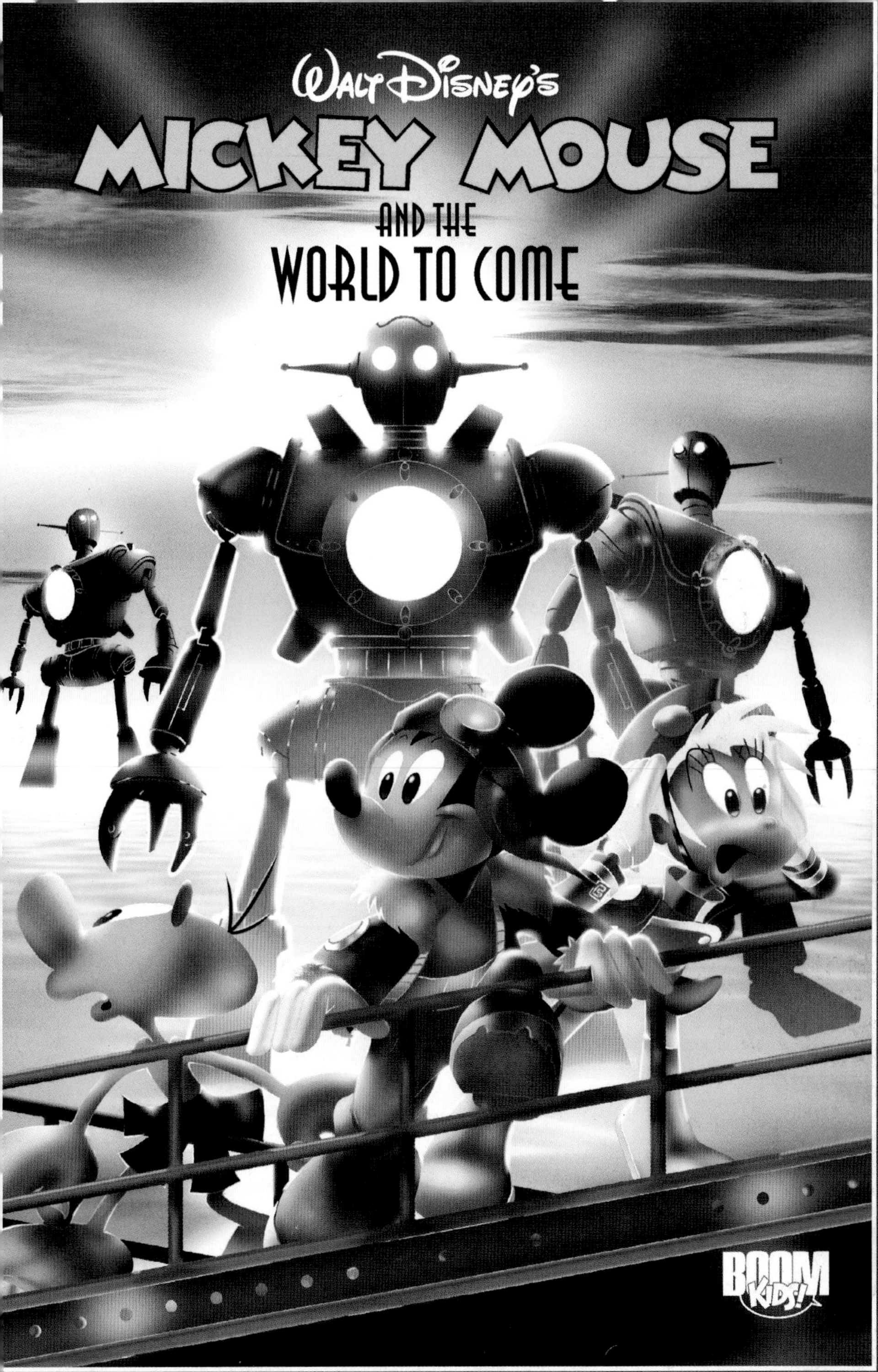
Walt Disney's
MICKEY MOUSE
AND THE
WORLD TO COME
BOOM KIDS!

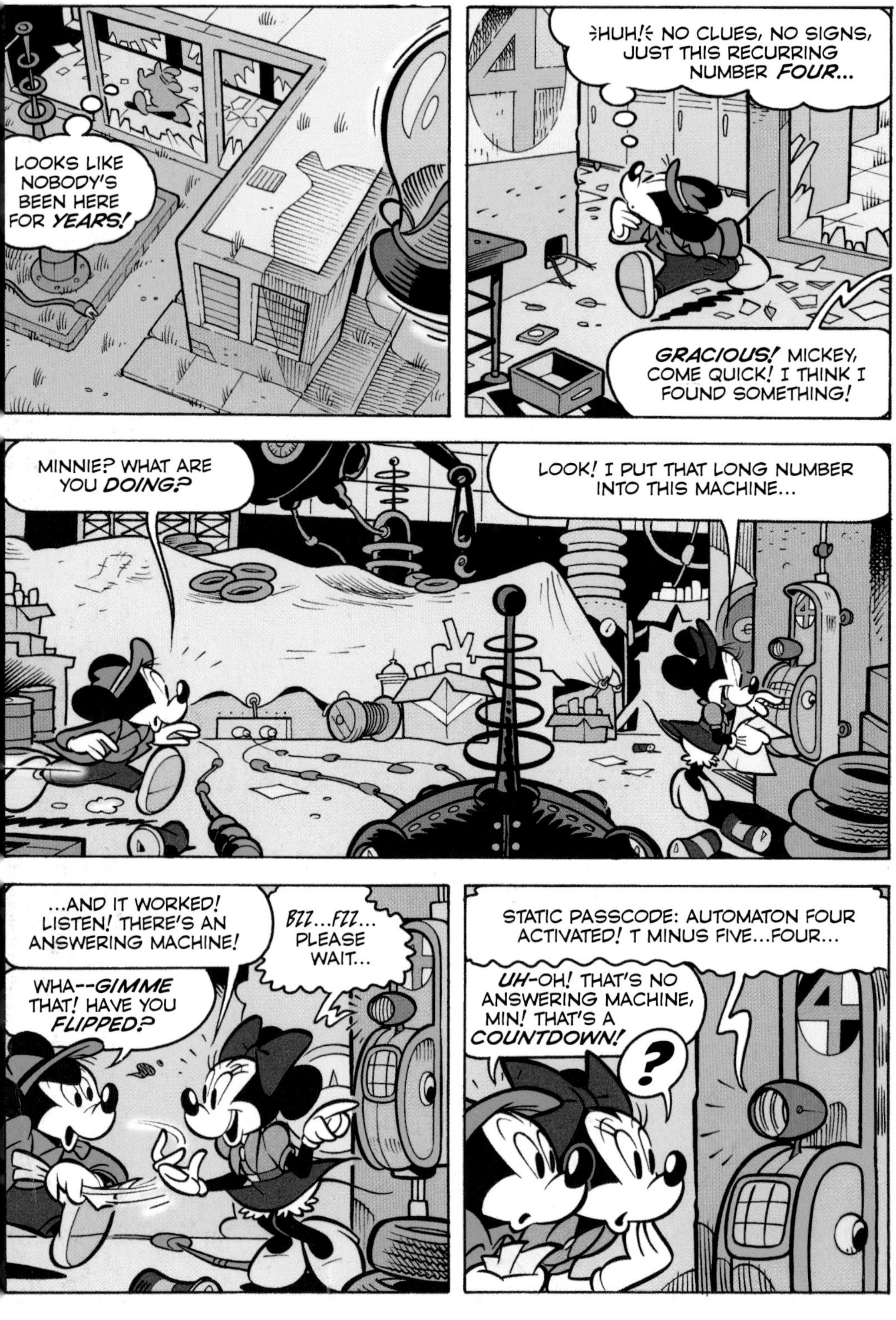
LOOKS LIKE NOBODY'S BEEN HERE FOR *YEARS!*
HUH! NO CLUES, NO SIGNS, JUST THIS RECURRING NUMBER *FOUR...*
GRACIOUS! MICKEY, COME QUICK! I THINK I FOUND SOMETHING!
MINNIE? WHAT ARE YOU *DOING?*
LOOK! I PUT THAT LONG NUMBER INTO THIS MACHINE...
...AND IT WORKED! LISTEN! THERE'S AN ANSWERING MACHINE!
WHA--*GIMME* THAT! HAVE YOU *FLIPPED?*
BZZ...FZZ... PLEASE WAIT...
STATIC PASSCODE: AUTOMATON FOUR ACTIVATED! T MINUS FIVE...FOUR...
UH-OH! THAT'S NO ANSWERING MACHINE, MIN! THAT'S A *COUNTDOWN!*
?

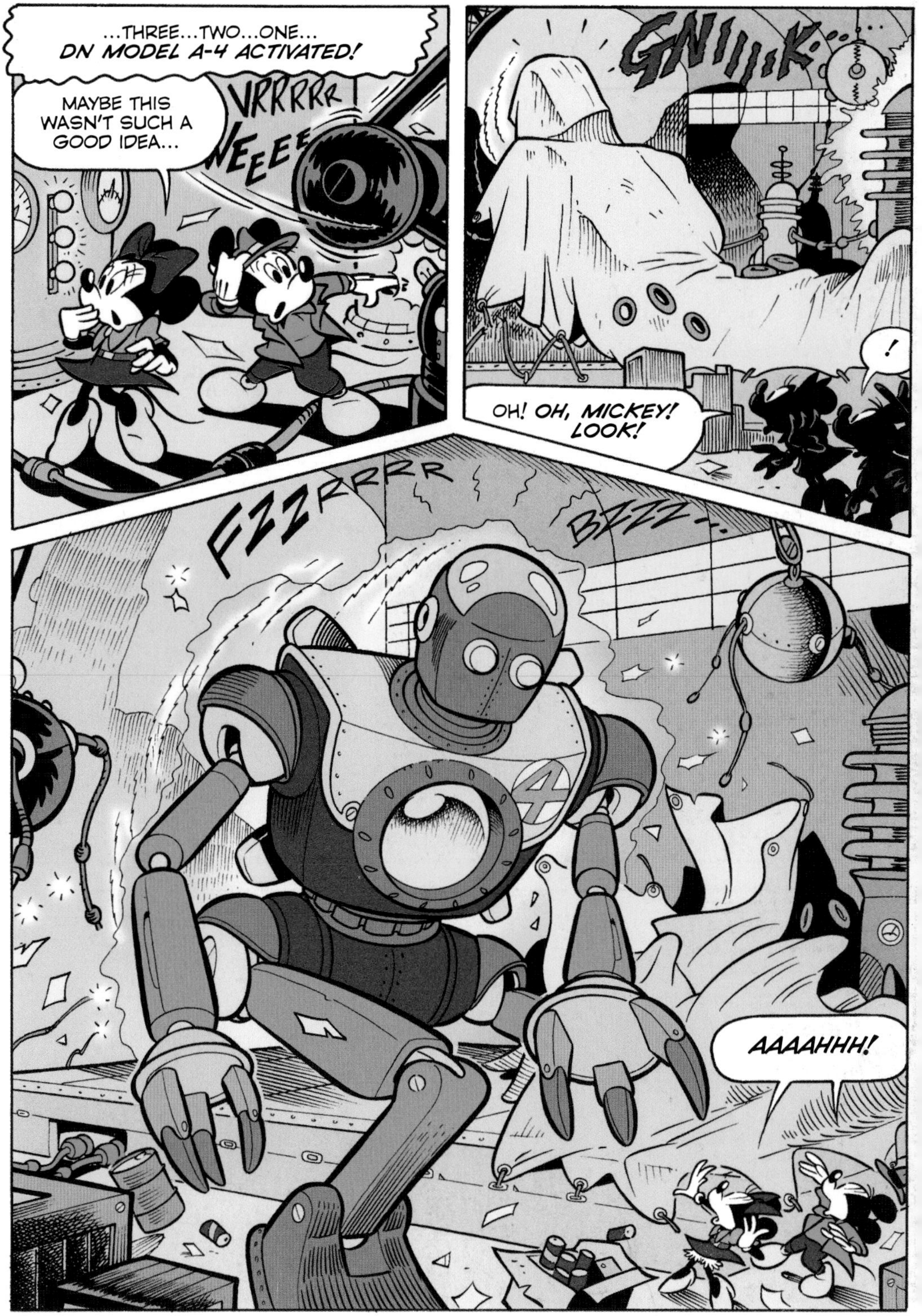
...THREE...TWO...ONE...
DN MODEL A-4 ACTIVATED!
MAYBE THIS WASN'T SUCH A GOOD IDEA...
VRRRRR
NEEEE
GNIIIIK...
!
OH! OH, MICKEY! LOOK!
FZZRRRRR
BZZZ...
AAAAHHH!

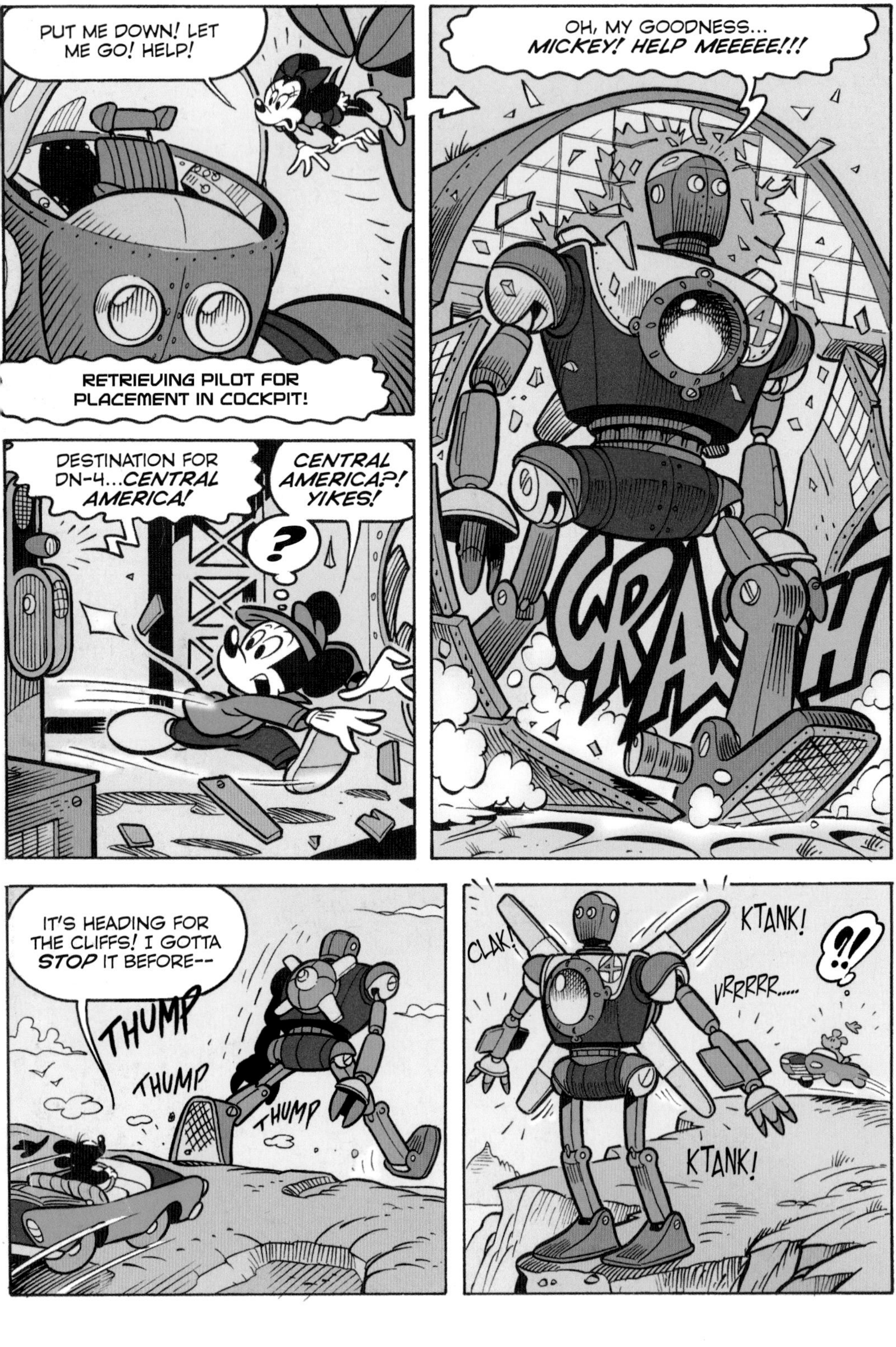
PUT ME DOWN! LET ME GO! HELP!
RETRIEVING PILOT FOR PLACEMENT IN COCKPIT!
OH, MY GOODNESS... *MICKEY! HELP MEEEEE!!!*
DESTINATION FOR DN-4...*CENTRAL AMERICA!*
CENTRAL AMERICA?! YIKES!
?
CRASH
IT'S HEADING FOR THE CLIFFS! I GOTTA *STOP* IT BEFORE--
THUMP
THUMP
THUMP
CLAK!
KTANK!
VRRRRR.....
?!
KTANK!

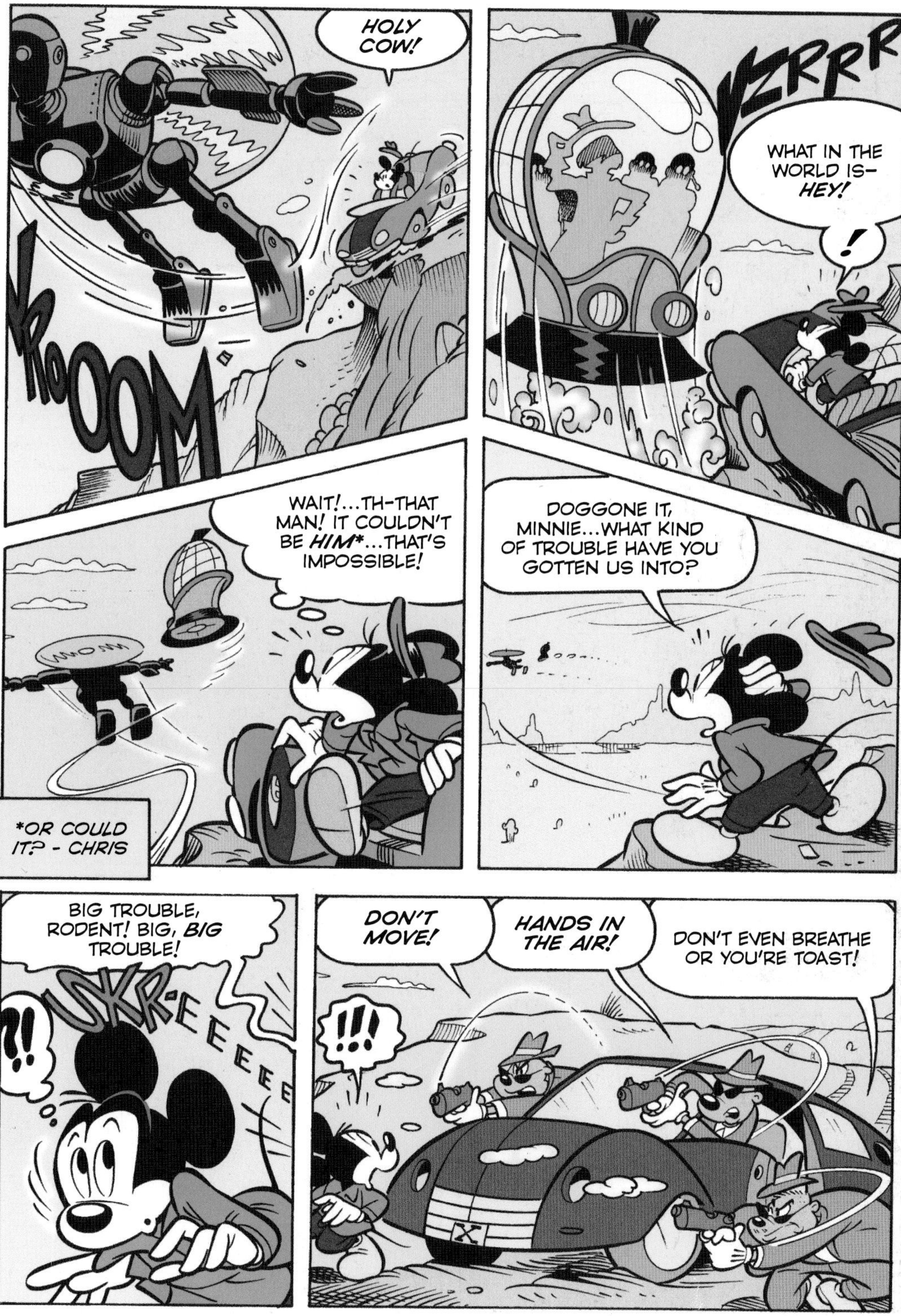
HOLY COW!
VROOOM
VZRRR
WHAT IN THE WORLD IS— HEY!
!
WAIT!...TH-THAT MAN! IT COULDN'T BE HIM*...THAT'S IMPOSSIBLE!
*OR COULD IT? - CHRIS
DOGGONE IT, MINNIE...WHAT KIND OF TROUBLE HAVE YOU GOTTEN US INTO?
BIG TROUBLE, RODENT! BIG, BIG TROUBLE!
SKR-EEEEEE
?!
DON'T MOVE!
HANDS IN THE AIR!
DON'T EVEN BREATHE OR YOU'RE TOAST!
!!!

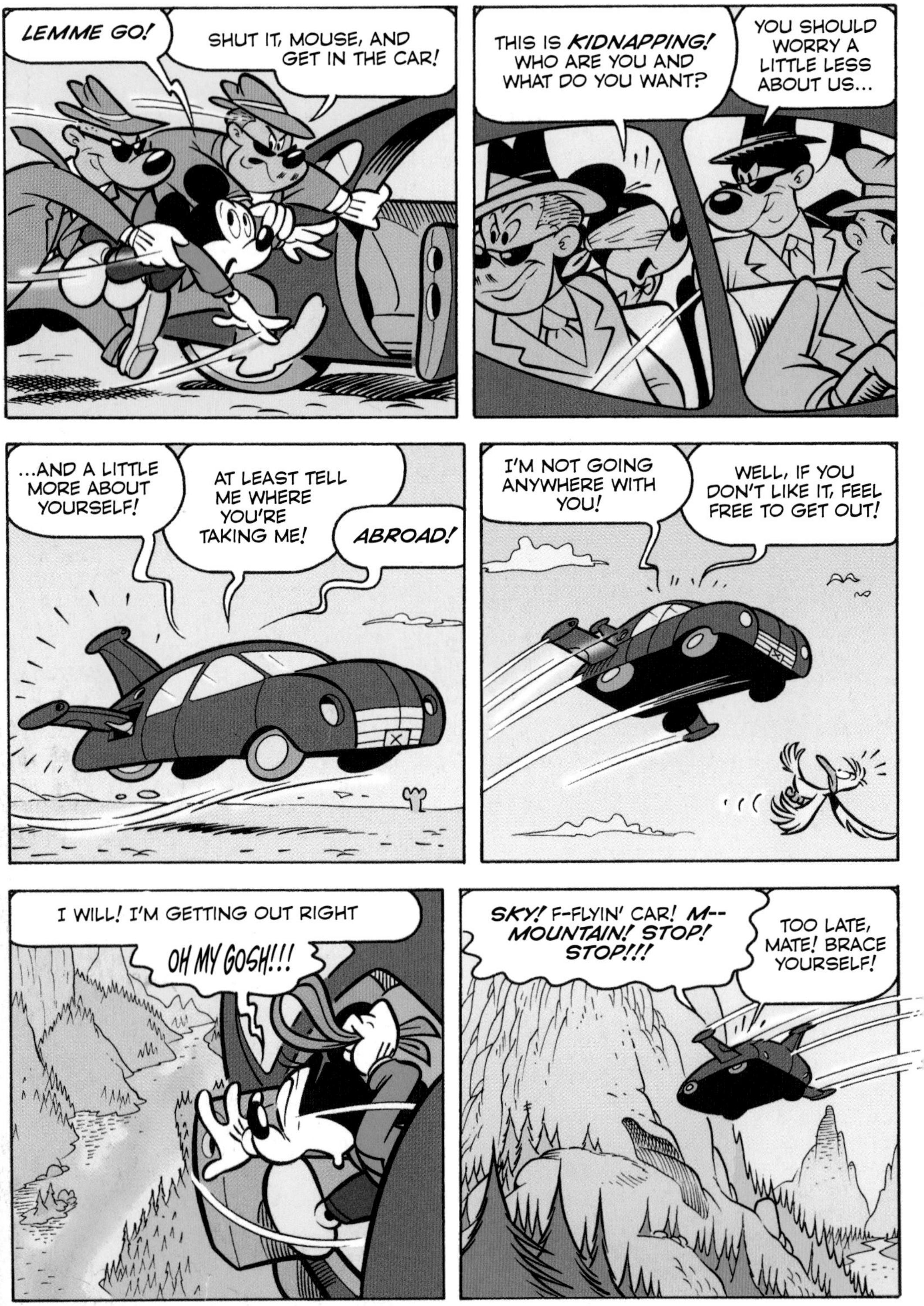
LEMME GO!
SHUT IT, MOUSE, AND GET IN THE CAR!
THIS IS KIDNAPPING! WHO ARE YOU AND WHAT DO YOU WANT?
YOU SHOULD WORRY A LITTLE LESS ABOUT US...
...AND A LITTLE MORE ABOUT YOURSELF!
AT LEAST TELL ME WHERE YOU'RE TAKING ME!
ABROAD!
I'M NOT GOING ANYWHERE WITH YOU!
WELL, IF YOU DON'T LIKE IT, FEEL FREE TO GET OUT!
I WILL! I'M GETTING OUT RIGHT
OH MY GOSH!!!
SKY! F-FLYIN' CAR! M-- MOUNTAIN! STOP! STOP!!!
TOO LATE, MATE! BRACE YOURSELF!

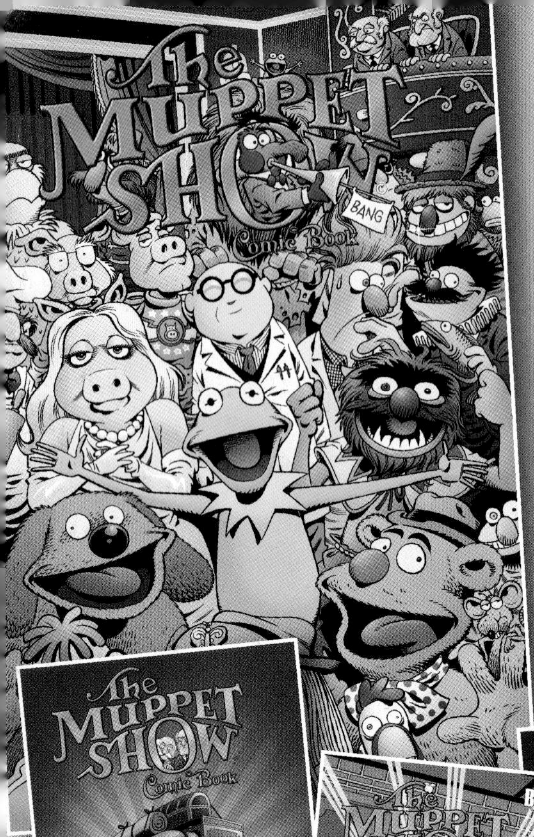
The Muppet Show
Comic Book
BANG

THE MUPPET SHOW COMIC BOOK: MEET THE MUPPETS

Collecting the first four issues of the Eisner Award-nominated THE MUPPET SHOW COMIC BOOK, written and drawn by the incomparable Roger Langridge! Packed full of madcap skits and gags, this trade is certain to please old and new fans alike!

SC $9.99 ISBN 9781934506851
HC $24.99 ISBN 9781608865277

THE MUPPET SHOW COMIC BOOK: THE TREASURE OF PEG-LEG WILSON

Scooter discovers old documents which reveal that a cache of treasure is hidden somewhere within the Muppet Theater...and when Rizzo the Rat overhears this, the news spreads like wildfire! Can Kermit keep everyone from tearing the theater apart?

SC $9.99 ISBN 9781608865048
HC $24.99 ISBN 9781608865307

THE MUPPET SHOW COMIC BOOK: ON THE ROAD

With the Muppet Theater destroyed, the Muppets take their act on the road...but with two very familiar hecklers in every town, will the show be a hit, or will our Muppet minstrels be run out of town in tar and feathers? Also: PIGS IN SPACE!

SC $9.99 ISBN 9781608865161

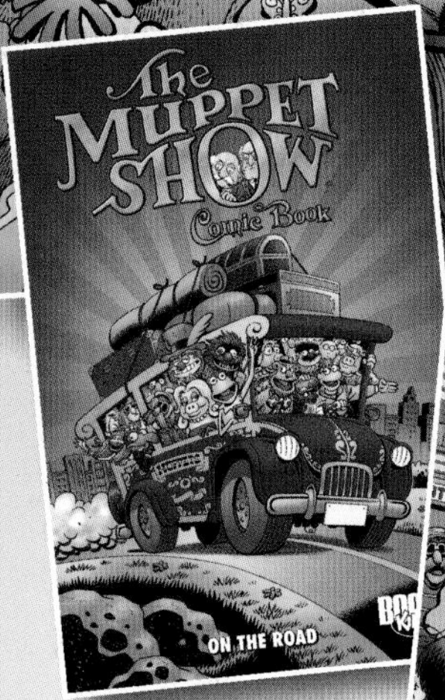
The Muppet Show
Comic Book
ON THE ROAD

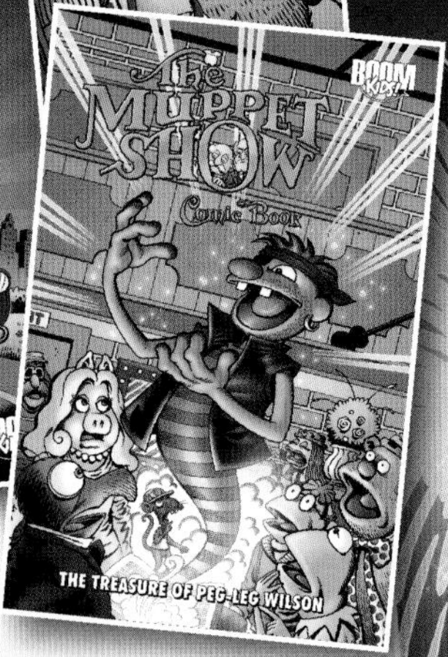
BOOM KIDS!
The Muppet Show
Comic Book
THE TREASURE OF PEG-LEG WILSON

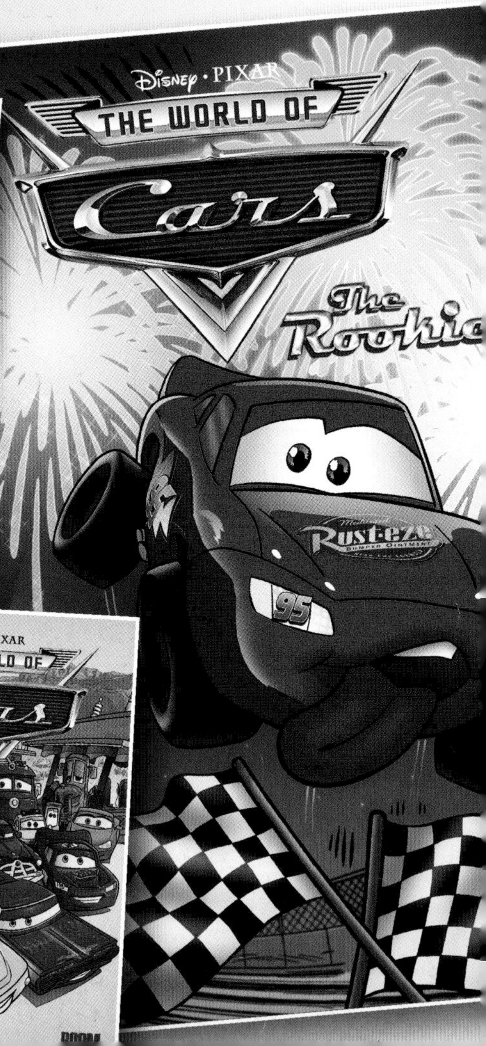
Disney · PIXAR
THE WORLD OF
Cars
The Rookie
Rust-eze
95

CARS: THE ROOKIE

See how Lightning McQueen became a Piston Cup sensation! CARS: THE ROOKIE reveals Lightning McQueen's scrappy origins as a local short track racer who dreams of the big time... and recklessly plows his way through the competition to get there!

SC $9.99 ISBN 9781934506844
HC $24.99 ISBN 9781608865222

CARS: RADIATOR SPRINGS

Lightning McQueen is hanging out with his friends at Flo's V8 Café when he realizes that everyone knows his story...but he doesn't know anyone else's! Lightning wants to know how his friends ended up in Radiator Springs...and more importantly, why they decided to stay!

SC $9.99 ISBN 9781608865024
HC $24.99 ISBN 9781608865284

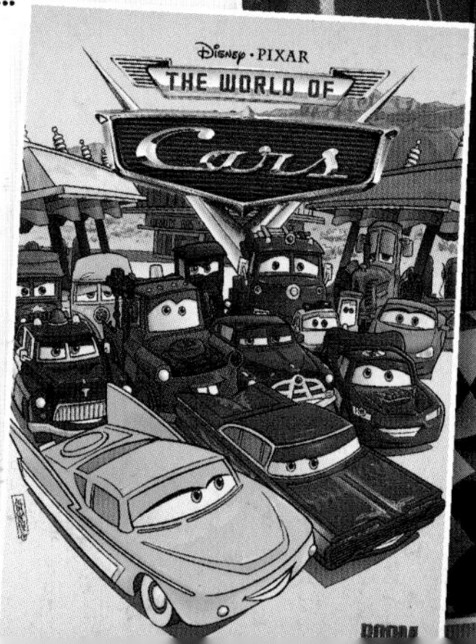
Disney · PIXAR
THE WORLD OF
Cars

WALL•E: RECHARGE

Before WALL•E becomes the hardworking robot we know and love, he lets the few remaining robots take care of the trash compacting while he collects interesting junk. But when these robots start breaking down, WALL•E must adjust his priorities...or else Earth is doomed!

SC $9.99 ISBN 9781608865123
HC $24.99 ISBN 9781608865543

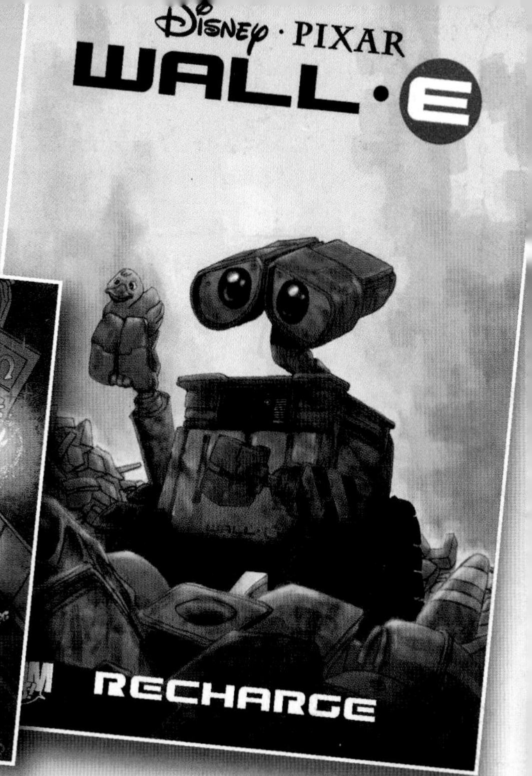
DISNEY · PIXAR
WALL·E
RECHARGE

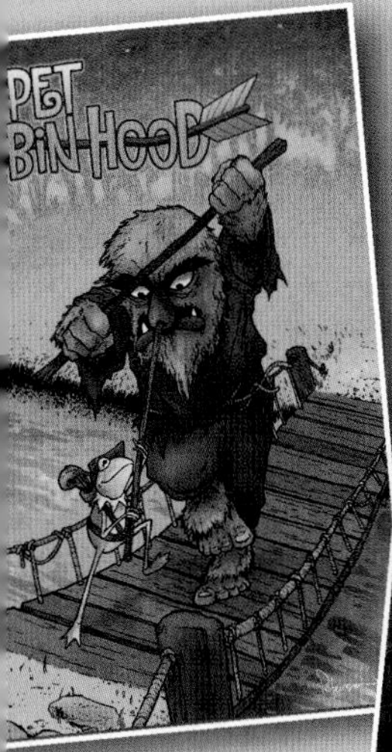

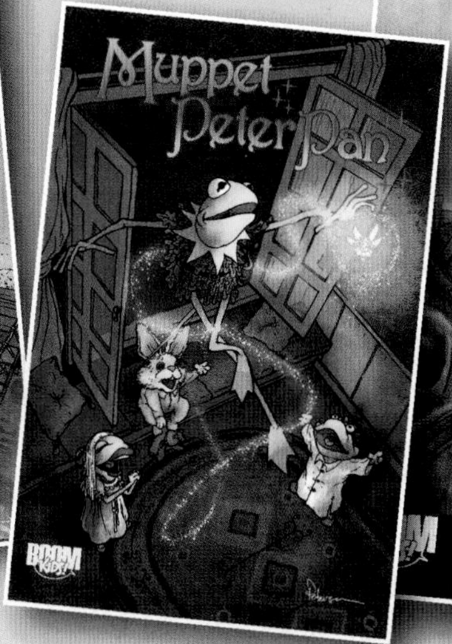
Muppet Peter Pan

MUPPET ROBIN HOOD

The Muppets tell the Robin Hood legend for laughs, and it's the reader who will be merry! Robin Hood (Kermit the Frog) joins with the Merry Men, Sherwood Forest's infamous gang of misfit outlaws, to take on the Sheriff of Nottingham (Sam the Eagle)!

SC $9.99 ISBN 9781934506790
HC $24.99 ISBN 9781608865260

MUPPET PETER PAN

When Peter Pan (Kermit) whisks Wendy (Janice) and her brothers to Neverswamp, the adventure begins! With Captain Hook (Gonzo) out for revenge for the loss of his hand, can even the magic of Piggytink (Miss Piggy) save Wendy and her brothers?

SC $9.99 ISBN 9781608865079
HC $24.99 ISBN 9781608865314

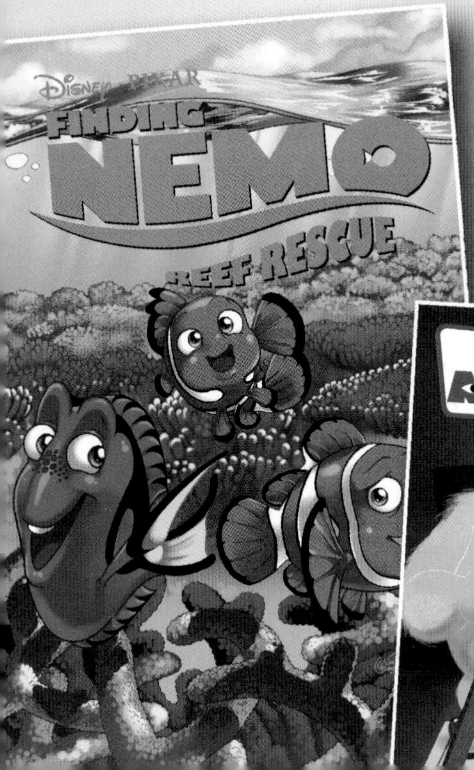
FINDING
NEMO
REEF RESCUE

FINDING NEMO: REEF RESCUE

Nemo, Dory and Marlin have become local heroes, and are recruited to embark on an all-new adventure in this exciting collection! The reef is mysteriously dying and no one knows why. So Nemo and his friends must travel the great blue sea to save their home!

SC $9.99 ISBN 9781934506882
HC $24.99 ISBN 9781608865246

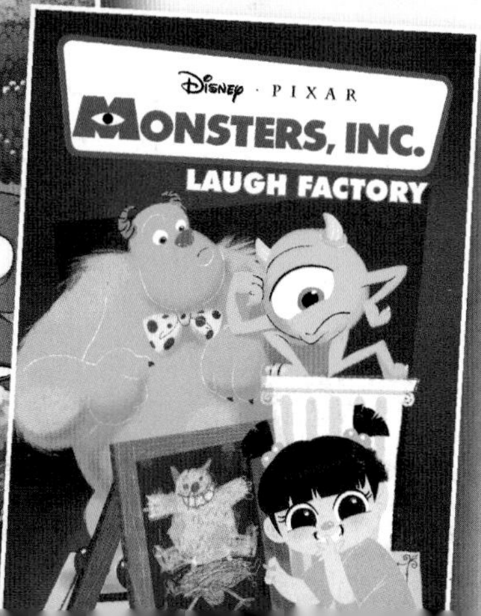
DISNEY · PIXAR
MONSTERS, INC.
LAUGH FACTORY

MONSTERS, INC.: LAUGH FACTORY

Someone is stealing comedy props from the other employees, making it difficult for them to harvest the laughter they need to power Monstropolis...and all evidence points to Sulley's best friend Mike Wazowski!

SC $9.99 ISBN 9781608865086
HC $24.99 ISBN 9781608865338

DISNEY'S HERO SQUAD: ULTRAHEROES VOL. 1: SAVE THE WORLD

It's an all-star cast of your favorite Disney characters, as you have never seen them before. Join Donald Duck, Goofy, Daisy, and even Mickey himself as they defend the fate of the planet as the one and only Ultraheroes!

SC $9.99 ISBN 9781608865437
HC $24.99 ISBN 9781608865529

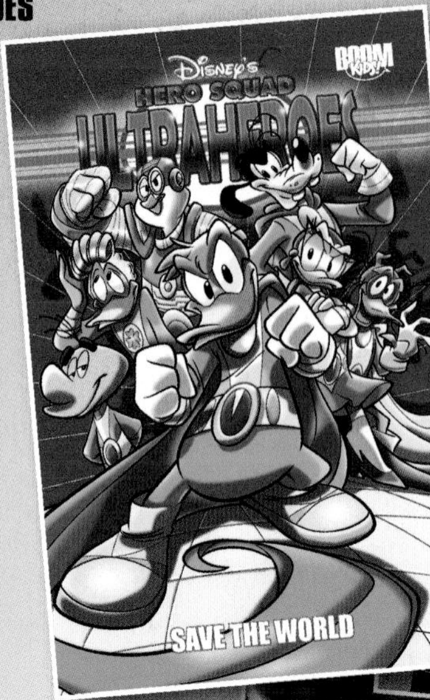
Disney's
HERO SQUAD
ULTRAHEROES
BOOM KIDS!
SAVE THE WORLD

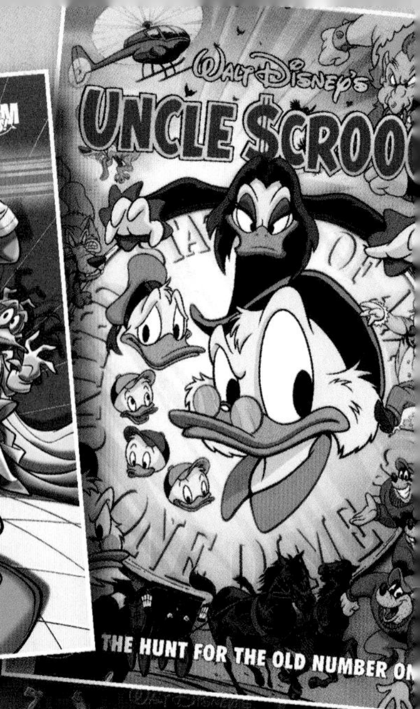
Walt Disney's

UNCLE SCROOGE: THE HUNT FOR THE OLD NUMBER ONE

Join Donald Duck's favorite penny-pinching Uncle Scrooge as he, Donald himself and Huey, Dewey, and Louie embark on a globe-spanning trek to recover treasure and save Scrooge's "number one dime" from the treacherous Magica De Spell.

SC $9.99 ISBN 9781608865475
HC $24.99 ISBN 9781608865536

WIZARDS OF MICKEY VOL. 1: MOUSE MAGIC

Your favorite Disney characters star in this magical fantasy epic! Student of the great wizard Nereus, Mickey allies himself with Donald and team mate Goofy, in a quest to find a magical crown that will give him mastery over all spells!

SC $9.99 ISBN 9781608865413
HC $24.99 ISBN 9781608865505

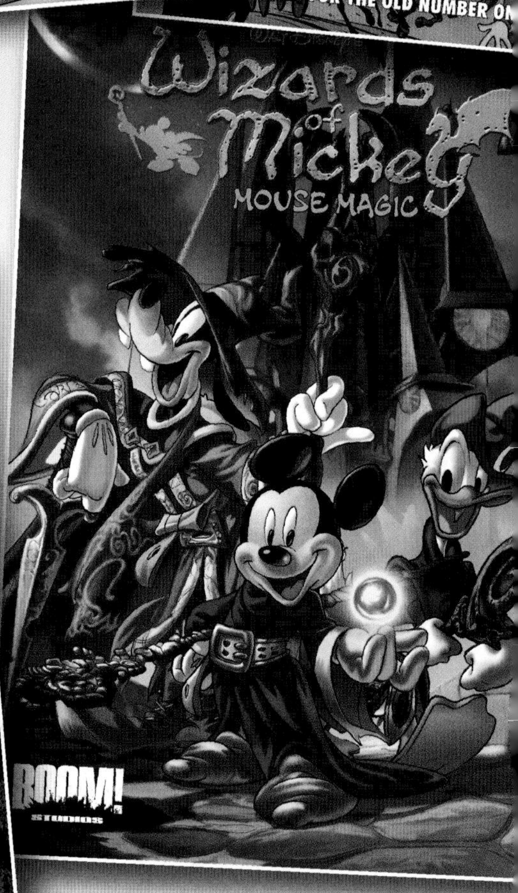
Wizards of Mickey
MOUSE MAGIC
BOOM! STUDIOS

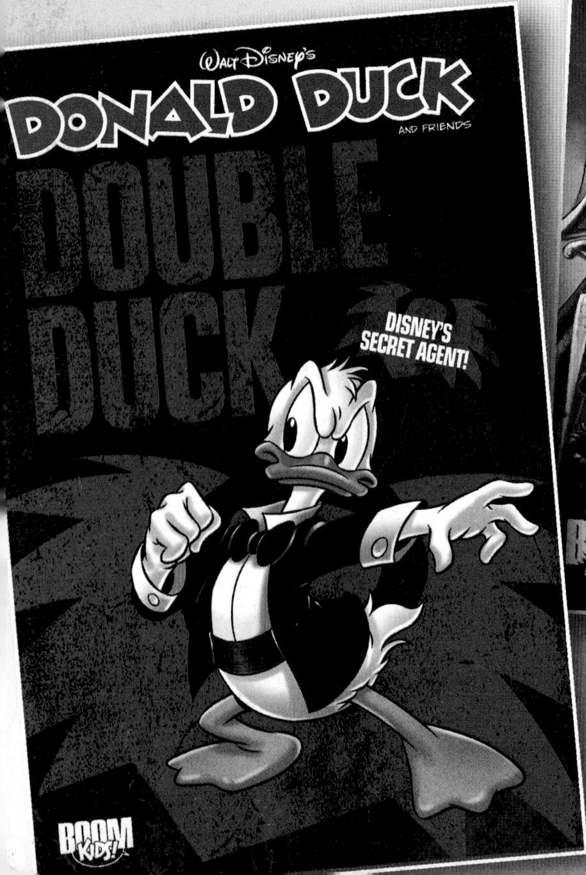
Walt Disney's
DONALD DUCK
AND FRIENDS
DOUBLE DUCK
DISNEY'S SECRET AGENT!
BOOM KIDS!

DONALD DUCK AND FRIENDS: DOUBLE DUCK VOL. 1

Donald Duck as a secret agent? Villainous fiends beware as the world of super sleuthing and espionage will never be the same! This is Donald Duck like you've never seen him!

SC $9.99 ISBN 9781608865451
HC $24.99 ISBN 9781608865512

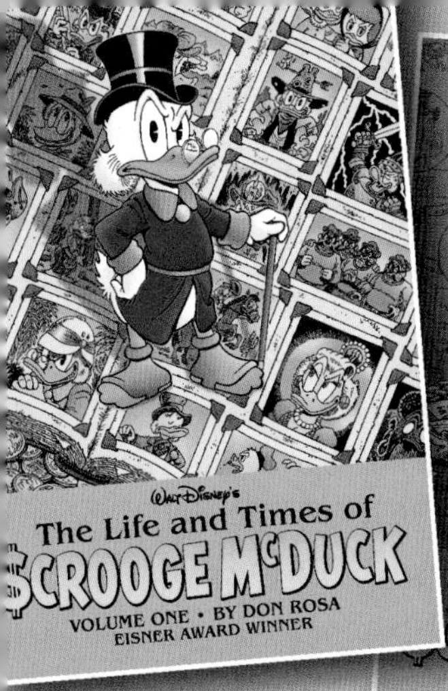
Walt Disney's
The Life and Times of
SCROOGE McDUCK
VOLUME ONE • BY DON ROSA
EISNER AWARD WINNER

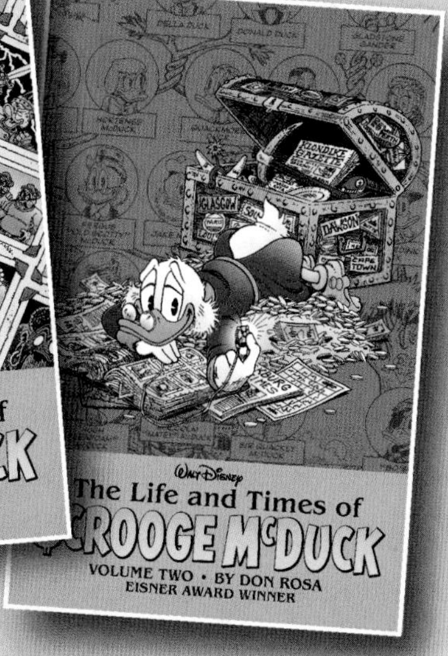
Walt Disney
The Life and Times of
SCROOGE McDUCK
VOLUME TWO • BY DON ROSA
EISNER AWARD WINNER

THE LIFE AND TIMES OF SCROOGE McDUCK VOL. 1

BOOM Kids! proudly collects the first half of THE LIFE AND TIMES OF SCROOGE MCDUCK in a gorgeous hardcover collection – featuring smyth sewn binding, a gold-on-gold foil-stamped case wrap, and a bookmark ribbon! These stories, written and drawn by legendary cartoonist Don Rosa, chronicle Scrooge McDuck's fascinating life.

HC $24.99 ISBN 9781608865383

THE LIFE AND TIMES OF SCROOGE McDUCK VOL. 2

BOOM Kids! proudly presents volume two of THE LIFE AND TIMES OF SCROOGE MCDUCK in a gorgeous hardcover collection in a beautiful, deluxe package featuring smyth sewn binding and a foil-stamped case wrap! These stories, written and drawn by legendary cartoonist Don Rosa, chronicle Scrooge McDuck's fascinating life.

HC $24.99 ISBN 9781608865420

MICKEY MOUSE CLASSICS: MOUSE TAILS

See Mickey Mouse as he was meant to be seen! Solving mysteries, fighting off pirates, and generally saving the day! These classic stories comprise a "Greatest Hits" series for the mouse, including a story produced by seminal Disney creator Carl Barks!

HC $24.99 ISBN 9781608865390

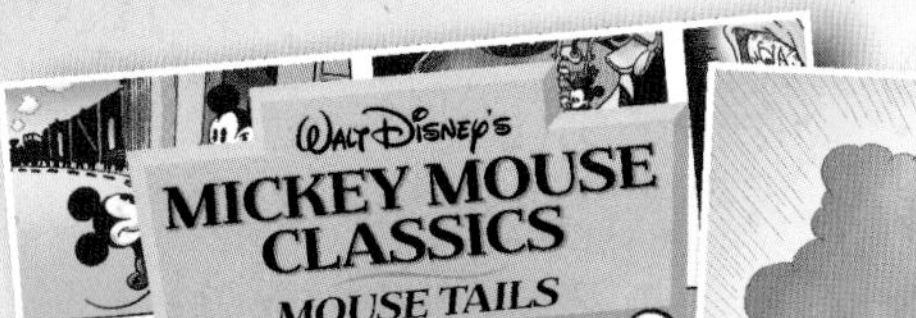
Walt Disney's
MICKEY MOUSE CLASSICS
MOUSE TAILS
BOOM KIDS!

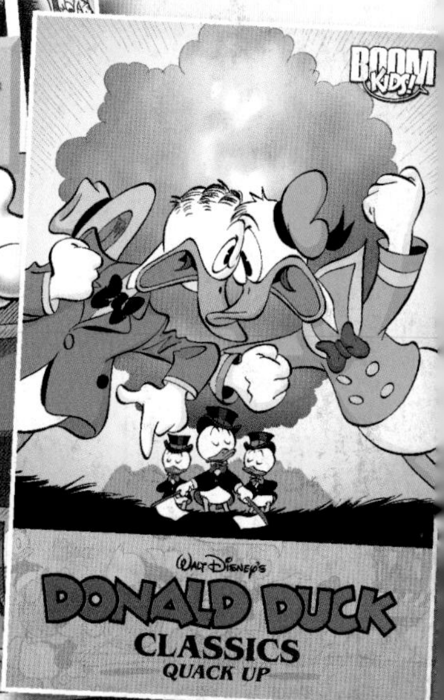
BOOM KIDS!
Walt Disney's
DONALD DUCK
CLASSICS
QUACK UP

DONALD DUCK CLASSICS: QUACK UP

Whether it's finding gold, journeying to the Klondike, or fighting ghosts, Donald will always have the help of his much more prepared nephews – Huey, Dewey, and Louie – by his side. Featuring some of the best Donald Duck stories Carl Barks ever produced!

HC $24.99 ISBN 9781608865406

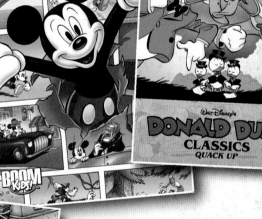

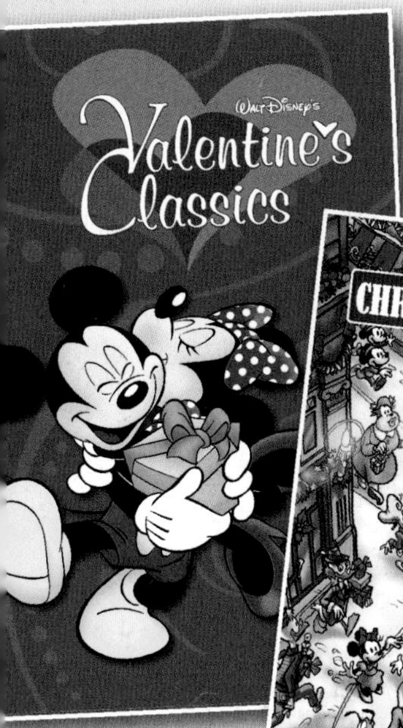
Walt Disney's
Valentine's Classics

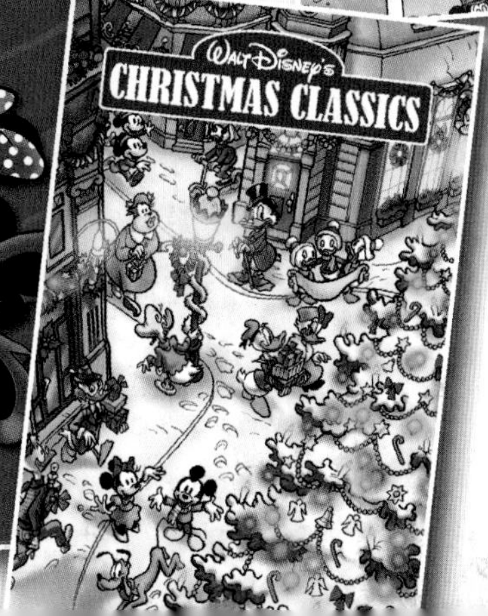
Walt Disney's
CHRISTMAS CLASSICS

WALT DISNEY'S VALENTINE'S CLASSICS

Love is in the air for Mickey Mouse, Donald Duck and the rest of the gang. But will Cupid's arrows cause happiness or heartache? Find out in this collection of classic stories featuring work by Carl Barks, Floyd Gottfredson, Daan Jippes, Romano Scarpa and Al Taliaferro.

HC $24.99 ISBN 9781608865499

WALT DISNEY'S CHRISTMAS CLASSICS

BOOM Kids! has raided the Disney publishing archives and searched every nook and cranny to find the best and the greatest Christmas stories from Disney's vast comic book publishing history for this "best of" compilation.

HC $24.99 ISBN 9781608865482

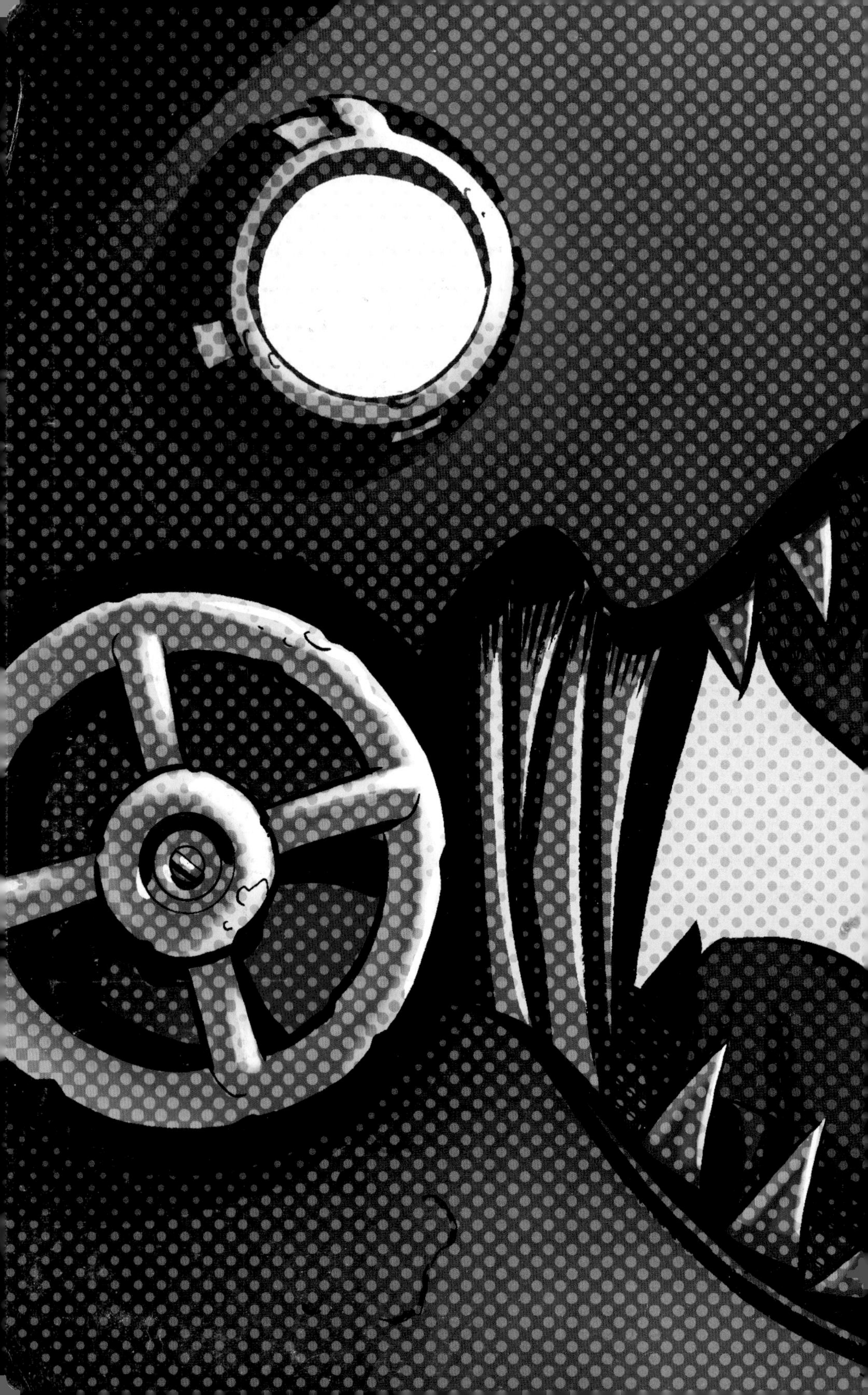